WALES:
THE IMAGINED NATION

WALES:
THE IMAGINED NATION

Studies in Cultural and National Identity

Edited by
TONY CURTIS

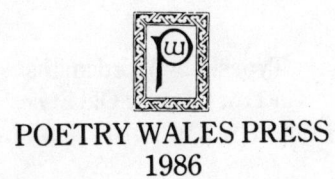

POETRY WALES PRESS
1986

POETRY WALES PRESS
56 PARCAU AVENUE, BRIDGEND, MID GLAMORGAN

British Library Cataloguing in Publication Data

Wales: the imagined nation:
studies in cultural and national identity
1. Wales – History
I. Curtis, Tony, *1946-*
942.9'07   DA720
ISBN 0-907476-53-8
ISBN 0-907476-54-6 Pbk

The publisher acknowledges the financial support of the
Welsh Arts Council.

Cover Design: **Jeane Rees**

Typeset by Wordsmiths
in 11pt Century Old Style
Printed by J.W. Arrowsmith Ltd.

CONTENTS

List of Illustrations

Introduction

Wales is a process.
Wales is an artefact which the Welsh produce.
The Welsh make and remake Wales
day by day, year by year, generation after generation
if they want to.

I first used those words by Gwyn A. Williams as an inscription for a long poem, 'Pembrokeshire Seams' in which I attempted to point out a unity between the industrial, coal-based Glamorgan where I now work and the national park coastal beauty of Pembrokeshire where I spent much of my boyhood. The seams of rich coal which are so obviously underpinning the modern history of east Wales are, less obviously perhaps, just as important to an understanding of the now uniformly rural Dyfed. Professor Williams forcefully made his point about Welsh national assumptions in a radio talk entitled 'When Was Wales?'. Many people were stirred by that talk and recent books around the same theme by Gwyn Williams and other notable Welsh historians. That question, "When was Wales?", and the considerations which the talk addressed, I realised, touched upon issues which had been raised in and by my own life.

Growing up in Carmarthen through the 1950's I had always assumed that I was Welsh. This despite the fact that I was not sure what that entailed, apart from the fact that Carmarthen was undoubtedly *in* Wales; despite the fact, also, that no-one in our house spoke Welsh. My grandfather, Jim Curtis, had left work on a farm in Berkshire before the Great War and come west with the G.W.R.. Gran had been a Barrah from Jeffreyston, a little village below the Landsker line in Pembrokeshire. Grandad Williams, a Welsh-speaking Bangor man, had lived in industrial Lancashire for over thirty years, attending a Welsh chapel in Earlstown the whole time. But he died before my first birthday and my mother was, and is, very much a Lancashire lass brought to West Wales by the Land Army in another War. Welsh lessons were, naturally, taught at my junior school in Carmarthen town, but our fiery Welsh teacher sprayed the front four rows when she demonstrated "ll" and, besides, legend held that she had broken the arm of a stuttering boy the previous year. The acquisition of a language in early life is often facilitated or baulked by such sets of accidental circumstances.

At the Queen Elizabeth Grammar School there was a language divide. I played for the junior rugby XV but never got to know several members of the team who were from the Welsh forms. We were, no doubt, a mixed bunch, but there is no shortage of rugby skills in Dyfed and, I remember, there was a little lad on the wing who seemed pretty fast. In any case, my parents moved to Pembroke-shire after my third year and I heard virtually no Welsh in school or outside for the next fifteen years. South Pembrokeshire, below the language and cultural line of the Landsker running through Haverfordwest, is exclusively Anglophone. Still, our games master had dropped the winning goal at Landsdowne Road in an international back in the early 1950's and twice a year we visited the mecca of the Arms Park, roaring with the thousands and mouthing convincingly the general sense of 'Mae Hen Wlad Fy Nhadau'. The people of South Pembrokeshire may speak with a hint of West Country burr, but their "Little England" is not to be easily dismissed as "beyond Wales".

If nationality is not necessarily linked to language, if it is neither simply a matter of geographical residency, then is it a matter of rugby and singing? Is Welshness a thing to be opted into, or out of? If Gwyn Williams is right, if we choose to "make" Wales, if we "want to", then out of what may we make Wales, and why might we "want to"?

Ernest Gellner in his *Nations and Nationalism* has several profound arguments in respect of national identity. He claims

> nationalism is a very distinctive species of patriotism, and one which becomes pervasive and dominant only under certain social conditions, which in fact prevail in the modern world, and nowhere else. Nationalism is a species of patriotism distinguished by a few very important features: the units which this kind of patriotism, namely nationalism, favours with its loyalty, are culturally homogeneous, based on a culture striving to be a high (literate) culture; they are large enough to sustain the hope of supporting the educational system which can keep a literate

culture going; they are poorly endowed with rigid internal sub-groupings; their populations are anonymous, fluid and mobile, and they are unmediated; the individual belongs to them directly, in virtue of his cultural style, and not in virtue of membership of nested sub-groups.

National identity is, then, founded on "cultural style". But this is not necessarily synonymous with real power for, by Max Weber's classic definition, a state is "that agency within society which possesses the monopoly of legitimate violence". Even allowing for the potency of cultural power groups within broadcasting, the press and the education system, Wales, by those terms, clearly has no separate entity from England. The national urge for self-identification, for the autonomy of character and individuality, if not of political and economic power, has, necessarily, to be achieved through the creation and maintenance of "cultural style".

Emyr Humphreys, in the first chapter of his eloquent and impressive sweep of polemic, *The Taliesin Tradition*, sees the survival and extension of an individual's dignity as intrinsically implicated in that individual's firm grip on a national identity:

> He must know both consciously and unconsciously that his own dignity as a human being is linked with the dignity of the national entity to which he belongs. He knows that this is a destiny from which he cannot escape and the mark of the hero in any myth is the degree of readiness with which he embraces his destiny.

In a bold, even Leavisite, projection from that premise Humphreys argues that

> Unless a people are certain of their identity and its values, they are fatally inhibited from exercising that degree of creativity which is necessary to reaffirm civilised values in the corner of the globe that they inhabit.

However, there seems to me to be a flaw in that last argument, for may not a people express its humanity, its "civilized values" in the *process* of questioning and working *towards* "the dignity of the national entity"? And are there not several startling examples from our recent history of the most uncivilized values imaginable materialising as a result of an over-certainty of national identity? The Twentieth-

Century Welsh may be split personalities in terms of political, geographical and cultural activities, but they have yet to systematic- ally kill other people in their struggle to define themselves.

Emyr Humphreys, while recognising the threat to his country from a largely ignorant, myopic, predatory Whitehall –

> Increasingly Wales did not exist in the bureaucratic mind as anything more than a geographical expression. In the 1950s the country itself was considered long overdue for economic dismemberment. It was an ideal site for a vast recreation area to meet the needs of the overcrowded English conurbations.

– does take heart from the resilience of the imagination, the "Taliesin Tradition" itself, in defending Wales from such pressures. He says:

> One of the encouraging elements that emerges from even the most superficial contemplation of Welsh history is the capacity of such a marginal society to generate and perpetuate so large a body of myth.

And further, this resilience is not merely a form of futile gesturing, for

> The myths of the Welsh were closely bound up with a living poetic tradition. This meant a degree of discipline in their formal arrangement and a social and political significance attached to their correct propagation. Myth-making is a recognised activity among defeated peoples. It is not only a source of consolation. Properly understood and used it is a most potent weapon in the struggle for survival.

What the present collection of essays attempts to do is to look closely at the various expressions of that need to define oneself and one's immediate context in terms of a Welsh national identity. This book responds to the question, "How do we imagine ourselves to be Welsh and where do we imagine Wales to be?"

Prys Morgan's opening chapter surveys the history of modern Wales and locates, from the Tudors to Lloyd George, manifestations of a deep-rooted, if at times fancifully expressed, need for Wales.

James A. Davies discusses Dylan Thomas, that most distinct poet and indistinct Welshman. Tony Bianchi argues that R.S. Thomas has been involved in a far more complex relationship with his readership than might have thus far been recognised. Tony Curtis considers some notable successors to the vastly differing work of these two Thomases, while Dai Smith sees in the flowering of fine novelists in the industrial hinterland of the 1930s a brave attempt to confront and order the evident collapse of the traditional foundation of modern Wales.

Carl Tighe, Peter Stead and Michelle Ryan are concerned that in the theatre, the cinema and in television Wales has consistently failed to project its essential concerns and has been overshadowed by the preoccupations of producers in England and America. John Hartley and Trevor Wright's detailed case-study of the media's treatment of Plaid Cymru exemplifies these arguments forcefully in the field of what might be assumed to be "objective" news coverage, but which is, in fact, "news" production.

Rod Jones sees that in the visual arts the physical fact of Wales has been mediated and distorted according to larger, dominant notions of beauty and truth, contributing to the material power which those ideas release.

Deirdre Beddoe argues that across the range of imagined realisations of Wales the treatment of women and their concerns, in particular, has been, at the least, inadequate and, at worst, derogatory; women have been subjected to a number of stereotyped roles that range from the beshawled harpist to the stolid Valleys Mam.

Here one locates the greatest irony: to preserve one's sense of a discrete identity one may construct a set of national characteristics which, in fact, caricature those underlying qualities which one hopes to secure. In this context of roles played for the benefit of powerful sections of society within Wales, as well as interested observers from outside, the following extract may serve as an interesting example. In 1932 Methuen of London published *In Search of Wales* by H. V. Morton. This was the fourth book in a series which had been "In Search Of" (and had, presumably, "found") England, Scotland and Ireland. Morton writes pretty well and the series was evidently a commercial success. However, he feels that this last task may well prove to be more difficult:

> Wales, I feel, is going to be interesting. She is, of the three
> sister nations which, with England, compose the British Isles,
> the smallest and the most mysterious. I wonder, as I find my

way out of London, what any man in the street would reply if I asked him:

"What does the word 'Wales' convey to you?"

He might possibly reply:

"The Prince of Wales, Lloyd George, the Eisteddfod, Snowdon, Welsh Rarebit..."

There he might stick. Perhaps a more literate member of the public might add:

"St. David, Fluellen, Parson Evans in *The Merry Wives of Windsor*, leeks, pictures of Caernarvon Castle in railway carriages, mine disasters, and Cardiff."

Someone might even recite the old libel that has stuck so hard to Wales and the Welsh:

> Taffy was a Welshman,
>   Taffy was a thief.

But I fear one would get no more except from a student of history. We in England do not hear so much of the glory of being Welsh as we do of the glory of being Scottish or Irish. I cannot remember one occasion on which a Welshman when drunk has hit his chest and announced to the company:

"I'm Welsh and – proud of it!"

The nearest thing to this were some of Mr. Lloyd George's early speeches about mountains and sunrise. And the Englishman, although he never boasts about being English, loves to hear a Scotsman bragging about Scotland and an Irishman crying about Ireland. Jock and Paddy are clear and definite characters, but Taffy is more elusive. His silence is strange. No comic papers have made him lovable, as they made Paddy lovable during centuries of Home Rule argument. No music-hall has developed him as a type which common people can recognize at sight, as they have, with pardonable fantasy, done to the Scot. Every one laughs in a friendly way at the parsimony of the Scot and the belligerency of the Irish, but no joke has been made up about the Welsh. This is significant. The impression that the Welsh are untruthful is definitely unkind. It must be admitted that a touch of the sinister is imparted to the thousands of apparently English Joneses and Williamses when they suddenly speak in a strange and difficult tongue. The Englishman, who hates the unfamiliar and the unexpected, begins to feel that

there is something queer and uncomfortable about Taffy. There
is something unnecessary, and – yes – sly, about this second
language, almost as if Taffy belonged to a secret society!

In a sense, Morton is continuing a tradition of visitors' impressions
of Wales, travellers' tales, which extends back to George Borrow,
and, it could be argued, to Giraldus Cambrensis. Though he has a
propensity to wax lyrical about "Ancient Briton" coracle-men and the
cockle-women of Penclawdd, "who look as if they are waiting for
Rembrandt to come and paint them", Morton is genuinely
sympathetic to the suffering of the people in the coal valleys and
seems stirred by their fortitude. Still, he is very much an outsider
and remains so after having written the book. There is a sense in
which such a visitor would welcome a "type" which "common people
can recognise at sight". He argues that the Welsh have not
succeeded in projecting a sufficiently clear image of themselves; what
the book does show is that Morton's journeying in that dismal year
of 1932 leads him to a fuller awareness of the complexity which
makes this people particularly unmalleable in his original terms. What
is crushed under the weight of an easy national or racial assumption
is the very colour of individuality which makes the area worth
distinguishing in the first place. Perhaps a present-day Morton might
be tempted to call in at Brunel House in Cardiff and allow the Wales
Tourist Board to hand him a packaged Wales on the spot.

Such problems necessarily exist: under pressure from an
economically and culturally dominant neighbour, it is predictable that
a small nation should construct a set of "national" characteristics as
a means of securing its survival. The most obvious distinguishing
feature of a Wales which is a small part of the United Kingdom and
a smaller part of the European Community, is the Welsh language.
Ernest Gellner argues a vital and precise role for the creation and
preservation of a "liturgical" language in the process of nationality:

> ...it is clearly advantageous to stress, sharpen and accentuate
> the diacritical, differential, and monopolizable traits of the
> privileged groups. The tendency of liturgical languages to
> become distinct from the vernacular is very stong: it is as if
> literacy alone did not create enough of a barrier between cleric
> and layman, as if the chasm between them had to be deepened,
> by making the language not merely recorded in an inaccessible
> script, but also incomprehensible when articulated.

It may not be too fanciful to argue that the Welsh language has just such a "liturgical" function within Wales today. It may well be that the language plays a more important part in determining the nature of society within Wales than in distinguishing Wales from the rest of the British Isles. On each side of the language divide in a Wales which is now widely bi-lingual in its public life, individual Welsh men and women claim their national identity either because of, or in spite of, that situation. This collection of essays directs itself to the fascinating confusions of life in Wales as it is reflected, distorted, created in the arts and the media.

On a cold February day in 1977, Oriel, the Welsh Arts Council bookshop and gallery in Cardiff, staged a lunch-time event. R.S. Thomas, the most influential and respected figure in Anglo-Welsh writing, had agreed to give a poetry reading. It was the first public engagement in the English language that R.S. Thomas had made for a number of years so the *Western Mail* was not too heavy-handed in its report, perhaps; Clive Betts wrote:

> One of the greatest poets writing in English crept into Cardiff last week. Twenty-four hours later a rather embarrassed R.S. Thomas slipped back out again to his parish squeezed between the mountains and the sea of Aberdaron... On the dot he launched with a few quick words of Welsh into a prepared list of readings, some of them poems still uncollected. On the dot, after frequent glances at his watch, he ended with the words, "Ah, well, it's time now," before autographing a few books and vanishing.

Oriel Gallery was packed that day; people filled the staircase to the bookshop, figures squatted right up to the feet of a rather perplexed poet. A number of well-known faces were in the audience – writers, broadcasters and, near the door, the man who had proved so elusive in my grammar school's rugby team, now readily recognisable, Gerald Davies, one of the most talented wing-threequarters ever to play for Wales, or any other team for that matter. An important section of the clan, one might say, had gathered. Perhaps here, at the feet of the poet and priest who had travelled from the farthest western corner of our country one might touch something that was indisputably, essentially Welsh. R.S. Thomas read, in a steady, low voice, the poems which have "expresssed the national identity of the Welshman" (see 'R.S. Thomas and His Readers'). The audience was attentive and stilled. There were no questions. As she left, a sixth-former remarked, "I never imagined he'd have a real English accent like that".

Tony Curtis

Barry/Barri. 1986.

PRYS·MORGAN

Keeping the Legends Alive

Keeping the Legends Alive

Gethin, one of the characters in Aled Islwyn's novel *Cadw'r Chwedlau'n Fyw* (Keeping the legends alive) published in 1984, says:

> "Wales hasn't got any history. She hasn't had a history for generations. Bumbling on, surviving from one century to the next. Romanticising the past... Keeping the legends alive, that's all recent Welsh history has been about... What sort of condition is a nation in that has to think twice before deciding where genuine historical events end and legends and fairy stories begin?"

Since the novel (which won the National Eisteddfod's prize in August 1985 for the best new novel) deals with Lois and her various lovers, such as Gethin, during the years 1969 to 1979, the characters in it have not had the benefit of reading recent books on Welsh history such as Gwyn A. Williams' *The Welsh in their history* or *When was Wales?* which break down the distinction which lies in Gethin's mind between a real and an imagined nation. Gethin is bitterly critical of the Welsh for deceiving themselves with reach-me-down heroes or unreal clichés about nonconformity, radicalism, male voice choirs and rugby. But historians have become more and more concerned with the role of imagination, myths, generalisations, images, clichés, in the cohesion of modern nations, states, or groups, emphasizing human activity in constructing these units or the deliberation and self-consciousness of such a process. This concern among historians contrasts with the older wisdom that states are organic growths, or unself-conscious occurrences over centuries. The new concern arises to some extent because all over the world one observes states large and small (e.g. the U.S.A. or modern African republics) which are human constructs, artificial agglomerations put together in a short time. Some might object that such thinking cannot be relevant to Wales, a land with obvious physical unity, (a mountainous Atlantic peninsula differing geographically from the plains to the east), historical unity (an awareness of the people's identity for two millenia) and linguistic unity (most of the people spoke their own language, Welsh, until around 1900), so that the observer could take an organic unity for granted. And the objectors would be right up to a point, but that would be half the story. The other half of the story is the subject of this essay, the role of myths, ideas, images and so on which have given the Welsh self-consciousness down the centuries and at times of challenge and crisis have, it may be argued, sustained the very existence of Wales. This latter half is particularly significant in the case of a people like the Welsh where the nation has not been coterminous with a political state. The process is a good deal more complex than that attacked by Gethin in the novel, it is not only a matter of keeping the legends alive, but also keeping alive through legends.

Even in the earliest centuries of Welsh history, a period stretching from the end of the Roman Empire up to the Norman Conquest, the subject is of importance although the Welsh had their own independent political institutions throughout the period. As far as can be judged from the patchy records of the period, the Welsh were defined as *Brython* (Britons), a name which had in Roman times been particularly associated with the native inhabitants of south and western Britain, and more often towards the end of these dark centuries, as *Cymry* (Welshmen, in modern Welsh) a word meaning something like fellow-countrymen, which also referred to the Cumbrians of Cumbria and Strathclyde. The link between the northern and southern Cymry was broken by the battle of Chester about 616 A.D., but the Welsh of Wales preserved an historical memory of what they came to call "The Old North" because many Welsh princely families claimed descent from Cumbrian leaders and because the earliest Welsh literature was composed in the lands which became southern Scotland. The Welsh were also given a self-awareness by being continually subjected to attacks from the Irish and Anglo-Saxons or English, and appear to have claimed to be the earliest inhabitants of the British Isles, now wrongly and unjustly attacked by wave after wave of foreigners, *Eingl* (Angles), *Saeson* (Saxons) and others. The invaders called the native inhabitants whose power they usurped the "Welsh", a word which came from the continental experience of the invaders, meaning a romanised foreigner, which seems ultimately to stem from a romanised Celtic tribe called the Velcae, somewhere in Germany. In the reign of Offa of Mercia, in the later eighth century, the English defined the Welsh even more precisely, for Offa built an earthen dyke from Prestatyn in the north to the Wye estuary in the south, a kind of Great Wall of China in miniature, the memory of whose builder was never forgotten. Offa's Dyke, then, can stand as an example of the way in which the Welsh were defined by their enemies and attackers.

Even in these early centuries, the Welsh used history and myth to sustain their spirit. There were myths of origin, for example the long-cherished Brutus myth, that the Britons took their name from an eponymous founder, a Roman consul Brutus, or, referring to the Romans' own belief in their Trojan origins enshrined in Virgil's *Aeneid*, the Welsh thought that the British might even have taken their name from an earlier eponymous hero, one Britto from Troy. There were also myths referring to the emergence of the Welsh from the ruins of the later Roman empire, such as the "Treason of the Long Knives", in which the British or Welsh leader Vortigern, in the middle of the fifth century, falls in love with the beautiful daughter (later called Rowena or Alice) of the Saxon leader Hengist, is invited with all the other British leaders to a great banquet with the Saxon leaders, who then owned no more than a coastal strip somewhere in the south-east, and then in mid-carousal Hengist gives a signal at which each Saxon leader draws a long knife from his buskin and slays the British leader sitting next to him at table, after which bloodbath, Vortigern is forced to concede large areas of southern Britain to the invaders for their permanent occupation. The Welsh could thus comfort themselves that the Saxons had only come through a plot, that the Almighty would never bless them, and in time the Welsh or British would regain overlordship over the whole island.

In these myths of origin or emergence, Vortigern was closely related to Macsen, or the Roman Imperial pretender, Magnus Maximus who led a brief revolt to try to capture the Western Empire in 383 A.D., the departure of whose legions symbolised for the Welsh the end of Roman rule in Britain and the beginning of a separate existence for the British or Welsh in these islands. Little is known of the real Magnus Maximus, but in Welsh myth he was connected with Wales through his wife Elen (supposedly from Segontium or Caernarfon) after whom stretches of straight road were called Elen's Causeways (Sarn Elen), and from whom were descended not only Vortigern but also many of the early princes and rulers of Wales. The legendary Elen was also jumbled up with

Helena, the mother of the Emperor Constantine, and this is because
the myths of origin were not only British and Roman in character but
also strongly Christian. The retreating, ever more constricted,
Welsh people were sustained by telling themselves that they were
the primary people of the British isles, their power had been
diminished by foul, not fair, means, that the origin of their
government and ruling families was Roman and Imperial, (just as the
ultimate origin of their race had been Roman or Trojan), and that they
had been Christians for centuries, perhaps since the visit of Joseph
of Arimathea to Britain, and that they were utterly different from
pagan Anglo-Saxons with their recent veneer of Christianity.

Following the first waves of barbarian invaders there came the
Vikings and then in the late eleventh century, the Normans, who
began their piecemeal conquest of Wales in the South in the 1090s
and ended it with the Angevin King Edward I's conquest of Gwynedd
in 1282. Between the eleventh and thirteenth centuries the Welsh
were defined by their enemies as a nation, now judged as primitive
and semi-barbaric by the sophisticated standards of the peoples of
the western European mainland. Geoffrey of Monmouth in the early
twelfth century, a Breton from Gwent who bridged the gap between
Norman and Welsh civilization, gave a new lease of life to the myths
and legends we have described, the Brutus and Trojan myths of
origin, adding to them many historical legends of the kings of Britain,
most remarkable of which were the tales of Arthur, which had not
been dominant in the Welsh myth before the twelfth century but
which now commanded attention, and which captured the imagination
of the Europeans. In the later twelfth century another Norman-
Welshman, Giraldus Cambrensis or Gerald the Welshman, shows in
his writings a profound consciousness of the differences between the
Welsh and their neighbours. Dr. Michael Richter has shown how
Giraldus led an unsuccessful attempt in the late twelfth century to
make Wales an archbishopric independent of Canterbury, and how
this campaign used the cult of St. David, thus greatly increasing the
fame of his cult, helping him to become the patron saint of the Welsh
people. In the same period the Welsh themselves were becoming
more keenly aware of a kinship or nationality that was superior to
their loyalty to local dynasty, Deheubarth, Powys, Gwynedd and so
on, and the word *cenedl* changed gradually in this period from
meaning a kin-group to something like its modern meaning of 'nation'.

Even before the conquest of 1282 the Welsh rulers wished to
be praised by being compared to all kinds of ancient Welsh heroes,

such as those rulers of the "Old North" praised in the earliest Welsh poetry in the sixth and seventh centuries; the Welsh lawyers sought to give sanction and status to their legal code by calling it after the name of Hywel Dda (Howell the Good) the lawgiver who was supposed to have codified the Welsh laws at Whitland (Dyfed) around 900 A.D., and the bards and musicians claimed in the twelfth and thirteenth centuries that their rules and regulations were codified by the king Gruffydd ap Cynan in the late eleventh century, a so-called "Statute of Gruffydd ap Cynan" still being respected in the sixteenth century. The difference is that after 1282 the Welsh adjusted this view of history to the conquest and more and more emphasized the prophetic or messianic dimension. The legends of conquest are still there, but now there is a sense of urgent search for a rescuer, a political saviour for the nation, a second Arthur who would return to avenge the defeats of the Welsh, or a second "Owain" (the most popular image of this mythical hero) who would rise up and drive the English from the island.

Norman Cohn has shown in a classic study *The Pursuit of the Millenium* how Messianic cults quickened the lives of common people in various countries such as Germany or the Low Countries continually in the later middle ages and sixteenth century, and Professor Glanmor Williams in his study of poetry, prophesy and politics in Wales has shown how mythical heroes troubled the Welsh imagination in the centuries after the conquest of 1282; for example in the fourteenth century the Welsh eagerly awaited the return of one of the descendants of the princes of Gwynedd, Owain of the Red Hand, from France, and how they were dumbfounded when the news came of his death abroad before he could return to his rightful kingdom. Around 1400 the Welsh thought that the "second Owain" must be Owain Glyndŵr (Owen Glendower) who rebelled against the English successfully for around ten years. In the middle of the fifteenth century the second Owain, the Son of Prophecy (*Mab Darogan*) was thought by many to be William Herbert, earl of Pembroke, but he was killed with the flower of the Welsh gentry at the Battle of Banbury 1469 in the Wars of the Roses: within a few years the young Henry Tudor had taken his place as the second Owain. How seriously nobles and rulers took popular or bardic prophecies is difficult to say: certainly Owain Glyndŵr consulted Hopcyn ap Thomas of Ynystawe (Glamorgan) as a "maister of Brut", that is, an expert on *Brud* or bardic prophecies, which were to a large extent historical myths and legends; Henry Tudor in 1485 is also said to have consulted Dafydd Llwyd of Mathafarn (Powys) before the battle of Bosworth. A vast amount of bardic poetry was composed in the fifteenth century, a good deal of it in praise of various political leaders, and a good deal of that uses history as propaganda, as a legitimator of action. Henry Tudor was glad to pose as the prophesied Welsh hero in 1485, though whether the corpus of Welsh myth meant a great deal to him after that date is a moot point. One can judge from the frequent passing references in fifteenth-century Welsh poetry to minor events or figures in Welsh myths (for example, minute details of the story of Vortigern's dealings with Hengist and Horsa around 440 A.D.) that the audience for this poetry was familiar with Welsh history and mythology, and that it frequently called upon history as comfort and solace, and it is hardly surprising that the English in this period suspected the Welsh bards of spurring the Welsh to rebellion by reciting tales of national heroes to them.

The fifteenth and sixteenth centuries are starkly constrasted periods in Welsh history, the one a century of rebellions and civil wars, the other the century of the 'Act of Union' 1536-42, and the Tudor Reformation. Henry Tudor, who became King Henry VII in 1485, certainly made use of Welsh myths and legends for a short time during his reign; in the Battle of Bosworth he used the red dragon as a standard, symbolising his claimed descent from the last Welshman to claim to be king over the British Isles, Cadwaladr the Blessed, and in a sense symbolising the aim of his Welsh supporters to avenge their ancient losses by setting a Welshman once again on a British throne. The Welsh bards aided Henry by acclaiming him as the second Owain, the Son of Prophecy, and he in turn used the Red Dragon of Cadwaladr as one of the supporters of the royal standard and called his eldest son Prince Arthur. Prophecies thus fulfilled are a two-edged sword, for after 1485 one important strand of Welsh myth was twisted by the ruler and woven into Tudor royal propaganda. The messianic legends, the myths of Vortigern and the Long Knives and all those mythological grudges of the past subsided and disappeared in the early sixteenth century, only remaining, if at all, as folk tales. The Brutus or Trojan myth of the origin of the Welsh was mocked and derided by historians such as Polydore Vergil (brought from Italy to England as the historiographer of the Tudor dynasty), though Welsh antiquaries tried to defend such myths bravely for two centuries or more. The most curious transformation of all during the sixteenth century was that which occurred to the Christian or ecclesiastical myth of the Welsh: at various points in the middle ages, the Welsh had sought to prove that their Christianity was older and deeper than that of the English, that the Welsh were the heirs of the early British church which had been founded by Joseph of Arimathea only shortly after Christ's death, that for centuries it maintained its independence against papal encroachment, and had its own saints and customs. But after the Tudor Reformation the English in their attempts to legitimise the newly-reformed Church of England, turned eagerly to the legends of the British church, free from papal control, and so Welsh myth was taken over and used to give a myth of independent origins to the Anglican Church, just as royal propagandists and scholars in the sixteenth century turned to Welsh traditions and borrowed the Welsh concept of a British realm founded by Brutus, applied it to the kingdom of England, and used it to justify the expansion of Elizabethan England over the whole of the British Isles, an expansion which became reality with the absorption of Wales 1536-42, the conquest of Ireland 1601, and the Union with Scotland 1603. Even obscure Welsh legends might be borrowed in this period by the English and used for new political circumstances. Professor Gwyn A. Williams has shown how the Welsh legend that Madoc, son of the Welsh king Owain Gwynedd, had discovered America about 1170 A.D. and had settled there with his companions, was used by Dr John Dee (Queen Elizabeth's magician, and a famous author) to justify the English claim to America and to contest the Spanish claim to that continent.

In general the Welsh during the sixteenth century saw their myths and legends absorbed into English history and tradition, taken over for the purposes of the vigorously expanding English state, or discredited and dismissed as fairy-stories by English antiquaries or Renaissance scholars. The Welsh ceased to have an independent history, although Welshmen struggled long to prove that the Brutus story was true, and new myths arose within the fold of Protestantism in this period. To compensate for the discrediting of Brutus, the Welsh began to claim that they had a more ancient eponymous hero than Brutus, namely Gomer (from the Book of Genesis), that *Cymru* was named after him, and that *Cymraeg* (Welsh) was really *Gomeraeg*; also that the Welsh language was one of the oldest in the world, that it was closely related to Hebrew, and probably spoken by the Patriarchs in the world's infancy. The Hebrew origin of Welsh was believed by scholars such as Dr. John Davies of Mallwyd (early seventeenth century) and by Puritan historians such as Charles Edwards (late seventeenth century). The loyalty of the Welsh was secured by the myths we have mentioned above, the belief that the Tudors were really the heirs of the ancient Welsh princes and kings such as Cadwaladr, or that the British or Welsh Church was the original basis of the independent Anglican Church, but it should be remembered that at a time when the Welsh language declined in status, and given official recognition only as one of the official liturgical tongues of Anglicanism, while being hounded out of secular administration, law and government, rearguard attempts were made by the Welsh to give it a new prestige by appealing to Old Testament history by way of compensation.

The lexicographer and almanacker Thomas Jones said in his preface to the Welsh-English dictionary he produced in 1688 and entitled *The British Language in its lustre* that the Welsh language was by then held in low esteem (in his words it was "regardless") and that the Welsh themselves were deprived of any kind of history, they were virtually "blotted out of the books of records" and unable to agree on the history of their origins as a people. The present writer has tried to show in *The Eighteenth Century Renaissance* that contemporaries in the late seventeenth-century felt that the life blood was ebbing away from Wales, Welsh history seemed to be regarded as an irrelevance, the language was becoming a mere *patois*, and traditional culture, which had long been preserved by local gentry, was now abandoned by them and was waning even among the more isolated common folk. The present writer has also tried to show that the 1680s and 90s were a turning-point in Welsh cultural history, when new social forms, long in the making, became clearly visible, a new middle class of leaders, new social attitudes, a new culture of literacy and so on, so that it is not surprising that this period should see the start of a vigorous process of creating a new image for the Welsh. This was the start of a complex movement which we might term the renaissance of things Welsh in the eighteenth century, and, while much of the movement was honest, scholarly, sober and realistic antiquarianism, the element of fantasy is often present. The licensed meeting of bards and musicians, an *eisteddfod*, had not been held since 1567, the bardic order which held together for so many centuries the world of Welsh history, legend and mythology, had disappeared by 1600, the professional bards had largely ceased their activities by the Civil Wars, and the last of them had apparently died in the 1690s. But in 1701 a group of poets held the first of the modern revived *eisteddfodau*, and, although they were feeble, amateurish affairs, the organizers of such moots early in the eighteenth century claimed that they were being held according to the "Statute of Gruffydd ap Cynan".

At a time when in 1689 the Council of Wales had been abolished, in 1690 the Gaels of Ireland and in 1715 the Gaels of Scotland were defeated and downcast and Brittany was isolated from the British Isles by the long French Wars of William III and Anne, this was the time a group of scholars, the most able of whom was Edward Lhuyd, keeper of the Ashmolean Museum in Oxford, put Welsh history on a completely new footing, by showing that Welsh was the daughter of the old British language, she in turn was the sister language of Irish, Gaelic, Cornish and Breton, and that they were all in turn daughters of an unnamed ancient language which was called by them Celtic, after the bands of warriors roaming Europe long before Christ, the scourge of Ancient Greece and Rome. The ancient warrior bands settled down and were eventually conquered by the Romans, and amongst the most striking defenders of the Celts of Gaul against the Roman conquerors such as Julius Caeser had been their sages or priests called the Druids. Edward Lhuyd was sober and cautious in his writings, but, like many of his Welsh contemporaries, he was moved by the sense of living continuity with the Classical World, especially since the main headquarters of the Druid cult was said to have been in Anglesey and that the Druids had led a dramatic last-ditch defence of the island with its sacred groves (the oaks of which contained the golden boughs of mistletoe) against the Roman armies. His Breton contemporary, the Abbé Pezron was certain that the Welsh and Bretons were descendants of the Celts, that their ancestors had held sway over much of Europe and the near East, that Breton and Welsh were the remains of the language of the Patriarchs; while Lhuyd's Welsh contemporary, Henry Rowlands (from the island of Anglesey) believed that the megalithic stone circles to be found all over Wales were Druid temples, the cromlechs were sacrificial altars, and one or two contemporaries even went so far as to suggest that the Welsh bards had been the successors of the ancient Druids. Lewis Morris, a leader of the early eighteenth century antiquarian revival in the generation after Edward Lhuyd, believed for example that Welsh folk verses (*penillion telyn*) sung to the harp contained scraps of Druidic wisdom.

Welsh writers who popularised the views of the scholars tended to emphasize some of these fantastical ideas at the expense of sober scholarship; it is important to remember that all over Europe in this period pure and bogus scholarship were inextricably intermingled. In

Wales this process had a powerful effect, for it gave the Welsh a sense of independent tradition or history, an antique Classical past of their own with their own Classical remains (Stonehenge and other stone circles), and a powerful motive for going back to neglected traditions and manuscripts. Did not old Welsh proverbs perhaps contain the Druids' wisdom? Earlier scholars (several in the mid-seventeenth century) had suspected such things, but such ideas were popularised in the eighteenth, by Theophilus Evans, for example, in his *Drych y Prif Oesoedd*, a history book of 1716. The process also had a powerful effect in Wales because it emphasised the sweeping grandeur of the ancient past of the Welsh people and language, so that, in comparison, the three or four centuries of decline and failure in recent times appeared a mere hiccup; the constricted size of modern Wales could be forgotten when the imagination roamed with the early Celts, gold-torqued, galloping on their glorious steeds on plains as far afield as Connemara and Galatia in Asia Minor; the miserable *patois* – what the satirist William Richards in *Wallography* (1682) had called the "Gibberish of Taphydome" – shone with a new brilliance when it was known that the Celtic mother-tongue had been intoned by the Druids. To peoples with little present, and no future, the discovery of the distant past was electrifying.

The present writer has in an essay in *The Invention of Tradition* tried to show how the revival of Welsh history lay at the root of the revival of so many other things Welsh in the eighteenth century, but that as the century advanced, and the scholars broadened the appeal of their movement so as to reach the common people, the element of fantasy, imagination, invention and bogus forgery, grew, and the element of sober realism declined. The simple reason for this is that the Welsh public had an enthusiasm for the past that could not be sustained or satisfied by the available evidence, or, if available, by the rather meagre and unsuccessful performance of the Welsh in past centuries. Let us take a few examples of the fields where imagination and myth took a strong hold.

Although there had once been a powerful Welsh musical tradition with native instruments such as the Welsh harp, this had died away in the seventeenth century. The musical manuscripts of the bards had quickly become unintelligible, the harp now fashionable was the triple harp (a version of the Italian baroque harp), imported melodies and songs abounded, and peculiarly Welsh ways of singing, such as *canu penillion*, were confined to a few tiny corners of remote mountain country. John Parry in his book *Ancient British Music* (1742) suggested that his collection of Welsh tunes really dated from very early times, perhaps from the days of the Ancient Druids. Harpists like Parry during the eighteenth and early nineteenth centuries helped to revive Welsh music, to make Welshmen collect or write music, by creating in the Welsh the illusion that their music was peculiarly national, peculiarly ancient, that their harp, for example, had nothing to do with baroque Italy, but was an ancient national instrument, and to be treasured for that reason. By the end of the eighteenth century Wales considered itself, and was known abroad, as the Land of Song.

The whole field of language and literature in Wales was transformed in the same way. The eisteddfod itself, revived in 1701, was always conscious of being a revival of a much greater institution in the past, always trying to live up to magnificent medieval princely moots held according to the Statute of Gruffydd ap Cynan, trying to revive the rules of prosody and alliteration laid down once and for all in the Carmarthen Eisteddfod in the mid-fifteenth century, trying to recapture the pageantry and grandeur of the last great eisteddfod held under Queen Elizabeth's patronage at Caerwys in 1567. It is in north eastern Wales, where the memory of the two eisteddfodau of Caerwys in the sixteenth century was strongest, that the most successful eisteddfodau of the eighteenth century were held (from 1789 to the mid-1790s), and these were held with the money and encouragement of the London Welsh, especially of the Gwyneddigion Society of London. It was the London Welsh throughout the eighteenth century who gave the lead in things Welsh, and it was they, the exiles long separated from the reality of things at home in Wales, who most readily turned to an invented Wales, a Wales of the imagination which they then gave to their native land. The greatest inventor of the Welsh past in the eighteenth century was not a London Welshman, but a stonemason from the Vale of Glamorgan, Edward Williams (1747-1826), historian, bard, scholar and many other things besides, an eccentric and a genius. He was a frequent visitor to London, working there for several years, and it was in London in 1792 that he launched on the world his Gorsedd of the Bards of the Isle of Britain. Edward Williams claimed that he and a friend (Edward Evan of Aberdare) were the last remaining bards of Britain, that he had received from the earlier generations by apostolic succession the whole of their ancient lore and liturgy, that he had a bardic name, Iolo Morganwg, and that since the line would soon come to an end, the whole bardic inheritance, inherited ultimately from the Ancient Druids, must be thrown open to the public. He accordingly held a druidic moot in London called *Gorsedd* (it had two literal meanings in Welsh, throne or mountain summit), and in the ensuing years he initiated groups of poets and scholars into what he said was a revived order of druids or bards. He envisaged the order of druid-bards as a permanent institution, a permanent supporters' club, as it were, for Welsh history, literature and language, it would found national institutions such as a Library and Museum, it would be a political pressure group (Iolo was a Radical and a strong pacifist and anti-slavery campaigner), and it would turn the eisteddfodau into a permanent institution instead of a series of intermittent events. Iolo had to wait until he was an old man, in the Carmarthen eisteddfod of 1819, before he managed to connect his Gorsedd with an important eisteddfod, but Iolo's Druido-bardism had a strong effect on popularising the eisteddfod, so that, quite contrary to expectations, the eisteddfod became one of the most successful Welsh institutions in the nineteenth century. Iolo's aims were strongly practical, but the means he adopted to convince his faint-hearted countrymen of these were sublime and fantastic, and involved him in elaborate fantasies, mythologising and downright forgeries.

The 1790s were the highpoint, in many ways, of the romantic imagination as far as things Welsh were concerned, and Gwyn A. Williams has clearly shown in his *Madoc* and his *In Search of Beulah Land* how powerful was the role of imagination and myth in the Welsh response to the American Revolution abroad and what he has called a crisis of modernisation of life at home. We have already mentioned the way in which the legend of Madoc's discovering America about 1170 was used to justify the Elizabethan empire in America. The legend reappeared in Wales in the eighteenth century, as interest in American affairs grew, and as the possibility grew of Welsh radicals taking bands of their fellow countrymen across the Atlantic to found free Welsh homelands in the New World. The height of this "Madoc fever" came in the 1790s, when books and pamphlets on the subject were published, Iolo Morganwg forged documents on the matter, an expedition to find the Welsh Indians (who were supposed to be the descendants of Madoc and his supporters, and were still speaking Welsh) was organized. The story has already been well told, and it is sufficient here to say that however unlikely the tale, and however much evidence there was to show that it was myth, it had a powerful effect on the Welsh imagination for decades, it helped to boost Welsh self-confidence by connecting the Welsh with one of the most dramatic events of the period, the American Revolution, it gave a motive for going out to settle in America (to contact the lost Madogians), and is a perfect example of the tendency noted in this chapter several times, of the Welsh to turn at times of crisis to fantasy and myth as motives or legitimators of action.

The 1790s were also the high-point of a tendency, growing throughout the later eighteenth century, to surround the Welsh language with fantastical theories. The greatest of the language mythologists was the grammarian and lexicographer – a London Welshman for most of his life – William Owen-Pughe. He adapted to Welsh many of the linguistic theories of the previous generations of scholars, inside and outside Wales, strongly believed that Welsh was the greatest and amplest language in Europe, the language of the Patriarchs and Druids, that it contained the clue to the origin of all other languages, that it could be analysed into short monosyllabic particles conveying essential concepts or ideas, and that these could be infinitely assembled and reassembled as in a kaleidoscope, to multiply vocabulary, and just as this process had happened to Welsh in the patriarchal and druidic past, so the same process must be undertaken today by contemporary linguists. Pughe in his grammar books totally reconstructed the Welsh language from top to bottom, and in his Welsh-English dictionary he not only described a vast amount of words (for he had read in minute detail all available Welsh manuscripts) but also invented an even vaster amount of words to convey every conceivable nuance of modern thought. For example, one word, *gogoelgrevyddusedd* conveys "some slight degree of superstitiousness". His aim was a practical one, to give status to Welsh and to give it a method of coping with the infinitely complex demands on all modern languages, but his methods of propaganda were fantasy and myth, and he himself was strongly motivated by the sense that he had discovered the clue, through Welsh, to the essence of primeval language, and to all Language.

The enthusiasts we have mentioned such as Iolo and Pughe were all interconnected, sometimes close friends, at other times bitter enemies, all deeply patriotic, but all sensitive to the developments of the Romantic movement in England and further afield. One of their greatest concerns was to make the Welsh common people think of themselves as a nation, and to give drama and colour to their drab existence. They saw that one of the most effective ways of making the people visualise or memorise their history was through a

Cambrian hall of fame, and so they brought all kinds of heroes to the attention of the people, hence the revival from 1770 onwards (in the case of the work of Evan Evans, poet and scholar, and Thomas Pennant, the naturalist and traveller) of the fame of the half-forgotten rebel prince Owain Glyndŵr. Thomas Gray had made famous the last of the Welsh bards surviving the supposed massacre of the bards by Edward I, he was now absorbed into Welsh tradition as an historical figure. The fourteenth century's chieftain from near Newport, Ifor Hael (Ivor the Generous) was made into a symbol of the generous patronage of the Welsh to poetry, and so Ifor became launched as a baptismal name, and Welsh workmen called their society of mutual aid the Order of True Ivorites (*yr Iforiaid*). Just as Robin Hood was revived in England, so the figure of Twm Sion Cati (Thomas Jones of Fountain Gate, Tregaron, Dyfed) now reappeared as a pranking, japing Welsh Robin Hood in Anglo-Welsh fiction in the early nineteenth century, returning within a brief time to Welsh tradition. Figures like this humanised, made palpable, the unknown territory of Welsh history.

In the same period and through the same methods, the myth-makers of the Welsh persuaded the people to see that each corner of the landscape of Wales was numinous, by publishing old tales and legends, or by sheer invention; thus they publicised the coast of Cardigan Bay as the Welsh Lyonesse or Ker-Ys, the landscape of the Lowland Hundred or *Cantre'r Gwaelod*, drowned by the sea because of the neglect of the drunken Seithennyn; thus they explained the placename of Beddgelert, now the haunt of Snowdonian tourists, as the "Grave of Gelert" the favourite hound of Llywelyn I, unjustly slain by the prince on the suspicion of having killed his baby, when in fact the faithful hound was blood-covered from attacking a wolf which was attacking the royal cradle. This was an invention, as far as can be judged. Until the end of the eighteenth century the Welsh eyed their own mountainous land with little regard, seeing its grim harshness and the poverty of its agriculture as a punishment, and recalling the loss, so many centuries before, of the flat fertile plains now in the hands of the fortunate English. Welsh patriots now took up the admiration for the wild landscape felt for the first time by English romantic tourists, pouring into Wales in the 1790s, and told the Welsh that Wales should be proud (not ashamed) to be the Land of the Mountains (*Gwlad y Bryniau*), for the mountains were fastnesses, the home of liberty, and radical patriots believed mountain air was the air of freedom. Was it a coincidence that, from the last quarter of the eighteenth century on, the great developments of the Industrial Revolution, which in Wales occurred in the mountainous parts (slate in Snowdonia, iron and coal in upland Glamorgan) caused the opening up of the remotest areas to modern change?

The patriot propagandists, such as Iolo Morganwg, were also successful in helping the common people visualise their country more clearly through what one might call a "heraldry of culture" for want of a better phrase, a complex of symbols and signs standing for Wales, a language of decoration made up of the Three Feathers of the Princes of Wales, the Red Dragon of Cadwaladr the Blessed, the Ancient Druid, the Cromlech and stone circle, the leek of St. David, the wild mountain goat of Snowdonia (this last an excellent symbol in caricatures of Wales). Iolo went even further than this in inventing a special bardic alphabet, *Coelbren y Beirdd*, a kind of Ogham-writing, which he claimed had been carved on sticks and stones by the bards when they were forbidden pen and ink by the English conquerors, and a set of bardic symbols such as the *Nod Cyfrin* (Secret Sign) of three bars showing past, present, and future, which is still used as the ideogram of the National Eisteddfod. In fact the eisteddfodau of the romantic period were a marvellous showcase for the heraldry of culture, the halls decorated with suitable national mottoes and symbols, the bardic chairs carved with Iolo's alphabet and the oakleaves and mistletoe of Druidic symbolism. A latecomer to this language of symbols for Wales was the Welshwoman in her *pais* and *betgwn*, shawl and tall black hat, largely invented or perhaps homogenised by Augusta Hall, Lady Llanover, out of many local female costumes, in 1834 and the following years, and very soon accepted as the symbol *par excellence* of the Welsh, a kind of Welsh Marianne or John Bull.

In this section we have only mentioned a few of the great achievements of the romantic period, from the 1770s to the 1840s especially, in firing the imagination of the English and Welsh, and shaping the self-image of the Welsh people, creating what was really a new national identity at a time when Wales was drawn inexorably into the maelstrom of British social, political and industrial life, and when many of the peculiarities of Welsh nationhood had either disappeared or become moribund. In yet another crisis of modernisation or crisis of identity, the Welsh had turned to their past, and where it was wanting, had effectively adorned or invented a Wales of the imagination.

While it lasted the Romantic adventure was exhilarating, but Wales itself was changing rapidly, indeed the romantic inventions we have just mentioned were a response or reaction to the changes, the common people were converted to various forms of nonconformity, concerning themselves with social and political causes, and Wales was becoming highly industrialized. All over Europe the age of Romanticism with its delight in the remote, the quaint, the curious, was giving way to the age of Reform, Progress and Improvement, nowhere more so than in England. For much of the seventeenth and early eighteenth centuries the Welsh appeared to be comical country bumpkins, for Puritans, Wales was one of the "dark corners of the land"; during the latter half of the eighteenth century the Welsh began to be admired by English travellers, scholars and reactionaries for those qualities of backwardness formerly satirised, an admiration copied by the Romantics in the following period. This admiration evaporated quickly in the 1830s and 40s, partly because the age had changed, partly because Wales itself was changing rapidly. Even so, it was still a backward country compared with cities (almost on the borders of Wales) such as Manchester, the pacemaker of the British Empire. In the 1830s and 40s we see one of those recurring crises of conscience of the Welsh people, as they are forced to reassess themselves, and readjust to a new world. In the event they set about to change their self-image, and invent a new picture of the idealised Welsh society.

The turning point was the crisis over Welsh education in the 1840s, a time of great sectarian bitterness, and soul-searching after a decade or more of fitful rioting and rebellions in various parts of Wales, a time when in 1846 the government sent commissioners to examine Welsh society and education, published in government Blue Books 1847. This led to a great furore in Wales itself, which by 1854 was dubbed, because of a political satire by R.J. Derfel, the "Treason of the Blue Books", on the pattern of the "Treason of the Long Knives", the ancient legend about Vortigern, Rowena, Hengist and Horsa. The hullabaloo is a perfect example of romantic legend-making giving way to political satire. In the period now opening, that of Victorian Wales, the Welsh devoted themselves to self-improvement, to gaining political rights, to establishing religious, educational and political institutions, to business, industrial hard work and success. The older romanticism of course did not disappear: the eisteddfod as an institution went from strength to strength, a Welsh national anthem (*Hen Wlad fy Nhadau*) was launched in 1856,

Victorian Welshmen recited and sang huge numbers of patriotic ballads on romantic historical themes. It was however a beleaguered culture, more and more engulfed by the triumphant force of Welsh nonconformist populism, the culture of the *Gwerin.*

The leaders of the earlier generation had been patriotic squires, successful middle class people such as merchants and craftsmen and, above all, rural clergymen, but the leaders of the 1840s and subsequent decades were nonconformist journalists, preachers, and radical politicians. In their hands the history of Wales was transformed into Nonconformist and Radical propaganda, ancient princes and mythological grudges were elbowed out by new heroes, great evangelists of previous times, John Penry the "morning-star" of the Welsh reformation, William Williams the hymnwriter of Pantycelyn, Thomas Charles of Bala the pioneer of the Sunday Schools; and the new bogeymen were vindictive Anglican magistrates, or Tory squires evicting poor tenants for voting according to conscience. In their hands the very image of Wales was transformed in the 1840s and 50s into the Land of Chapels, Land of Revivals, Land of Assemblies (the *Cymanfaoedd* were either religious synods or evangelical hymn-singing sessions), Land of Great Privileges (the privileges of having been visited so often by the Holy Spirit in the great revivals), Land of the Great Choirs (the harp was now forgotten, or restricted to pubs and Romany gypsies, and chapel choirs were more respectable national symbols), Land of the White Gloves (Welsh judges were supposed to have no cases to try, hence their gifts of white gloves, so Wales had turned over a new leaf after the age of the Merthyr Rising, the Newport Rising, and the Rebecca Riots, 1831-43), and perhaps most complex and difficult to explain, Wales was also becoming the Land of the *Gwerin.*

Gwerin in Welsh means a mass, so the word means the masses of common people, as opposed to the aristocrats or clergy. Nonconformist and Radical publicists came to use this word more and more frequently as the nineteenth century advanced, excluding the aristocracy from the Welsh nation entirely, and most Anglicans for good measure, and the nation became a nation of the *Gwerin,* poor labourers, craftsmen, merchants, even capitalists, together with their printers, preachers, publicists, performers, all united in their Welsh self-consciousness as expressed in the life of the chapel. The Welsh saw themselves as the most virtuous and hard-working people in Europe, in farm, mine and factory, the most God-fearing, the best at observing the Sabbath, the most temperate and abstinent with

regard to drink, the most deeply devoted to educational improvement and to things of the mind, the most constant in their support
in country and town for the Liberal or Radical political cause, the
most classless and egalitarian in spirit. The *Gwerin* thus embraced a
very broad spectrum of the Welsh people, at their most anglicised
the *Gwerin* were merely a Welsh aping of Victorian middle class
mores, but at their least anglicised, the leaders of the *Gwerin* could
be very anti-English and anti-capitalist: an example of this is the
Patagonian Venture 1865, whereby Michael Daniel Jones and others
organized a settlement overseas, outside the British Empire (in this
case on the frontier regions of Southern Argentina), of Welsh
farmers freed from the oppression of Anglican English-speaking
squires at home. The *Gwerin* publicists were also concerned with
political action at home, and we should not forget that the
image-making was not merely a matter of giving the Welsh
self-esteem, but also a spur to a particular kind of political activity.
As to the *Gwerin* view of history, it was in the main recent history,
that of the rise of nonconformist causes from the seventeenth
century onwards (hence the celebrations throughout Wales in 1862
to commemorate the Great Ejection of 1662), but by the late
nineteenth century, when the leaders showed a greater historical
sensitivity, they portrayed the *Gwerin* of Wales as the true heirs of
Welshness, the only people who remained faithful to the old language
and things Welsh, and the abiding people of the land of Wales, the
people who had a moral right to the soil of Wales because they had
worked longest on it (or under it, in the case of miners), and were
no birds of pasage like the Vikings, Normans or English squires. This
last image appealed greatly to the late nineteenth century Welsh land
reformers such as Dr E. Pan Jones of Mostyn (Clwyd). We have
mentioned the commemoration in 1862 of the Great Ejection of 1662,
but this had little significance for large areas of Wales under the
domination of the Methodists. The Methodists were the most
assiduous of all the sects in creating a special interpretation of Welsh
history, which measured everything according to whether it aided or
hindered the Methodist revival, hence Wales before 1735 was sunk
in pagan darkness.

Innumerable biographies of nonconformist heroes great and small
were produced, even marble statues of a few of the most famous
such as Daniel Rowland at Llangeitho; by contrast when a statue of
one of the greatest of medieval Welsh princes, Llywelyn I, was put
up in Conwy 1884 he was commemorated not as an independent

prince but as founder of the Abbey of Aberconwy. There was no difficulty in putting up a memorial to the translators of the Welsh Bible (1588) at St. Asaph in 1888. A statue to Llywelyn II at Cilmeri, where he was slain 1282, was discussed continually from 1856 onwards, but Hywel Teifi Edwards has shown that not until 1902 was a monolith put up at Cilmeri – and then by an English squire Stanley Bligh, at his own expense.

Since other chapters in this book will discuss the images of Wales during the twentieth century, we will not concern ourselves with the present century, but our story cannot close without one further, and confusing, development which took place in very late Victorian and Edwardian Wales, the period which Kenneth O. Morgan has called the "Rebirth of a Nation". The publicists of early Victorian Wales had struggled to recreate the image of the country in the face of the hostility and scorn of progressives and modernists, and by the 1880s they had succeeded remarkably, Wales had come to accept its *Gwerin* image of respectability, and the Welsh were seen by the other nations of Britain as a respectable partner, it also fitted the aims of Radical leaders who were at great pains to emphasize the common interests of master and man in industry in the struggle against clerical and landlord privileges. In the same period (1880-1914) Wales had become a rich country, with a rapidly expanding population, and so could express its nationality in material terms more lavishly than ever before. The Wales of the *Gwerin* in this period began to copy the other nations and movements of Europe in celebrating its history in more lavish and colourful ways. Welsh language drama was revived from 1879 onwards, and many of the plays written by men like Beriah Gwynfe Evans drew on historical themes. The *Cymru Fydd* movement of moderate nationalism was a political failure in 1895, but it had a strong cultural effect in helping to revive Welsh history, as one sees from the work of Llywelyn Williams, Owen M. Edwards, J.E. Lloyd and others. The Gorsedd of Bards in the same period had their ceremonial made grander and more colourful, their regalia more ecclesiastical and splendid, designed now by Sir Hubert von Herkomer and Sir Goscombe John. There was also a revival of interest in Celtic contacts, with Pan-Celticism in the air. Cardiff became if not in name at least in fact a Welsh capital, its City Hall (1904) containing for the first time a Welsh pantheon of marble statues to heroes such as St. David, Boadicea, Hywel Dda, Giraldus, Llywelyn the Last, Dafydd ap Gwilym, and so on, next door to which was founded (1907) a

National Museum.

The high point of the movement, Imperial Welshness as we might term it, in a sense came with the election of a Liberal government in 1906, dedicated among other things to put forward a programme of Welsh radical demands such as the disestablishment of the Church in Wales, and the establishment of institutions for Wales such as the Museum and Library (1907), though many Welshmen felt that David Lloyd George himself with his astounding rise to world statesman from a classic *Gwerin* background was the true high watermark. It is certain that Lloyd George did as much for Welsh pride and self-esteem as any of the romantic or radical publicists of the previous hundred years. Lloyd George was also responsible for the ceremonial highpoint of the movement of Welsh Pageantry of the 1890s and 1900s, that is the Investiture of the Prince of Wales at Caernarfon 1911. It was an astounding display of wonderful ceremonial and bad history, all the clichés of the eighteenth and nineteenth centuries were rolled into one, royal ceremonial full of plumes and dragons, druids and bards, Welsh regiments, Welsh choirs, hundreds of girls in red cloaks and tall black hats, lavish decorations (Lloyd George replaced the leek with the more elegant and refined daffodil as his preferred Welsh national symbol), a monument to a special kind of Wales, part *Gwerin* Wales, part Imperial Wales – and on both those the sun was about to set. In a sense it might be suggested that the lavish pageantry of Imperial Wales from the 1890s had arisen because the sun was already setting. Lloyd George was as conscious as anyone of the failure of Cymru Fydd 1895, of the profound divisions in the field of Welsh labour relations which rent asunder the populist compromises symbolised by the *Gwerin* ideal, leading to new trades unions 1898 and at almost the same time to the rise of the Independent Labour Party. He was also aware of the foreign immigration into Wales, the rapid decline of the Welsh language between 1870 and 1900, and he must have been aware of the deep unease amongst earnest chapel folk from the 1890s onwards, which led to the brilliant but all too brief evangelical revival led by Evan Roberts in 1904 and 1905. At the time of its greatest material prosperity, Imperial Wales was in the midst of a crisis of Welshness and this time (because it was rich and because European states were doing the same thing) Wales turned to appeal to the imagination through ceremonial and monumentality. Even while all this pageantry was going on the images of a new Wales were being created, for by 1905 the Welsh were giving their country a new image as a sporting nation, above all as the nation of rugby football, an utter contrast with the last fling of Victorian non-conformity in 1904-5 or Imperial Welshness in 1911.

What can be said in conclusion about the appeal to an imagined and ideal Welshness down the ages? We are bound to return to the point at which we started, and ask with the novelist's character Gethin, whether the Welsh are doing little more than "keeping legends alive"? There is in all countries an element of cultural inertia, the tendency to keep things going simply because they have been there for so long. Many of the features mentioned in this chapter can still be found in some residual form long after their original relevance has disappeared, hence Welsh schoolgirls still don their "Welsh costumes" on March the first, hence the Welsh Rugby Union still uses the three ostrich plumes of the medieval Principality as its ideogram, hence the crowds at international matches still sing, even if they have no other connection with chapels, the hymns popular in chapels eighty years ago.

We have of course in this chapter emphasized the role of myths and images and bogus inventions in times of crisis, usually a crisis of identity, but in fact the grouping of people known as "Wales" is a palimpsest of ideas, layer on layer built up over the ages, and the group loyalty or awareness is the cumulative result of this process. Hence the impression of "keeping the legends alive". The impression has perhaps been created up to this point that Wales as such does not really exist, it is a purely artificial construct, as Gwyn A. Williams suggests is true of most European nations; they are, he says, constructed during the nineteenth century, and if we want Wales to exist, we have to make it. But a careful consideration of our evidence shows that in order to succeed a lie must be a half-truth or a white lie, that is to say, the images, myths and clichés which have the most powerful effect are made up in part from real elements, although adorned with imagination. Iolo Morganwg indulged in all kinds of forgeries but in the main they were fantasies constructed out of real facts, even his druid-bards were virtually, if not really, the heirs of the Ancient Druids, who were the earliest known intellectuals to defend the Celtic peoples. Lady Llanover's "Welsh costume", although bogus, was made up from all sorts of genuine folk costumes. The *Gwerin* as an ideal may make us into too upstanding and worthy a people, but there were many individuals in the last century whose lives resembled the vision, it was just that the idealists turned the whole pint of milk into cream. In the twentieth century it may be that

not every Welshman plays rugby, but more of us play rugby, in
proportion, than do in most other countries, certainly more than
enough to make a good cliché.

E.J. Hobsbawm has shown that the myths and images of the kind
we have mentioned are found in all countries and since they are used,
he says, as legitimators of action and as social cement, they are
inextricably intermingled with what older historians would call "real
history", and in the case of Wales, a people whose very existence has
been precarious for centuries, it is hard to see how they would have
survived at all without this elaborate structure of ideas. In Aled
Islwyn's novel Gethin bitterly bundles up fairy stories with St David,
Bishop Morgan, "The Three of Penyberth" (the nationalist arsonists
of 1936) with miners, rugby and choirs, a substitute for history –
"Legends are the shrouds of corpse-like nations". But in reality they
are the bones and sinews of living nations. As another Welsh writer,
Waldo Williams, has put it: "What is being a nation? Keeping house
in a cloud of witnesses".

FURTHER READING

S. Anglo 'The British History in early Tudor Propaganda', *Bulletin J. Rylands Library*, xliv (1961).

R. Bromwich *Trioedd Ynys Prydain in Welsh Literature and Scholarship* (Cardiff 1969).

E.T. Davies *Religion and society in nineteenth century Wales* (Llandybie 1981).

O. Ellis 'Welsh music: history and fancy', *Transactions of the Honourable Society of Cymmrodorion, 1972-3* (1974).

G. Evans *Land of my fathers* (Swansea 1974).

D. Greene *Makers and forgers* (Cardiff 1975).

D.W. Howell *Land and people in nineteenth century Wales* (London 1977).

W.J. Hughes *Wales and the Welsh in English literature from Shakespeare to Scott* (London and Wrexham 1924).

R.T. Jenkins and H. Ramage *History of the Honourable Society of Cymmrodorion 1751-1951* (London 1951).

A. Johnson *Thomas Gray and the Bard* (Cardiff 1966).

F. Jones *The princes and principality of Wales* (Cardiff 1969).

I.G. Jones *Explorations and explanations* (Llandysul 1981).

T.D. Kendrick *British antiquity* (London 1950).

D.M. Lloyd (ed) *Historical basis of Welsh nationalism* (Cardiff 1950).

D. Moore 'Cambrian antiquity' in Boon and Lewis (eds), *Welsh Antiquity* (Cardiff 1976).

K.O. Morgan *The Rebirth of a nation: Wales 1880-1980* (Oxford 1982).

P. Morgan *Eighteenth-century Renaissance* (Llandybie 1981).

P. Morgan *Iolo Morganwg* (Cardiff 1975).

P. Morgan 'From a death to a view', in Hobsbawm and Ranger (eds), *The invention of tradition* (Cambridge 1983).

P. Morgan 'From long knives to Blue Books' in R.R. Davies et al. (eds), *Welsh society and nationhood* (Cardiff 1984).

P. Morgan 'The Gwerin of Wales' in Hume and Pryce (eds), *The Welsh and their history: select readings in the social sciences* (Llandysul, forthcoming).

F. Payne *Welsh peasant costume* (Cardiff 1964).

I.C. Peate 'Welsh Society and eisteddfod medals and relics', *Transactions of the Honourable Society of Cymmrodorion, 1937* (1937).

M. Richter 'Giraldus Cambrensis: the growth of the Welsh nation', *Nat. Lib. of Wales Journal*, xvi (1970), xvii (1971).

D. Smith (ed) *A people and a proletariat. Essays in the history of Wales 1780-1980* (London 1980).

G. Thomas *The Caerwys eisteddfodau* (Cardiff 1967).

D. Williams *John Evans and the legend of Madoc* (Cardiff 1963).

G. Williams *Welsh reformation essays* (Cardiff 1967).

G. Williams *Religion, language and nationality* (Cardiff 1979).

G. Williams 'Prophecy, poetry and politics' in Hearder and Loyn (eds), *British Government and administration* (Cardiff 1974).

G.A. Williams *Madoc: the making of a myth* (London 1980).

G.A. Williams *In search of Beulah land* (London 1980).

G.A. Williams *The Welsh in their history* (London 1982).

G.A. Williams *When was Wales?* (Harmondsworth 1984).

JAMES A. DAVIES

A Picnic in the Orchard: Dylan Thomas' Wales

A Picnic in the Orchard:
Dylan Thomas' Wales

In the early summer of 1914 David John and Florence Thomas, with their eight-years-old daughter Nancy, became the first occupants of 5 Cwmdonkin Drive, Uplands, Swansea. They moved out of rented accommodation in Montpellier Street, nearer the town centre, into what, years later, their famous son described as "a mortgaged villa in an upper-class professional row".[1]

The description is revealingly pretentious and not wholly accurate. As part of a letter from Dylan Thomas, then twenty-one, to Wyn Henderson, that sophisticated and maternal friend of writers and artists, it was written to appeal and impress. D.J. Thomas doubtless had a mortgage but Cwmdonkin Drive was hardly "upper-class". Rather, it was a new street in a Swansea suburb – the Uplands – that, during the first three decades of this century, became a thriving and fast-expanding *bourgeois* world.

The expansion was a major manifestation of a fundamental change in Welsh society: the rise of its middle class.[2] Effectively, this meant the social advancement, through brains, education and determination, of working-class boys like Dylan Thomas' father. "D.J." was born in Johnstown, near Carmarthen, in 1876, the son of a railway guard. He won a scholarship to University College of Wales at Aberystwyth, took a first-class honours degree in English, and became senior English master at Swansea Grammar School. This achievement gave him little pleasure; schoolmastering was less than he felt he deserved.[3] But, given his background, he had done well. And in moving into newly-built Cwmdonkin Drive he established himself as a middle-class, home-owning, professional man. Most of his contemporaries back in Johnstown would have found the odour of drying plaster in the rooms of No. 5 to have been the sweet smell of comparative success.

In smaller Welsh places this new middle-class did not always detach itself physically from the community it served: as late as the

1950s professional men often lived in the same valley streets as miners and steelworkers. Nonetheless, in the years after 1914 like began to cling to like in, for example, the retirement ghettos of Colwyn Bay, Llandudno and Tenby, and the intellectual *laagers* of Aberystwyth and Bangor. But apart from Cardiff, in its Radyr, Rhiwbina, and Roath Park suburbs, and possibly Newport, only Swansea was big enough to create and sustain a vigorous and socially self-sufficient middle-class world. In between-wars-Wales, a country still mainly rural or socially mixed, Dylan Thomas' Swansea was a new and rare phenomenon.

It was almost wholly English-speaking. A few could speak Welsh, even fewer did so. Welsh belonged to the old, poor, rural world from which many had escaped. English was the passport not only to social and material advancement but also, for D.J. Thomas and others like him, to a vibrant language, a greater literature, and a bigger world. "D.J." certainly did not hark back nostalgically and guiltily to some muddy linguistic womb (nor did his son)[4] and his attitude was typical of most other first-generation migrants to that brave new world of urban gentility. Certainly he was not a happy man: to bitterness at his lack of further professional advancement were added strains within his marriage. But his rages, drinking, and bad language within the home – reminders of earthier antecedents – his contempt for pseudo-gentility, his eventual choice of "literature instead of life",[5] were not manifestations of cultural deprivation or the loss of roots, but expressions of dissatisfaction with the point he had reached and of hot desire to move ever further away from the world of his youth. Caitlin Thomas recalled, maliciously but shrewdly, that "no blue-blooded gentleman was a quarter as gentlemanly as Dylan's father",[6] and so fingered his frustrated social and related intellectual ambitions.

They were hardly furthered by his marriage to Florence Williams, whose parents had come from Carmarthenshire to working-class St. Thomas on Swansea's east side. Possibly "D.J." was forced to marry her; certainly it now seems a most unlikely match. As Florence Thomas she became a kind, loving, thoughtless, slightly feckless wife and mother, with no intellectual interests whatsoever, who increasingly got on her husband's nerves, and who retained strong links with St. Thomas and with the peasant world from which her family had come. Most importantly, she was unable, through character or conduct, to offer her children any admirable alternative to her husband's *bourgeois*-intellectual yearnings. In being what she

was she fostered contempt for urban and rural working-class life.
The Uplands was a "sophisticated middle-class suburb".[7] Its
inhabitants were often much concerned to protect their new-found
social status by keeping up appearances, worshipping regularly,
living moderately. Within the Uplands itself were private junior
schools, churches and chapels, a cinema, a respectable pub, a busy
shopping centre. Swansea Grammar School and the new University
College were within walking distance. The area was supported by a
thriving urban cultural infrastructure – much good music, fine
amateur and professional theatre and sport, an art gallery, a
museum, local newspapers, further cinemas and pubs – as well as
fine large shops; the town centre and its institutions were geared to
the affluent *bourgeoisie*. For, above all else, Swansea's western
suburbs remained comparatively affluent through difficult times: they
were relatively unscathed by the economic depression and mass
unemployment of the 1920s and 1930s that devastated much of
Wales and forced many to leave for England and beyond. D.J.
Thomas bought too many books and, probably, drank too much beer
to make ends meet easily; he taught evening classes and occasionally
borrowed from relatives, whilst his wife – who hardly ran a tight
domestic ship – paid tradesmen in rotation. But his job was secure,
the mortgage always paid; they continued to employ a living-in maid.

Dylan Thomas' Swansea was an unusual Welsh place but it was not
an alien wedge, a "Little England" beyond financial exigencies and
the language of heaven. It was Welsh enough; from south-east Wales
it looked very Welsh indeed. It was, probably, less sure of itself than
a comparable English area and, certainly, less generally affluent. Its
social parameters were more Welsh than English in being less harsh:
the occupation-range was wider – Thomas' close friend, the painter
Alfred Janes, was the son of a green-grocer – and a school-teacher,
for example, had more status. Yet as a middle-class enclave it
probably felt itself to have more in common with, say, parts of Bristol
than, say, parts of Tonypandy.

For the young Dylan Thomas this was Wales. It was the country
where he grew up, went early to Sunday-school, to private school
near his home, and then to the grammar-school. He acted in plays,
watched films at the Uplands Cinema, played and watched cricket,
and idled on the sands. He read his father's books in the study of No.
5 and was spoiled by a doting mother.

His reaction against this world is well-known and need only be
briefly described. Firstly, he began to write poetry, to fill the famous

notebooks. In itself this was a rejection of *bourgeois* norms and compounded by much of his poetic material: 'I see the boys of summer', for example, attacks sexual repression, the lack of sensual fulfilment as

>   the boys of summer in their ruin
>   Lay the gold tithings barren,
>   Setting no store by harvest, freeze the soils;

and insists on the urgent need to challenge conventions before death, "The sleepy man of winter",[8] makes its drastic appearance. Again, another fine early poem, 'Why east wind chills', argues against provincial complacency as the poet hears

>   content and 'Be content'
>   Ring like a handbell through the corridors.[9]

The simile, a memory of the grammar-school, places that middle-class institution firmly behind the impulse to restrict that is the essence of the suburban genteel.

These – and there are others – were confident but, at the time, confidential assertions. Less confidentially but no less confidently his letters told others what he thought of his birthplace. Geoffrey Grigson learned that Thomas lived "in the smug darkness of a provincial town", Pamela Hansford Johnson that Swansea was a "blowsy town...a dingy hell" with "unutterable melancholy blowing along the tramlines". To Swansea itself he announced that

> In this overpeopled breeding box of ours, this ugly contradiction of a town for ever compromised between the stacks and the littered bays, the Philistines exercise an inevitable dictatorship.[10]

Such hostile gestures were supported by outrageous personal behaviour: Thomas refused to work at school, paying no attention to any subject save English, played truant frequently, failed his exams, became an uncommitted and unsuccessful local journalist, drank too much too often, insulted the locals and, it is said, developed a liking for sleazy sex. He could hardly wait to leave for bohemian London "paved with poems".[11]

And yet...even such nonconformity was essentially conformist: in seeming to reject *bourgeois* attitudes Thomas only demonstrated another kind of conventional behaviour. He offered the stereotyped bohemianism that Swansea suburbanites expected of an English-language POET. For in those thoughts that do often lie too deep for teenage *angst* or wild defiance to affect them he was profoundly and permanently influenced by his middle-class upbringing. Caitlin Thomas was one of the few who realised that, despite appearances to the reckless contrary, her husband longed for "bourgeois respectability and armchair comfort"[12] and that he worried constantly about the *declassé* and poverty-haunted life he seemed fated to lead. As he told Gwen Watkins: "All we want is the little semi-detached with the little regular income".[13] Hence, also, his worries about appropriate clothes: he could, for example, fret about clean shirts when Caitlin visited him in London. She herself recalled with amazement his insistence that she dress with moderation for a visit to Carmarthen market.[14] At one time Thomas travelled daily to London from temporary homes in Sussex and Buckinghamshire to work for film companies; though a bowlered and pin-striped commuting Thomas is not quite acceptable the picture is not wholly preposterous. Much is summed up in a letter to Daniel Jones, his closest friend:

> We must, when our affairs are settled, when music and poetry are arranged so that we can still live, love, and drink beer, go back to Uplands or Sketty and found there, for good and for all, a permanent colony; living there until we are old gentlemen, with occasional visits to London and Paris, we shall lead the lives of small-town anti-society, and entertain any of the other members of the WARMDANDYLANLEY-WORLD who happen to visit the town...Jones and Thomas, that well known firm of family provisioners, shall not move out of their old town. So be it.[15]

'Warmley', Jones' family home in Sketty, is, here, the centre of a Swansea that is "the one real world",[16] where Jones and Thomas would live as gentlemen of leisure and means, travelling a little, entertaining visitors who belonged to their social circle, and being mildly and confidently anti-social. Thomas' fantasy is blatantly class-based, a reminder of his pretence at living in an "upper-class" row, of his compulsive gestures towards the moneyed and gentlemanly life – membership of London clubs, private schooling for

his children, a propensity for taxis – and of "D.J."'s thwarted
ambitions.

Thomas' Wales, then, in being identical with his Swansea, was a
small place, for the Swansea that formed him was, at least until his
mid-teens, mainly the town-centre and the western suburbs. As a
journalist he knew the old Strand area near the river and the dockland
streets close to the sea, parts of the town then full of slums,
disreputable pubs, and the sexual promise of a busy port. But of most
of Swansea, in particular of the reeking industrial, working-class
areas that had made the town "the metallurgical centre of the
world",[17] he knew very little, despite the fact that his mother's
relatives still lived in St. Thomas. In Thomas' stories that other
Swansea is no more than a place of odd behaviour and sexual
suggestiveness: in Manselton lives Daphne, the widow over whom
Mr Roberts, once a brewery executive now fallen to an insurance
collector, had come a cropper; in St. Thomas, apart from relatives,
was George Hooper's aunt, who could see through walls, and
possibly Lou who, despite, or perhaps because of, her fairground
ornaments and rose from Woolworth's, captures Jack's heart in
respectable Victoria Gardens before whisking him home to lascivious
romance.[18] Outside the ordered and reassuring suburbs was an
uncontrollable, disconcerting and confusing world.

Thomas' knowledge of geographical Wales is similar to his
knowledge of Swansea: he knew very little of most of it. Wales north
of Aberystwyth he visited only once when, during the last months of
his life he wrote a piece for the B.B.C. on the Llangollen
International Eisteddfod. North Wales, he wrote with typical South
Walian indifference, was somewhere above Harlech, "just a bit
further on, one way or the other".[19] He knew only a little more of the
South Wales valleys, although he had appeared in amateur dramatics
in Gwaen-cae-gurwen in the Amman Valley and in Trecynon, near
Aberdare. The Valleys were part of

> a strange Wales, coal-pitted, mountained, river run, full so far
> as I knew, of choirs and football teams and sheep and story-book
> tall black hats and red flannel petticoats, [that] moved about its
> business which was none of mine.[20]

Occasionally he wrote of valley-people in familiar places: a fortune
teller from Aberdare and a Fat Man from Treorchy on a fairground,
a collier from Blaina ringing the bell on the strength machine; in a

Swansea pub is a drunk from Dowlais with mine-damaged buttocks, in another are "Toop little Twms from the Valleys" on the verge of vomiting; in Paddington Station buffet is "a deacon from the Valleys on a mean blind, with his pocket-book sewn in his combs".[21] Such references are minor elements in Thomas' work, providing material for slightly grotesque satire.[22] Much the same can be said of his treatment of other South Wales towns: Llanelly is an adjunct of the Valleys, full of short, aggressive, hard-drinking, leek-wearing rugby fans;[23] Bridgend, Neath and Newport, "with their lakes and luxury gardens, their bright, coloured streets roaring with temptation",[24] are the improbable stops on Gwilym Jones' religious tour. The capital, Cardiff, hardly features, possibly, to judge from the semi-autobiographical *Adventures in the Skin Trade*, because Thomas too often passed through behind the frosted window of the London train's toilet.[25]

None of these places meant much to Thomas; outside Swansea few did. One exception was Gower, where he camped as a boy and, as a young man, enjoyed "walking alone over the very desolate Gower cliffs, communing with the cold and the quietness".[26] In 1949 only Rhossilli's lack of a pub prevented him choosing its Old Rectory in preference to the Boat House at Laugharne. The other great exception was Dyfed which, in Thomas's day, was Cardiganshire, Carmarthenshire and Pembrokeshire. The first meant New Quay and Talsarn, where Caitlin took the children for part of World War Two, and sorties to Aberystwyth. The last meant excursions to such places as St. David's or Tenby, using borrowed, chauffeured cars. Carmarthenshire, importantly, meant the triangle formed by Carmarthen town itself, Laugharne and Llanstephan.

His mother's family were from Llangain and Llanybri, between Carmarthen and Llanstephan. Despite migrations to Swansea they remained thick on the ground. Thomas spent childhood holidays not only on his aunt's farm, the famous "Fernhill",[27] but also at Blaencwm, where other relatives owned cottages. ("D.J." inherited one and lived in it for part of his retirement; his penniless son with family were inevitable visitors.) Blaencwm was peasant Wales, damp and squalid, and Thomas hated it. It was "a rat-infested cottage in the heart of Wales", "a breeding box in a cabbage valley" in an "inbred crooked county" in the "agricultural depths".[28] A description of a night walk from Llangain to Llanstephan is revealing as well as fascinating:

It was a fool of a night. The clouds were asses' ears. The moon
was ploughing up the Towy river as if he expected it to yield a
crop of stars. And the stars themselves:- hundreds of
bright-eyed urchins nudging each other over a celestial joke. It
is a long road to Llanstephan, bounded by trees and farmers'
boys pressed amorously upon the udders of their dairymaids.
But the further I walked the more lonely it became. I found the
madness of the night to be a false madness, and the vast
horseplay of the sky to be a vaster symbol. It was as if the night
were crying out the terrible explanation of itself. On all sides of
me, under my feet, above my head, the symbols moved, all
waiting in vain to be translated. The trees that night were like
prophet's fingers. What had been a fool in the sky was the wisest
cloud of all – a huge, musical ghost thumping out one, coded
tune. It was a sage of a night, and made me forgive even my own
foolishness.[29]

Thomas wrote this in November 1933. He had already produced
near-final versions of 'And death shall have no dominion', 'Why east
wind chills', 'Before I knocked' and 'The force that through the green
fuse drives the flower'; he was writing his first important short story,
'After the Fair', to be published in the *New English Weekly*. Already
he was a mature and accomplished writer. Yet this extract from a
letter is remarkable for being almost wholly lacking in a sense of
appropriate style: it is pretentious, over-written, conventionally
romantic in its rather desperate search for sermons in clouds. But,
inadvertently, it dramatizes alienation: the young man walking to
Llanstephan and able to respond to the wild beauty of the night and
country life around him only in a contrivedly "literary" and
part-facetious way is an apt paradigm for Thomas at Blaencwm. He
felt at home only on "the bound slope of a suburban hill, the Elms,
the Acacias, Rookery Nook, Curlew Avenue... the aspidistra, the
provincial drive, the morning cafe, the evening pub."[30] All else,
almost, was a foreign land.
    The exceptions are New Quay, Dyfed, and Laugharne. From
September 1944 to early summer 1945 the Thomases lived in a small
bungalow, a "wood-and-asbestos pagoda"[31] called "Majoda", just
outside New Quay. There, during the war's last winter, Dylan
Thomas found a temporary refuge in this "cliff-perched town at the
far end of Wales".[32] New Quay, then as now, was a quiet respectable
place to which middle-class people retired and which came briefly to

life as a summer seaside resort. Thomas often avoided paying his
rent – usually, his landlord suspected, by hiding in the lavatory – and,
in their cups, he and Caitlin had tremendous quarrels; they were both
nearly murdered by a drunken captain with a sub-machine gun who
thought his wife too familiar with them. But such episodes, especially
the machine-gunning, were infrequent as Thomas established a
routine that took him, most nights, to the Black Lion, and led to some
of his finest poems: 'A Winter's Tale', 'A Refusal to Mourn', 'This
side of the truth', 'The Conversation of Prayer', 'Lie still, sleep
becalmed', and much of 'Fern Hill' and 'In my craft or sullen art'. Not
since adolescence had he been so prolific. Suddenly he had again
found the right combination of subjects and circumstances. To his
London friend, T.W. Earp, he satirized New Quay as a tight,
puritanical world with some hypocrisy and much suppressed
sensuality, hearing

> from the Welsh lechered
> Caves the cries of the parches and their flocks. I
> Hear their laughter sly as gonococci. [33]

In *Quite Early One Morning* he anticipated *Under Milk Wood* in
describing with sharp affection a town full of retired sea-captains,
singers, ministers, teachers, maids, often obsessively concerned
with neat appearance. [34] Here was a smaller, saltier version of the
Uplands.

As for Laugharne: Ferris writes of it before World War Two as a
small eccentric town with a "raffish air" and a "reputation for fighting
with fists and knifes", [35] more like the setting of *West Side Story* than
a Georgian backwater in Wales. Caitlin Thomas, however, recalls its
genteel puritanism, with "'perfect Lady', their highest term of
praise", that revealed its iron hand to the young widow: its "rigid
dictates" tried to condemn her to

> a gentle spell of desultory gardening, inelegantly stooping in
> hand-woven tweed skirt, strung about with raffia baskets,
> chamois leather gloves and secateurs...Or delicate water-
> colours of detailed split-in-half, botanical plants...And in the
> evening, whist drives...[36]

Under Milk Wood catches something of this side of Laugharne life in
references to "watercolours done by hand", to Mrs Ogmore-

Pritchard's "spruced and scoured dust-defying bedroom", and to the disapproving "Thou Shalt Not" on the bedroom wall.[37] Caitlin Thomas, as an aristocratic Celt who "didn't care a bugger what anyone thought",[38] always tended to get up middle-class noses and so, in New Quay, Laugharne, or amidst the "pinched penny-pricing gentility"[39] of the Uplands, brought out their governing prejudices.

In Laugharne's Boat House, as in New Quay, Thomas was able to write poems: his fine final flowering included 'In the White Giant's Thigh', 'Do not go gentle', 'Poem on his Birthday', 'Prologue' to the *Collected Poems*, as well as *Under Milk Wood*. Further, it seems no accident that in neither place did Thomas behave with consistent outrageousness; he tended to conform to imposed social limits, leaving his "roaring boy" image for London and the U.S.A. The firmly cushioning middle-class ethos of both small towns accommodated and controlled a productive daily routine. In "Boat House Laugharne" he did nothing much in the mornings, apart from visiting his aged parents installed opposite Brown's Hotel, before crossing the road for drink and chat. Then

> Muzzily back to late lunch, of one of our rich fatty brews, always eaten alone, apart from the children…Then…up to his humble shed…and bang into intensive scribbling, muttering, whispering, intoning, bellowing and juggling of words; till seven o'clock prompt.
>
> Then straight back to one of the alternative dumps…to spend the rest of the evening in "brilliant repartee". That was a sample day…[40]

Years earlier, Thomas had described the "Provincial Rhythm"[41] of a typical Cwmdonkin day: up late, reading by the fireside, midday drinking in the Uplands Hotel, a delayed lunch before an afternoon and early evening usually spent drinking and reading until the pub called again. Laugharne, as another New Quay, had become an estuarine Uplands.

Thomas was infamous for disparaging his country: "Land of my fathers, my fathers can keep it"[42] is only one such remark. Each small Welsh industrial town, he wrote, was "a festering sore on the body of a dead country"; the "emptiness of Wales" was that of a country "completely peopled by perverts"; it was "this arsehole of the universe, this hymnal blob, this pretty sick, fond sad Wales"; more traditionally, Wales was "mean, green, horse-thieving".[43] He protests too much, of course, but one cannot argue that such expected insults simply mask an inner core of patriotic affection. Rather, they often disguise his indifference to much that was Welsh. Despite youthful rebellion and later, more occasional outbursts, his roots were deep in new middle-class surburbia; home and homeland meant the Uplands-centred Swansea of his youth and the imitations found in two small coastal towns. His Wales was there; the rest, geographically speaking, when not wholly unknown did not matter much.

A sense of Wales as a *bourgeois* bastion in the west was fundamental to Thomas' career. The extent to which it permeated his creative imagination is seen in four areas of his work in which he explored Welsh themes. Firstly, in the early prose-fiction he creates two strange rural worlds called "Jarvis" and "Cader".[44] The former is vaguely located in, it seems, the Carmarthenshire countryside; the latter, an area including "Capel Cader", "Cader House", "Cader Marshes" and "Idris Water", suggests Cader Idris, in Gwynedd, but becomes dislocated when the narrator of 'A Prospect of the Sea' views "the Jarvis peaks, and Cader peak beyond them to the edge of England". Both worlds are alike: in both Thomas conflates his varied experiences of Welsh country places.

What emerges is a sinister and menacing place of crystal-ball gazing, dancing witches and surrealistic arbitrariness. It is, too, rampant with sexuality: "he climbed alone up a stone stairs to the last tower. He put his mouth to her cheek and touched her nipple. The storm died as she touched him." Rural Wales is a Freudian land of phallic towers and feminine hills. It is also a violent land where sex means lust and is rendered in brutal metaphors: "She has put a knife in my belly and turned my stomach round", thinks the boy of the girl whom he loves on a hill. That violence is further stressed in dreams of mutilation and, importantly, in a recurring concern with the Crucifixion: "the death of Christ on a tree he loved most", Thomas writes of the gardener in 'The Tree', "...He would sit in his shed and read of the crucifixion"; in 'The Visitor' is the kind of woman who "had washed the body after it had been taken off the tree, with cool and competent fingers that touched the holes like ten blessings"; the child in 'The Tree' crucifies the Idiot in his garden. The cruelties of the punishment are stressed and savoured. And all such violent acts and imaginings are reflected in the violence of nature:

From their holes in the flanks of the hills came the rats and

weasels, hairs white in the moon, breeding and struggling as
they rushed downward to set their teeth in the cattle's throats...
Now the sheep fell and the flies were at them. The rats and the
weasels, fighting over the flesh, dropped one by one with a
wound for the sheep's fleas staring out of their hair.

But the action, strange as it is, invariably takes place in such solidly
middle-class settings as impressive country houses sited advantage-
ously to look down on the surrounding land: 'The Tree' is set in a
house with a tall tower and with extensive grounds tended by a
gardener with a potting shed; 'The Lemon' is in a house on a hill, a
large house with a central hall, corridors, and "too many rooms"; in
'A School for Witches' is the parsonage, and "Cader House", where
the doctor lives, is a "nice, square house" with "inner rooms". The
exception, in 'The Enemies' and 'The Holy Six', is Mr and Mrs
Owen's "small house with one storey, in the middle of the valley".
Yet this, too, is a *bourgeois* outcrop: Mr Owen has the bungalow built
because he finds and likes the spot during a country walk and is
sufficiently mobile and affluent to act upon desire.

To these houses come Anglican clergymen: the country rector,
the "Reverend Mr Davies", to the Owens, the Reverend Rhys Rhys
to his own vicarage. In the garden of the large house of 'The Tree',
in an idyllic moment as remote as a Seurat Sunday, the old gardener
tells Bible stories to the mistress' young son. But the clergymen are
old, tired and weak, dominated by sensual Vices or their own
disturbing inner compulsions. The gardener's stories move inevitably
to Calvary. Religion cannot counter the prevailing atmosphere of
darkness, cruelty and lechery in a fallen world, a ruined Eden, in
which the tangled weed-filled garden is a recurring symbol. In 'A
Prospect of the Sea' is inevitable retribution: as the girl entices the
boy into the sexual sea an old man builds an ark, creatures move, and
rain starts to fall.

When he wrote these stories Thomas' experience of rural Wales
was restricted to life at Blaencwm, Fernhill and Johnstown. Thus his
use of socially superior settings instead of his relations' small farms
and damp cottages, and of Anglican clergy for the nonconformist
ministers who generally, in Wales, attended to those like or below
his own family, reveal the extent to which his work remade other
Welsh areas in terms of the social patterns and aspirations of
Swansea's suburbia. The settings and much of the social detail in
these early stories spring from the same impulse that led him to

boast of living in "an upper-class professional row". The symbols of ruin, the drift towards destruction, dramatise Thomas' ultimate rejection of that foreign land he tried to make familiar.

"Jarvis" and "Cader" evade precise topographical placing until the moment in 'A Prospect of the Sea' when the boy in the grass with a girl grows afraid: "If he cried aloud to his uncle in the hidden house, she would make new animals, beckon Carmarthen tigers out of the mile-away wood to jump around him and bite his hands". Suddenly we are near Fernhill and in the imagined remembered world of Thomas' childhood holidays. In this last, in 'A Visit to Grandpa's' and the three Fernhill pieces – 'The Peaches' and the poems 'After the Funeral' and 'Fern Hill' – is another response to Welsh affairs.

'A Visit to Grandpa's' is about paternal relations in Johnstown. The holidaying young boy observes a world made strange: "Dan Tailor stepped from his window where he sat like an Indian priest but wearing a derby hat...an old woman by the gate of a cottage...ran inside like a pelted hen". Grandpa rides horses in his dreams and wants a Llangadock burial. He is found walking to his grave "like a prophet who has no doubt".[45]

'The Peaches' opens *Portrait of the Artist as a Young Dog* with a journey into darkness: young Dylan's Uncle Jim drives him through the night from Swansea to stay at "Gorsehill" farm. The journey is from a "warm, safe" world to a world in decline:

> The ramshackle outhouses had tumbling, rotten roofs, jagged holes in their sides, broken shutters, and peeling whitewash... There was nowhere like that farm-yard in all the slapdash county, nowhere so poor and grand and dirty as that square of mud and rubbish and bad wood and falling stone...

Physical dilapidation is accompanied by cultural and personal decay. Uncle Jim is a drunkard who takes the farm-stock to pay for beer and relaxes in a broken bardic chair; his son, Gwilym, training for the ministry, preaches to terrorise and exploit young Dylan and his friend Jack, and masturbates in the field lavatory; Aunt Annie is a pathetic and ineffectual figure. The weed-filled garden returns as familiar symbolic comment on this graceless world.

Young Dylan is "a royal nephew in smart town clothes, embraced and welcomed". He feels superior to and distances himself from this ruined rural outpost. His affiliations are with middle-class Wales that is genteel Swansea and nowhere is this seen more clearly than in the ending. For 'The Peaches' centres upon the visit of Jack Williams, Dylan's rich Swansea friend, who stays at "Gorsehill" for only one night, during which he is frightened by Uncle Jim's drunken threats, before ringing his mother to take him home:

> Mrs. Williams sent the chauffeur for Jack's luggage.
> Annie came to the door, trying to smile and curtsy, tidying
> her hair, wiping her hands on her pinafore.
> Mrs. Williams said, "Good afternoon", and sat with Jack in the
> back of the car and stared at the ruin of Gorsehill.
> The chauffeur came back. The car drove off, scattering
> the hens. I ran out of the stable to wave to Jack. He sat
> still and stiff by his mother's side. I waved my handkerchief.

Annie reacts with ingrained servility: Mrs Williams is a disliked but superior stranger. Dylan feels no familial loyalty. His only concern is to retain friendly contact with his Swansea world and with that moneyed, powerful part to which he fervently wished to belong.

'After the funeral (In memory of Ann Jones)',[46] the poem that Thomas began when his aunt died in 1933, is a moving and compassionate response to an individual and the representative of a way of life. As Walford Davies has pointed out, there is "a recognition of the wilder inheritance that lay behind the suburban tidiness of his parents' home";[47] Conran detects Thomas' uncertain relationship to both his aunt and her world.[48] That uncertainty, a theme of the poem, manifests itself in doubts about appropriate style, whether the "grand style" or "bardic" utterance is suitable for Ann's commemoration. Here is a typically *bourgeois* reluctance to raise the voice: the poem's abrupt transition from the extravagant gesture to the deeply-felt yet tightly controlled and *simpler* response to Ann's life ("Her flesh was meek as milk...") is a move, not altogether sustained, into a different *social* register. Further, Ann Jones' "scrubbed and sour humble hands", evidence of a harsh, puritanical and subservient Welsh rural life, become in death "these cloud-sopped marble hands" that, writes Thomas, "storm me forever over her grave". "Storm" is a crucial image in pointing to the poet's struggle to remain aloof and to the strength of his suburban defences. He is more the affected tourist than the empathetic exile now returned; certainly he is, even here, as much the observer as was young Dylan in 'The Peaches' and 'A Visit to Grandpa's'.

'Fern Hill'[49] is about remembered empathy; it reveals more significant patterns of thought. As a child, recalls the poet, he was "prince of the apple towns" who "lordly had the trees and leaves/Trail with daisies and barley". He was "honoured among wagons" and "among foxes and pheasants"; he was both pursuer and controller, "huntsman" and "herdsman". That is, childhood was hierarchical, almost feudal. Whilst exploring the solipsism of youth the poem demonstrates the inescapable influence of an upbringing in a world of gradations and pretentions. Memories are coloured not only by aging but by a sense of superior social class. 'Fern Hill' is the rural dream of a man from the Uplands brought up by "D.J." and used to a living-in maid.

"D.J.", in his aspiring suburban self, is a crucial source of Dylan Thomas' special kind of Welshness. Of Thomas' three most important poetic responses to his father, two can serve as introductions to the third. 'I fellowed sleep'[50] ends with fathers triumphing in parental competition for the son:

> There grows the hours' ladder to the sun,
> Each rung a love or losing to the last,
> The inches monkeyed by the blood of man,
> An old, mad man still climbing in his ghost,
> My fathers' ghost is climbing in the rain.

This packed final stanza is ambitiously concerned with mystical aspiration, evolution, ideas of life and death, and the fathers' influential presence. But such impressive ideas depend upon the simple *bourgeois* cliché of upward mobility, of "climbing the ladder". This text/sub-text link anticipates effects in Thomas' finest work.

'Elegy'[51], his final and unfinished poem, celebrates "D.J."'s strength of character:

> Too proud to die, broken and blind he died
> The darkest way, and did not turn away,
> A cold kind man brave in his narrow pride
>
> On that darkest day. Oh, forever may
> He lie lightly, at last...

'D.J.' is admired for his middle-class virtues of restraint and brave reserve. In the manner of his dying he exhibited qualities different in degree but not different in kind from those that sustained respectable life in the suburbs of west Swansea, where folk valued privacy and, too often, hid tensions and troubles behind a front of normality heroically cultivated. The poem's main structural and rhetorical devices in themselves dramatise control and restraint. The poem is in quatrains divided into triplets; the consequent tension between stanza-form and rhyme-scheme, and between the sentence with its emotional momentum and the imposed stanza-form, suggests an impulse towards fragmentation but with a stronger stress on the poet's controlling hand. Patterns of alliteration, internal echoes, near-repetitions, and clearly-developing symbolism, strengthen that hand in mastering grief. Thomas' obsessive concern with formal problems, his choice of poetic structures of amazing strictness, are, here as elsewhere, a consequence of his upbringing, a reflection of the ordered and authoritative structures that, regardless of his own behaviour, filled his formative years.

'Do not go gentle into that good night',[52] the most famous of the "fatherly" poems, combines the cited qualities of the other two. Firstly, the strict intricacies of the villanelle contain a deeply emotional subject in, paradoxically, a clamping yet intensifying context. This last, the poetic form, is in creative tension with the poem's ostensible purpose: though Thomas' father is urged to reject conventional behaviour, to put aside "gentle"-manly conduct and to "rage", the poem's rigid formality insists on the great and continuing power of those very conventions. Secondly, the special suggestiveness of the diction links a powerful sense of death, the facing of death, and ways of living lives, with reminders of prosaic suburban existence. Line one contains "gentle" with, to repeat, its second sense of "gentlemanly" or "genteelly", and "good night", which is both a morally charged euphemism for death *and* the casual late-evening farewell of Uplands acquaintances. In line two "close of day" certainly evokes life's end but also echoes "close of play" to recall Thomas' love of cricket fostered by regular watching at the county ground below Brynmill. In such words and phrases, as in further references to "gentle" and "good night", the poem excavates a potent sub-text that is also exposed in the simple moral insistence of "right" and in the use of "wave", a gesture of farewell *and* part of sea-imagery that, with "green bay", not only symbolises existence but recalls Swansea's coastal setting. Against the reference to "wild men...who caught...the sun in flight" that early love of cricket again presses, as does Thomas' implied disapproval – the pun on "sun" – of his own behaviour. The simple, mainly monosyllabic diction – the language really used by suburbanites – and the poet's suggestive evasiveness – death is only mentioned once; it is the "light" that is "dying" – are other strong reminders that to confront his father was, for Thomas, to explore his own roots in a profoundly-experienced middle-class world which, in the deepest sense, he never left.

The main "Laugharne" poems of the Boat House years are near-mythic responses to the countryside and rural life: 'In Country Sleep', 'Over Sir John's hill', 'In the White Giant's Thigh', 'Poem on his Birthday' and 'Prologue' to the *Collected Poems*.[53] These are not always responses to *Welsh* rurality: 'In the White Giant's Thigh' almost certainly depends on the poet's memories of the Cerne Abbas figure near Ringwood, in Hampshire, where he had often stayed at his mother-in-law's home. The countryside of this poem is no different, in essence, from that of the Laugharne-located poems of the remainder of the 'In Country Heaven' sequence for, in his closing years, Thomas was not celebrating a new-found affinity with a land tilled by previously despised forebears but using the countryside and the sea as metaphors to explore the relationship between life, creativity, and death. In doing so he again reveals his own persisting sense of identity.

If, as has been suggested, poetic formality is, in Thomas' work, expressive of the ordering, conforming impulse essential to middle-classness, then these late works are the most *bourgeois* of poems. They are all tightly controlled, fiendishly strict. 'Poem on his Birthday', for example, alternates lines of six and nine syllables. 'Prologue', famously, rhymes the first and last of its one hundred and two lines, then the second and penultimate, until the central two lines form a rhyming couplet: "A most difficult technical task...", Thomas wrote ruefully, "Why I acrosticked myself like this, don't ask me".[54] Related to the exercise of external authority via form and structure is a thematic desire for order and pattern: 'Over Sir John's hill' views instinctive natural violence in terms of the legal system; in 'In Country Sleep' the poet visualises nature as a process with "purpose and control", as a "'designed', 'true', 'sure', 'shaped' and 'ruled' universe".[55] Again, these are confident poems packed with authoritative statements: "Never and never/...Fear or believe"; "the women of the hill/Love for ever meridian;"; "Heaven that never was/Nor will be ever is always true". The tone and affirmatory stance assert *bourgeois* confidence. A further way in which Thomas turns back to his Uplands upbringing is in his use of nursery rhymes and stories, most notably in the "Mrs Bond" references in 'Over Sir

John's hill', and in the use of *Red Riding Hood* and *Beauty and the Beast* in 'In Country Sleep'. Links with a world of warm beds, a doting mother, adequate means and sufficient order, are intensified by the tendency, for example, in 'In the White Giant's Thigh', to view a disordered, even violent, world – here, the natural one – from a position of seeming security. Thomas has remained the observer; he has become, as T.H. Jones noticed, an even more objective one.[56] 'Prologue' offers forceful illustration. From a land of "castle keep...plumbed bryns...Hollow farms", birds, and "animals thick as thieves", all sinking beneath an undefined flood, Thomas stands apart with "Wales in my arms". The mysterious rural world is carefully separated from what he regards as his country; the latter seems to be loved and is certainly embraced; significantly, in also connoting cradling, it is associated with upbringing.

As early as 1934, in his short story, 'The Orchards',[57] Thomas embalmed his idea of Wales. The story has powerful biographical elements: the central character, Marlais, has Thomas' middle name and his first name is recalled in Marlais' journey across Wales to the sea.[58] He steps from his "top-storey room in the house on a slope over the black-housed town" where "cloud...bursts in cold rain on the suburban drives", leaves "the great stack forests" and the "long dead of the stacked south" of the country, the scenes of industrial waste, and moves over the "water-dipping hills" to

> the sea-village road where the blossoms of the orchards hung over the wooden walls...into a clump of villages. He laid himself down in the grass, and noon fell back bruised to the sun; and he slept till a handbell rang over the fields. It was a windless afternoon in the sisters' orchards, and the fair-headed sister was ringing the bell for tea.
>
> He had come very near to the end of the indescribable journey. The fair girl, in a field sloping seaward three fields and a stile from Marlais, laid out a white cloth on a flat stone. Into one of a number of cups she poured milk and tea, and cut the bread so thin she could see London through the white pieces. She stared hard at the stile and the pruned, transparent hedge, and as Marlais climbed over, ragged and unshaven, his stripped breast burned by the sun, she rose from the grass and smiled and poured tea for him.

The whole story translates, without strain, into autobiography:

Thomas turns away from suburban Uplands, from industrial Swansea and the smoky south, to head west into rural Wales only for us to discover that, as always in Thomas' life, despite his journey and changed, disreputable appearance, in his end is his beginning. The picnic in the orchard refers us back to the Uplands of authoritative, scholastic handbells, clipped hedges, mingled sexual allurement and maternal/domestic comfort, sandwiches cut with ineffable gentility, and glimpses of wider, metropolitan horizons. A *bourgeois* upbringing is recreated in a field.

Thomas' work was shaped by that upbringing and always reflected it; and in his life he was most at ease when he could function within familiar parameters once thoughtlessly rejected but remaining insidiously influential. His great importance as a writer depends in part on his middle-class affinities, on demonstrating, in 'Do not go gentle', for instance, links between seemingly prosaic existence and deep feelings, strong emotions, the imaginative potential of suburban man. He was one of a large and growing social group. Marlais' picnic is a microcosm not only of Dylan Thomas' Wales but of the known and loved country of many named Davies, Evans, Williams and Jones.[59]

NOTES

1. *Selected Letters*, ed. Constantine Fitzgibbon (Dent, 1956), p.167. I refer to this volume as *SL*.
2. See, e.g., Kenneth O. Morgan, *Rebirth of a Nation: Wales 1880-1980* (New York & Cardiff: O.U.P. & U.W.P., 1981), pp.125ff. & *passim*; Gwyn A. Williams, *When Was Wales?* (Harmondsworth: Penguin, 1985), p.265 & *passim*.
3. For basic biographical information on Dylan Thomas and his parents I have drawn on Constantine Fitzgibbon, *The Life of Dylan Thomas* (Dent, 1965), and, particularly, Paul Ferris, *Dylan Thomas* (Harmondsworth: Penguin, 1978).
4. Roland Mathias, 'A Niche for Dylan Thomas', *Poetry Wales*, vol.9, no.2, Autumn 1973, pp.51-74, interprets Thomas' life and work in terms of cultural dislocation consequent upon a lack of contact with "the older Welshness of Wales" (p.54). Despite Mathias' odd notion that the "real Wales" (p.53) was rural and Welsh-speaking, the article has some fine insights. I consider that "the language" was never much of an issue for Thomas.

5.   Mathias, p.55.
6.   *Leftover Life to Kill* (Putnam, 1957), p.57.
7.   Peter Stead, 'The Swansea of Dylan Thomas', *Dylan Thomas Remembered* (Swansea: The Dylan Thomas Society Wales Branch, 1978), p.22.
8.   *The Poems*, ed. Daniel Jones (Dent, 1971), pp.91-2. I refer to this edition as *PDJ*.
9.   *PDJ*, p.56.
10. Respectively: *SL*, pp.18, 43-4, 135, 92.
11. 'The Fight', *Portrait of the Artist as a Young Dog, The Collected Stores* (Dent, 1983), p.159. I refer to the work as *Portrait* and to this volume as *CS*.
12. *Leftover Life to Kill*, p.64.
13. Ferris, p.164.
14. *Leftover Life to Kill*, p.57.
15. Daniel Jones, *My Friend Dylan Thomas* (Dent, 1977), pp.42-3.
16. *ibid* p.41.
17. *The Swansea Directory 1929* (Swansea: The Bart Cronin Advertising Agency Ltd, 1929), p.65.
18. Respectively: 'Where Tawe Flows', 'Extraordinary Little Cough', 'One Warm Saturday', *Portrait, CS*, pp.181 & 183-4, 166, 219-238.
19. *SL* p.203.
20. 'Reminiscences of Childhood' (second version) *Quite Early One Morning*, Aldine Paperback edition (Dent, 1971), p.8.
21. Respectively: 'After the Fair', 'Holiday Memory', *CS*, pp.2, 2, 309; 'One Warm Saturday', 'Old Garbo', *Portrait, CS*, pp.225, 213; *Adventures in the Skin Trade, CS*, p.255. "Toop" (*CS*, p.213) is a phonetic version of the Welsh word "Twp", meaning "stupid".
22. Respectively: 'Jarley's', *CS*, p.350; *Under Milk Wood* (Dent, 1957), p.6; 'The Holy Six', *CS* p.101; 'Laugharne', *Quite Early One Morning*, p.70.
23. 'Where Tawe Flows', *Portrait, CS*, p.184; *Adventures in the Skin Trade, CS*, p.285.
24. 'The Peaches', *Portrait, CS*, p.128.
25. *CS*, pp.246-8.
26. *SL* p.27.
27. The name of the farm is "Fernhill" (one word); Thomas' poem is 'Fern Hill' (two words).
28. Respectively: *SL*, pp.34, 278, 279, 52.
29. *SL*, p.53.
30. *Letters to Vernon Watkins*, ed. Vernon Watkins (Dent and Faber & Faber, 1957), p.23.
31. *SL*, p.266.
32. 'Quite Early One Morning', *Quite Early One Morning*, p.20.
33. *PDJ*, p.179.
34. *Quite Early One Morning*, pp.19-20.
35. *Dylan Thomas*, pp.164-5.
36. *Leftover Life to Kill*, p.17-18.

37. Respectively: *Under Milk Wood*, pp.2, 14, 3.
38. Ferris, p.164.
39. *Leftover Life to Kill*, p.56.
40. *ibid.* pp.36-7.
41. *SL*, pp.26-7.
42. Quoted in *Adam*, no.238 (1958), p.68.
43. Respectively: *SL*, pp.35, 86, 143, 350, 283.
44. Quotations and references in this and the next six paragraphs are taken from *CS*, pp.5-48, 54-71, 87-103, 109-114.
45. Quotations from this and the next two paragraphs are taken from *CS*, pp.122-143.
46. *PDJ*, pp.136-7.
47. *Dylan Thomas*, Walford Davies, Writers in Wales Series (Cardiff: UWP, 1972), p.46.
48. Anthony Conran, *The Cost of Strangeness* (Llandysul: Gomer Press, 1982), pp.180-87.
49. *PDJ*, pp.195-6.
50. *PDJ*, pp.101-2.
51. *PDJ*, pp.216-17.
52. *PDJ*, pp.207-8.
53. Respectively: *PDJ*, pp.197-201, 201-3, 203-5, 208-11, 3-5.
54. *SL*, p.377.
55. Walford Davies, p.78.
56. *Dylan Thomas*, Writers & Critics (Edinburgh: Oliver & Boyd, 1970), p.102.
57. *CS*, pp.41-48.
58. The name 'Dylan' is from *The Mabinogion*. He is "the rich yellow-haired boy" who "made for the sea" and became known as "Dylan Eil Ton" (Sea son of Wave). See *The Mabinogion*, trans. Gwyn Jones & Thomas Jones (Dent, 1976), pp.63-4.
59. This essay occasionally draws on the introduction to my *Dylan Thomas's Places* (Llandybie: Christopher Davies, 1986), by kind permission.

How to Write Anglo-Welsh Poetry

John Davies

It's not too late I suppose...
You could sound a Last Post or two,
and if you can get away with saying
what's been said, then do.

First, apologise for not being able
to speak Welsh. Go on: apologise.
Being Anglo-*any*thing is really tough;
any gaps you can fill with sighs.

And get some roots, juggle names like
Taliesin and ap Gwilym, weave
a Cymric web. It doesn't matter what
they wrote. Look, let's not be naive.

Now you can go on about the past
being more real than the present –
you've read your early R.S. Thomas,
you know where Welsh Wales went.

Spray place-names around. Caernarfon.
Cwmtwrch. Have, perhaps, a Swansea
sun marooned in Glamorgan's troubled
skies; even the weather's Welsh, see.

But a mining town is best, of course,
for impact, and you'll know what to say
about Valley Characters, the heart's dust
and the rest. Read it all up anyway.

A quick reference to cynghanedd
always goes down well; girls are cariad;
myth is in; exile, defeat, hills...
almost anything Welsh and sad.

Style now. Nothing fancy: write
all your messages as prose then chop
them up – it's how deeply red and green
they bleed that counts. Right, stop.

That's it, you've finished for now –
just brush your poems down: dead, fluffed
things but your own almost. Get
them mounted in magazines. Or stuffed.

TONY BIANCHI

R.S. Thomas and His Readers

R.S. Thomas and His Readers

In 1972 Jeremy Hooker cautioned us against laying too much stress upon those poems of R.S. Thomas concerned with "the condition and identity of Wales" and the "primal sanctities of its rural way of life".[1] Wales, it seemed, was now, and indeed had all along been a metaphor for the poet's "inner tensions": a cause of them, too, perhaps, but always subordinate to the real focus of interest, namely the "quarrel with the self". Thomas himself remarked, as early as 1968: "I became rather tired of the themes about nationalism and the decay of the rural structure in Wales",[2] and again in 1975: "I used to propagandise on behalf of Welsh Country Life and...the Welsh identity; well, now I've wrung that dishcloth dry".[3] A balanced, detached reading of the poet's output since the publication of *The Stones of the Field* in 1946 does, indeed, tend to confirm Hooker's view that "the definition of his work largely on the basis of...these preoccupations falsifies not only the whole but also the centre of his poetry". Even in 1972, Hooker was confident that such a "half-truth really is a straw man by now...", and most English critics have been content to leave the argument at that and, now that Iago Prytherch has "vacated the stage for God", simply await the next instalment of "surprises", "obsessions" and "fundamental questions".[4]

All the more surprising, therefore, that on May 14 1983 the *Western Mail* should welcome the poet to Cardiff on the occasion of his seventieth birthday as "a man whose genius has found expression in the search for [the] ancient simplicities of rural Wales". Surprising, too, that R. Gerallt Jones, in introducing an evening of celebration at the Sherman Theatre some days later, should acclaim R.S. Thomas as above all else a poet "who has expressed the national identity of the Welshman". The audience of five hundred – surely the biggest that any contemporary Welsh poet could command – seemed to concur.

Of these two responses to R.S. Thomas' work – that of the

detached academic seeking objective meaning and that of the "common" Welsh reader gathering usable images – it is the second with which this discussion is concerned. What follows, therefore, is not a study of R.S. Thomas' poetry, nor even of his attitude to Wales. It is, rather, an examination of how a very small part of his work has lent itself uniquely well to serve the interests of a particular readership in Wales. That readership – product of a re-alignment of cultural and class interests since the last war – has succeeded in constructing and institutionalising a fixed reading of Thomas' poetry quite independently of the growing range of academic interpretations of his work. More than any other English-language writer in Wales, R.S. Thomas has been reconstructed in the image of his own audience. The following discussion is a preliminary attempt to trace the features of that audience and to define the central role played by R.S. Thomas in its development.

Centrality is something which Welsh critics have been very ready to grant R.S. Thomas. In Roland Mathias' view, he "has affected the minds and hearts of a whole generation of people, particularly students, teachers, lecturers, professional men. He has changed their attitude towards the essential Wales over a period of something like forty years".[5] So complete has been the process of his institutionalisation that he now appears as a natural object in other poets' landscapes: "At sunset we climb Uwchmynydd/to a land's-end/where R.S. Thomas walks"[6]; "his sole-voice toiling like a sea bell under that drowned land"[7]; "He sits/writing by a north cliff/watching aliens in the lost/parishes..."[8] – and also, of course, as the object of parody, as in Peter Finch's 'A Welsh Wordscape'.[9] His work is quoted with remarkable frequency to illustrate, clinch or simply to leaven an argument, be its subject literary, historical, political or even sociological. Gwyn A. Williams' *When Was Wales?* (1985), a major one-volume history of the Welsh, is topped and tailed with Thomas' 'Welsh History' and 'The Welsh Hill Country' while Bud B. Khleif in *Ethnic Boundaries, Identity and Schooling* quotes 'If You Can Call it Living' to illustrate some "socio-economic and identity issues".[10] Thomas has also been institutionalised, in a stricter sense, through the school curriculum. For eleven years between 1970 and 1983, he was the only Welsh poet represented on the WJEC English Literature O-Level syllabus. Approximately twenty-two per cent of all Welsh candidates for this examination studied his work each year during this period, while it was studied generally at sixty-six per cent of all Welsh secondary schools – a short way behind Dylan Thomas, who scored seventy-three per cent, but well ahead of the next challenger, Emlyn Williams, who mustered a mere fifteen per cent.[11]

The precise nature of Thomas' appeal has depended to some degree upon the language of his audience. Many critics of Anglo-Welsh literature have seen him as a cornerstone of a canon which they themselves are still in the process of constructing. Peter Elfed Lewis affirmed that "the achievement of R.S. Thomas in itself justifies the Anglo-Welsh poetic tradition...and confirms that this tradition does have its identity".[12] Raymond Garlick, in his *Introduction to Anglo-Welsh Literature* (1970) – a pioneering attempt at constructing an historical native tradition in the English language – counterpoints the work of Thomas with that of Morris Kyffin, George Herbert, James Howell, Rowland Watkyns, John Dyer, Edward Davies, Morgan Llwyd and others, thereby lending Thomas an almost messianic aura. Harri Webb has dubbed him "Prifardd of English-speaking Wales"[13] and Tony Conran its "prophet",[14] while Randal Jenkins has seen in him something of an Anglo-Welsh T.S. Eliot.[15] Critics of literature in Welsh, on the other hand, have claimed Thomas for their own. For *Y Fflam*[16] and Alun Llywelyn Williams,[17] it was Thomas' identification with an historic, Welsh-speaking and rural Wales which entitled him to be regarded as a Welsh poet, despite his language. Even a hostile reading like that of Dafydd Elis Thomas[18] confirms the received image of Thomas as above all the purveyor of a Wales which is "essentially rural" and "profoundly historical". For Prys Morgan, his definitive contribution has been "the defence of the Welsh language and nationhood, through the medium of English":[19] a view echoed by John Rowlands,[20] and by Ned Thomas for whom Thomas' Welshness as a poet is synonymous with the degree to which he can translate "the Welsh language culture" into an appropriate English idiom.[21]

At bottom, however, these alternative views of Thomas are inseparable. Since the last war, the identity of Anglo-Welsh literature has been premised upon the perceived seniority and organic continuity of Welsh-language literature. Within this consensus, R.S. Thomas has been useful to both camps because he has provided the means of acknowledging a national literature in English which yet derives its legitimacy from its subordination to the older literature. This analysis was first advanced, understandably, by a Welsh-speaking intelligentsia jealously pressing its claim that it and it alone could speak for the whole of Wales. Saunders Lewis' lecture, *Is There An Anglo-Welsh Literature?*, averred in 1937 that, as literature is the product of an organic community and industrialism the destroyer of such communities, no national literature in English, the language of industrial Wales, could possibly emerge: its very existence signalled the "undirected drifting of Welsh national life", and its Welshness was a borrowed and tenuous one. In 1953 Aneirin Talfan Davies[22] reinforced the image of the Anglo-Welsh writer as "translator", contending that "the perpetuation of the Welsh language is the *sine qua non* of any culture that can be called *Welsh in Wales*": the Anglo-Welsh writer looked at Wales "through the refracting windows of a foreign language" which was incapable of apprehending the "soul" of Wales. Waldo Williams, the Welsh-language poet, declared his agreement with this position in an early issue of Raymond Garlick's *Dock Leaves*,[23] seeing the Welshness of the Anglo-Welsh writer as a "compensatory" and "synthetic" response to the loss of Welsh: Welsh literature in English was the literature of an unstable social "predicament", whose key was the fate of the Welsh language. D. Tecwyn Lloyd,[24] an important and frequent commentator in Welsh on the field, elaborated this view in 1967: Anglo-Welsh literature was the affliction which attended "detribalisation" – "and there is no future for such a thing as that". Bobi Jones,[25] Professor of Welsh at Aberystwyth and the most significant ideologue amongst contemporary critics in Wales, was still developing this analysis in the 1970's, in line with a growing interest among nationalists in colonial literatures and in the internal-colonialist rendition of the Celtic "fringe". Anglo-Welsh literature, according to this reading, was a "perversion of normality...a grunt or a cry or an odour rising from a cultural wound of a special kind..." – it was an "interesting colonial product", whereas literature in Welsh was "a *complete* literature".

Remarkably, many Anglo-Welsh writers assented to this sub-ordinate role. Raymond Garlick, as we have seen, constructed a distinct Anglo-Welsh canon which he nevertheless held only to be Welsh "at one remove",[26] and only Welsh at all because of "seepage" (Tony Conran's term) of certain key attitudes and predispositions from the culture of the Welsh-speaking community – a point later reinforced in the two introductions to the field, by Raymond Garlick and Glyn Jones, and more recently in the introduction to the major anthology, *Anglo-Welsh Poetry 1480 - 1980*. Whatever their eagerness not to "play Esau to the Welsh poet's Jacob",[27] for much of the post-war period Anglo-Welsh poets have also looked forward, with John Tripp, to the day "this dry/English pen, this arrogant/

instrument, will no longer/be required",[28] an attitude fundamental to that "poetry of exile" observed by Tony Conran in the 1960's. Conran himself, in 1963, hailed three new Anglo-Welsh writers as "strangers" and "exiles",[29] striving to re-enter the fold through commitment to the (Welsh) language and political nationalism. This trend reached its apogee in Harri Webb's declaration (made, disconcertingly, on 1 April 1985) that he would cease contributing to the "load of old rubbish" which was Anglo-Welsh literature and concentrate on the "kernel" of the Welsh identity, the Welsh language.[30] R.S. Thomas, following MacDiarmid's notion of a "stop-gap anti-English literature in Scotland",[31] argued in 1946 that Anglo-Welsh literature "might simply be a phase in the re-cymrification of Wales",[32] still maintained in 1978 that the Anglo-Welsh writer "speaks a foreign tongue",[33] and throughout this period became the natural focus for this whole complex of attitudes.

The construction of Anglo-Welsh literature since the last war has, however, been much more than merely a formation of abstract attitudes and definitions. It has provided the material with which a new cultural intelligentsia has attempted to mould itself in Wales: not yet sufficiently confident or entrenched to challenge the established Welsh-speaking intelligentsia (thus the deference), but aware of a vast English-speaking readership for whom they must "become a voice, drawing them back to the tradition from which they have become separated and, in so doing forging a new tradition, establishing a new literature..."[34] The Irish literary renaissance was an early model for these aspirations: H. Idris Bell,[35] in 1922, toyed with the notion of a new "Anglo-Welsh movement" headed by a Welsh Yeats, an idea which R.S. Thomas himself took up in 1946.[36] In the same year the nationalist historian A.W. Wade-Evans looked to an "Anglo-Welsh literary movement...on the Anglo-Irish model" for the "resurrection of Wales".[37] Keidrych Rhys, a prime mover in this new orientation of Anglo-Welsh writing, was fully aware of the difficulties attending such an aspiration. "The Anglo-Welsh 'intelligentsia'", he wrote "is so inorganic as scarcely to be more than a group who happen to be connected with a single region. [They] can't make their opinions and influence felt on any particular matter as the Irish can or could through their Academy of Letters".[38] In keeping with the consensus outlined above, however, the formation of such an "Anglo-Welsh movement" would for Rhys be no more than "a stage on the way back to the use of Welsh for literature" and an agent "in securing sympathy in the better English minds for Welsh cultural ideals and aims". Once more, the very basis of an organic English-speaking literary intelligentsia – its potential readership – is paradoxically ignored. Instead, this gathering of "displaced souls"[39] has sought coherence by establishing what Allen Upward called "syndicates of intelligence". Accordingly, Keidrych Rhys' short-lived Cymdeithas Cymru Newydd provided, in 1939, the first attempt to institutionalise an English-speaking intelligentsia within a national context. It was followed, in the mid-sixties, by the Guild of Welsh Writers,[40] and subsequently by the English section of Yr Academi Gymreig and the Welsh Union of Writers. The achievements of these bodies has been piecemeal, however, and they have failed to force major inroads into the vital area of education. Despite Raymond Garlick's[41] thesis that the English literature of Wales finds its historical continuity as the expression of the professional classes, this was a junior intelligentsia, lacking the social and professional cohesion of its Welsh-speaking counterpart. Of the forty-three Anglo-Welsh poets anthologised in *The Lilting House,* twenty-four were either born or spent a large part of their lives or careers outside Wales. Fifteen teachers provided the only significant professional grouping and there were only three lecturers: one an Englishman, the others exiled for much of their lives in Australia and the Middle East. By contrast, of the forty-two poets represented in J.P. Clancy's *Twentieth Century Welsh Poems,* nineteen were lecturers and there were also sizeable groups of ministers and journalists: all primary positions for the reproduction of ideology.

This nascent Anglo-Welsh "aristocracy of intellect",[42] marginalised by an "Athenian" Welsh-speaking elite[43] and excluded from positions of cultural influence, understandably found its options highly circumscribed. In the event, a distinct Anglo-Welsh grouping did emerge, but only by seeking to emulate its Welsh-speaking counterpart or through a cruder piggy-backing by which it won a borrowed status which left the problems of readership once more unresolved. The euphemisms for this process, much vaunted in the 1960's, were "reconciliation"[44] and "rapprochement".[45]

Why did the new Anglo-Welsh find the exclusive claims of the Welsh-language elite so irresistible? The answer to this paradox lies partly in the "desperate need of an emerging middle-class...to find a range of attitudes and a life-style".[46] More importantly, however, it is to be found in the remarkable strength of the Welsh literary elite itself. This strength derived from three factors: the emergence in the post-war period of a new Welsh-speaking middle-class, served by its

own intelligentsia and promoting itself through ethnic solidarity, of
which literature constituted a major component; a coherent ideology,
borrowed variously from English Romanticism, cultural anthropology
and elements of a perceived Welsh tradition, again primarily literary
in orientation; and finally, the reproduction of this class and its
ideology through new institutions and education. The two complementary processes involved in the formation of this new class, as
Glyn Williams and John Lovering have shown, were economic
marginalisation and the expansion of the service sector in Wales –
although the appearance for the first time in this period of a sizeable
indigenous agricultural bourgeoisie cannot be discounted in considering the continuing ruralist orientation of this class.[47] Exclusion
of the traditional local petit-bourgeoisie from new economic formations has led to a reliance on "the idea of local community integration
and solidarity as the basis for the retention of their own power".[48]
Vis-à-vis the new, predominantly English migrant bourgeoisie, this
response has developed into a specifically nationalist ideology. At the
same time, public expansion since the war – in contrast to earlier
development patterns, which "dramatically hindered the growth of a
bourgeoisie in Wales" – has "generated several new 'quasi-
bourgeois' niches".[49] Employment in Professional and Scientific
Services, which comprises the elite of this sector, doubled between
1951 and 1971. As Khleif,[50] Williams[51] and Lovering[52] have argued,
these new, middle-class clusters have also been associated with the
growth of nationalism. The alliance of these two groups, the one
traditional, the other novel, under a nationalist umbrella has helped
forge a "knowledge class" of remarkable coherence. Moreover, as
Khleif has pointed out,[53] the emergence of this ethnically assertive
elite has occurred at a juncture in the history of late capitalism at
which professional intelligentsias or "information men" have come to
possess a leading economic role. "In Wales, as elsewhere", states
David Bevan in his study of S4C personnel, "the new ethnic
resurgence in this post-war period was spearheaded by a vociferous
middle-class using language as a symbol of its separateness in its
quest for mobility and advancement".[54]

    Although its role was a new one, however, this "knowledge class"
did not emerge ab nihilo: "in Wales", as Khleif observes, "the new
university-trained class has been a reinforcement of the Llenorion,
that is, the cultured or literary class...which used to be a smaller
class before the Second World War".[55] Given the traditionally literary
orientation of the Welsh intelligentsia, it was natural that any new

intellectual grouping seeking legitimacy should define itself in literary terms. The sometimes odd consequences of this fact are well illustrated in the proclamation of J.E. Daniel, Saunders Lewis' successor as president of Plaid Cymru: "It is in the poetry of Taliesin and Dafydd Nanmor...far more than in the Special Areas Acts or Five Year Programmes that the salvation of Wales is to be found".[56] Less boldly asserted, however, this has been the fundamental position of most literary commentators in Wales since the war. When Yr Academi Gymreig appealed to the Welsh Arts Council in 1984 to reconsider its policies for literature, R.S. Thomas was amongst the fifty-three signatories to a public letter which accepted as axiomatic that "the very existence of a Welsh identity has always rested on the strength of the Welsh literary tradition". Ned Thomas's *The Welsh Extremist* – the "little red book"[57] of seventies cultural nationalism – was an important vehicle for promoting this fetishisation of Welsh literature, "which after all is modern Welsh thinking",[58] and of that "small and dedicated intelligentsia, mainly writers", without whom Wales "would be just another group of history's passive victims".[59] A more recent exposition of Welsh identity sustained, even "saved from premature extinction",[60] by "professional story-tellers, poets, the bardic tradition, the church and men of learning"[61] is to be found in Emyr Humphreys' *The Taliesin Tradition*. Many of the same author's novels are explorations of the function of a Welsh intelligentsia in the twentieth century and have won for him a recognition from Welsh-language critics similar to that accorded to R.S. Thomas.[62]

The social and ideological provenance of this literary clerisy remains largely unexplored. This is mainly because there exists no scientific critique of Welsh culture,[63] while a distinctive Welsh sociology has only begun to emerge. Indeed these deficiencies themselves reflect the disproportionate amount of intellectual capital which has been invested in literary production in Wales. What is agreed, however, is that the first Welsh-speaking middle-class elite in Wales (as distinct from its London-based precursors) arose from the unique mid-Victorian conjuncture of an exclusive, rural, nonconformist populism and British imperial expansion. In the event, the aspirations of this new middle-class, spearheaded by the educational campaigns of Hugh Owen, found rapid and abundant realisation through assimilation in imperial destiny. At the same time, a cultural rearguard survived through resisting in the name of Welshness, both Anglicisation and the process of modernisation with which it was seen to be synonymous. Ironically, this latter faction articulated its ideals in the terms of the only ideology to which it had access: that of anti-philistine sections of the English intelligentsia.

This crucial alignment was clinched with the entry of the very first contingent of Welsh nonconformists into Oxford in the 1880s. Oxford University, during this decade, was for the first time assimilating large numbers from the lower middle-classes of all regions in Britain – both from "old petty-bourgois groups and new salaried occupations [who] came to see each other as in some ways in a similar situation".[64] The sudden appearance of these groups and the hitherto unassimilated changes taking place in society outside the University walls, provoked much self-questioning as to how adequately education was "providing a national intelligentsia for the needs of the later nineteenth century".[65] In answering this question, and in defining a national function for these new elements, Arnold's commitment to Volksgeist – to a national spirit expressed in language and literature – played a major role:

> It is essential to recognise that Arnoldian *Bildung* enters a university system...when that system finds its students in the petit-bourgeoisie and even in the working classes. The Arnoldian and Leavisite discourse of culture became powerful because it allowed literature to impose its values on students who had no power basis outside the institutions and who came to be shaped by them.[66]

O.M. Edwards and his fellow members of Cymdeithas Dafydd Ap Gwilym, busy discovering the riches of their own national literature and conscious of their position as intellectual vanguard of an emergent class, were extremely receptive to this transformation of literature into a new and accessible locus of power.[67] From a different perspective, however, this valorisation of culture signified the recoil of elements within the English intelligentsia to a state of crisis in British capitalism. As a result, an earlier "entrepreneurial ideal" rapidly became discredited by "the counter-revolution of the ideals of empire, aristocracy, gentry and rural romanticism",[68] so that this period has since come to be seen as the source of "the suffocating 'traditionalism' of English life".[69] The new Welsh elite, poring over its Arnold and Ruskin,[70] resolved its contradictions by ascribing to Wales itself the features of this new English traditionalism: in particular its nostalgia for a pre-capitalist past, its desire to establish a vanguard of "the remnant" and its appropriation of Culture as the ideological focus for an "enobled, transformed middle class".[71] An idealised Wales, in accordance with Arnold's own elevation of "Celtic spirituality" as the antidote to English philistinism, thereby became the very embodiment of *Gemeinschaft*, while modernisation was externalised and distanced as a British phenomenon which could be pursued or ignored without implicating the "essential" Wales. Within this perspective, as O.M. Edwards noted approvingly, the Welsh language would retain a subaltern role as the vehicle of a "great literature", while English would be promoted as "the language of Empire and of commerce".

The consequences of this ideological alignment have been threefold. Firstly, an educational elite inclined towards Saunders Lewis' view that "culture and modern civilization cannot survive together",[72] has obstructed the growth of a scientific and industrial intelligentsia in Wales. Parity in numbers between arts and science degrees, attained in England in 1903, was not achieved in Wales until 1956.[73] In 1953[74] the Welsh educational establishment could still maintain that "it is true and obvious that industrialism has been an alien factor in the pattern of our lives". It invoked Arnold and Eliot in defence of the "organic unity" of Welsh culture, which was "indissolubly bound up with the Welsh language"; and it looked upon the English-speaking majority as a deracinated mass whom it was necessary "to imbue...with a realisation of their Welsh heritage". The pattern of academic achievement in Wales since the last war illustrates a continuing bias against scientific and technological study and also the remarkable degree to which young Welsh students are still conscripted into the literary intelligentsia. Thirty per cent of Welsh students studied arts subjects at A-level in 1982, while nineteen per cent studied sciences; the corresponding figures for England were twenty-four per cent and twenty-one per cent respectively. While almost seven per cent of Welsh A-level students studied English literature, over eight per cent of the Welsh-speaking group studied Welsh literature; eight per cent of candidates studied English Literature throughout Great Britain. At degree level, nearly four and a half per cent of all students read English, while again over eight per cent of Welsh-speaking students read Welsh.

Secondly, successive generations of Welsh critics have followed the orientation of this clerisy and located their reading of Welsh literature within the dominant discourse of English criticism. As Dai Smith has argued, Ned Thomas' *The Welsh Extremist* echoes "that canon of English tradition which looked in various ways for a century or more, to defend an organic, *natural* English civilization against the destructive tendencies of 'mechanised mass life' or 'industrial civilization'".[75] Even Saunders Lewis' criticism, replete with "principles", "standards", "learning", "tradition", "organic continuity" and appeals for "learned men to raise the intellectual level of the people", is frequently no more than an elegant reworking of Eliot and Leavis.

The third consequence of this alignment is perhaps the most serious. The culture debate was not, of course, peculiar to England. Indeed, the terms in which it was most frequently conducted – *Kultur* and *Zivilisation, Gemeinschaft* and *Geselschaft* – were most fully developed by a German academic mandarinate and the anti-capitalist romanticism with which it, too, resisted modernisation.[76] The feature which did make England unusual, however, was the debilitating restriction of this discourse within the terms of two disciplines wholly inadequate to the purpose: literature and social anthropology. As has been argued elsewhere,[77] no other native disciplines capable of analysing the totality of national life – particularly sociology, history and political economy – have emerged in modern Britain. And while anthropology might have provided some critical context in which to question some of the pre-conceptions of the literary elite, its mode of development restricted it to a role wholly complementary to that of literature.

Functional anthropology emerged as a tool of imperialism, which required coherent, unified models of subject groups for the purposes of efficient administration. This "totalisation without contradictions",[78] when subsequently developed as an academic discipline in the west, took as its subject such putative "stable, homogeneous and undifferentiated" peasant communities as that studied in the celebrated work of Arensburg and Kimball in Ireland. In Wales, this research was championed by the "Aberystwyth school", headed by Alwyn D. Rees, who rendered an essential, ahistorical Wales in terms of the supposed "completeness of traditional rural society", set against the "formless masses of rootless nonentities" of modern urban civilization.[79] Change and conflict were, from this perspective, alien and could therefore be dismissed as un-Welsh. The true "Pays de Galles", according to the classic formulation of Rees' colleague, E.G. Bowen, was "indissolubly linked" with the "isolated farmstead", the people's "love of music, poetry, philosophy and religion", and the Welsh language ("the very medium of life itself").[80] In extending the currency of these ideas, Rees became "the last great ideologue of a decadent Welsh *weltanschauung*, equipped to bestow the cachet of academic social science upon his version of the O.M. Edwards myth".[81] In this way, the Welsh anthropologist joined the post-war nationalist intelligentsia and "took on the mantle of the defender of the faith".[82]

In England, direct liaison between cultural anthropology and literature was limited (although it was vigorously promoted by Q.D. Leavis and underpinned her work on the "reading public"). In Wales, a much less rigid intellectual division of labour allowed the two practices constantly to overlap, as Rees's editorship of *The Welsh Anvil* and *Barn* indicates. Their intellectual monopoly tended, moreover, to colonise space within other disciplines, including theology (best illustrated by the Welsh Church Congress of 1953, at which the literary critic, H. Idris Bell, invoked Rees in support of his appeal for a "truly national Church" to express the "Welsh soul") and philosophy (in the shape of that "prophet of the Welsh cultural revolution", J.R. Jones[83]). The stultifying consensus which resulted bestowed upon literature in the Welsh language the same all-embracing, seamless role ascribed to English literature by the 1921 Newbolt Report and, later, by the *Scrutiny* school a humanist surrogate for religion, a "bond of national unity" between the classes, and the last bunker of the rural organic community. J.E. Daniel's claims for Welsh literature were, in this context, no odder or more original than Merton Professor Gordon's remark in the 1920's that "England is sick...English literature must save it".[84]

Anglo-Welsh literature clearly had no function or legitimacy within this national mission. Without a prescribed constituency, it had to forge one of its own. In many ways, it is this ultimate ingredient of the "organic community" – Q.D. Leavis' "homogenous reading public" – which has been most elusive to the Welsh writer in English. Like *Scrutiny*, writers in Welsh have worked in the conviction that a "public could be rallied, a key community of the elite", drawn "from those typically 'independent' social groups, the small farmers and shopkeepers...and from their sons and daughters in the teaching profession".[85] In this, for all the reasons described above, they have been relatively successful. In a more strictly literary sense, too, a culture of protective exclusion has generated what Wordsworth called a "co-operating power in the mind of the Reader". A shared ideology and class position meant that readers willingly adopted positions inscribed for them in the text, in order not only to understand the work itself but also to confirm their participation in the social formation signified by that work. Since the 1930s, in particular, a number of formal features have come to characterise this compact between the writer in Welsh and his "adequate reader". The collaborative "we" of Gwenallt's 'Wales', the internal dialogue in J. Kitchener Davies' 'The Sound of the Wind That is Blowing' and T.H. Parry Williams' 'Hon', the "you" of J.M. Edwards' 'The Blacksmith', the apocalyptic voice of Waldo Williams' 'Preseli' and Gerallt Lloyd Owen's 'Cilmeri', the elevation of the "small band" in Prosser Rhys' 'Cymru' – all of these devices, together with the more literally collaborative traditions of praise and elegy, successfully define and inscribe the reader as an active participant in the discourse of rural decline and cultural resurgence. This is not true of all poetry in Welsh, of course: much popular traditional verse constructs its ideal reader, not through conscious solicitation, but simply through the ritual rehearsal of established motifs and forms. Outside of this ideological consensus, the Welsh language poet may be as uncertain of or as indifferent to a *specific* readership as one would expect any post-Romantic English writer to be.

The Welsh poet in English has rarely been sufficiently confident of what the reader is bringing to the act of reading the poem to inscribe for him or her such a clear role with such minimal device. When adressing subjects concerned with Wales – particularly issues of community, history and culture – the poet has faced quite fundamental problems. Given that a range of key concepts has been defined according to the requirements of a particular intellectual stratum, that these definitions have become the dominant ideas within the whole discourse of nationality, and that they are sanctioned by an English literary tradition in which most Anglo-Welsh writers have been educated, there remains little room for manoeuvre. The poet can, like Donald Davie,[86] appeal to that part of the academic community "committed...to the idea of 'minority culture'" – an audience so specific that the poet's voice *ipso facto* becomes representative. This option is severely hindered, however, by the absence of an institutionalised professional group of Anglo-Welsh scholars, enjoying the respect of its peers. He can cut his losses and, like Gillian Clarke or Leslie Norris, create a "poetry of personal definition and point of view".[87] He can, with Vernon Watkins, construct a supra-personal "I" and become his own audience, or, as in Harri Webb's 'Climeri', resort to some form of atavistic romanticism and thereby find in history the idealised audience which he would wish to find in the present. Or he can attempt to engage his reader through more structural methods, perhaps in combination with one of these positions. A range of such devices becomes evident for the first time in the work of Idris Davies, where the crude apostrophising and rhetorical questioning of earlier Anglo-Welsh poets gives way to a complex dramatic and ironic method in which the implied author's voice is only one of many and the reader is compelled to define his own position from a wide, though weighted, range of options. Since 1945, however – if we accept that Dylan Thomas won many readers but failed to create a coherent readership – the dominant voice in the attempt by Anglo-Welsh writers to define an audience (a tradition, a canon, a set of values, etc.) has been that of R.S. Thomas. It is in his work, or rather in a small section of that work, that an English-speaking readership in Wales has been able, for the first time, to recognise itself *as* a specific and corporate readership.[88]

The prerequisites for Thomas' achievement were in part ideological and in part formal. Ideologically, R.S. Thomas was perceived as cherishing all of those positions definitive, as we have seen above, of the ethnic resurgence of the Welsh-speaking middle-class: an hostility towards science[89] and urban life[90] as un-Welsh; an equivalent elevation of rural values;[91] an essentialist or ahistorical concept of nationhood, based on a selective view of the past and notions of an organic tradition;[92] a belief in the importance of an elite in defending this ideal,[93] of which the Welsh language is the embodiment;[94] a view of the English-speaking Welsh as alienated[95] and needing to align themselves with these values to overcome this alienation;[96] and above all, the elevation of culture, literature and even "taste" as the surrogate religion which informs these convictions.[97] As a profile of R.S. Thomas this is, of course, highly selective; in addition, its main features derive from models (from Wordsworth to Eliot) which are not Welsh at all, and biographical circumstances such as the poet's upbringing in a town where almost eighty per cent of the population still spoke Welsh must make of the poet's sense of estrangement something more than just an acquired cultural posture. Whatever their provenance, however, these positions were compatible with an embedded consensus amongst the post-war Welsh-speaking intelligentsia. This group, defined through the disciplines of literature and anthropology, and consolidated through a new professional mobility and advancement, adopted R.S. Thomas as its "honorary white" and used him as a point of reference by which to distance or exclude other Anglo-Welsh writers of more dubious allegiance.[98] Institutionally and intellectually subordinate, an aspiring Anglo-Welsh intelligentsia acquiesced in this prescribed hierarchy in order to gain legitimacy. That collective acquiescence could not be realised, however, merely by the isolated reader's passive assent to a set of positions enunciated by the poet: rather, a whole readership had to be engaged as an active and conscious subject in the discourse. This, at bottom, was a formal problem. R.S. Thomas, in offering an answer to that problem, became the first Anglo-Welsh poet successfully to interpellate his English-speaking readership within the discourse of cultural nationalism.

The poems in which this interpellation was most tellingly effected are, not surprisingly, the most often anthologised in Wales. (Selections made by English editors generally move more freely outside this core.) Six major anthologies of Anglo-Welsh verse have appeared since Thomas's move to Aberdaron in 1967, the point at which he is generally taken to have set aside his earlier preoccupations for "conversations or linguistic confrontations with ultimate reality".[99] They are *Welsh Voices* (1967), *This World of Wales* (1968), *The Lilting House* (1969), *Twelve Modern Anglo-Welsh Poets* (1975), *The Oxford Book of Welsh Verse in English* (1977) and *Anglo-Welsh Poetry 1480 - 1980* (1984). If we add to these the influential O-Level set text, *Ten Contemporary Poets* (1963), a canon of some fifty poems emerges. Of these, however, ten poems appear on at least three occasions[100] and six of these – 'The Welsh Hill Country', 'A Peasant', 'Welsh Landscape', 'The Hill Farmer Speaks', 'Cynddylan on a Tractor' and 'Welsh History' – appeared in Thomas' first two collections, dated 1946 and 1952. Two others, 'Iago Prytherch' and 'A Blackbird Singing', belong to the 1958 collection, *Tares*, and while 'Welsh Testament' and 'A Welshman at St. James' Park' are slightly later poems, they are both firmly rooted in the preoccupations of earlier work and employ methods of engaging the reader which are characteristic of the first period.

Thomas employs several methods of inscribing for his reader an active role in these poems. The most important and recurrent of these are all common strategies for reader-inscription and have been discussed extensively elsewhere.[101] They include, in particular, marginalisation of the subject, careful manipulation of point-of-view, and subversion of expectations. 'A Peasant', the most frequently anthologised of all Thomas' poems, demonstrates each of these techniques. The subject, Iago Prytherch, is a solitary, liminal being reminiscent of Wordsworth's "silent monitors". The reader is enticed into following the poem's intense scrutiny of his marginal existence by the implied author's omniscience and declaratory manner ("be it allowed...", "So are his days spent...", "see him...", "There is...", "Remember him..."), by constant repetition of the third person pronoun, and by a reversal of the reader's pastoral expectations: the perception of the peasant as "half-wit" breaks what Wordsworth termed the "formal engagement" between author and reader upon which pastoral "habits of association" are based. Having engaged the reader as willing observer, the poem clinches his sympathy and ascribes him a specific identity by a simple device of shifted viewpoint. Insecure in his own point of view because of frustrated expectations, the reader is suddenly offered an alternative but negatively weighted vantage-point, identified as a "refined/But affected sense". The lack of pronominal reference here (does this "sense" refer to an outside "them", to the implied reader, or to an aspect of the implied author?) allows the reader to ponder his own position, as though he were not directly involved in the discourse, until the following line ("Yet this is your prototype") invites him, now that his ground is shifting, specifically to disassociate himself from this alternative. The implied reader's incorporation in this discourse is completed by the rite of passage which the poem enacts: a process of separation and discovery whereby the reader is taken from his given point in society (unspecified, but implicitly alien to Prytherch's world), undergoes a process of re-orientation and is finally received into a new society for which Prytherch is the prototype ("The first man of the new community" of 'Temptation of a Poet') – not now merely "fixed in his chair", but "enduring like a tree". The poem has weaknesses with respect to its "writerly" quality (that is, its scope for reader-collaboration): the repeated exhortations, for example – like Wordsworth's "But deem not this man useless – Statesmen!" – show some desperation in the poet's search for an audience, and the terms of anti-pastoral suggest a little too much cold comfort on the farm, threatening to subvert expectations simply with incredulity or laughter. Nevertheless, the poem remains sufficiently open and deft to engage the reader in a willing act of allegiance. Though the object of that allegiance is only insinuated here, it is pointedly Welsh (as early as the first line an ironic distance is implied between Prytherch and a more heroic Welshness associated with his name), it is tribal ("stock") and perhaps subject to attack ("impregnable fortress"), and it is synonymous with a timeless "naturalness", however "stark".

In the later 'A Welsh Testament', this celebration of roots is subjected to critical scrutiny. Here, as in 'The Hill Farmer Speaks', however, the subject speaks in his own voice and the reader is inscribed by implied dialogue ("All right, I was Welsh..."), by questions ("Does it matter...?") and by direct address ("My word for heaven was not yours..."). As in 'A Peasant', a third element is then introduced ("men sought us..."), which is differentiated from the implied reader by the third person pronoun ("them") and by distancing ("I saw them stare...I saw them stand..."). It transpires, however, that "they" address the subject in the same way as did the implied reader ("You are Welsh"), so that the reader is then implicitly included in the judgement on the alien intruder. The implied reader's position, having been one of privileged interlocutor, from this moment becomes insecure. Is he synonymous with the tourist whose eyes place "strong/Pressure on me"? Is he the agent of the subject's escape from the "prison" or "museum" of history, language and religion? Does he aspire to that condition himself ("Did the door open/To let me out or yourselves in?")? The poem closes on an enigma, and while it is clearly "about" the subject's disafection with his "drab role", it is also concerned with the observer's inability to address that fact and the problem of Welshness with which it is associated. A notion of Welshness is systematically dismantled by one of the *volk*. The observer remains either alienated or, if so moved, incorporated into the drama only as a further subject of elegy.

Like 'A Peasant', 'A Welshman at St. James' Park' works through the presentation of opposites between which the reader must make a choice. "Gardens" are contrasted with "wildness", "the exiled subject", "I", with an amorphous, regulated, "public". The implied reader's allegiance is won through an identification of Wales with the margin ("I think of a Welsh hill/That is without fencing") and the implied author with those Welshman, "Bosworth blind, who left the heather/And the high pastures of the heart" to fight for an English monarchy with which the park has since become associated. The ideal reader understands the poem, threfore, by acknowledging his Welshness; but in doing so must also accept that that Welshness is synonymous with a rejection of urban society and of the mass, mindless materialism implied by the image of birds "seduced...by/bread they are pelted with". The reader's seduction is completed by the poem's negation of a certain kind of gentile suburban pastoral, to which the author proffers his own idyll as a "true", rugged alternative ("sinews of stone/The curved claws").

'A Blackbird Singing', otherwise a very different poem, employs a similar stratagem of reader-persuasion. It differs from 'Ravens' (also in *Pietà*) and the much earlier 'Wales' and 'Maes-yr-Onnen', in refraining from ascribing specific historical associations to the animal in question (the blackbird which, in its role as historian, is derived from *Culhwch and Olwen*). As in most of Thomas' later poetry, the code by which the audience is inscribed in the work is under-determined and the individual image given greater autonomy. The first section is impersonal ("it seems..."), unspecific ("dark places..."), expresses uncertain wonder ("a suggestion...as – though...") and is strongly metaphorical ("the notes'/Ore were changed to a rare metal"). In contrast, the second section is personal ("You have heard...") and places the reader in a concrete and literal environment ("alone at your desk...green April...work...mild evening outside your room"). Having thus been lured into sharing the revelation described, the ideal reader more easily accepts the proffered resolution of these opposites in the final section's depiction of the bird as historian. This resolution's credibility, it must be emphasized, is almost wholly a consequence of the poem's strategy of seduction: without the central section, which defines the appropriate distance between mundane observer and miraculous subject, the reference to "history's overtones, love, joy/And grief" would seem what in fact it is – a grandiose abstraction and an overburdening of the symbolic capacity of the subject. The absence of active verbs in the last section, too, conceals from the reader that he is being told anything – that history, for example, is relived and renewed through tribal memory, that it is transformed by art and that its meaning lies outside chronological time – which is not self-evident.

'Welsh History', by contrast, is declamatory and unambiguously propagandist. Its appeal, however, is based upon a simple, not to say crude, use of the same devices already noted. As before, the implied author's authority as historian is built up through repetition of unelaborated statements in the past tense ("We were...we fought...kings died...bards perished"). The reader is incorporated into the subject through the almost incantatory repetition of "we" and, in the first section, by marginalisation ("were always in retreat...", "our ultimate stand/In the thick woods") and exclusive of others ("the stranger"). He is then gradually insinuated into a prescribed identity associated with defeat, isolation, race ("blood and birth"), "ineptitude" at all but poetry and music, and national awakening. The highly abstract nature of these associations and the demands they make of the reader are disguised not only by being couched in the language of indisputable historical fact but also by the careful interpolation of mundane, tangible objects (grass, bones, woods, ford, thorn and bramble, hands, rags, mud houses, crumbs) so that essentially rhetorical statements borrow a sense of material solidity. Suitably inscribed within the historical scenario, the reader is ready to accept the final, if ambiguous, change in tense and register ("we were a people, and are so yet...").

'Welsh Landscape' has proved almost as popular, although perhaps for different reasons. Tony Conran has suggested that this "nasty" poem has been "remembered and quoted by those who would destroy any future for Wales".[102] Moelwyn Merchant, however, sees in it only a rejection of "false mythology",[103] while for the editors of *Twelve Modern Anglo-Welsh Poets*[104] it expresses the poet's impatience "about the narrow-minded inactivity of Welsh people". For Roland Mathias,[105] this bitterness is simply the obverse of the poet's commitment to a fight against tremendous odds and, like the work of Gwenallt in Welsh, was an indispensable ingredient in the creation of an Anglo-Welsh audience. There is much to be said for each of these interpretations, although the vehemence of the first tends to bear out the truth of the last. They vary so considerably, however, because the reader is placed in an ambivalent position over which the author, for once, exercises insufficient control. He is encouraged by the opening subterfuge ("To live in Wales is to be conscious..." is really only subjective musing masquerading as objective statement) to alienate himself from the familiar world (that of "the machine") and share the various perceptions (of "red sky", "sped arrows", language, cries in the night, etc.) which identify an essential Wales. In all this, the implied reader is at once sensitive witness, victim and outsider, for whom the language is "strange to the ear". None of these roles, however, is compatible with the judgemental voice of the last ten lines, which is thus rendered ambiguous. Does it declare the historical Wales bankrupt (so let's give up the ghost) or bogus (so let's get to the real nub of the matter)? Does the sudden shift from wonder to derision indicate a loss of control, a rash, indeed disingenuous attempt to effect a closure while the real problem remains unsolved? Or is it simply an expression of the discrepancy between a sensed Wales and an allegedly real Wales? It is, paradoxically, *because* of this uncertainty and the uneasiness caused by a surge of contumely in which that reader suddenly cannot be inscribed (and which, for that reason, the real reader questions), that the poem compels its audience to take up positions around questions of historical and cultural nationalism. The difficulty, of course, is that the poem provides a seductive entry into this discourse but fails to offer a means of qualifying or replacing it when it is found wanting.

By one means or another, each of these poems – and 'The Welsh Hill Country', 'Iago Prytherch' and 'Cynddylan on a Tractor' can be read in similar ways – succeeds in cajoling readers into constructing encoded positions as though for themselves. Each associates the reader with a number of negatively inscribed positions (concerned with exile, outsiders, the machine, the public, England, affectations, etc.) from which he is enticed into accepting certain alternative values (nature, Wales, history, etc.). In every case, however, the reader's removal from one set of values to the other is either incomplete or impossible to achieve. In 'A Peasant', 'A Welshman at St. James' Park', 'Iago Prytherch' and 'The Welsh Hill Country', the effect of marginalisation of the subject ("too far for you to see") by a privileged narrator is to inculcate in the reader an attitude of awe, whilst at the same time holding him at arm's length, alien and impotent. In most of the remaining poems, the reader is led to view Welshness itself as something "other" – as part of a selective history, a selective "remnant", or a timeless natural world, all of which "prototypes" exclude the reader's own experience, indeed derive their very power from that sense of exclusion. For the reader, Wales is never "here now, but there":[106] like Thomas himself, it is transformed into a distant object of "awe" and "reverence", "on a peninsula".[107].

The above discussion has shown that a core of Thomas' work has succeeded in engaging an English-speaking readership in Wales in a discourse from which it has been historically excluded – but engaging it, finally, only to render it impotent. We have seen, too, that this process of engagement and exclusion is inseparable from an established hierarchy of intelligentsias and readerships in Wales. R.S. Thomas' earlier poems, preoccupied with margins and boundaries, historically and culturally allusive, have been used to fix and perpetuate this hierarchy. They have also been placed within a tradition of bitter pastoral elegy – a genre uniquely capable of engaging both English-speaking and Welsh-speaking readers – which an insecure middle-class has used to forge an identity distinct from both an alien Welsh proletariat and an alien British bourgeoisie.

Thomas' role in this process can be usefully compared with the reception of Dostoevski in Germany after the First World War. As Leo Lowenthal has demonstrated, Dostoevski "served as an ideological crutch for members of the German middle classes, providing them with a series of myths that made sense to individuals caught between a powerful upper class and a rapidly rising proletariat".[108] Commentators in a wide range of disciplines – literary, medical, political, religious, scientific and philosophic – together extracted certain "basic meanings" from Dostoevski's work which, though quite distorting of the original, offered "an imaginary solution whereby such middle-class groups can avoid a real analysis of the problem of transforming the social system".[109] Before the war, the dominant interpretation stressed the novelist's "myth of inner life"; subsequently, with the dispossession of the middle classes, the same author was pillaged for his purported "myth of national life". Although in Wales the general social configuration is different, a divergence of critical responses to R.S. Thomas' work does testify to similar social modes of reception. While English critics like Dyson and Alvarez have celebrated Thomas' "quest for self-knowledge" and "inner landscape of atonement", a Welsh intelligentsia, seeking through a resurgent ethnicity to win a concessionary role on the fringes of the British state, has been much more concerned with the incorporation of his work into a useable literary canon. In literary terms the results of this process have been mixed. Thomas's influence was much to be seen in the chronic long-sightedness of Anglo-Welsh poets in the 1960's, groping through "seven hundrend and fifty years of darkness"[110] for the glimmer of "a sunken past".[111] Too often, this preoccupation devolved into the mere exchange of one cliché for another, into pastiche,[112] and into the sublime awfulness of Bryn Griffiths' "stones, nudging the stranger to a vague knowledge of guilt".[113] Strangely, few have attempted R.S. Thomas' successful strategies of reader inscription: Meic Stephens' 'Ponies, Twynyrodyn' and Gillian Clarke's 'Blaencwrt' are rare exceptions, and simpler, more rhetorical or more personal modes have often been preferred. More generally, the work of R.S. Thomas has, for the English-speaking section of this elite, been employed to define a notion of "national life" in which it can take up a distinct but subordinate role which excuses it of any need to examine its real position, or that of its audience, within the social order.

And finally, we have seen that, for all of these reasons, no intelligentsia organically related to a broad English-speaking constituency in Wales can create itself within the terms of the dominant literary discourse – a discourse within which Wales' leading novelist in English can still declare that "the only function of English in Wales is to serve and safeguard the Welsh language".[114] For those who believe that "the idea of an organic intelligentsia is essential to the history of the Welsh"[115] and that their survival requires the restitution of such an intelligentsia,[116] a fundamental reorientation of concerns is indispensible: a reorientation already evident in the fields of history, sociology and, to a degree, nationalist politics.[117] R.S. Thomas' work has been used – within the context of a wide range of prescriptive notions concerning the "Welsh heritage"[118] – to delay the execution of this task in the literary arena and to condemn most of the Welsh to a marginal existence in which they are permitted only a vicarious identity.

NOTES

1.   *Poetry Wales*, vol.7, no.4, Spring 1972, p.93.
2.   *R.S. Thomas: Selected Prose*, ed. Sandra Anstey (Poetry Wales Press, 1983) p.110.
3.   *Critical Writings on R.S. Thomas*, ed. Sandra Anstey (Poetry Wales Press, 1982) p.136.
4.   *ibid.*, p.136.
5.   *Western Mail*, May 14 1983.
6.   Gillian Clarke, *Selected Poems* (Carcanet, 1985) p.93.
7.   Duncan Bush, 'In Wales', in *Green Horse*, ed. Meic Stephens and Peter Finch (Christopher Davies, 1978) p.32.
8.   John Tripp, *Passing Through* (Poetry Wales Press, 1984) p.16.
9.   *Green Horse, op.cit.*, p.64.
10.   Bud B. Khleif, *Ethnic Boundaries, Identity and Schooling* (New Hampshire, 1975) p.30.
11.   Don Dale Jones, *An Inquiry into the Teaching of Anglo-Welsh Literature in the Secondary Schools of Wales* (Welsh Arts Council, 1978).
12.   quoted in *Poetry Wales*, vol. 6, no. 1, Summer 1970, p.4.
13.   *Poetry Wales* Spring 1972, *op.cit.*, p.123.
14.   Anthony Conran, *The Cost of Strangeness* (Gomer, 1982) p.229.
15.   *Poetry Wales*, Spring 1972, *op.cit.*, p.104.
16.   *Y Fflam*, No.11, 1952, pp.43-4.
17.   *Y Llenor a'i Gymdeithas* (BBC, 1966).
18.   *Poetry Wales*, Spring 1972, *op.cit.*, p.60.
19.   *Wales: A New Study*, ed. David Thomas (David and Charles, 1977) p.282.
20.   *The Arts in Wales 1950-1975*, ed. Meic Stephens (Welsh Arts Council, 1979)

p.206.
21. *The Welsh Extremist* (Y Lolfa, 1973) pp.117-18.
22. *The Welsh Anvil*, V, 1953, pp.19-31.
23. *Dock Leaves*, Winter 1953, pp.30-35.
24. *Transactions of the Cymmrodorion*, 1967, pp.57-80.
25. *Planet* 16, pp.12ff.
26. *Dock Leaves*, Michaelmas 1951, p.3.
27. Raymond Garlick in *The Lilting House*, ed. Meic Stephens and John Stuart Williams (Dent and Christopher Davies, 1969) p.xxi.
28. John Tripp, *Collected Poems* (Christopher Daviews, 1978) p.111.
29. *The Cost of Strangeness*, *op.cit.*, p.302.
30. *Western Mail*, 2 April 1985.
31. *Lucky Poet* (Methuen, 1943) p.201.
32. *Selected Prose*, *op.cit.*, p.33.
33. *ibid.*, p.172.
34. Raymond Garlick, in *Dock Leaves*, Michaelmas 1951, p.4.
35. *Welsh Outlook*, August 1922.
36. *Wales*, vol.6, no.3, pp.93-103.
37. *ibid.*, p.30.
38. *Wales*, Oct-Dec 1943, pp.6ff.
39. Anthony Conran, *Formal Poems* (Christopher Davies, 1960) p.28.
40. see John Tripp, *Planet* 24/5, pp.77-81.
41. Raymond Garlick, *An Introduction to Anglo-Welsh Literature* (University of Wales Press, 1972) p.79.
42. *Formal Poems*, *op.cit.*, p.28.
43. Raymond Garlick, *An Introduction...*, *op.cit.*, p.79.
44. Raymond Garlick in *The Lilting House*, *op.cit.*, p.xxi.
45. Meic Stephens in *Poetry Wales*, vol.3, no.3, Winter 1967, p.7.
46. *The Cost of Strangeness*, *op.cit.*, p.64.
47. Glyn Williams, 'Economic Development, Social Structure, and Contemporary Nationalism in Wales', *Review*, V, 2, Fall 1981, p.283.
48. *ibid.*, p.306.
49. *Crisis of Economy and Ideology*, ed. Glyn Williams (BSA/SWSG, 1983) p.68.
50. *Social and Cultural Change in Contemporary Wales*, ed. Glyn Williams (Routledge, 1978) pp.102ff.
51. Glyn Williams and Catrin Roberts, 'Language, Education and Reproduction in Wales', in Bruce Bain, ed. *The Sociogenesis of Language and Human Conduct* (New York, 1983) p.509.
52. *Crisis of Economy and Ideology*, *op.cit.*, p.69.
53. after Bell, *Social and Cultural Change...*, *op.cit.*, pp.106-7.
54. David Bevan, 'The mobilisation of cultural minorities: the case of Sianel Pedwar Cymru', *Media, Culture and Society*, 1984, 6, pp.103-117.
55. *Social and Cultural Change...*, *op.cit.*, p.108.
56. J.E. Daniel, *Welsh Nationalism – What It Stands For* (London, 1937) p.40.
57. Dai Smith, *Wales! Wales?* (Allen and Unwin, 1984) p.156.

58.   *The Welsh Extremist, op.cit.*, pp.41-2.
59.   *ibid.*, pp.11-12.
60.   Emyr Humphreys, *The Taliesin Tradition* (Black Raven Press, 1983) p.46.
61.   *ibid.* p.24.
62.   see Alun Llywelyn-Williams, *Y Llenor a'i Gymdeithas, op.cit.*, and Derec Llwyd Morgan, 'Emyr Humphreys: Llenor y Llwyth', *Ysgrifau Beirniadol* VII (Gwasg Gee, 1973) pp.285-303.
63.   see D.Glyn Jones in *Ffenics*, vol.1, no.4, Spring 1963, pp.35-45.
64.   John Oakley, in Francis Barker et al, eds., *Literature, Society and the Sociology of Literature* (University of Essex, 1976) p.21.
65.   J.P.C. Roach, 'Victorian Universities and the National Intelligentsia' in *Victorian Studies*, Dec. 1959, p.139.
66.   Simon During, 'On Cultural Values and Fascism', in *Southern Review* vol.17, no.2, July 1984, p.176.
67.   This whole field deserves further investigation. As R. Tudur Jones observes, "It is astonishing how little scholarly work has been done on the influence of English culture on Wales". (*Ffydd ac Argyfwng Cenedl*, vol.2 (Tŷ John Penry, 1982) p.41).
68.   Colin Leys, in *New Left Review*, no. 151, May/June 1985, p.21.
69.   Perry Anderson, 'Origins of the Present Crisis', *New Left Review*, no. 23, 1964, p.34.
70.   see *Y Llenor*, 1942, p.28, on the reading tastes of T.E. Ellis, and Alun Llywelyn-Williams, *Y Nos, Y Niwl a'r Ynys*, and Thomas Jones, ed., *Astudiaethau Amrywiol* (UWP, 1968) pp.145-7, on the influence of English literature on other members of Cymdeithas Dafydd ap Gwilym.
71.   Matthew Arnold, quoted in Terry Eagleton, *Criticism and Ideology* (NLB, 1976) p.106.
72.   *Y Faner*, 12 Feb. 1949.
73.   see G.W. Roderick and M.D. Stephens, 'The Influence of Welsh Culture on Scientific and Technical Education in Wales in the Nineteenth Century', *Transactions of the Cymmrodorion*, 1981, pp.99-108.
74.   Central Advisory Council for Education, *The Place of Welsh and English in the Schools of Wales* (HMSO, 1953).
75.   *Wales! Wales? ibid.*, p.157.
76.   see Michael Löwy, *Georg Lukacs – From Romanticism to Bolshevism* (NLB, 1974), p.30.
77.   Perry Anderson, 'Components of the National Culture', *New Left Review*, no. 50, May/June 1968, pp.3-57.
78.   *ibid.*
79.   Alwyn D. Rees, *Life in a Welsh Countryside* (UWP, 1950) p.170.
80.   E.G. Bowen, 'Le Pays de Galles', *Transactions of the Institute of British Geographers*, no.26, 1959, pp.1-23.
81.   *Crisis of Economy and Ideology..., op.cit.*, p.34.
82.   Graham Day, 'The Sociology of Wales: Issues and Prospects', *Sociological Review*, vol.27, no.3, 1979, p.451.

83. Pennar Davies, *Y Brenin Alltud* (Christopher Davies, 1974) p.100.
84. quoted in Chris Baldick, *The Social Mission of English Criticism* (Clarendon Press, 1983) p.105.
85. F.R. Leavis, quoted *ibid.*, p.222.
86. quoted in David Trotter, *The Making of the Reader* (Macmillan, 1984) p.136.
87. *The Cost of Strangeness, op.cit.*, p.167.
88. *ibid.*, pp.222-3.
89. *Selected Prose, op.cit.*, p.167.
90. *Y Fflam*, 5, 1948, p.10.
91. *Selected Prose, op.cit.*, p.24.
92. *ibid.*, pp.37, 46.
93. *ibid.*, p.165.
94. *ibid.*, p.153.
95. address at Llangefni National Eisteddfod, Wednesday, 3 August 1983.
96. *Selected Prose, op.cit.*, p.33.
97. *Y Faner*, 4, March 1977.
98. *Planet* 16, p.14.
99. *Critical Writings on R.S. Thomas, op.cit.*, p.133.
100. Simon Barker (*Powys Review* 15, 1984, p.68) notes the monotonous recurrence of Thomas' anthologised poems but ascribes no special significance to this.
101. see, in particular, David Trotter, *op.cit.*
102. *The Cost of Strangeness, op.cit.*, p.223.
103. Moelwyn Merchant, *R.S. Thomas* (UWP, 1979) p.26.
104. Don Dale-Jones and Randal Jenkins, eds., *Twelve Modern Anglo-Welsh Poets* (University of London, 1975) p.180.
105. *The Arts in Wales 1950-75, op.cit.*, p.216.
106. R.S. Thomas, *Frequencies* (Macmillan, 1978) p.26.
107. John Tripp, *Passing Through, op.cit.*, p.16.
108. Robert C. Holub, *Reception Theory* (Methuen, 1984) p.46.
109. Leo Lowenthal, 'The Reception of Dostoevski's Work in Germany', in Robert N. Wilson, ed., *The Arts in Society* (NJ, 1964) p.144.
110. *The Lilting House, op.cit.*, p.116.
111. *ibid.*, pp.170-71.
112. *ibid.*
113. *ibid.*, p.195.
114. *Western Mail*, 8 August 1985.
115. *Efrydiau Athronyddol*, vol. XLVII. 1984, p.20.
116. *ibid.*, p.21.
117. It is the increasing cross-fertilisation of these three disciplines that has made a preliminary critique of the fetishisation of literature and tradition in Wales at all possible: see Dafydd Elis Thomas, *Traddodiadau Fory* (Llys yr Eisteddfod Genedlaethol, 1983).
118. see Roland Mathias in *Green Horse, op.cit.*, p.19.

TONY CURTIS

Grafting the Sour to Sweetness:
Anglo-Welsh Poetry in the last twenty-five years.

Grafting the Sour to Sweetness: Anglo-Welsh Poetry in the last twenty-five years.

How can I write
impartially of a land that I love?

John Tripp: 'Vulnerable's Lament'

Poetry has held a more central place in Anglo-Welsh literature than in the literatures of most countries. This may be explained by the theory of cultural and linguistic "seepage" from the older tongue, its Eisteddfodau and the bardic tradition. Anthony Conran, and Emyr Humphreys especially, have argued for a Taliesinic influence. But there is too the sense of a peculiarly poetic strength in the English language when it is given voice in a Welsh accent – Richard Burton, Anthony Hopkins, Emlyn Williams and Dylan Thomas himself testify to that. Certainly, notions of natural musicality in Wales and the Welsh inform some expectation of lyricism from our country. There are also a range of socio-economic reasons for the predominance of poetry over novel-writing and the performance of contemporary theatre which are discussed elsewhere in this book. Writers choose their own themes perhaps, but having chosen that theme a writer will, naturally, be drawn to an existing audience. The main thrust of investment by the government, through its Welsh Arts Council, has been supportive of poetry (when, that is, there is money left over from its huge subsidy of the Welsh National Opera, that "flagship of the arts" in Wales). One thinks of the "Dial-a-Poem" scheme, the Writers on Tour scheme which favours poets in its format, as well as direct subsidies to magazines which, necessarily, feature poems and short fiction. *Poems and Pints*, which B.B.C. Wales produced for the television network, and the recent S4C and Channel 4 *Wales – Landscape and Legend*, (for which the present writer acted as Script Consultant), all point to the malleability of poetry and poets in terms of the media.

Writing in Wales, as far as the majority of outsiders are concerned (and certainly as far as the Wales Tourist Board is concerned), means Dylan Thomas. The writing of poetry from and about Wales since the war has been dominated however not by the loud music of Dylan's "sullen art" but by R.S. Thomas and Idris Davies.

The genius of Dylan and his friend and fellow visionary Vernon Watkins created an enduring body of work located in the first instance in a Swansea and Laugharne of the imagination, and in the second instance in the Gower and the seascape still held in Taliesin's gaze, that metamorphic spirit of poetry, what Emyr Humphreys has called "the crucible of myth". Still, neither writer addresses himself to the matter of Wales as an industrial and agricultural region, or as a bilingual nation. Vernon Watkins worked assiduously to extend a body of visionary writing which he could trace across Europe and many centuries. His poetry was consciously "defending ancient springs"[1] in the neo-platonic tradition, which Kathleen Raine argues, is at the centre of much of European literature; though his fine poem 'The Collier' suggests that his particular voice could articulate the needs and protests of the industrial valleys. Dylan Thomas, as an ambitious, professional writer, looked to London and America. He is reputed to have said, "The land of my fathers, my fathers can keep it".[2] And there is no doubt that he was prepared to manipulate the idea of Wales and Welshness for his audiences.

The other major figure from the mid-century was David Jones, who lived in London and there constructed his classic reaction to the Great War, *In Parenthesis*. In that book, and the later works *The Anathemata* and *The Tribune's Visitation*, David Jones succeeded in placing Wales in a conception of Christian Europe which spanned twenty centuries. But neither his concerns nor his style could be said to have influenced the poets of Wales who followed, with perhaps the exception of Roland Mathias.

Though the 1950s saw the posthumous *Selected Poems* of Idris Davies, the elevation into myth of Dylan Thomas and the establishment of Vernon Watkins, R.S. Thomas and Dannie Abse as notable additions to the poetry lists from London, it was not until the second half of the next decade that a substantial number of new voices emerged. With these voices there appeared a sense of the poet's role in evoking Wales as an entity. The poet takes on the mantle of remembrancer: it is a role informed by the example of the exiled miner Idris Davies from his teaching post in London as he exorcised the ghosts of his early days in Wales, the Strike of 1926 and the depression years of the 1930s. Also, there was the strong, insistent moral stance of R.S. Thomas, the Cardiff-born priest, uprooted and transformed by his experiences in his parishes in the west and north. The act of memory was to be a national responsibility, a political commitment now.

It is interesting to note that these new voices from Wales in the 1960s – Raymond Garlick, John Tripp, Leslie Norris, John Ormond, Harri Webb, Robert Morgan, John Stuart Williams, Gwyn Williams, Alison Beilski, Tom Earley – included no-one under the age of forty. Roland Mathias has claimed that

> ...a pronounced feature of Anglo-Welsh writing is its avoidance of precocity, an avoidance which in itself underlines the slow growth from unconfidence and a determination to experience life in some fullness before seeking to comment upon it. Dylan Thomas, in writing some 350 poems in his little red notebook before he was nineteen, was an outrageous exception. Much more characteristic are David Jones and Gwyn Williams, who wrote scarely at all in their twenties and early thirties. [3]

As a generalisation, that view is surely disproved by the example of a number of younger, prolific poets emerging through the 1970s, such as Robert Minhinnick, Mike Jenkins, John Davies and Tony Curtis, and I find it more useful to stress the correlation between the writing and the means of its publication. From 1965 onwards *Poetry Wales* magazine existed. Its founder and editor, Meic Stephens, soon afterwards became the Assistant Director, Literature of the newly established Welsh Arts Council. In a short space of time there was a new, lively outlet for poetry and an organizing structure for the support of writers and their publishers. At the same time Wales itself was in the throes of a vibrant, and occasionally violent, debate concerning its national identity and, especially, the place of the Welsh language in the nature of that identity. Anglo-Welsh poetry from this point on addresses itself constantly to such questions. Poets such as Robert Morgan, John Tripp, Leslie Norris, Harri Webb, Sam Adams and Meic Stephens were building a body of work which recalled their roots, the heritage of life in the industrial valleys. The essence of community life, its practices and peculiarities, is evoked and the threat to human loyalites and groupings stressed as the coal industry declines and the valleys' population is transformed and eroded.

The response of these poets is akin to that of Seamus Heaney who, especially in his first two books, feels dislocated from his roots by his education and his success in the world. From an early poem such as 'Digging' right through to the recent *Station Island* he is wary of the distance which writing may place him from the action. There is certainly something of that need to justify poetry in a world of telegrams and anger to be found in Anglo-Welsh poets too. John Tripp in particular has a number of such poems. One can also trace characters of a justified belligerence, from the voice of John Ormond's 'Cathedral Builders' – the workman witnessing the pomp and circumstance of a cathedral's consecration looks up and says, "I bloody did that", – through to the trespassing teenager in Robert Minhinnick's 'J.P.'

With the exception of Robert Morgan, who like Idris Davies left the pit to train as a teacher, the poets of this 1960s "second wave" and later are a generation removed from the working-class and the Welsh language. They share with Seamus Heaney that acute sense of their having removed themselves from the traditional working practices of the community in which they still perceive their roots. There is a sense in which yeterday's wrongs are still being fought. The clear-cut morality of capitalist and work-unit, owner and miner, the tentacled beast of Lewis Jones' *Cwmardy* and the heroic individual who fights to survive in its land structure much of the work. These are moving and powerful issues to inspire novelist and poet alike.

The stress on individuality within a strong community structure – workforce or chapel – a resolve strengthened by the radicalism of the last century, surely informs much of the poetry produced from the industrialised south-east of Wales. There is, in fact, a sub-genre of character poems: fathers, relations, "butties" – all assume representative value. Examples of this form of writing are numerous but the following are readily to hand in the Garlick and Mathias anthology and *The Valleys*[4] from Davies and Jenkins: Robert Morgan's 'Blood Donor'; Sally Jones' 'Community'; Meic Stephens' 'Elegy' series; John Tripp's 'The Doctor'; Leslie Norris' 'Elegy for David Beynon'; Harri Webb's 'Not to be used for babies' and 'That Summer'; and John Ormond's 'My Grandfather and his Apple-tree'.

John Ormond's 'My Grandfather and his Apple-tree' is the most ambitious and the most successful of "character" poems. In concentrating on the life of this one man the poet summarises the whole broad sweep of social change in South Wales from a predominantly rural economy to the accelerating expansion of industrial communities in the coal valleys that created a "Klondike" in Wales.

John Ormond's grandfather begins life as "A wild and drinking farm-boy" who is sobered first by marriage and then by his move to the working life of a miner, leaving his farm

> For dark under the fields six days a week
> With mandrel and shovel and different stalls.

The abrupt change of work-experience is seen literally in terms of black and white, light and darkness. These and other polarities extend through the poem: the "whitewashed cottage" is paid for by his toil in "the night vein"; the "bleeding white" of his tree-grafting is bound by the strips from his "working flannel-shirt and belly bands." It is the distinction between the sweet and the sour, of course, that is central to the poem. By drawing on the apple-tree – one of the archetypes in Kathleen Raine's definition of the "Tradition" – as a focus John Ormond pulls together the dilemmas of both social change and personal destiny. The farmboy and "a miller's daughter" establish themselves in both the mining community and the institution of marriage; the young man has to compromise himself in both respects. The cattle stall is exchanged for the working stall biting into the coal seam; the fresh air of the countryside for the claustrophobia of work underground. The "whitewashed cottage" seems the setting for a perfect, new start, but the "sudden" rent effectively locks the young man into a strictly-defined role and commitments.

Still, "All light was beckoning" him back into the natural world and he responds by cultivating a garden of "neat greens". However, the tree at the centre of his chosen Eden proves too sweet for a man who has worked to place himself in the front rank of chapel society: "it budded temptation in his mouth". Just as he has collared himself in with respectability, he now signals his elevation to the role of chapel deacon by binding up the apple-sweetness, grafting it to a branch of cooker, strapping "the bleeding white of junction" with pieces of his old working clothes. The union is sealed with "clay from the colliery" and so the circle of his working life as a statistic in the South Wales industrial complex and as a prime mover in the chapel sphere is closed.

Such a completion and an ordering proves to be a condemnation, a confinement. As in Blake's 'Garden of Love' the "joys and desires" have been bound up with briars, and the fact is here compounded by the miner's own volition in the process. Blake's work emphasises the incumbent responsibility of the individual as strongly as it criticises the tyranny of Church and State. So it is in 'My Grandfather and his Apple-tree'. John Ormond's poem works effectively at several levels: as an historical poem; as a family remembrance; it is an allegorical treatment of the life of a man as a social, economic and religious animal; the whole is a brilliantly sustained metaphor with a strong narrative structure. At its close one is left with the widowed miner brooding through his retirement years, regretting the lost sweetness of life, nettled around with sourness, devoid of juice.

One way of gauging the accomplishment of that poem is to compare it with the companion pieces from John Ormond's *Requiem and Celebration*. With the exception of 'My Dusty Kinsfolk' – a poem whose execution surmounts that rather weak title – the other poems such as 'Sonnet for his Daughter', 'For his Son, Unborn', 'Portrait of his Father' and especially, 'Portrait of his Grandfather', are examples of family remembrance heavily-laden with echoes of Dylan Thomas' sound effects:

> ... In his chaptered hand
> A seed of a century broke to a branch of death,
> Each leaf a cross to loss in a candled dark.

> 'Portrait of his Grandfather'

and again,

> From his gentle craft and his loins I woke
> Hammered to words in the active midnight:

> 'Portrait of his Father'

It seems strange that John Ormond should be so dominated by Dylan's voice so far into his middle age. An exact contemporary of his, Dannie Abse, had been similarly affected by what he described as "these noisy echoes" in his first collection, *After Every Green Thing*; but that had been in 1948, and in his subsequent work Abse found and held his own voice. Perhaps the long publishing silence of John Ormond had left him comparatively unpractised. In 1973, four years after *Requiem and Celebration*, John Ormond's *Definition of a*

Waterfall appeared from O.U.P. He was then fifty and this, only his second collection, was, in effect, a "selected poems". Those weaker pieces in which Ormond's own voice had been drowned, were excluded as was the long, final poem from *Requiem and Celebration* so reminiscent of Vernon Watkins. John Ormond's reputation and his influence on younger poets is notable; it is a position held by virtue of a handful of strong poems from that second collection: 'My Grandfather and his Apple-tree', that finely-realised memory, 'The Key', 'The Cathedral Builders', the celebration of landscape and Wales 'Ancient Monuments', the love poem 'Design for a Quilt' and the title-poem 'Definition of a Waterfall', itself.

Though John Tripp is almost the same age as John Ormond, and though both men had journalistic experience in London before establishing themselves as published poets in Wales, where John Ormond's writing has been considered, meticulously drafted, with the poems emerging at an almost frustratingly slow rate, John Tripp continues to be prolific, varied and often colloquial, with an emphasis on performance and immediacy. Indeed, much of Tripp's work is dominated by an anger and impatience. Over the last twenty years he has been one of the most frequently published and publically visible of poets in Wales. He presented an arts programme in the days of T.W.W. and held a regular spot on the *Poems and Pints* series for B.B.C. Wales T.V. in the early 'seventies. Books, recordings and frequent readings of his work established John Tripp, through the 1970s particularly, as a leading voice not only in Anglo-Welsh poetry, but also as a pithy commentator on the politics and social changes in Wales. Here was someone who could take poetry out of the classroom, off the page and into the pub and club. With the possible exception of Harri Webb, and that briefly, no-one seemed to voice the needs of what poetry-conscious public there was in Wales more than John Tripp.

For twenty years John Tripp's subject has been, essentially, Wales itself. He writes always patriotically, sometimes aggressively, sometimes with a persuasive wit. His return to Wales in the mid-sixties at one stroke gave him an obvious theme and an audience for those nationalistic concerns. However, as a monoglot, John Tripp's support for the growing language campaign was always that of an outsider. The dilemma is made clear in his poem 'Outsider'. Tripp imagines one "Thomas" at the National Eisteddfod:

> Yet he is 'Anglo', dipped in England's sewer,

worse than a Michigan tourist, odd as an Eskimo,
roaming like a campless Arab
through the heart of his people.
All that his fingers touch, his mind bites at,
                                                    give voice to Wales,
all his verse will strain to bridge the gulf.

The deeper irony is that Tripp's obvious audience is precisely that
eighty per cent of the population of Wales which is unable to define
or proclaim itself Welsh through the language. Unlike R.S. Thomas,
Raymond Garlick, Bobi Jones, Meic Stephens and, more recently,
Peter Finch, Nigel Jenkins and Gillian Clarke, John Tripp has never
acquired the language; as a journalist in England and a professional
writer, he realised that his voice was, necessarily, to work through
the medium of English.

In two key early poems, however, it is apparent that Tripp wants
to argue for a Wales that is somehow separate, independent, in some
way a haven for traditions, practices, virtues even, that remain
largely unspecified. In 'A Received Culture'[5] and 'Diesel to
Yesterday'[6] there is a strong emphasis on the border, a distinct line
drawn geographically, historically and culturally between England and
Wales. The poet feels

                        like a stunted
Welsh Canute, trying to stem the swill from the east
washing over us. Behind me it runs
into bogs, too putrid to fertilise this desert.

The dominant culture of an alien, colonising neighbour has denuded
and emasculated Wales and the Welsh,

soon their stock to be sucked through the Severn Tunnel.

In the previous year, 1968, appeared one of R.S. Thomas' most
caustic political poems, 'Reservoirs'. There the Welsh are accused
of complicity, through their indifference, in the destruction of their
language, and with it their most valuable heritage. They watch the
English

                    ...elbowing our language
Into the grave we have dug for it.[7]

The Welsh, claims Tripp, are even betrayed by the good fortune of men who should be their natural leaders,

>   ... Good loyal Henry
> then sliced up the language to keep his realm intact.

Tripp, and the other Anglo-Welsh poets, he implies, are scribbling "in invisible ink/on dissolving paper...on the futile quarto" because they are writing poetry, and that in the English language.

This sense of guilt persists to the present. Only recently Harri Webb (whose marvellous satire 'Synopsis of the Great Welsh Novel' is included in this book) is reported in a *Western Mail* article[8] to have turned his back on any further writing in English, declaring "I don't believe that writing in English about Wales matters very much any more". He goes on to sound off in no uncertain manner: "Anglo-Welsh literature is, more or less, a load of old rubbish. It has only marginal relevance to Wales now... I believe that Welsh is the kernel. I don't believe you are a real Welshman until you speak the language. Without it, you cannot properly be Welsh". Whilst he holds a nationalist position in politics, Webb tempers his stance by arguing that "All nationalists are idolators. They offend against the Second Commandment – 'Thou shall not make unto thyself graven images'. They place their country alongside God. But when you look around for alternatives, there aren't any". Even allowing for the liberties of the press, and perhaps Webb's tactics of provocation, this is an intriguing performance. It touches several sensitive nerve-endings for the Anglo-Welsh.

It is, though, inconceivable that John Tripp could take such a stance. The language issue apart, Wales for him embodies a set of ideals and traditions, not exactly pastoral, which are the antithesis of modernity and a vague, undefined "English" materialistic influence. This distaste is more colloquially expressed, but just as severe as that of R.S. Thomas in poems such as 'Reservoirs', 'The Fair' and the sequence *What is a Welshman?*[9], but Tripp doesn't sustain the same invective against technology which R.S. Thomas develops from the very early 'Cynddylan on a Tractor' to the "machine" of the *H'm* poems. Tripp is determined to warn "...against frivolous excursions/from the tainting of eastern zones". He says that he often wishes there were border-guards, a sort of Check-Point Charlie with "...this frontier sealed/at Chepstow". Such fantastic images are too often repeated to be dismissed as merely tongue-in-cheek rhetoric, or the excesses of performance poetry. If one looks at other work produced in the late sixties and early seventies one finds that John Tripp was not alone in this apparent extremism.

Raymond Garlick is one of the most strident of such voices. An Englishman by birth and a Catholic by faith (an ancestor was martyred for his faith in Derby in 1588) Garlick is one of those who was drawn to the landscape and traditions of Wales, the country of his childhood summers. He opted into a Welsh identity, as have other notable literary figures from Edward Thomas, Richard Hughes and David Jones through to Jon Dressel and Chris Torrance. Saunders Lewis, the central figure in a matrix of literature and politics in Wales, was himself born in Liverpool. Raymond Garlick was the founder of *Dock Leaves*, later to become *The Anglo-Welsh Review*, and an enthusiastic protagonist of Anglo-Welsh literature through his publications and his teaching at Trinity College, Carmarthen. His support for the nationalist and Welsh language causes was determined and vociferous, particularly during the late 1960s and the early 1970s. Although he, like Harri Webb, repudiates quite unequivocally, the violent extremes of the nationalist movement:

> In Wales we shall never see
> a terrible beauty born.
> ...a freedom hacked out here
> is a freedom without worth.

> 'Matters Arising'

Garlick's poetry employs at times the most emotive referents of any writer in post-war Wales at this time. His period of teaching in Holland lead him to draw analogies between the two small countries. Images of oppression, particularly of the Nazi occupation, are used as models for some equally horrific impending fate in Wales. He can leap from:

> the tall boots bruising
> the sunlit lawn;
> doom at the door
> in the cold of dawn.

> 'Fourth of May'[12]

to the image of Wales as a crucified nation:

> I think of this
> and remember Wales,
> the size of Holland.
> Don't let the nails
>
> of crucifixion
> be hammered there –
> employed by hands
> half unaware.

'Fourth of May'

Language protesters are betrayed by the courts in terms of Pilate's treatment of Christ in 'Passion 1972',[13] to my mind, one of the least well-judged of his poems.

Garlick, like several of his contemporaries, makes use of the tainted history of the Welsh foot-soldiers pressed into the service of their English kings – 'Agincourt' and 'Cywydd I Llansteffan',[14] in common with John Tripp's 'Saint Fagan Fight' and 'Defeat in the North',[15] portray the Welsh as victims of a military system, pawns in a larger strategic power-game played by their English masters. Unlike Tripp, Raymond Garlick has not continued to publish into the 1980s. There may be a range of explanations for that fact. However, the publishing climate would be supportive of his work were he to present it and one might suggest that his output has waned with the dissipation of that protest and passion of the 1960s.

It is John Tripp who embodies the qualities of protest, drawing on the achievements of both R.S. Thomas and Idris Davies, and carries some essence of the 1960s forward into the 1980s. However, there are signs that Tripp himself may be running out of steam. His most recent collection, *Passing Through*,[16] still exhibits the qualities of anger and pathos, wit and self-effacement which have characterised his work over twenty years. But now the latter qualities dominate. Tripp's gaze has always been hard and straight; moving back from London to tackle "the social, political and cultural shambles of Wales when I returned"[17], he enlivened the performance of poetry and articulated a range of needs for audiences who felt betrayed, confused and, briefly, patriotic. He can be quite objective about that time now. "Besides the patriotism, which is still there but not as

strong as it was before the disastrous Referendum on Devolution in
'79, other Welsh aspects of my work are an authentic sense of place
and a genuine concern for the underdog, the marginal people in our
botched society, the neglected and forgotten. At our best, we *do*
care".[18]

It is that sense of caring which does attract in John Tripp's work.
But this "gnarled bard", having lost the ready focus of the nationalist
struggle, can sometimes fall back too heavily on himself:

> Years of trains and buses
> and their hopeless connections
> have dulled my edge.
> What I choose to remember
> is that I do it, that still
> somehow it is worth doing.

And he ends the same poem with "...To pass the time/I start to write
this...". At its best, John Tripp's work combines the controlled
strength of the American "confessionals" and the compassionate
cuting edge of the late novelist and broadcaster Gwyn Thomas.
'Connection in Bridgend' and 'Second Coming' work well in this vein.
However, too many of the poems in *Passing Through* seem too
obviously willed into being, and then barely worth holding on to.

> the fire went out in my belly.
> Outnumbered, I surrendered with bad grace.

>   'White Flag'

The book's cover is pertinent: the scene is Cardiff station and a train
is departing. A figure sits immobile on the platform seat, not getting
on any train, waiting for the destination board to flick up other
directions.

Gillian Clarke first published in 1970, encouraged by her husband
who, redeeming a poem in draft from her wastepaper-basket, sent
it to Meic Stephens. Stephens' response was positive and Gillian
Clarke threw herself into the writing of poetry with enormous
energy. She wrote and published very frequently through the 1970s,
also becoming Reviews Editor for *The Anglo-Welsh Review* and then
succeeding Roland Mathias as editor in 1976. Gillian Clarke was
quickly established as a leading Welsh poet and her first full-length

collection *The Sundial,* published by Gomer Press in 1978, has proved the most successful book of poetry from a publisher in Wales for many years. Her *Selected Poems* (Carcanet, 1985) encourages one to consider the development of a poet over fifteen years, working in Wales to considerable effect in terms of critical acclaim, audience response and book sales.

The commitment to poetry, for Gillian Clarke, was linked with her growing recognition of the importance of Wales to her life. Living in suburban Cardiff, she was spiritually inhabiting a more rural, Welsh-speaking world to the west. The act of writing involved in the deepest sense a confrontation and acceptance of her essential Welshness. In 1970 the context of publishing in Wales and the concern to voice Welsh issues, to proclaim a specific Welsh identity, provided a receptive ground for Gillian Clarke's growth as a writer. In a recent interview[19] she acknowledges this:

> My loss of Welsh has been a very strong tension in my writing. But English is my mother tongue, and it is the tongue I was educated in. But being a woman and Welsh and therefore in two senses not wholly ready to count myself as one of the grown-ups, not easily able to feel I was permitted to be myself, to be a writer, an artist, I was a very late developer. Many women, particularly in Wales, are late developers as writers. I didn't begin writing properly until I was thirty, by which time I had long been learning Welsh. So, while I grew through childhood and adolescence without Welsh, I already knew a lot of Welsh before I began to write openly. I began to write and to post poems because of the existence of the Welsh magazines written in English, like *The Anglo-Welsh Review, Poetry Wales,* and others. Those magazines gave me a sense of my own ability to join the ranks of the writers within them, writers who seemed to be giving me, written down, my own world.

That process, as a woman and as a writer, has been steady and determined. Gillian Clarke's themes remain constant, her destination fixed. She still works under the influence of Yeats, the Romantic poets and, of her contemporaries, Ted Hughes and Seamus Heaney especially. The influence of Hughes and Heaney is clear in much of her best work; but these poems *are* her best work because she has learned from and assimilated, rather than merely imitated, those poets. It would be crude misrepresentation to assign the birth and death imagery of poems such as 'Scything', 'Ram' and 'Welsh Blacks' to Hughes alone; just as it would be churlish to credit Seamus Heaney for 'The Water-Diviner' or 'Chalk Pebble'. Still, these two powerful poets inform Gillian Clarke's work as they do many of their contemporaries and it is interesting to compare Gillian Clarke's work with Hughes' 'Thought Fox' and its mystical aesthetics; her use of the Welsh language with the poems from Heaney's *Wintering Out*, and his own fascination with the elements and the poet's need to name them in poems such as 'The Diviner'[20] and the 'Shelf Life' sequence from *Station Island*.[21]

Whilst she has been swayed and carried on by the musicality of Yeats, Gillian Clarke, unlike Tripp and Garlick, has avoided the direct voicing of political concerns. She is not a poet of instant responses and, though she has written to commission, notably from the B.B.C. and the R.S.C., one cannot imagine her producing work such as R.S. Thomas' *What is a Welshman?* or the protest poems of Raymond Garlick in the early 1970s. She is far less direct than her contemporary Sally Roberts Jones. Sally Jones does not have the lyrical strength of Gillian Clarke, but she has constantly addressed herself to the matter of Wales. Like Raymond Garlick and John Tripp, Sally Jones' arrival from London in the 1960s was a significant opting into a Welsh identity. In poems such as 'Community', 'Language Protest, Llangefni' and 'Tryweryn'[22] her concern for the survival and integrity of a Welsh Wales is clear. It is interesting to compare 'Tryweryn' with Gillian Clarke's 'Clywedog'.[23] Where Sally Jones is angry and ironical –

> All's for the best – rehoused, these natives, too,
> Should bless us for sanitation and good health.
> Later, from English cities, see the view
> Misty with hiraeth – and their new-built wealth.

Gillian Clarke is lyrical and ironical –

> And walls a thousand years old.
> And the mountains, in a head-collar
> Of flood, observe a desolation
> They'd grown used to before the coming
> Of the wall-makers. Language
> Crumbles to wind and bird-call.

All this is not to say that her poetry is merely content to hold a traditional, lyrical ground in a pastoral landscape. Her long poem 'Letter From a Far Country' succeeds as a feminist polemic where more directly aggressive voices have repelled those they would seek to change. Her work as a whole also exists against, and contributes to, a Wales that is, for her, as for R.S. Thomas the core of everything that she knows. To this end she is driven by the need to reclaim a lost heritage that is encoded in a languge to which she must lay claim; an inheritance that may only be realised by the continuing act of naming. She finds her material in the landscape and in specific records such as a *Cofiant*. [24]

> The one in my family was written by a man who bears my own
> father's name, John Penri Williams. It was published in 1895, and
> was written about his father, my great, great grandfather, the
> Reverend Thomas Williams who was born in 1800 in the Llŷn
> peninsula in North Wales. The *Cofiant* shows that they had not
> moved from that rural community and were still living in the
> same family farm as they had been for many, many generations.
> Further research told me that the family living in this farm had
> descended from the minor gentry – and although its well known
> that in Tudor times gentlemen made up genealogies to fill up the
> empty hours, nevertheless, if we are to believe the particular
> Tudor gentleman in my family, then this little tribe of farmers
> was descended from the Welsh princes. Whether they were or
> whether they weren't is irrelevant, because it contains in any
> case a marvellous image of what has happened to Wales. The
> genealogy is a thing of great beauty, there are marvellous
> names: Gwynedd, Madoc, Angharad and Princess Nest.
> Suddenly in 1725 an English surname is imposed.

Over the last ten years more and more of her time has been spent away from Cardiff, renovating and finally, in 1984, fully occupying a cottage remotely placed in Dyfed, in one of the most strongly Welsh-speaking areas of Wales.

There is an appropriateness, even an inevitability, in that move. The cottage, Blaen Cwrt, had been the setting and the subject of one of her strongest early poems. This describes and celebrates the renovation of the place, "Some of the smoke/Rises against the ploughed, brown field/As a sign to our neighbours in the/Four fields of the Valley that we are in". A claim is being made to enter that community, to turn one's back on the "brochure blues or boiled sweet/Reds" and opt for "Nettles tasting sour and the smells of moist/Earth and sheep's wool". Nettles in Gillian Clarke's work are more likely to be those of Edward Thomas than John Ormond. The much-maligned Georgian qualities exemplified in Thomas' work have been more constructive than the modernism of Eliot and Pound as far as Anglo-Welsh poetry is concerned.

Just as Edward Thomas in celebrating the rural life of pre-war England protested the immorality and absurdity of the Great War's carnage, so Gillian Clarke's creation of a rural landscape in the west of Wales serves to underline implicit arguments concerning the way she feels we, especially we who wish to call ourselves Welsh, should conduct ourselves. 'Blaen Cwrt' is a place where "air spins", smoke "curls like fern"; where there is "a thick root". Images build up an impression of an organic, holistic state of being and, in response, even "Our fingers curl on/Enamel mugs of tea, like ploughmen". The poem closes with a summation of the qualities of Blaen Cwrt that has the weight and some of the naiveté of a manifesto.

> It has all the first
> Necessities for a high standard
> Of civilised living: silence inside
> A circle of sound, water and fire,
> Light on uncountable miles of mountain
> From a big, unpredictable sky,
> Two rooms, waking and sleeping,
> Two languages, two centuries of past
> To ponder on, and the basic need
> To work hard in order to survive.[25]

Gillian Clarke is not only drawing a parameter around the physical and imaginative territory which she wishes to occupy, she is dedicating herself here to the the task of poetry and the cause of her Wales with a crusading zeal. It is a zeal which is predicated in the dislocation which urban life has occasioned and in this respect she is following in the steps of R.S. Thomas (she literally does this in 'Fires on Llŷn'). But where Thomas' landscape is a harsh tutor, testing and undermining any easy belief in a benevolent creator, Gillian Clarke's nature, while it can be instructive in its constant offerings of mortality, is closer to Wordsworth's maternal Nature. Bones, eggs, skulls, proliferate in Gillian Clarke's poems, but they are seized upon as *objets trouvé*: the ram's "helmet" skull could be "a vessel for blackberries and sloes" until the "Night in the socket of his eye" insists a harsher lesson. "Sheep's Skulls" are sought like mushrooms and it is only later that one assumes a closer significance –

> On the rose
> Patina of old wood it lies
> Ornamental in the reflection
> Of a jar of wheat stalks.

There is a sense in which Nature, and natural truth is "out there"; one brings it back to one's world, the security of one's day to day living, where it resonates and disturbs.

In her treatment of this nature of Wales, this instructive landscape, Gillian Clarke involves even her sense of her womanhood. Her long title poem from *Letter from a Far Country* is set in motion from an immediate, urban, domestic situation, but from that life in the Cardiff suburb of Cyncoed the poet projects herself out and back into a quite different

> ...landscape. Hill country,
> essentially feminine,
> the sea not far off.[26]

Blaen Cwrt is now an

> ...innocent smallholding
> where the swallows live and field mice
> winter and the sheep barge in
> under the browbone...

which holds the secret of its former owner's suicide. Again and again it is Nature's revelation of our mortality which quickens the impulse to shape one's life to a natural cycle.

In the earlier 'Harvest at Mynachlog' the same point is underlined, though on this occasion there is no questioning of the woman's role and the farmer's son who flashed through "the boasting sky" over those same fields in a previous year

> ...died minutes later
> On an English cliff.

That "English" seems in itself to be inconsequential, perhaps arbitrary. However, it does fit into a pattern of derogatory comparisons between England and Wales which underpin Gillian Clarke's poetry.

In 'Fires on Llŷn',[27] written in 1984, the poet walks on the Llŷn peninsula in North Wales receptive to the special resonances of that area and linking them with the violent history of the almost-visible Ireland across the sea. She has explained in some detail the poem's genesis:

> Many things which seemed unconnected were in my mind when I wrote it, though I was only aware of some of them. The year I was born, 1937, three men, out of deep-felt belief that what they were doing was right and in what they saw as the interests of peace and of their small country, Wales, set fire to an R.A.F. bombing school in North Wales, in Llŷn, the north-west peninsula which reaches far out into the Irish Sea. The Welsh poet R.S. Thomas lives in Llŷn, and about five years ago I heard him interviewed on the radio and he said that he believes in God because sometimes he finds the form of a hare on the mountainside, and although the hare has gone the form is still warm. He called it God's absence. It is an idea which has occupied me ever since. In the Llŷn peninsula more and more of the houses and farms are becoming holiday cottages, occupied for only a few weeks every year, while many local people are homeless. In the past few years anger about this, and about the breaking-up of Welsh speaking communities, has taken a frightening turn – holiday cottages are burned down in what the media have called 'The Arson Campaign'.[28]

What is clear from that is the poet's awareness of wider, and often specifically political, events which are subsumed into her work more often than might be generally assumed.

In 'Fires on Llŷn' the sanctity of the land's end at Uwchmynydd is broken by the thoughtlessness of "Three English boys":

> Over the holy sound Enlli
> is dark in a ruff
> of foam. Any pebble or shell
> might be the knuckle-bone
> or vertebra of a saint.

Three English boys throw stones.
Choughs sound alarm.
Sea-birds rise and twenty thousand saints
finger the shingle
to the sea's intonation.

Those English boys, by their casual actions, set in motion a line of
imagery and cross-reference that links the two Celtic countries, both
with histories of subjugation by the English. The "fires" at the
poem's end are explained as the sun's flash upon windows rather than
the work of the Welsh-language militant arsonists, but the poem has
by that time established a complexity of fearful associations, and
guilt, and anger. In more senses than one the poet has been playing
with fire. In what way can the "sea's mumbled novenas" convincingly
resolve the multiplicity of social and political dilemmas which the
poem has touched upon?

'Miracle on St. David's Day' loads even more spiritual weight onto
Wales. The poet is conducting a writer's visit to an asylum. She
estabishes some sense of her audience of inmates in rather clumsy,
generalised terms –

I am reading poetry to the insane.
An old woman, interrupting, offers
as many buckets of coal as I need.
A beautiful chestnut-haired boy listens
entirely absorbed. A schizophrenic

on a good day, they tell me later.
In a cage of first March sun a woman
sits not listening, not seeing,not feeling.
In her neat clothes the woman is absent.

Included in this introduction to the inmates is the central subject of
the poem, "A big, mild man" with "labourer's hands". It is this "big,
dumb labouring man" who rocks to the rhythm of the poems and
then, affected, transported by the sound, he rises to recite
Wordsworth's 'The Daffodils'. The poem becomes significant as a
positive act of memory, a lucid evocation of his past, his lost
innocence. The fact of his utterance too is a moment of clarity
focussed in his fogged brain.

The incident, it cannot be denied, was a remarkable one; it

underlines the power of poetry, albeit learned by rote "Forty years ago, in a Valleys school", to touch areas of our emotional needs which the mind, even a healthy mind, can work hard to avoid. However, in her re-creation of the incident and her weighting of the elements in the poem, Gillian Clarke overloads the piece. The title makes a claim for our patron saint's intervention which is, to say the least, unquestioning. The risk she takes in quoting surely the most frequently-quoted lines in English poetry is obviously a calculated one, but just as obviously, it must finally appear as heavy-handed.

The poem closes with a transcendent image of daffodils that are, by now, the flower of poetry itself, "their syllables/unspoken", the spirit of nature animated by "the big, dumb, labouring man's" act of speech, and the emblem of Wales (courtesy of Lloyd George). It is as if the daffodil were being made to function as does T.S. Eliot's rose:

> And all shall be well
> All manner of thing shall be well
> When the tongues of flame are in-folded
> Into the crowned knot of fire
> And the fire and the rose are one.

> 'Little Gidding'

But that triumphant conclusion to the *Four Quartets* stands on the achievement of those quartets, and the body of Eliot's poetry as a whole. 'Miracle on St. David's Day' has not earned its ending, and, again, one is asked to accept a set of corollaries from its Welsh setting that may, in fact, be far from acceptable.

This poem, which opens so effectively – its first stanza pointing out "the rumps of gardeners between nursery shrubs" – manages, remarkably, to proceed to its transcendent resolution with no further sense of irony. That irony would have helped to press the intriguing elements of the story and the descriptions of its setting into a more acceptable form. Gillian Clarke's work may not be consciously, or even obviously, politically-charged, but, in fact, her entire aesthetic is heavily weighed by passionate convictions regarding Wales, and pre-supposes such feelings in her audience.

Of the younger poets active in Wales at the present, Mike Jenkins (b. 1953), Robert Minhinnick (b. 1952), Nigel Jenkins (b. 1949) and Steve Griffiths (b. 1949) are most specific in their political alignments. John Davies (b. 1944) is another notable voice. Griffiths, after his interesting early sequence of poems concerning Anglesey, is now based in London where he works as a social worker. His concerns are with Tripp's "underdogs", but his focus has, necessarily, moved away from Wales.

John Davies, though resident for a number of years in Prestatyn, North Wales, continues to return to his native Cymmer and Port Talbot, as does his poetry. He is no card-carrying party man, but he does claim an affinity with the working people of that major steel town. He regrets the decline of the industry and the community which it raised in 'In Port Talbot' where only

> rust is eager and red-haired

> in no-man's land, this town,
> my town, whose thunder's the sound
> of thunder running down. [29]

The elegiac theme is worked in more detail in his latest collection, *The Visitor's Book* (Poetry Wales Press, 1985) which opens with a section of poems that deal with loss. John Davies mourns both relatives and familiar characters from the community of his childhood, as one would expect, but he also raises questions about the loss of Welshness. The process is regretted but recognised as the consequence of large and complex forces.

> And when at last shared work's vibrations cease,
> sharing itself will fade (as in the mining villages nearby)
> with Keir Hardie's dream, with Bethanias long since ghosts,
> down history's shaft. Difference and indifference will untie
> taut bonds of work that cramp yet forged here a community;
> then old South Wales will have to start a New. Meanwhile
> reverberations still, slow leavings, long goodbye.

Davies has recently returned from a teaching exchange in the State of Washington where he wrote a number of poems on the native Indian culture and its stubborn, fitful survival under the pressure of colonisation. There is a sense in which the poet was encountering there something not altogether unfamiliar.

Robert Minhinnick has attracted more critical attention and praise than any of the other new poets of the 1980s, with the possible exception of Oliver Reynolds. From his first full collection, *Native Ground*[30] to his third and latest book, *The Dinosaur Park*, he has established himself as an accomplished image-maker with a perception of characters in their immediate social context. He is more engaging than Reynolds, described by Peter Porter in *The Observer* of 6 October 1985 as "an impressive recruit to the New Heartlessness". Certainly, Reynolds' first collection, *Skevington's Daughter*, published by Faber in the September of that year, has a coolness about it. There is a section of poems with Welsh phrases as their titles, but in these and many other poems he seems to be outside of his subject-matter, manipulating words, rather than conveying feelings which would draw the reader into an emotional commitment.

Minhinnick's political standpoint is not flown like a flag, but, rather, implicated in the strong emotional loyalties he expresses towards his characters. His "native ground" has specific roots in the life of his grandfather, an "Old socialist... Labouring on a magistrate's estate". It is interesting to compare this poem with 'J.P.', where the justified angers of the grandfather are re-kindled by the grandson. Minhinnick does remain clear in striking his own course, though he recognises the limitations of the old man's understanding –

> The spittle of your politics
> Flies free, a special sour phlegm
> Reserved for Tories and the Nationalists,
> Those two distinctive enemies
>
> In your black and white world

but wants to share, at least, his independence of mind.

In his latest book, *The Dinosaur Park*, (Poetry Wales Press, 1985), he engages the vacuity and despair of a contemporary society, particularly observed in the working people, miners and steel-workers he sees at leisure in the resort town of Porthcawl, where Minhinnick now lives. Poems such as 'The Coast', 'The Resort' and 'The Dinosaur Park' see him charting the decline of a society which has lost its way, which no longer seems in control of its destiny and which turns a hard face towards its people. The final section of the sequence 'The Resort' closes with an image that defines the problem:

Our culture has its midden on the sands.
The bottles lie around the beach like empty
Chrysalids, sea-holly holds the strewn plastics
In a green pincer. So we embrace our time,
And in ones and twos the people tread the shore
Gazing about them, each with a question.

Robert Minhinnick's implicit socialism grows out of Wales, his "native ground", but does not specifically engage the matter of Wales itself. It seems that more often the younger poets are less concerned with the task of defining and defending Wales in terms of a separate nation than the poets of the "second wave" in the 1960s. They are, though, quick to recognise the way that Wales has had a special place in the development of Western capitalism and British imperialism and that the steady transformation of those forces underlies the social problems that confront and engage them in contemporary Wales.

Mike Jenkins' first collection, *Rat City*,[31] dealt with his experiences of life in Belfast, his wife's home town, and he has carried the republican convictions learned there back to Wales. Over three further collections of poetry he has developed a voice which deals sympathetically and angrily with both the history of the Merthyr area where he now lives and the iniquities of contemporary Britain, which he perceives fully as a comprehensive school teacher in a disadvantaged town.

In poems such as 'Dic Penderyn on Aberdare Mountain', 'Lewis Lewis on the Convict Ship' and 'Chartist Meeting, Heolgerrig'[32], he effectively re-creates significant moments from the history of the Valleys, while the long title poem from his third collection, *Empire of Smoke*,[33] is an ambitious, impressive panoramic presentation of the Merthyr area and its heritage –

I was born in the crater of this town
below a ring of tips and heaps
which glower down.
I felt the past like valleys
mapping out the nerves
of many of its people
and saw the paralysed expressions
of museum exhibits: like Richard Crawshay
piggish and puffed with fowl and port
turning you servant with his eyes

and dreaming of an empire of smoke
to replace the fickle clouds.

The inheritance is at Dowlais Top,
a black planet of scattered mounds
where hardly a tuft of grass
can take root.

This sequence and many of his other historical re-creations have the
well-realised tone of John Tripp's 'Imaginary Conversations' from
The Loss of Ancestry. Jenkins seems intent on pushing the form
further and it is interesting to note that 'Empire of Smoke' is
dedicated to the Caribbean poet Derek Walcott, who visited Wales
in 1980 to receive the Welsh Arts Council's International Writers
Prize. In that same year *The Star-Apple Kingdom* appeared from
Cape and this book, with its extensive use of the dramatic
monologue, had a clear influence on several poets.[34] Such visits
highlight the openness of younger Anglo-Welsh poets to a wide range
of international influences.

Empire of Smoke opens with a poem in memory of the Aberfan
disaster of almost twenty years before, 'He Loved, Light, Freedom,
and Animals', a piece which can stand beside John Tripp's 'Narrative
for Victims' and Leslie Norris' 'Elegy for David Beynon' as one of the
few convincing poems from a host of responses to that tragedy.
Certainly, like John Tripp, Mike Jenkins may be seen to be speaking
for "the underdog, the marginal people in our botched society, the
neglected and forgotten", but his poetry is focussed and quickened
by his closer proximity to such a society.

Wales, for both Mike Jenkins and Nigel Jenkins, is the particular
immediate context of more universal issues. Merthyr's history and
economic decline is the place where Mike Jenkins sees the forces of
capitalism and democracy at odds. Nigel Jenkins too is committed to
Wales in terms of his personal life and his principles. His 'Never
Forget your Welsh'[35] is a rollicking piece of satirical wit, a shotgun
blast which scores hits against hypocrises and corruptions at both a
national level:

                    vultures of unthink
                    Thatcher their queen
                    come to the Patti and
                    told us

go
Maggie Maggie Maggie
Charles and Di
orgasmic grovel
glee-faced serfs no
tongue like a Taff's
for lavish licking of the royal arse

and in the particular context of his native Swansea's local government
scandals of the 1970s

Wynford Vaughan Thomas
by appointment to
the sheep of Wales
will keep the people's memory
clean

arise
Sir Neddy Seagoon
arise Gerald Murphy
two years inside for getting caught
then HTV
scrubs the prison soup
from his chin.

Nigel Jenkins has been a member of the Communist Party but
"became disillusioned by its very soft line on Wales. I was hostile to
the emphasis on democratic centralism. I wanted the Communist
Party to play a leading role in achieving Welsh independance".[36] He
was on the point of joining the Welsh Republican Movement (of which
Mike Jenkins was already a member) but the police actions of the
early 1980s virtually closed the movement down.

His current work includes a long-term series of 'Triads', based on
a traditional Welsh format of remembrancing and commentary
achieved through groupings or multiples of three. The earliest of
these have appeared in *Radical Wales* in 1985, a magazine to which
he and Mike Jenkins regularly contribute. More obviously than Mike
Jenkins, Nigel Jenkins is attempting to capture the sort of audience
to which Garlick and Webb addressed themselves in the early 1970s.
Nigel Jenkins is a continuing admirer of Harri Webb's work in
particular, but the fact that both Harri Webb and Raymond Garlick

have indicated that they intend addressing that audience no longer
may call into question the continued existence of such an audience
and the efficacy of such an approach.

In general, the younger Anglo-Welsh poets have avoided the sort
of polemic which assumes a Welsh national identity. Their work
evokes the particular situation of their roots and the towns in which
they live: Merthyr, Prestatyn, Port Talbot, Swansea, Anglesey,
Porthcawl. There is no unquestionable Wales, rather, they must
work from the immediate context, the known. Emyr Humphreys has
written of "the sense of disorientation prevailing among the majority
who have been deprived of the language and the opportunity of
inheriting the history and traditions that go with it".[37] These poets
embody that confusion and their writing returns again and again to
define and clarify that confusion.

What is clear though, is that over the last decade the task of
transmitting a fresh, iconoclastic reappraisal of Wales to the Welsh
has been excellently performed by historians such as Gwyn A.
Williams, Prys Morgan, Dai Smith, Kenneth O. Morgan, Hywel
Francis and Glanmor Williams. Wales is not what we assumed it to
be. Simplistic assumptions of "national pride", a self-regarding
"national" identity, are not to be allowed to go unquestioned. Rather,
such assumptions point to needs which we share with many other
peoples and which will have to be continually addressed if we are to
find ourselves. In the contemporary context writers face a harder
task than even those raised by the ferment of the language campaign
and the Devolution Vote, issues which served to focus much recent
writing and to justify its polemic. Now Wales has its own fourth
channel and its bi-lingual cheque books. However,the task still
remains of voicing the situation of the eighty per cent who are outside
the language, who, for a complexity of reasons, turned their backs
on the chance for Devolution, but who still feel a deep need to call
themselves "Welsh". Anglo-Welsh writing and, in particular, the
strong tradition of Anglo-Welsh poetry, will, no doubt, play a notable
role in addressing that need.

NOTES

1. See *Defending Ancient Springs*, a collection of essays by Kathleen Raine. London, O.U.P., new edition, 1985.
2. Quoted by Geoffrey Grigson. Under "Dylan Thomas" in *The Penguin Dictionary of Modern Quotations*, Harmondsworth, 1984.
3. Introduction to *Anglo-Welsh Poetry 1480-1980*, edited by Raymond Garlick and Roland Mathias. Bridgend, Poetry Wales Press, 1984.
4. Poetry Wales Press, 1984.
5. *The Loss of Ancestry*, Swansea, Christopher Davies, 1969, p. 14.
6. *Collected Poems 1958-78*, Swansea, Christopher Davies, 1978, pp.13-14.
7. *Selected Poems 1946-68*, London, Rupert Hart-Davies, 1973.
8. Tuesday April 2nd, 1985.
9. Christopher Davies, 1974
10. London, Macmillan, 1972.
11. *Ten Anglo-Welsh Poets*, edited by Sam Adams, Manchester, Carcanet, 1974, p.90.
12. *Twelve Modern Anglo-Welsh Poets*, edited by Dale-Jones & Jenkins, London, University of London Press, 1975, p.172.
13. *A Sense of Europe*, Llandysul, Gomer Press, 1972.
14. *ibid.*
15. *Collected Poems*, p.116.
16. Poetry Wales Press, 1984.
17. Interview with Susan Butler in *Common Ground*, edited by Susan Butler, Poetry Wales Press, 1985.
18. *ibid.*
19. *ibid.*
20. *Selected Poems 1965-75*, London, Faber & Faber, 1980, p.24.
21. Faber, 1984.
22. *Writing in Wales: A Resource Pack*. Edited by Tony Curtis and Cliff James, Cardiff, The Welsh Academy/The Welsh Arts Council, 1985.
23. *Selected Poems*, Manchester, Carcanet, 1985.
24. *Common Ground*, interview with Susan Butler.
25. *Selected Poems*.
26. *ibid.*
27. *ibid.* But see also the drafts in *Writing in Wales*.
28. *Writing in Wales*.
29. *At the Edge of Town*, Gomer Press, 1981.
30. Christopher Davies, 1979.
31. Edge Press, 1977.
32. *The Common Land*, Poetry Wales Press, 1981.
33. Poetry Wales Press, 1983.
34. For example, see 'Gulf Stream' in *Poetry Wales*, vol.18 no.1 and 'Pembrokeshire Seams' from *Letting Go*, Poetry Wales Press, 1983,

both by Tony Curtis.
35.   *Practical Dreams*, Newcastle, Galloping Dog Press, 1983.
36.   Interview with Tony Curtis, October, 1985.
37.   *The Taliesin Tradition*, London, Black Raven Press, 1983.

Synopsis of the Great Welsh Novel

Harri Webb

Dai K lives at the end of a valley. One is not quite sure
Whether it has been drowned or not. His Mam
Loves him too much and his Dada drinks.
As for his girlfriend Blodwen, she's pregnant. So
Are all the other girls in the village – there's been a Revival.
After a performance of Elijah, the mad preacher
Davies the Doom has burnt the chapel down.
One Saturday night after the dance at the Con Club,
With the Free Wales Army up to no good in the back lanes,
A stranger comes to the village; he is, of course,
God, the well known television personality. He succeeds
In confusing the issue, whatever it is, and departs
On the last train before the line is closed.
The colliery blows up, there is a financial scandal
Involving all the most respected citizens; the Choir
Wins at the National. It is all seen, naturally,
Through the eyes of a sensitive boy who never grows up.
The men emigrate to America, Cardiff and the moon. The girls
Find rich and foolish English husbands. Only daft Ianto
Is left to recite the Complete Works of Sir Lewis Morris
To puzzled sheep, before throwing himself over
The edge of the abandoned quarry. One is not quite sure
Whether it is fiction or not.

DAI SMITH

A Novel History

A Novel History

There is, as every schoolboy knows in this scientific age, a very close chemical relation between coal and diamonds. It is the reason, I believe, why some people allude to coal as "black diamonds". Both these commodities represent wealth; but coal is a much less portable form of property. There is, from that point of view, a deplorable lack of concentration in coal. Now, if a coalmine could be put into one's waistcoat pocket – but it can't! At the same time, there is a fascination in coal, the supreme commodity of the age in which we are camped like bewildered travellers in a garish, unrestful hotel.

Joseph Conrad, *Victory* (1915)

The rapid transformation of the south of Wales into a central node of the world economy effected more than the material change which, as a minor by-product, brought the young Pole, Joseph Conrad, to Cardiff in 1885 on a ship looking for a cargo of coal. It created a culture which made the region "a problem" for the continuity of other Welsh traditions and moving beyond basic needs to human desires for community, turned the social experience into an idea which the post-1918 world would brutally test. The "fascination in coal" was, as an older Conrad knew, dependent on the social and historical relationships it produced, sustained and abandoned. The novels written directly about industrial South Wales have been heavily burdened by the weight of a history so immense in its implications as to be almost insupportable.

In the year Conrad's opening words in *Victory* were published the war-time government of Britain succumbed to the illegal, unofficial strike of South Wales miners. The Minister of Munitions, David Lloyd George, travelled to the Coal Capital of the world, Cardiff, to surrender. He, and his government, conceded the point that the "supreme commodity of the age" required digging. He knew, too, that there was no greater concentration of coal for the British Navy than in South Wales. There was, for a moment, workers' control of the "supreme commodity". It was a fact which another Welshman gleefully pounced on, for the obverse side of Caradoc Evans' biting denunciation of peasant Wales was his hope for proletarian Wales:

> These strikes in Wales have a deeper meaning... The people are awakening. Nonconformity is bitten with its own teeth. Some Welsh towns and villages contain more picture palaces than chapels. That fact, and the fact of his riotous rebellions, may prove that, although the Welsh miner is still a creature of many primitive instincts, he is willing to begin at the beginning.[1]

One year later it was precisely this overthrowing of a cultural overlordship (Welsh, nonconformist, sanctified by rurality) and the embracing of alien gods (non-Welsh, socialist-syndicalist, rootless) which was to be emphasized by the Commissioners appointed to investigate the causes of industrial unrest in South Wales. But, first, they insisted on underlining a material fact, one as unpalatable in Welsh reality then as it has been in some Welsh minds ever since: "coal-mining stands out as pre-eminently the most important of the industries of Wales... In South Wales...it directly employs a larger proportion of the population than any other industry, while its needs have to be supplied and its output handled by large numbers engaged in the transport industry...indirectly it has contributed materially to the establishment and development of a variety of industries which, in its absence, could not possibly have attained their present large proportions...it is the very basis of the great shipping industry of the South Wales Ports, and...from 1841 downwards the population of Cardiff has...increased 10,000...for every additional million tons of coal shipped from its port...to use a colloquialism, "Coal is King". The public have been too slow to realise the significance of this fact; they are far from adequately realising it even yet, but the miners themselves are fully conscious of the supreme position which their industry occupies".[2]

What was of grave concern, beyond immediate industrial strife, was the manner in which this vast concentration of miners (over a quarter of a million by the War's end) and its urban-industrial framework (two out of every three people living in Wales) seemed to be by-passing the religious, educational and political institutions considered "proper" by organized society. In the light of the subsequent history of the coalfield the immediacy of that threat, even more than the undeniable long-term dislocation of Welsh life, has been underplayed. The power of that work-society to enact revolutionary change within itself as a prelude, many hoped, for change beyond its limiting framework caused anchoring ropes to fray and snap. The evidence, down to the mid-1920s, confirms the Commissioners' fears – one of them, Vernon Hartshorn, resigned the Presidency of the South Wales Miners' Federation in 1924 on the grounds that "Bolshevism" had taken over – that the normal – in politics, in society, in the union, in culture – was being challenged, and even on occasion replaced, by alternatives that, in the crucible of intense struggle, can justly be labelled "surreal". Expectations were subverted.

New expectations were not fulfilled. The society which had been force-fed until *all* its shoots were luxuriant now withered. Between 1921 and 1935 the estimated net loss of population in this industrial region was 314,000. In the 1920s alone, when a thousand people a year left Merthyr Tydfil, the biggest town in Wales as late as the 1870s, the population fell by over twelve per cent.[3] The incidence of mass long-term unemployment was the highest in the British Isles. Poverty was endemic. More commissioners came to observe and document the misery. The political threat had virtually ceased to be an issue by 1929 when the Minister of Health was informed that

> without something like a miracle it will be several years before the many thousands who must leave the area can be transferred to work elsewhere, and that in the meantime a large number of men, even if a steadily diminishing one, must remain exposed to the demoralising effects of idleness. That the danger is serious is clear when it is realised that a considerable number of the unemployed have not worked in a mine since 1921, while many more have been idle since 1926... The situation is, we believe, without parallel in the modern history of this country.[4]

And, having delivered their facts wrapped up in sanctimonious homilies, the investigators declared there was "no solution". Others were less inclined to write the whole thing off though, as survey followed report, little enough was done and, even at the end of the 1930s, poor Merthyr was recommended by the experts of the

Political and Economic Planning group as only fit for the scrap-heap. Even the three thick volumes of 1937 entitled *The Second Industrial Survey of South Wales* (like the first, of 1932, a detailed analysis by experts from University College of South Wales and Monmouthshire) plumped, amongst a welter of expansionist suggestions, for the grim conclusion that "if 80,000 insured workers were bodily removed from South Wales, there would remain an ample supply of labour to cater for the needs of all industries, while still leaving about twelve per cent of the total labour supply wholly unemployed".[5]

This history, of "great dream" and "swift disaster" in Idris Davies' coupled phrases[6] at the end of the 1930s, had to be understood in order to be assimilated. Politicians and economists turned somersaults in the 1930s to see if standing on their heads would help in a world-turned-upside-down. Photographers saw South Wales as a peculiarly focused example in the miasma of a general malaise, and sought images to deliver up its frozen state. Poets either escaped into a surrealism of effect whose sociological implications for the nature of inter-war Welsh life have been little understood – like the work of Dylan Thomas, that Welsh Huckleberry Finn who could never quite get back to the raft – or mooned over a society fit only for keening: "I watch the clouded years" said Alun Lewis in 1941,

> Rune the rough foreheads of these moody hills,
> This wet evening, in a lost age.[7]

By then it was, indeed, a "lost age". Conrad's "supreme commodity" ruled no more and the hotel, so far as South Wales was concerned, was more drab than "garish", more derelict than "unrestful". The Thirties was the lynch-pin decade in the last century of Welsh history. Enough had already happened to require a literature for that history. The novel seemed the form best suited to pull that history into a significant shape. However, almost nothing of any real value had been written in prose fiction about South Wales before the 1930s. What had been done moved, rather uneasily, from romantic novelettes to quasi-documentary accounts of provincial or regional life as if the latter was a curiosity to enliven the conventional plotting. In Joseph Keating, writing before the 1920s, the two were combined.[8] Later, and especially in Jack Jones' novels, the silver-spoon romanticism is dropped in favour of a Zola-esque slice-of-life but the notion of the South Wales coalfield as an unknown territory to be revealed or explained to the sympathetic reader remained. It is there explicitly in the straight documentary like James Hanley's *Grey Children* (1937) and, also avowing authenticity as its motive force, in B.L. Coombes' influential autobiography *These Poor Hands* (1939). Writers who did not want to be so severely circumscribed by established traditions of writing about areas like South Wales were still almost overwhelmed by the sheer force of their raw material: single-industry communities, a male bonded world, political and industrial strife, life underground, raucous popular culture, evangelical religion, tragedy, disasters, explosions, illness, unemployment. If the result was often itself stock melodrama it is scarcely surprising. One possibility was to view these things at one remove but the magnetic pull of the subject was as damning in fiction as in life. Irony trivialised no less than involvement.

In order to give the fiction – the imaginative re-ordering of the chaos that had overtaken people in South Wales – its true weight of purpose, writers had to break the fetters of that provincialism which labelled their concerns as parochial as they were geographically limited. There was, in Wales, no metropolitan perspective to adopt. Novels on city life would only emerge, haphazardly, much later. Besides, their challenge to the dominance of an industrial urbanism (to the conflation indeed of Valleys/industrial/South Wales/coalfield as an adjectival description of Welsh-writing in English) would, for a long time, languish in a client relationship to the greater creative impulse of the cities' hinterland. Individual removal from the coalfield's maelstrom was a fictional device employed by a number of writers. Rarely, however, did the individual manage to reflect back upon the communal or class story which this was designed to probe. Family histories were favoured vantage points between the extremes but, again, seemed destined to evade the artistic difficulty of using an established model of prose-fiction to represent matters which had not generally found their way into the novel except via a naturalism which would prove self-defeating the moment it tried to reach for an historical analysis. That perspective was no more than an inadequate observation of individuals and events over time.

If a generation of Welsh writers (and it is strictly a counter-factual supposition) had come to maturity *before* 1920 then their writing would have been as "open" as the historical pattern of South Wales had been to that point from the 1880s. As it was, we must date them from 1930 as fictional recorders and acknowledge, as in many different ways they did, that their subject was sharply restricted. Their task, and in advance of any possible historiography, was to reflect on their society's impasse. Through varied styles and intentions we can detect this common thread. It is one that in South Wales goes beyond the immediate concerns of the proletarian novel of the 1930s or the documentary form or even the historical Romance. The problems of constructing fictions about the majority human experience in Wales stemmed from the junction box of the 1930s. The reasons, then, for this problem are to do with a lack of tradition of writing about working-class life as much as with the particular development of native South Walians capable of using what tradition, notably in English, was available. The 1930s was for South Wales a decade of confluence – of languages, literature and generational emergence – in this sense too. The subject was immense. Self absorption was often frenetic. It is not ideal, perhaps, that the Welsh novel in English came of age during this "lost age", but the achievement was by any judgement considerable. Merely to cite a roll-call of the number of titles is to re-emphasize how productive a decade it was for the novel in Wales, and how insistently these works clung to similar themes: Jack Jones – *Rhondda Roundabout* (1934), *Black Parade* (1935) and *Bidden to the Feast* (1938); Rhys Davies – *A Time to Laugh* (1937) and *Jubilee Blues* (1938); Goronwy Rees – *A Bridge to Divide Them* (1937); Gwyn Jones – *Times Like These* (1936); Lewis Jones – *Cwmardy* (1937) and *We Live* (1939); Richard Llewellyn – *How Green Was My Valley* (1939).

That last is, of course, the last laugh the 1930s continues to have on this region of Wales which is substituted, here, for a national life it has apparently betrayed. Undoubtedly, insofar as Wales is popularly imagined outside, and sometimes inside Wales, it is the lilting cadence of Llewellyn's brilliantly titled book that summons up the familiar images. More seriously, it is no coincidence that in the 1930s Llewellyn utilised the mythology of a Fall-from-grace to explain the bewildering pattern of Welsh industrial history since it was only by reference to the past that the dog-days of the Thirties could be understood and only by a distortion of that past's meaning that the decade could be consigned to meaninglessness. The latter was the inevitable response on the part of those who read it in the 1930s though those years are not chronicled in the novel. Llewellyn's work retains its grip because its dystopian message can always be conjured away by the utopia of its Edenic Past. Its vacuousness lies in its attempt to make political fantasy the cause of the desolation, for which the flight of his protagonist is, inevitably, the sole salvation. It is an "if only" book: *if only* men had not overthrown their leaders, *if only* there had been no immigration into Wales, *if only* the Welsh had left before all this happened. Which is where, naturally, this Welsh *Looking Backward* begins.[9]

Nonetheless, the novel is not really an historical novel nor even a novel about actual history (in the way Alexander Cordell's successive epics since *Rape of the Fair Country* (1959) incorporated genuine historical events, or in the manner in which Gwyn Thomas, almost pre-empting "magical realism", transmitted the 1930s into the 1830s in his masterpiece *All Things Betray Thee* (1949));[10] rather it is a novel designed to echo a contemporary sensibility about the enormity of loss. This feeling is shared by almost all these Welsh writers. It is there most strongly, though in a contrasting fashion, in Gwyn Thomas whose adult years were haunted by those possibilities to effect change which he had sensed, as a child, in the 1920s. Gwyn Thomas rarely wrote about the 1920s. When he did recall those years it was, more often than not, by assuming the wonderment of a child at what he then saw and allying it to his numb fury at all of what followed for industrial Wales. His most haunting symbol for an almost tangible loss is the gazooka, that home-made mouth-instrument which the jazz-bands of the striking colliers turned into a collective note of plaintive defiance. Only in the work of Gwyn Thomas has the rebellion of that twanging, buzzing threnody been understood. These Gondoliers, Carabinieri, Toreadors, Zulus, Gauchos, Sultans, Spuds, Chinamen, Legionnaires and Grenadiers created a politics of inversion within the vulgarity of a shared popular culture. Their carnivals echo pre-industrial days of communal disorder. Gwyn Thomas' "rodneys" and "clowns" are never more disturbing than when they refuse to be just "voters". The gazookas, blown in their thousands, signal in their wailing eloquence a recognition of coming defeat even in the middle of a "new excitement":

> By the beginning of June (1926) the hills were bulging with a clearer loveliness than they had ever known before. No smoke rose from the great chimneys to write messages on the sky that puzzled and saddened the minds of the young. The endless journeys of coal trams on the incline, loaded on the upward run, empty and terrifyingly fast on the down, ceased to rattle through the night and mark our dreams. The parade of nailed boots on the pavements at dawn fell silent. Day after glorious day came up over the hills that had been restored by a quirk of social

conflict to the calm they lost a hundred years before.

When the school holidays came we took to the mountain tops, joining the liberated pit-ponies among the ferns on the broad plateaux... For our mothers and fathers there was the inclosing fence of hinted fears, fear of hunger, fear of defeat.

And then, out of the quietness and the golden light, partly to ease their fret, a new excitement was born. The carnivals and the jazz bands.

...We formed bands by the dozen, great lumps of beauty and precision, a hundred men and more in each , blowing out their songs as they marched up and down the valleys, amazing and deafening us all. Their instruments were gazookas, with a thunderous bringing up of drums in the rear.[11]

That 1957 story (based on a radio play) moves into a comic view that was typically sandwiched between "the rapture" of its beginning and a "basic disbelief" –

We were like an army that had nothing left to cheer about or cry about, not sure if it was advancing or retreating and not caring. We had lost.

However, on another occasion, and still mesmerised by that Time-out-of-Time, Gwyn Thomas considered another fantasy:

Imagine if, instead of gazookas, they had carried rifles![12]

The image was not entirely a mere fancy in one man's mind. One novella, building on the actual violence of the interwar years and published in 1937 when numbers of Welsh colliers had already volunteered to "fight Fascism" in Spain, turned the entrenched despair of the 1930s into an impulse for armed revolution. This was Glyn Jones' bravura fable 'I Was Born in Ystrad'.[13] Here the catharsis of struggle, through an uprising against the State, is a fictional by-pass for the dead-end of contemporary Wales. Glyn Jones blends naturalism and surrealism to convey the state of Depression Wales. The rhetoric of its argument is designed to lead to the one logical alternative apparently left to a people now, in 1937, itself officially declared "surplus to use". Glyn Jones does not bother to refute this designation. On the contrary, he emphasizes the hopelessness of any practical way out of the morass. Glyn Jones' first-person narrator,

Wyn, speaks in the haunting, wistful tones and uses the tactile imagery which will later infuse all of Glyn Jones' prose: the legendary invocation is present, from the start, in the origins of our storyteller. His father was a collier, but his forebears were "independent peasant farmers from the West" and, on his mother's side, the squirearchy and wise-woman are invoked until we go all the way back to "the native princes". The child is gifted with a sense of smell and touch. It is when his inner eye, temporarily corrupted by university education, begins to see *beyond* what he sees that action must follow.

The story provides a ready-made contrast between the unspoiled mountain country to the north and the "steaming earth-crack of the Ystrad Valley", but there is a brooding fascination with the industrial glamour of the Valley-in-work which Glyn Jones transforms into a stunning word-scape.

> The first town dirties the water. Between the blown silks of smoke one sees the township huddled narrow against the river, houses terraced like bent rod-iron along the mountain sides, saving flat silt for pits and railways, long rows of grey streets spiney with vertebral chimneys curving over the shell-folds of the hills parallel to the river bed, or struggling into the mountains...
>
> Farther down, where the river runs like a length of opened vein, deep through the divided flesh of the hills, the stalks of two black stacks unravel into horizontal smoke, and the pit is bannered with it... Men move over the sequined earth lifting the steel tip of a boot across the little tram rails, talking, hanging the coco-nut fibre bag or the feed bucket over the brown pony's neck, knocking the cage up at the pit-mouth... The fine dry drizzle of coal-dust has settled on sparkling skin and steel. Dug and shovelled lump coal is shoved out packed in the chalked trams, and by the locomotive sheds the pit sidings swerve towards the railroads shining like tightwire into the sun... The boiler house siren hoots the day shift up and the pit road chatters like a drumskin with the heavy boots hail-showering over it.
>
> I saw this, and more, when I was young, accepting it, fascinated by it. But since I see the track precede the wheel: where there are fifty pits someone will find the bones of the little wren, and under the concrete of the engine-room there is a crocus that will burn holes in it.[14]

Ystrad is Merthyr, a place that *did* revolt in 1831 and where, by 1937, the industrial past seemed as pre-historic as the timeless world the story invokes constantly. The narrator can never really lose himself either in that childhood of time or in the world of Art and Intellect. The latter becomes despised as inimical to working-class, Valleys' life:

> Daily it becomes clearer that my...great love of grandeur and sensuousness and style in all things were bringing about in me a subtle, spiritual betrayal of my people. I did not even notice in these years of satisfied sensuous craving that indifference to the sufferings and aspirations of the class from which I had sprung is the almost universal condition of English poetry...
>
> Later on, when I got back to the Valleys, I became a bit saner and I began to take immense pleasure in arranging lists of dates like the following – 1830-1835: 'Paracelsus', 'Lady of Shalot', 'Lotus Eaters', Reform Bill, Factory Legislation, Unrest in Ireland. 1842-50: 'Bells and Pomegranates', 'The Blessed Damozel', Coal-mine and Factory Legislation, Chartists at Kensington Common. Revolutions in France, Austria, Germany and Italy.[15]

And in Wales? Glyn Jones' narrator, confronted in Cardiff by a poverty that seems to compound passivity and to emphasize a political divorce from the "socialist" Valleys, turns to secret, conspiratorial activity whose end is violent upheaval. The story unfolds like a jerky newsreel. Guerrilla warfare, it seems, may as well flash onto the screen as all the other absurdities. At least it is activity for the people who had "lost faith in one political party after another" whilst, on the fringes,

> Who could believe in empty clichéists and windbags like the local communists...or the Welsh Nationalists with their summer schools for spooners?

This alternative through rebellion ends in yet more defeat but it is a defeat made acceptable by the exertion of will and the triumph of love. Finally, the narrator, on the mountain above the valley, lies down as sacrificial flesh until

> at last the vultures lift their beaks out of my eaten eyes.

There is nothing quite like this anywhere else in the literature about industrial Wales. The present was exorcised by Glyn Jones by breaking its back on the wilful rhythm of his prose-poetry. It is a feverish chant. The past has lost all meaningful resonance. The future remains strictly unimaginable. It was a common plight. Even in Lewis Jones' epic rediscovery of working-class history, in *Cwmardy* and *We Live*, the martyrdom of his hero, Len, in Spain and then the projected politics of a class-conscious people are little more than shadows of the past through which they have already lived.[16] Other novelists deliberately pulled up short of treating the abysmal decade into which industrial Wales had fallen.

Gwyn Jones' scrupulously weighted novel of 1936, *Times Like These*, surely intended its original readers to reflect on the failure of the half-decade which ends, in 1931, its fictional account. The mining family in this story move through the travails of political and industrial upheaval after "the short-lived boom" of 1924. Jenkinstown and the community surrounding it are seen from within through a thick, descriptive account of family life, leisure and the straightforward yet forlorn hopes for marriage and children. Against all this, querying it and threatening it, is a public life – the foreground of political decisions based on the coal industry's troubles, the background of elections and labour parliamentarianism – in which the Biesty family and their neighbours must, like it or not, play a part. Yet the Valleys are always somehow separate from these events which remain less vital than the intimate, sharply-observed life of household and community. The last words of the novel –

Everything do seem so useless, somehow

– echo Stephen Blackpool's plaintive cry in Dickens' *Hard Times* (1854) that it is "Aw a muddle!", yet the characters in Gwyn Jones' microcosm of South Wales clearly survive by virtue of their social integration. And this is achieved despite a diminution of what had once passed for a fuller life:

More than ever Jenkinstown made news out of trifles. At one time there had been trips to Cardiff to see the City play football or to visit the shops and theatres; there had been holidays at the seaside, though these shrank progressively from the duration of a fortnight to a day; there had been a glimpse of other places, and other folk, of other ways of life, before the return to the

familiar and intimate things of Jenkinstown; and even then there
was no lack of curiosity about births, marriages, deaths and
accidents; but by 1931 the miners and their families were so cast
back upon themselves for entertainment and interest that the
most trivial happenings were magnified for weeks.[17]

That species of introspection was also a reversal of the
perspective that had once been enjoyed. South Walians had hitherto
confidently expanded their view of themselves and the world. It was
this rumbustious enjoyment of possibility which, over-riding all
manner of individual and communal set-backs, informs the colourful
history poured out in Jack Jones' early novels. Later on his novels
shade imperceptibly into an effect of merely local colouring, amateur
chronicling and sentimental effusiveness. Throughout his writing
career he moved away from the contemporary or near-contemporary
to highlight the greater interest in what had already occurred. The
novels became encyclopaedic, replete with the flotsam and jetsam of
a world that always seems to be rushing towards a future which, we
cannot but reflect in our own attainment of it, is so much less worth
possession than the one we can only read about.

Jack Jones makes his case most powerfully in the vivid *Black
Parade* (1935). The schematic clashes of opinion and personality in
his earlier work, *Rhondda Roundabout* (1934), here give way to a
richly textured panorama of South Wales from the 1880s to mid
1930s. Once again there is an exactitude about dates (the 1898 strike
which founds the S.W.M.F.; Keir Hardie's election in Merthyr as
Wales' first Socialist M.P. in 1900; the Minimum Wage Strike of
1912; the closure of the great Dowlais Iron Works in 1930; and,
finally, the by-election in Merthyr in 1934 that sees S.O. Davies, for
Labour, defeat the ILP and Communist candidates), which
increasingly turns the novel into an historical diorama against whose
whirling images the characters – very much a family story again – are
seen, less and less, in the round. They observe and remark on these
major events – deaths in War, the rhetoric of A.J. Cook in 1926 and
Lloyd George in 1929 – but their own strength of interest for the
reader lies entirely in their youthful intermingling with a society,
c.1880 – 1900, once as youthfully poised as themselves. The public
events which serve as historical signposts do not signify the shape
of a history so much as the early sense of novelty which makes the
lives of Saran and Glyn and Dai and Harry vibrate with an excitement
also buzzing within their late nineteenth century Wales. For this is

Merthyr at its climactic peak where nonconformity and its perceived enemies (the pagan, the secular, the shiftless) jostle for power. The Chapel and the Public House *both* symbolise a striving for control.

The latter's existence is not quite the unbuttoned anarchy it might seem. The 1881 Act, about to ban drink on Sundays in Wales, is extolled in Zoar Chapel by the preacher, Sylvanus, but then who but the brickworks' girl Saran and her lover Glyn are the real creators of South Wales' new power? And this, in their chapel-going *and* working *and* drinking, is something they know and act out in an integral sense. Neither their own depicted lives nor the social framework of those lives is separated out by Jack Jones to make a fictitious divisiveness that would be reserved for the later fictions of historians. Historians' narratives all too often fail to reproduce that simultaneity of experience:

> Everybody was singing – all kneeling afterwards before God in Zoar – again all sang – then all listened to the reading of God's most comforting Word – and sang again – Sylvanus bowed his head in prayer as the collection was taken – *then*:
>
> "Before I submit for your consideration my interpretation of the messages delivered by Isaiah to King Hezekiah, I want to say a word regarding the work of a social character still to be accomplished by nonconformity, which is the only militant religious body of our times. We have won, despite the Established Church, the battle for Sunday closing in Wales, and very soon now there will not be a single drinking-den open on the Sabbath... soon we shall marshall our forces for the fight to free Wales of the chains that bind it, chains which were forged and clapped on us for the benefit of the Established Church.
>
> Wales to-day with its great mineral wealth, is the foundation-stone of the rapidly growing British Empire , which is expanding amazingly: – and the most important factors in this expansion are the coal and steel of South Wales – and the men who produce them, of course...

Things were warming up in the Albion, one of the three pubs practically on the doorstep of Zoar Chapel. Those patronising the Albion on Sundays, and most week-nights as well, were able to follow the services almost as well as those in the chapel itself, for not only could they hear the singing, but also what the preacher was saying once he reached peroration point.

"Being here's like having one's drop of beer in the chapel", some of
the chaps used to say, but there were others, especially the domino
players, who disliked the "noise", as they called it, made by those in
chapel when they were considering whether to play the double-six or
the six-four next...

> "A great preacher", said Glyn as they left the chapel.
> "Not so bad" said Saran, "once he began talking from
> the Bible, but when he was on about the drink I thought
> little of him, I see no harm in a man having a drop of beer
> if only he keeps himself tidy".[18]

Saran, the brick-yard girl, is Jack Jones' organizing principle. She is
not idealised. Her life of unremittingly hard labour is shown to wear
her down, piece by piece, into old age but her maintained balance,
between acceptance of work and snatched pleasure, is present in her
portraiture from the beginning. It is exactly that idea of a poised
personality as representative of a wider society that other writers,
and Jack Jones himself as he approaches his own time in his fiction,
do not convey. They cannot suggest it because, in the 1930s, the
balance has been lost. However, for Jack Jones, born into late
Victorian South Wales, the aura of expectation, which others
abandon or fantasise, was a palpable reality. The inhabitants of *Black
Parade* discover themselves not in work or the family – these are the
given situations from which they start – but on the street where life
is consumed, identities amongst strangers exchanged in a Wales of
enormously high immigration, and where individual preference or the
wilfulness of personality is asserted *against* the forming moulds of
religion, education or respectability. This is the freedom within
Capitalism. The enticing, transient taste of a South Wales arrayed in
all this consumerist glory was never better done than by the gulping
prose of Jack Jones whose heroes do not waste time on the
mountains *above* the Valleys:

> Then off down to the town of a hundred delights. All sorts of
> sport from cock-fighting to bare knuckle fighting in secret
> places, and foot, cycle and pony racing in the Big Field where
> the sports were due to commence at 2.30 sharp, but the gates
> were opened at noon for anyone who wanted to go and have a
> drink and a snack at either of the four big marquees erected for
> the day... Still, plenty of time before we go there thought the

brothers.

"What about a drink?" said Dai as they neared The Black Cock.

"Plenty of time for that, too" Glyn told him.

"Let's have a walk around town first."

So they walked round, first to see the new sensations in the Iron Bridge fairground. Then back through narrow streets crowded with people going here, there and everywhere. To the Eisteddfod which had already started at the Temperance Hall; to singing festivals about to commence in two of the largest chapels; to the fairground; to the registery office to get married, and afterwards into one or other of the numerous pubs to drink the health of the young couples in good beer at twopence a pint.

...The brothers, having completed their tour of inspection, were back in Pontmorlais...[and]...into the crowded Black Cock they turned...into the long bar, at the end of which the battle-scarred Harry was seated in the midst of admirers listening to Twm Steppwr playing 'A Sailor Cut Down in his Prime' on the concertina...[and]...entertaining the company... with those improvisations for which he was famous in a hundred townships of the five largest mining valleys...[and]...rendering his scandalous song-portraits, after each of which the company in the bar roared laughingly the seemingly innocent refrain:

> Did you ever see?
> Did you ever see?
> Did you ever see-ee
> Such a thing before?[19]

The detail of the actual history can thus unfold in a literal fashion in Jack Jones' novels because it all fits into a pattern dictated by the survival of appetite for life. Saran holds everything together by bringing new generations to life and ushering others out. The novel's throb of continuity is in its end:

> "S'long, Harry bach", she murmured as she stood and watched
> the funeral out of sight around the corner. Then she swallowed
> hard and led the way back into the living room.[20]

Yet the assertion is transfixed by the material transfer of the past into the present since only in the past itself does a kind of freedom of choice remain. Lewis Jones carefully dissected the illusoriness of this freedom, without ever sacrificing the liveliness inherent in its existence, in *Cwmardy* (1937). He then re-asserted the necessity of that freedom, this time against Capitalism, and of its agent, the new political consciousness which he dramatised in *We Live* (1939). At the end of that novel, too, an old couple, Big Jim and Siân, survive to offer continuity, and hope, beyond the sacrificed generation of the intermediate, hopeless 1930s. Only one Welsh writer refused any chronological consolations. The author was Gwyn Thomas and *his* 1937 novel was refused publication for almost fifty years.

Sorrow For Thy Sons[21] marked a new departure – albeit a hidden one until now – in the fiction written about South Wales. Gwyn Thomas began in the mid 1930s to seek out a form, and a style to serve that form, which would be as savagely abrupt as the fate visited upon his society. South Wales is "a slaughterhouse" whose victims are its own children. South Wales is orphaned from the hopefulness of its own near history and deprived of any exit into the future. The only escapes offered are ones which willingly renounce the best possibilities once examined for use by the community. So of the three brothers in the novel, one, Herbert, can survive by embracing the role of a subservient, lickspittle in a shop; Hugh, educated out of his class in university, remains umbilically attached to his society and yet incapable of acting from within it – he physically leaves; Alf, unemployed collier, is not able to begin a new generation with his love, Gwyneth, and is also incapable of being anything other than a denizen of this benighted land. The brothers are, when the book begins in 1930, on their own – only photographs of relatives serve to connect them to the past. The work which made the valley is finished and Alf, apart from picking for coal on the slag heaps, will never work again. Alf, who is most nearly an embodiment of the Valley's past life, does attain a kind of grace by virtue of some selfless acts of kindness and love but these are, on his part, counter-balanced by an unfathomable depth of bitter anger and unassuageable contempt for others. The 1935 marches against the National Government's Unemployment Act are given due weight and, to an extent, offered as an example of what "the people" *en masse* are still able to do, but nothing flows from this which will enact major changes. It is an isolated instance of heroism in spite of hopelessness.

The bleakness is a constant. What proved most unacceptable to the readers at Gollancz was the lack of any uplifting proletarian presence to redress the unrelieved gloom. There are workers who exploit workers in this novel; the worse the misery and the more petty the act (selling charity clothes, gathering waste coal on a tip when a butty lies injured) the greater the betrayal of any vestige of human solidarity. Gone, too, is any glimpse of delight in the place or high days and holidays. The novel is a catalogue of a thousand species of despair served up in an unrelenting documentation of misery.

However, the apparent transparency of the prose disguises the book's formalistic purpose. The novel's importance really lies in its attempted break with the naturalistic conventions that had usually dictated the structure and intentions of the working-class novel. Gwyn Thomas does not yet relinquish the detail of place and time which allows us here to locate his fiction in an actual history but already he is trying to strip that history to the essentials which, he suggests, holds his characters in its grip. The grip is terrible because it knows no release other than death. There is no development. This is the end of the line: there are no ancestors and no descendants. Hell is a continuity of present existence. The novel is a tragedy from which there is no bolt-hole. Whatever may happen subsequently that tragedy, for the novel, has already marked South Wales irredeemably. The Commissioners were right in their diagnosis and so, for Gwyn Thomas, the novelist's answer lies in declaring oneself a citizen of Hell.

Gwyn Thomas confronted head-on the dilemmas for the novel inherent in writing collective history as the acknowledged channel for individual, subjective experience.[22] He did not solve the problem in *Sorrow For Thy Sons* because his protagonists stayed too rooted within an actual framework and, therefore, were obliged to act and speak in righteous indignation. What they also possessed, though, was Gwyn Thomas' developing insight that only a degree of detachment could give them the freedom to comment (subjectively) on their collective selves (the history undergone). The voices in this first novel were not yet suffused with irony and equipped with that hyperbolic wit whose extravagance would match and mock its subject matter. This would come in the burst of fictional writings he published just after the War: *Where Did I Put My Pity?*, *The Dark Philosophers* and *The Alone to the Alone*. The voice had been honed to express the conscious sensibility which Gwyn Thomas believed to be the great discovery, the one true gift, of the inter-war years to his people. The 1949 disquisition on all of their history, *All Things Betray Thee*, is dedicted simply 'To The Valley and Its People'. Its insistence is that the defeat of their human potential which they have, no matter in how mitigated a fashion, directly suffered can only be offset by the consolation of self-knowledge. From that echo the void can be made to fill up with sound. He filled his own novels of this period with music and musicians, harpists, singers and the melancholy bands of gazooka players whose ghostly hooting lies behind so much of his frenetic, punchy dialogue. Naturalism is left far behind as he gives voice to these voiceless. Both the music and his verbal pyrotechnics deliberately affirm the depth and the universality of South Wales' history. Mere detail could not convey this. The history could not be shown whole without discovering a language adequate to the task.[23] The 1930s defied easy fictional treatment because the readily available genres of writing automatically made meaning subservient to their demands of form and style. Gwyn Thomas accepted South Wales' freezing hell of historical immobility. In so doing he gave himself the detachment to comment on its absurdity from within the joke which an unexpected historical process had played on South Wales.

The reversal of expectation, which serves as a key motif in all his later work, was established early. In *Sorrow For Thy Sons*, a "leader of Welsh Thought" visits Hugh's grammar school and addresses the assembled boys:

> The visitor was pausing. He didn't appear to be out of breath. He was bending over the table, swinging his big, well-prepared head from left to right, doing the same with the outstretched index of his right hand and smiling as if he had adopted every one of the one hundred and fifty boys present. When he started to speak again, there was a deliberate benevolence in his voice, that caused a softening in the faces of the boys.
>
> "Now I come to what is the essential part of my message to you. You are being given a good education. Use it to the best of your abilities. Become citizens of that world of opportunity which is around us. Most of you were born in this valley. Its hills have been your horizon. Do not let that be so forever. Have courage to look beyond the hills. I am not asking you to sacrifice your local patriotism. Oh dear, no."
>
> The visitor laughed as if he had said something ridiculous. The dour look on the faces of his listeners did not alter. They saw no joke in what had been said.
>
> "Oh dear, no. To love one's birthplace is a grand and noble

thing. But these things must be looked at, my young friends, not in the light of any sentimental loyalties, but in the light of your future welfare, your future happiness. That is the important thing. Let me give you a word of warning – These valleys were once prosperous. Their prosperity is waning and will, I fear, continue to wane. They will not, I fear, continue to afford facilities in the future to absorb you all when you have finished school and college. Do not let that daunt you. There are trouble-makers in these valleys, trouble-makers whose activities account for so much of the discontent and industrial idleness to be seen here, who will try to sow the seed of discontent in your hearts merely because you might fail to find employment in the towns where you were born. Pay no attention to these. Being themselves worthless and unsuccessful they try to poison others with their worthless doctrine of failure. I ask you again, look beyond the hills that have cradled you since birth. Take the world in your stride."

What gives *Sorrow For Thy Sons* its quite startling resonance in the 1980s is the relevance of its satire. It has been as if the social tragedy – pit closures, strikes, high unemployment, loss of morale, investigation and sympathy from outside, governmental indifference – has been re-enacted. Gwyn Thomas' masterly translation of that previous waste of human lives into a corresponding fiction of black, farcical comedy is, however, unrepeatable. Its genesis lay in the historical relationship once existing between inter-war Wales and the material processes which had shaped that culture. The link was so binding that Gwyn Thomas, developing a choral voice, could avoid the conventions of dramatising, or showing, in favour of the moral passion of telling, or discussing. In the 1940s such fictional rhetoric *could* conceivably address the present in the interests of a future.

The contemporary, shrinking world of the coalfield only relates to both its previous selves in that superficial way which allows it to be packaged in Tourist Board images for consumption. The phrase forever hung around the neck of the Valleys only requires an adjectival substitution to keep every copy-writer's cliché on the top of the file – "How Green/Red/Black Was My Valley". Or, as one of Alun Richards' characters spluttered, "How Green Was My *What*?" This dissonance between a half-baked mythology of Valleys' history and, from the 1950s, a rapidly changing life, put a dramatic distance between an alleged public persona and the actual perception people

had of themselves. What the latter was, or is, may still be taken as
in dispute. For Gwyn Thomas, in the 1950s and 1960s, the
displacement, as he saw it, into a kind of mindless affluence led him
to a wry, occasionally manic comedy in which the philosophic
clowning of his earlier fiction lost its bite. It is no simple coincidence
that as the society he had known, in all its intricacies, became
directionless – now imitative of what it had once been in its political
energies – so he gradually ceased to write novels. For those writers
who did wish to project individual histories within a social landscape
the novel form itself still beckoned. Very few questioned the form in
order to accomodate their subject. Even fewer wrote about
contemporary life in an industrial society that did now, at last, appear
to have reached its end. The rise and rise of the "Poets of the
Valleys" and of their more plodding brothers and sisters, the
"committed historians", was not matched by an equivalent band of
novelists, those still uniquely equipped recorders of our human fate,
who seemed to have been off to such a good and fecund start in the
1930s.

The exceptions who prove this rule are Ron Berry (b.1920) and
Alun Richards (b.1929). From quite different perspectives, and in
sharply contrasting styles, they have brought the relationship
between a changing people and an enchanted, decaying history up to
date. They have also found a way out of the dark forest of Cliché and
the deceptive maze of narrative History. The latter, in particular, has
its authoritative tones questioned and its credentials quizzed in this
work. Unlike so many others held in thrall by the unquestionable
drama of the history these two writers, accepting that weight, ease
the burden by making it, in their fiction, open once again. In place of
the shut down world of the 1930s, and the husks of imagination it left
across a wide array of creative endeavour, they make the past a part
of our imagined future precisely by seeing it as shapeless, in its
actual present, as our own recent experience has been. The paradox
is that human will, agency to choose, is thereby restored. If the
outcome is uncertain then the form to convey our complexity must
somehow be shaped to that uncertainty.

Ron Berry's novel of 1968, *Flame and Slag*, took the irreverent,
absolutely contemporary characters of his earlier books a stage
further into their own dissolution, in a future that would outstrip the
desperate "nowness" of the 1960s. He did this by confronting them
with their past. Rees is a collier in Caib colliery, a pit whose own
future has been assured by the N.C.B. but which will, nonetheless,

close. He marries Ellen, daughter of John Vaughan, one time official
of the Union Lodge and now, in old age, returned to Daren. After a
land-slip hits his house John Vaughan dies. Rees discovers his journal
and the narrative plays around his increasingly difficult relationship
with Ellen, and with the immediate life of Daren, by using the journal
as a book within a book, a history within a history, a past within a
present where the future is both cursed and unknowable. From
Rees' reflections on the journal (what *he* knows independently of *its*
facts) and his moving through the events of 1960s Daren, Ron Berry
constructs a labyrinthine narrative that reveals the layers-upon-
layers of a real history. Its fiction is designed to expose the fictive
imperatives which, in their own times, oil the wheels of human lives.
Like Faulkner he works the rounded nature of life into the linear song
of narration. This is Rees Stevens:

> While changing into pit clothes I took on one of those
> pre-cautionary moods: Hark at Reeso. Mrs. Stevens's bingo
> card philosopher, vaunting his lot. Five shifts a week until I'm
> sixty. See our kids educated all the way, see them head out into
> the shrinking world... But yourself, Rees, you'll spit coaldust
> long after your teeth drop from your gums. Spit up the old stuff
> like Dai and Glyndwr Stevens.
>   Yuh.
>   Humming *Miss Otis regrets* as I entered Caib lamproom,
> spinning my brass check across the metalcounter for lamp 967,
> the *Miss Otis* tune unconsciously reviving, finding its place inside
> my head as we crammed back, chest and rib-sides in the cage,
> old Lewsin Lewis Whistler softly, thoughtlessly, trilling the *Riff
> Song* and brazen-headed Charlie Page handing out Mintoes to
> everybody. Mintoe odour pervading the roadway as we walked
> in alongside Andrew Booth's boon, the trunk conveyor belt
> travelling back to pit bottom. Andrew's two younger brothers
> were Coal Board men, white fingered and collared seven days
> a week... both childlessly married to Aberystwyth University
> girls, young Plaid Cymru wives who canvassed Daren at local
> elections, enthusiastically futile against sanctioned fellow
> travellers on Daren's hundred per cent Labour borough council,
> utterly futile against a die-hard nucleus of Communist voters
> who abused the two Nationalists as if they were degenerate
> debs. Pairing themselves, B.A. Aber. below B.A. Aber., they
> sent a telling letter to the *Western Mail*, revealing their

experiences in the Earl Haig Club where a conclave of primitive
Socialists educated the ladies, regaled them with coal-face
adjectives, an old Arnhem paratrooper among these life-beaten
veterans from Tredegar Bevan's Janus-faced idealism.

And this is John Vaughan's journal:

It was Twmws Ivor Cynon who cut the actual first sod on April
21st 1923. Mr. Joseph Gibby the owner put the shovel into
Twm's hands for him to have a go, make the start of Caib pit and
the reason we called it CAIB comes from Twmws's grandfather
who was a blacksmith very clever at making a caib, which is the
Welsh name for mattock... I am referring to 1923, exactly 23
years after they drove the railway tunnel under Waunwen but
long before the senior school and the Earl Haig and Daren
Co-operative on Harding's Square, actually Daren was only
quarter as big with gas lamps no further than Dick Harding's
stables. It was like another kingdom in those days as compared
to these days, any honest man would say there are vast
differences. For instance until Caib raised steam coal we were
still working house coal seams half-way up the mountains and
every summer you would see brown squirrels in the Avenue
trees. What I can claim without fear of contradiction is that we
were happier. Much happier all round as regards being
neighbours sharing and sharing alike. Nothing resembling what
came after, for instance, the Schiller Award in 1933 made even
brothers enemies to each other.[25]

The journal goes on piling up its memory, allowing itself to wander
where a thought strikes an incident or a name back into life, defying
the file-card ordering of a history into just a record. Ron Berry holds
it all together in this remarkable tour-de-force. It is a novel *about*
history as much as it is concerned with the stuff of the history. And
it writes full-stop to that line of novels which we can trace from the
1930s.

Alun Richards moves away from the limits inherent in that
obsessed tradition by refusing to be swamped by a history that has
for so long demanded such exorcism. He achieves this considerable
feat by recognising how the obsession has distorted the cultural
texture of South Wales. He makes the point, to great and telling
comic effect in his collections of short stories *Dai Country* (1973) and

The Former Miss Merthyr Tydfil (1976); he exposes the deliberate usage made of the past for rapid commercial or aesthetic ends. In his novels the territory of urban and industrial Wales – brought to a fictional juxtaposition rarely seen – is explored as if it were fresh rather than exhausted material. The wider range of occupations and pursuits taken up by his characters confirm their removal from the socio-economic stereotypes who, black-faced, unemployed, or militant, stalk our fictional worlds (and certainly inhabit our soap operas). His Wales is a society of gradations in status and attitude which belies the monolithic assumptions of so many observers. A different kind of novel, a comedy of manners almost in a mainstream English-language tradition, is therefore open to him.

There were complaints, even before the traditional industries and communities of the coalfield were slowly dismantled in the wake of the Second World War, that the existence of middle-class society had been ignored too readily. There had been in abundance, after all, landed farmers, lawyers, colliery managers, school teachers, shopkeepers, engineers, clerks and officials. There was a fabric of golf clubs, social institutes, private functions, horse shows, residential streets of some standing and a discrete world-within-a-world (the "joking rich" they were sometimes called, though this is to underestimate the wealth of people for whom, even in the stricken 1930s, "Town" meant London not Cardiff or Swansea). This section, rooted in the land *before* industry or at a tangential remove from industry itself, created a distinct society – "their" Grammar Schools, "their" rugby club committees, "their" parts of public houses, "their" districts of the valleys, "their" social and familial circles – which has scarcely surfaced in our novels or our historiography. Nor did they only flourish in larger conurbations like Aberdare or Pontypridd or Maesteg. These groups had their sub-groups in all the middle-sized townships of the Valleys. They often set their public tone. Their provocative existence – between Capital and Labour – was a catalytic agent in the explosive Tonypandy disturbances of 1910 from whose fall-out they sheltered for half a century.

Although these people are treated in our fiction by writers such as Rhys Davies, and are constantly discussed in the novels of Gwyn Thomas, they have generally and peremptorily been shuffled to one side. Nor is this entirely wilfulness or a retrospective vindictiveness for, in essence, these groups were the original cultural fakers (is it just coincidence that so many of the administrators and manipulators of opinion in Wales in the 1980s are sons-of-the-manse or descendants of teachers? Where else would their inherited role now take them?). Their own, semi-detached sense of themselves was firmly related to the process of industrial capitalism which had actually brought human South Wales – via iron, tinplate, steel and coal – to its pre-1914 apogee. They were, by then, literally swamped by the working-class all around. And it was this class which made the political and social initiatives that marked out South Wales for two generations. Those who lament the imbalance in our written fiction are on the same wavelength as those 1917 commissioners who bemoaned a lack of order in the whole of the coalfield's development. It is one of the subtle strengths of Alun Richards' work that it holds both issues in its grasp.

Nowhere is this revelation presented more acutely than in his 1973 novel, *Home To An Empty House*. At first glance the novel, with sections devoted to the separate perspectives of his male and female characters, is an elegant dissection – a cut here, a slash there – of a marriage-on-the-rocks. The setting could be anywhere. Or almost anywhere. A first-person narration by a woman is a rare enough event in a South Walian novel to make the reader wonder. Indeed, Alun Richards makes no bones about his novel being about the sort of life, of teaching and ill health and sex and its discontents, you could imagine in any older, British urban place. He is surely right to emphasize that this is where we have washed up.

The history is, however, still there to consider. Walter, Connie's disaffected husband, is convinced the Welsh prefer remembering to living; Aunt Rachel survives but keeps her tenderness for one touch of the hand of a boy who died in the Great War; and Ifor, the older man to whom Connie turns, is the scholarship-boy who cannot ever again connect his life to his memories (he is Hugh in *Sorrow For Thy Sons*, he is the tortured, working-class boy to be "elevated", socially and scholastically in Alun Lewis' novel fragment of 1939). His one hope is self-awareness, and it is this that the uncomprehending Connie can elicit:

> ...I had done so much in my life to disguise my origins, and cloak my real feelings...meeting her was the beginning of a new awareness in myself. Her directness startled me at first, then took on the role of the surgeon's knife. She was no respecter of persons, and free of that awful Welsh trait of ingratiation which I encountered daily. In a curious way, it was as if I had come full circle to re-encounter in her the directness of the *werin*, that

valley sharpness, the same truculence and insolence of the colliers I remembered as a boy. She affected to despise sociology and professed a total indifference to things Welsh. She could not understand that I was the pip squeezed from the orange, the product of both, victim and assassin.[26]

Except, of course, she does not feel the need to understand. For her it was "meaningless in terms of my present". Connie is the first generation to whom the past is something other people had, strictly, now, a mere history:

Then I was suddenly confronted with the Welsh thing. Rachel on about the past, Ifor on the English, blaming them for the destruction of his own roots. I'd never thought about it before. Somehow I always associated Welshness with quarreling committees, with things going wrong, little political men with vested interests and families of unemployable nephews screwing money and jobs out of the State for their own special, personal causes. And the Language that nobody spoke much in the towns, unless it was to get on in the BBC or Education...[and]...the more emotive things...like a cottonwool fuzz at the back of the mind...Rachel spoke of men like Bevan who had passed on, leaving a name for greatness, but in the bleak towns they left behind them, nothing was substantially changed there anymore than it was anywhere else. Rachel harped on it like a Jewish matriarch. We were powerless, corrupting ourselves daily. The people had lost their will to be and only existed to be used by profiteers of one kind or another.[27]

Connie wants to believe that "it had nothing to do with me" but when, at the very last, Walter leaves both her and Aunt Rachel

the hardest thing of all to accept was my unimportance, my loneliness, just being me.[28]

This novel confronts directly the emptiness from which the new beginning must be made. No easy filling up of the vacuum of contemporary South Wales is on offer. Rhetoric is facile. Dismissal is cheap. The ideologies of accommodation to a Greater Wales or a Lesser Britain is tintinnabulation without a symphony. To imagine now is, at one and the same time, to admit the dreadful sense of completion, of an historical process ended, and yet affirm the refusal to lose the common memories which make human beings transmitters as well as receivers. To lose the thrust of that paradox is to lose the enormous gain which will accrue to our fiction by embracing the ambiguous, the ambivalent and the uncertain. Neither the heroic nor the disclaiming stance is appropriate. What we now have is a tradition, in English about Wales, for us to quiz rather than either dismiss, as so often has happened in our universities, or celebrate in a knee-jerk counter-response to academic philistinism. We do not need The Great Welsh Novel since it will remain, in the interstices of our welcome complexity as a people, the mythical beast which is also The Great American Novel. Within the body of English-language literature, especially now that the last century of this Welsh life has been both documented and imagined so exhaustively, there is an available substitute for that holistic tradition which is, whether in reality or in fiction, necessarily unattainable. The alternative is style, an articulation of life dependent on vision and voice. It is what Irving Howe, writing of "Jewish American authors" a generation removed from Yiddish, called

the yoking of street-raciness and high-culture mandarin.[29]

There could be no better description of the tonality of the best voices raised, and yet to be heard, from within our own novel history.[30]

NOTES

1.   'The Welsh Miner' (1916), *Fury Never Leaves Us: A Miscellany of Caradoc Evans*, ed. John Harris. Poetry Wales Press 1985, pp.155-6.

2.   *Commission of Enquiry into Industrial Unrest*, No. 7 Division, 1917, pp.4-5, 11-12.

3.   *The Second Industrial Survey of South Wales*, Vol 1, University Press, Cardiff 1937, pp.15-16.

4.   *Report on Investigation in the Coalfield of South Wales and Monmouth*, 1929, pp.9-10.

5. *Second Industrial Survey*, Vol. 1, p. 389.
6. Idris Davies, 'Do You Remember 1926?', *Gwalia Deserta*, Dent, 1938.
7. Alun Lewis, 'The Mountain over Aberdare', *Raiders' Dawn*, Allen & Unwin, 1942.
8. Keating published four novels set in "the Welsh mining valleys" between 1900 and 1917. That of 1905, *Maurice*, was first subtitled "a romance of light and darkness", and then, in the edition of 1912, re-titled "a romance of a Welsh coal mine". See Brynmor Jones' *A Bibliography of Anglo-Welsh Literature*, 1970.
9. Consult Dai Smith, *Wales! Wales?*, Allen & Unwin, 1984, pp. 110-123.
10. See Dai Smith: 'Breaking Silence: Gwyn Thomas and the "pre-history" of Welsh working-class fiction' in *Artisans, Peasants and Proletarians: Essays for Gwyn A. Williams*, ed. Clive Emsley and James Walvin, Croom Helm, 1985.
11. Gwyn Thomas, *Gazooka*, Gollancz, 1957, pp. 64-5.
12. Gwyn Thomas in conversation with the author.
13. Glyn Jones 'I Was Born in Ystrad', *The Blue Bed and Other Stories*, Jonathan Cape, 1937.
14. *ibid.* pp. 16-19.
15. *ibid.* pp. 21-23.
16. See David Smith: *Lewis Jones*, University of Wales Press, 1982.
17. Gwyn Jones: *Times Like These*, Gollancz re-print, 1979, p. 290.
18. Jack Jones: *Black Parade*, Hamish Hamilton, 1948 edition, pp. 57-59.
19. *ibid.* pp. 61-64.
20. *ibid.* p. 312.
21. Gwyn Thomas' *Sorrow For Thy Sons* will be published by Lawrence & Wishart in 1986.
22. The problems are dissected in Raymond Williams' *The Welsh Industrial Novel*, University College, Cardiff Press, 1978.
23. See Dai Smith: 'The Early Gwyn Thomas' in *Transactions of the Honourable Society of Cymmrodorion*, forthcoming, 1986.
24. Ron Berry: *Flame and Slag*, W.H. Allen, 1968, pp. 50-51.
25. *ibid.* pp. 32-33.
26. Alun Richards: *Home to an Empty House*, Gomer, 1973, p. 147.
27. *ibid.* p. 182.
28. *ibid.* p. 240.
29. Irving Howe, *Celebrations and Attacks*, Andre Deutsch, 1979, p. 25.
30. Two outstanding novelists who have used South Wales' history since the 1930s as a "control factor" in novels principally about other matters (a sectional intelligentsia's attempt to understand their own role in twentieth century Wales; the inter-relationship between political activists in the coalfield and intellectuals who are connected politically through historical crisis points) are Emyr Humphreys and Raymond Williams. They seem to me to understand acutely the importance, for their different purposes, of the "novel history" I have discussed but Emyr Humphreys' novels (*Flesh and Blood*, 1974; *The Best of Friends*, 1978; and, most recently, *Salt of the Earth*, 1984) are not part

of that fictional tradition or its history, whilst Raymond Williams deliberately moved beyond close consideration of a "felt life" to examine its wider dissemination in the life of the mind, of art and politics (notably in *Loyalties*, 1985). Their fictive reflections are a re-working of the meaning of history, and a subject for another time.

PETER STEAD

Wales in the Movies

Wales in the Movies

The British have never really come to terms with motion pictures. There has always been a British Cinema but it has never been able to establish for itself a recognisable and legitimate place within its own culture. There has been criticism from abroad, François Truffaut once suggested that there was "a certain incompatability between the terms 'cinema' and 'Britain'", but it was British audiences, exhibitors and critics themselves who were first to point out that British films were far too closely tied to music hall and theatrical conventions and that even at their best they tended to be somewhat stilted and wooden, the end-product of worthy endeavour rather than genuine creativity. The contrast was always with the unmistakable energy and effortless naturalism of the Hollywood movie as well as with the intriguing complexity and thoroughly national style of those European films that were shown in the London art houses.

As far as the masses were concerned the most obvious feature of the movies was the domination of Hollywood. The essential fact was that the relatively large British audience contributed substantially to the profitability of American films and so American producers tenaciously held on to their domination of the British market. Meanwhile British producers who were all too fascinated by the American example found themselves caught between making expensive films for the largely hostile American market or falling back on humbler films that might with luck make a small profit at home. The American film industry rested on an understanding between Wall Street and Hollywood whilst in London's Wardour Street the British film industry found it difficult to achieve independence when faced with the sheer size and wealth of the Hollywood empire. Tony Garnett was once to observe that "to be an Englishman in the film industry is to know what it's like to be colonised".

Audiences knew little about the high finance and politics of the film industry but they knew what they liked and there was no doubt that they very much liked what Hollywood had to offer. Welsh audiences, just like those throughout Britain, mostly went to the cinema to be entertained and it was pure entertainment that Hollywood guaranteed. In general films were popular because of their very sure social touch. Certainly, they only dealt with a limited range of social and emotional situations but in these films there were actors and actresses who seemed to exist in their own right and who exuded a kind of classless energy and confidence. The problem with English films was that theatrically trained actors and especially actresses had difficulty in injecting pace, wit and style into the depiction of a society that perhaps even in real life was too formal to lend itself to the conventions of the movies. Whatever the reason, Welsh audiences like other regional and working-class audiences in Britain accepted the fact that they would not see themselves in the movies unless it was in the guise of music-hall types brought in occasionally as humble policemen or railway porters to relieve the predominantly middle-class metropolitan and middle-brow drama.

To the film historians Britain must necessarily be seen as a film colony and Wales as on the periphery of that colony. What mattered more to the Welsh audiences of the past was that they were an integral and equal part of Hollywood's scheme of things with full and cheap access to the quality product that the studios were offering. For most of this century Welsh filmgoers would have thought it absurd to talk in terms of a specifically Welsh cinema or even to look for any serious depiction of Wales in the movies. Even now it is tempting to think of 'Wales in the Movies' as a non-subject or as a study that would have to rely on such trivial snippets as D.W. Griffith's pride in his Welsh ancestry (quite incredibly, Rodney Acland found that the great man had a "lovely Welsh-American accent") or Charlie Chaplin's recollections of his early days touring Wales, or possibly with the descriptions of the visits Randolph Hearst and Marion Davies made to St. Donants. The true film "fan" delights in trivia and would love to read of how *The Young Winston* was shot at Brynamman, *Arabesque* at Crumlin Viaduct and somewhat mysteriously *An American Werewolf in London* on the Brecon Beacons, but this kind of film history was put firmly in perspective by the Bangor housewife who was all too aware that *The Inn of the Sixth Happiness* had been filmed in Snowdonia and whose only comment on the film was that if Gladys Aylward had come to her for advice then the Chinese adversaries could easily have been avoided and "they would have arrived safely in Llanberis in only a fraction of the time"! To think in these terms is to confirm that Wales was on the periphery and can offer only footnotes to any history of film. In fact the situation is a little more complex for just occasionally Wales has broken into the movies, or rather it has been a case of film-makers sometimes wanting to use Wales for their own purposes. Certainly there are points to be made which contribute to an understanding of the forces that have shaped and constrained British Cinema generally.

A writer on Irish cinema once commented on the irony that the nearest Ireland had ever come to an indigenous film industry had been in the years before 1914. In a sense the same is true of Wales and quite justifiably Wales is given an honourable mention in all the standard histories of early British cinema. Many attempts have been made to identify the individual inventors and pioneers of film and cinema, but what is important and indisputable is that the commercial exhibition of motion pictures spread rapidly outside the innovating centres of Paris, London and New York in 1896 and the years that followed. The urban masses showed a great appetite for this new diversion and a whole army of entrepreneurs frenetically set about producing films and improvising places of exhibition. The earliest shows were in music halls or hastily converted shops (the famous "nickelodeons" in America) but it seems that after the initial craze there was a decline in the number of theatrical exhibitions and in Britain at least the initiative passed to travelling showmen who exhibited films in temporary but ornate booths. One such showman was Walter Haggar of Aberdare who had his own camera and who shot scenes in South Wales which would then be shown in his booth at the various fairgrounds throughout the area. What is fascinating about these years is the way in which the public demand for more and better films inspired the more enterprising of the showmen to move on from simple local shots to the production of fiction or feature films, and Haggar duly emerged as a distinguished and successful film-maker well aware of the kind of narrative melodrama that audiences favoured. Film historians have described films such as his *The Salmon Poacher, D.T.'s or The Effect of Drink* and especially his *Life of Charles Peace* as being as good as anything produced in Britain in that first decade of the new century and equally they have been impressed by the commercial acumen that enabled him to sell as many as four hundred and eighty prints of one film and to negotiate an agreement with Gaumont to distribute his films outside South Wales. Haggar had developed that same understanding of the popular taste that was generating a film industry in and around New York but which was soon to migrate to Hollywood. South Wales was booming in much the same way as America's East Coast and Mid-West and it is not too absurd to ask why Haggar's remarkable talent for making popular story-telling films did not become the basis of a permanent film industry. Why Hollywood and not, say, Barry Island? Of course it was all a question of finance and of the new pattern that emerged as producers, directors and exhibitors fought to maximize profits. As better films were made so there was a new boom in the construction or adaptation of motion picture theatres or kinemas and the trend now was for exhibitors to hire rather than buy their films and to hire from distributors who could offer mass-produced studio-made films at a cheaper rate than individual film-makers. Haggar could not compete with well-equipped studios nor with international distributors and so he sank whatever funds he had into the opening of permanent kinemas. He opened his first theatre in Aberdare in 1910 and like his fellow exhibitors throughout Wales he looked around for the best and cheapest films and found that increasingly they came from France and more especially America. As kinemas mushroomed in Wales, in 1914 there were twenty-one "picture theatres" in Cardiff and nineteen in Swansea, so audiences found that perhaps as much as eighty-five percent of what they saw was foreign.

Whatever hopes there were for a recovery of British film production were destroyed by the First World War. The great Silent Cinema of the 1920s was almost entirely a product of Hollywood and of the films seen by British audiences only about five per cent were home made. Not surprisingly Wales slipped out of film history and was glimpsed now only very occasionally in the newsreels. There were shots of the miners' disputes in 1921 and 1926 and of the accompanying poverty but the newsreel companies were soon encouraged to avoid such contentious stories and to concentrate on more festive events: Cardiff's annual Corpus Christi procession became almost the most regularly filmed event in the British calendar. In any cinema programme the newsreels would lead on to the main feature film and in these vastly popular fictional melodramas there would be no shots of Wales, but there were occasionally some Welsh faces and members of the audience might well have recognised Edna May Davies, Mary Glynne, Sam Livesy, Hannah Jones, Yvonne Thomas or several other actors and actresses all of whom had gone from Wales to the stages of London's West End and then into British films. Perhaps the best known of this colony of Welsh actors were Lyn Harding, a dark six-footer from Newport who starred in several British and American films and Edmund Gwenn from Glamorgan, a keen rugby follower and much acclaimed stage-actor who made many British films before becoming one of Hollywood's best-known character actors and who was not far short of eighty when in 1956 he starred in Alfred Hitchcock's *The Trouble With Harry*. Towering above all these performers in the 1920s though was Wales's own super-star Ivor Novello, who had been born Ivor Novello Davies in Cardiff in 1893 and who had later left Oxford University to become a well-known actor, playwright and composer. With his pale skin, dark hair and what were always described as "soulful" brown eyes, Novello was a natural for movie melodrama and he soon developed into the only British matinee idol who could compete with Hollywood stars in terms of spirituality and sexuality. His best known part was in *The Lodger*, the 1926 film with which Hitchcock established his credentials as a master of the macabre, although the young director was somewhat less than enchanted with the way in which Novello's star-status prevented any suggestions being made that the character he played was really Jack the Ripper. Novello's star shone brightly for a while but his trip to Hollywood to work with Griffith did not go so well, and neither was he able to adjust to the coming of sound.

It was in the 1930s that Wales really made its film debut. That decade saw an intense politicization of the cultural debate in Britain and as intellectuals and creative artists began to appreciate the values of the proletariat so increasingly the Welsh miners who had previously been thought of as undisciplined hotheads now became to many the classical expression of a long-suffering and democratic working class community. The largely unofficial but nevertheless very effective code of film censorship prevented both the newsreel and feature-film companies from depicting the politics of working-class communities but the new political dispensation and cultural debate made it inevitable that Welsh miners would make it into the movies, albeit in a highly controlled way. The miners were visited first by members of that group of documentary film-makers who believed that they were in the process of creating a new film genre that would halt the insidious influence of Hollywood's make-believe. The group had been inspired by John Grierson who combined the political scientist's sense that film could be used to educate and inform the masses with an aesthetic appreciation of the deeply poetic and humanist images of the North American director Robert J. Flaherty. Grierson argued for films that would offer "a creative treatment of actuality" and his organising flair also led him to suspect that he could find official and commercial sponsorship for such films even in the context of Britain's strict film censorship. He created the conditions which allowed the making of sponsored documentaries and he brought together directors who were convinced that, notwithstanding bureaucratic funding and mundane subject-matter, films of real feeling could be made. More radical directors like Paul Rotha were also determined to make their images as political as the format allowed. For this group the Welsh miners were a natural subject.

The sponsored documentaries that were made in South Wales made no reference to the politics of the area and said nothing about the South Wales Miners Federation and yet they did depict many of the problems connected with unemployment and they did allow the unemployed themselves to directly address the outside world. It was highly unusual for ordinary people to speak to the camera let alone the citizens of a highly politicized community like South Wales. Certainly in these documentaries the unemployed South Wales miners made their well-rehearsed comments in a very stilted way but at least they were being allowed to communicate. In 1937 Donald Alexander, who had first come to South Wales as a Cambridge undergraduate to shoot a miners strike on 16 mm, produced a film called *Eastern Valley* which dealt with the relief work organised by the Quakers at the top of the Monmouthshire Valleys. In this short film one unemployed miner explains that he was working now "not for a boss but for myself and my butties", whilst an old-timer admits that although mistakes had been made "a new interest in life" had been generated by the Quakers. The best known Welsh documentary was *Today We Live* which was made in that same year of 1937 for the National Council of Social Service. The Welsh scenes in this film were directed by Ralph Bond and they told a story in which the unemployed miners of Pentre debate whether or not to cooperate with the voluntary relief agencies. It is obvious that these unemployed miners had been coached, (Rotha was later to explain that "they were told the gist of what they had to say but put it into their own words") but nevertheless, the difficulty of dealing with poverty and boredom of living on a shilling a day are movingly conveyed and it is not surprising that the film was so well received in the art-houses of London and New York. It was a rare treat to hear the unemployed speak but the film made its impact not only because of the dialogue but also through the stunning images of life in the depressed Valleys. Bond's assistant on the film was Donald Alexander and his shot of the unemployed searching for waste coal on the slag heaps was not only the highlight of *Today We Live* but was destined to become the most famous image of the Depression as far as Britain was concerned. The sequence was "cannibalized" in many later films and was used even more than the sequences of underground and pit-head activity that had been shot a few years earlier by Alberto Cavalcanti. Alexander's slag-heap shots became an icon of proletarian hardship and played the same part for British intellectuals as the monochrome still-photographs of Dorothea Lange and Walker Evans were playing for their American counterparts.

The documentary film-makers had achieved a real breakthrough although they were constrained by their scheme of sponsorship and also by problems of distribution. Rotha, Bond and Alexander never knew whether their films would be seen outside of London's West End and New York's Museum of Modern Art. The commercial cinema had a stranglehold and, on the whole, exhibitors were quite happy to give their audiences a diet of Hollywood films interspersed with British comedies and with newsreels which had now become essentially tabloid and never dealt with political or individual issues unless there was some sentimental human-interest angle. As the Socialist cause strengthened in the 1930s so several groups attempted to challenge the commercial cinema by producing independent films and by arranging independent outlets. In particular the Communist Party attempted to make independent newsreels and to organize the showing of classic Russian feature-films. Undoubtedly what we may term an alternative film culture came into existence in the London of these years but this culture had hardly any impact in Wales. The independent newsreels, which in any case only consisted of badly shot silent sequences of marches and demonstrations, were rarely shown in Welsh halls and it was only with the greatest difficulty and expense that the Soviet classics were shown. In these years the limitations imposed on commercial newsreels by censorship and on the independent film groups by both censorship and expense were somewhat cruelly exposed by the more sophisticated, explicit and controversial treatment of the South Wales coal trade in the American newsreel, *The March of Time*.

In south Wales there was one kind of institution which seemed to hold out the possibility of an independent cinema and that was the miners' institute. Throughout the coalfield there were a number of these institutes and workmen's halls that operated as cinemas, which were controlled by local committees and which could have been used as outlets for political and Soviet films. The evidence suggests that at least some of these halls did attempt to introduce independent and radical films into their programmes, but in general the story of their efforts serves only to remind us of the many problems facing those wishing to challenge the commercial cinema. These miners' halls operated as genuine cinemas in competition with other local cinemas and so they had full 35 mm facilities. This meant that they could not show most of the independent films and newsreels which were made on 16 mm whilst at the same time they were covered by the ban on the showing of the 35 mm versions of Russian films (this ban did not extend to 16 mm versions). There were many ironies and obstacles but one suspects that in any case the audiences in these halls were eager to see the same kind of movies that were shown in other cinemas.

During the 1930s Hollywood captured the masses but increasingly its films were also appealing to critics and intellectuals. Educated film-goers were now beginning to appreciate those qualities which the masses had always detected and in particular they were at last spotting that there were forms of social realism in American cinema. Together with this realisation there came a new awareness that it was precisely this quality that was lacking in British films and by the late 1930s there was a crescendo of demand for a fuller sense of Britain in British films. When, in 1938, a reader named David Thomas wrote to *The Daily Worker* urging British producers to come out of their stupid world of make-believe and to start looking at the drama of everyday reality such as was to be found in the pits he was virtually speaking for the vast majority of critics and film-goers alike. Even as Mr. Thomas wrote, things were changing. The constant sniping of critics, the dissatisfaction of directors and above all the relaxation of censorship as war became inevitable all sanctioned the emergence of a social cinema. This was a real turning point in British film history, but, hardly surprisingly, it was Hollywood which both inspired and encouraged the change. The dark days of Depression had taught Hollywood that there were audiences for films that admitted that not all was right in the world, and then the election of Roosevelt in 1932 had for a while at least encouraged producers to make films that attacked certain evil and corrupt practices in American life. Whatever radicalism seeped into American cinema was virtually killed off by 1936, but films like *I Am A Fugitive From a Chain Gang* and *Black Fury* had inspired a new realism that lingered on even as the social message became muted. The British studios duly noted the lesson that there were audiences for social problem films and that, in any case, the censors were becoming more lenient. It was in this context that films like *South Riding* and *Pygmalion* were made but in the end it was the direct injection of American money that accounted for the real breakthrough. Following the 1937 Quota Act, American companies began to establish their own studios around London so that they could make "British" films and it was under this dispensation that M.G.M. made *The Citadel* in 1938.

Several British critics thought that *The Citadel* was one of the best British films ever and comments were made about the very apparent American production values, about the emergence of Robert Donat as a Hollywood-type star and about the way in which the film offered a real sense of London and South Wales. Hollywood loved middle-brow best-sellers (libraries and book-stores provided free publicity) and A.J. Cronin was very keen for his story about the ideals and ambitions of a young doctor to be filmed. He could never have foreseen that the film would be so well made; there were some early location sequences which rooted the story in the south Wales that the Documentary directors had discovered, there was first-class acting from Donat, Ralph Richardson and Emlyn Williams, who had also contributed some authentic Welsh dialogue, and there was also a convincingly detailed denunciation of the evils of private medicine. Britain was ripe for such a socially mature film, but the inspiration was largely that of Hollywood. The director, King Vidor, was well known in Hollywood for making social problem films that reflected his own brand of rural populism: he was very much for the common man and very much against the sharp-practices of all corporations and vested interests. *The Citadel* offered a fuller view of South Wales than any previous feature film, but it was essentially using the area for its own purposes. These purposes were largely determined by the demands of melodramatic narrative, but Vidor was also able to convey his own philosophy. The film was mainly concerned with the salvation of its hero: the Christian knight, now masquerading as the Anglo-Saxon individualist, had to discover his true self by pointing the masses towards a higher good. There was no room in this scenario for organised protest or trade unions and so the stupid miners are shown to be willingly held back by the Aberalaw Medical Aid Society, which was used to illustrate all the evils associated with any guild or syndicate of workers. At one point, the young doctor's wife comments, "Did anyone ever try to help the people and the people not object?".

The American lesson was that social problems could provide a magnificent subject for melodrama and once the studios sensed that the censors were not against experimentation they rushed to make their social films and in particular to use the photogenic coalfield. In 1939 Carol Reed filmed *The Stars Look Down*, another Cronin story set in a mining district. The original novel had made an outspoken plea for the nationalization of the mines and although Reed was later to claim that he had not been interested in the politics of the story, he could hardly duck the main issue. There are some remarkable sequences in the film that stress the need for a fairer and more efficient running of the coal industry. As so often in feature films though, the main concern is with the salvation of the hero and once again the union is depicted as a reactionary, vested interest. The film like the novel is set in the Durham coalfield but American critics were always to describe this as a film about Wales and the mining shots do indeed have a Welsh feel to them. The main Welsh element in the film comes in the form of Emlyn Williams who brilliantly creates the character, Joe, who is used as a foil to the hero, Davy, (Michael Redgrave). Whereas Davy realises his true destiny by leading the miners, Joe escapes from the coalfield and chisels his way through the Depression as a salesman. It was no accident that Emlyn Williams played such vital roles in both these Cronin films for this Oxford-educated North Walian was a very hot property in those years. His play, *Night Must Fall* had done well in the West End and, and, more crucially, on Broadway before Hollywood had filmed it in 1937 and so his name was as well-known to American producers and audiences as any other in the British film world. With the British studios so reliant on uninspired writers and bland actors, Emlyn Williams rapidly forged a career as a master of sharp dialogue and as a character actor who could blend charm and a feline opportunism with a thoroughly ambivalent sexual narcissism.

The Stars Look Down was a little too radical for the censors and its release was delayed until the outbreak of war. The same fate befell *The Proud Valley* which had been made at Ealing Studios by the young Penrose Tennyson. In contrast to the two Cronin films this story was set entirely in a Welsh pit village and throughout the idiom of the film was meant to be South Walian. A black sailor (Paul

Robeson) comes to work in a Welsh pit and is recruited to sing the solo bass part in the local choir's performance of Mendelsohn's *Elijah* before he joins in the protest to save the pit from closure and then finally helps to save lives in a pit disaster. At this time Ealing were in the process of developing a new repertory style that was meant to encompass the whole range of British social and regional types and this was to mean the depiction of the Welsh very much in terms of music-hall stereotypes. *The Proud Valley* was a key film in the evolution of this idiom and in particular it is worth noting definitive female performances by Dilys Davies and Rachel Thomas and the dialogue, which in part was written by that master of Welsh soap opera Jack Jones, who also acted in the film. Not only are there long sequences of low comedy and melodrama but the film also fudges the main political issues, for there is no place in the script for a miners' union and all the protests and initiatives are prompted by the spontaneous brain waves of individuals. The original script had the miners themselves taking over the abandoned pit, but the censor insisted on a less radical but perhaps more realistic conclusion in which the pit is saved by the new demands of war. At the core of the film is Paul Robeson's David Goliath and the singing of the miners who surround him. One either loves or hates what Robeson and the choir have to offer. Graham Greene hated Robeson's Uncle Tom-like figure, whilst, more recently, John Osborne has spoken of how many people at that time saw Robeson (who had already formed friendships in South Wales whilst raising funds for the Spanish Republic) as a "Blakean figure of goodness". The choir boasts that "you can't stop us singing" and that at least is true; one either finds that cloyingly sentimental or a powerful expression of community. We must remember that the censors did not want unions and so choral singing became one way of suggesting solidarity.

The miners had become politically and artistically fashionable and so it was perhaps inevitable that there would be first a blockbuster novel and then a blockbuster film. Richard Llewellyn had already worked as a screenwriter before he began what was to be his very filmic novel *How Green Was My Valley*. The Hollywood producer Daryl F. Zanuck could see that if only the politics would be left out then this would make a very effective melodrama. Eventually and almost by chance the movie fell into the hands of director John Ford who had recently converted Steinbeck's *The Grapes of Wrath* into the classic film of the American Depression. The work of John Ford is just like choral singing in that it either works for you or it doesn't. His film of Llewellyn's novel is set in a mythical Shangri-La which is part Irish, part North Walian but mostly just the land of nursery rhymes and whatever real Welshness the film has is contributed by just one actor (Rhys Williams) and by a choir. On one level this is pure Hollywood schmaltz and yet Ford's belief in family and community is so powerful and his photography is so aptly poetic that we are taken right out of the make-believe world. As always Ford, inspired by a nostalgia for the land of his ancestors, is depicting a mythical peasantry, but there will always be some Welsh filmgoers who will see his film as perhaps the ultimate tribute to all that was best in the old Welsh communities.

Such was the transformation in British films that by 1940 Graham Greene was complaining that pit disasters and shots of winding gear had become clichés, but many other critics were hoping that the War would encourage an even fuller social cinema. Quite obviously there would be new opportunities for documentary film-making although there was a certain amount of unease about dependence on official patronage. Wales, for example, was given a new official image of being an area that had suffered in the Depression but which was now contributing much to the war effort, as at the same time it benefitted from the new emphasis on full employment and reform. In the Ministry of Information's *Dai Jones – A True Story* (1941) an umemployed miner with a somewhat exaggerated Welsh accent makes his way to London in time to rescue a child in the Blitz – the point being that "Dai Jones is still digging, not for coals but souls". The poet Dylan Thomas hated the War but working on official films provided useful income and one of his best efforts was *Green Mountains, Black Mountains* which paid tribute to the Welsh war effort and which included a montage of Depression shots accompanied by a Dylan poem which boldly warned that "it shall never happen again".

The most interesting British films of the period were made by the young poet and painter Humphrey Jennings. The essence of his message was that the War and the new commitment to reform that it had necessitated would eventually allow both a material and cultural fulfilment for all sections of the population. His message was expressed most satisfactorily in *Fires Were Started* which followed the activities of the London Fire Brigade. In other films Jennings depicted various regional sub-cultures and he showed a particular fondness for Welsh mining scenes. In 1943 he wished to commemorate the Nazi atrocities in the Czech village of Lidice and to do that he made a film about the supposed Nazi takeover of a Welsh mining community. *The Silent Village* offered a loving, poetic and deeply moving portrait of the profoundly held democratic and communal values that Jennings found to be characteristic of the semi-rural pit village of Cwmgiedd, but perhaps the film tells us more about the idealism of a young English aesthete attempting to come to terms with the strangeness of the proletariat. As William Empson suggested this kind of middle-class approach to the workers was really "a version of the pastoral".

What film critics liked most about the war years was the way in which documentary techniques and themes spread to feature films. It was felt that British films were becoming more realistic and that in particular there was a more satisfactory depiction of lower-class and regional types. There was a good deal of self-congratulation in the British industry especially as there was a related feeling that American films were deteriorating and losing their social touch. This smugness somewhat disguised the fact that there had been no real breakthrough in terms of social sophistication. There were no real sequels to *The Stars Look Down* or to John Baxter's 1941 film *Love on the Dole* which had been perhaps the frankest film about the Depression. The most highly-praised films in the War were usually those that showed ordinary people contributing to the war effort either in terms of military or home-front activities albeit with a certain amount of good-humoured complaining about shortages or about bureaucracy. These were good days for salt-of-the-earth character actors who could deliver music-hall one-liners even as they put their shoulder to the wheel. Stanley Holloway and Tommy Trinder gave a Cockney lead and they were followed by an assorted army of regional types with Clifford Evans or Mervyn Johns contributing the Welsh accent. There was a Welshman in every squad but ironically the best known South Walian of those years was Naunton Wayne who had teamed up with Basil Radford to assert that nonchalant English superiority that was carrying the nation through the War.

In 1945 the critical consensus was that British cinema was poised for its greatest ever breakthrough. Hollywood was floundering, whilst at last British directors had found their natural subject – namely the British people. Films such as *Millions Like Us* and *Waterloo Road* had opened up new social themes and had suggested the way that British Cinema should follow. Some great British films were made in the late 1940s but there was never to be a full renaissance. The reasons for this are complex but they are overwhelmingly commercial. The truth was that Hollywood still dominated. For a while the Labour Government totally excluded Hollywood films as they attempted to improve the trade deficit but of course British studios could never produce sufficient films for the quite massive and record film audiences of those years, and in any case the Americans fought hard to retain their lucrative British outlet. But the influence of Hollywood went beyond that of market dominance for an ever present awareness of America encouraged British producers like Korda and Rank to believe that Britain's only hope was to make expensive films that would do well in America. This perpetual desire to play Hollywood at its own game did more than anything to prevent the development of a truly national film style. The contrast was with Italy where in the devastation of the post-war years a new breed of directors just went into the streets to make neo-realistic films that took the art-houses of the world by storm. The films of Rossellini and de Sica suggested that perhaps the British failure was as much artistic as commercial.

Meanwhile not all British films were made with Americans in mind, for there were always to be British "B" films which attempted some degree of social realism and there was also Ealing Studios which under Michael Balcon was attempting to discover some kind of English style. What Ealing tried to do, perhaps as an antidote to Hollywood, was to celebrate traditional English qualities and to hold up a mildly eccentric and anarchic middle class comedy of manners as a challenge to the bureaucracy of the modern world. Ealing's world was decidedly Home Counties English but it was quite prepared to use stock regional types. They were to have a great success exploiting the Scottish idiom in films such as *Whisky Galore* and *The Maggie* but they were somewhat less fortunate with Wales. Their interest in Wales went back to *The Proud Valley* and to Clifford Evan's role as *The Foreman Went to France* (1942) but their big Welsh film was *A Run For Your Money* which was released in 1949. Clifford Evans' story of the two miners who win a trip to London was partly scripted by the novelist Richard Hughes and the star cast was headed by Alec Guinness, but the film never really achieved the charm of Ealing's Scottish efforts. What the film did do was to define the way in which the Welsh would be depicted in so many films throughout much of the 1950s. The cryptic sharpness of Meredith Edwards, the nervous Chapel decency of Donald Houston and the Celtic zaniness of Hugh Griffith were to be repeated or copied in a whole succession of minor films. This was all pure music-hall, it was the world of Eynon Evans and of radio's *Welsh Rarebit* and perhaps we should see it all as providing low-comic relief for the drab Britain of the 1950s. As much as anything it reminds us of how severe was the cultural crisis in Britain and how urgently the new departures in popular culture were needed. Welshness was hopelessly parodied in the movies and the only moments worth recalling are those brilliantly manic cameos provided by Hugh and Kenneth Griffith.

The Ealing style defined a whole era in British Cinema but there had been other possibilities. Jill Craigie's *Blue Scar* (1948) set out to examine the somewhat ambivalent responses of the miners to nationalization. Bad editing gave undue prominence to the soap opera plot and ensured a rather confused ending but for nearly an hour the film brilliantly depicted the reality of everyday life in the Valleys. Undoubtedly, in filming Howard Spring's novel *Fame is the Spur* the Boulting Brothers were hoping to emulate the earlier success of the Cronin films, but 1947 was a long way removed from 1939. Like so many film people in the post-war years the Boultings associated Socialism with bureaucracy and restrictions and this was very evident in their depiction of the Labour politician whose story is told in the film. Similarly audiences so used to rationing and shortages were in no mood for social realism and they showed little interest in this very ambitious story which included interesting and detailed sequences of trade union activity in South Wales. Back in the heady pre 1914 days of miners' protest the hero, Hamer Shawcross (Michael Redgrave again), helps to inspire a riot in South Wales, but then later, as an established politician, he is sent back to ensure that the miners support the Government during the First World War: of course his change of position is duly noted by the miners and cruelly exposed by Kenneth Griffith's heckling. Emlyn Williams was always really more interested in the macabre and mysterious than in realism and his *Last Days of Dolwyn* (1949) suggested that music-hall Welshness lent itself more fruitfully to the gothic rather than to pantomime. Paul Dickson's *David* was quite rightly acclaimed at the Festival of Britain for the lovingly documentary way in which it told the story of a self-made Welshman, a chapel-going working-class poet, but it was revealing that this deliberate attempt to counter the Ealing style had restricted itself to the experiences of a young boy and of an old man.

In all those one-off films the emphasis had been on the traditional and there was very little here to challenge the period's need for stereotypes and the prevailing insularity and mediocrity of British cinema. When the change came it came, as was always the case with British cinema, as a response to external stimuli. The first challenge to Britain's most middle-brow culture came from young people themselves, from musicians and from novelists and dramatists and only later did film companies jump on the bandwagon. As film directors once again rediscovered working-class communities and regional accents it was the North of England which became the reference culture and Albert Finney who became the spokesman for proletarian independence. South Wales was not as fashionable as it had been twenty years earlier but Welsh charisma could still be used to sustain the kitchen-sink atmosphere. Richard Burton was a little too old to be a hero for the new youth culture but he was not an inappropriate choice to play Jimmy Porter in the 1959 film of that London Welshman John Osborne's play *Look Back in Anger*, whilst Rachel Roberts created a stunning persona as a long-suffering, neglected and frustrated working-class housewife in two of the era's best films, *Saturday Night and Sunday Morning* and *This Sporting Life*. The real Welsh challenge to Finney came from the Rhondda's Stanley Baker whose lip curling, jaw-rolling, working-class resentment and truculence was brilliantly harnessed by the American director Joseph Losey in three of his early British films between 1959 and 1962 (*Blind Date*, *The Criminal* and *Eve*) and then later in *Accident*. These were good years for Welsh stars (and we should not forget that actor-director Ray Milland was at the height of his career in Hollywood) but precisely because of their star-status these actors could plan their careers without any reference to a specifically Welsh cinema. These big names belonged to international audiences, although Stanley Baker was shrewd enough to see the commercial possibilities in the story of how the South Wales Borderers had resisted at Rorke's Drift. *Zulu* (1964) has been described as a Welsh Western and I once heard a group of football supporters at Ninian Park all agree that it was the greatest film ever.

The great world of the movies really came to an end in the 1970s as audiences declined and the studios switched to television work. The classic years of Hollywood gave way to a new pattern in which corporations financed blockbusting movies and left independent directors to scramble around for backing which might come from a variety of sources, including television. There followed something of a bonanza for independent and non-studio films and although films like *Jaws* and *E.T.* monopolized the main commercial cinemas the true film afficionado could find many delights at film festivals, film

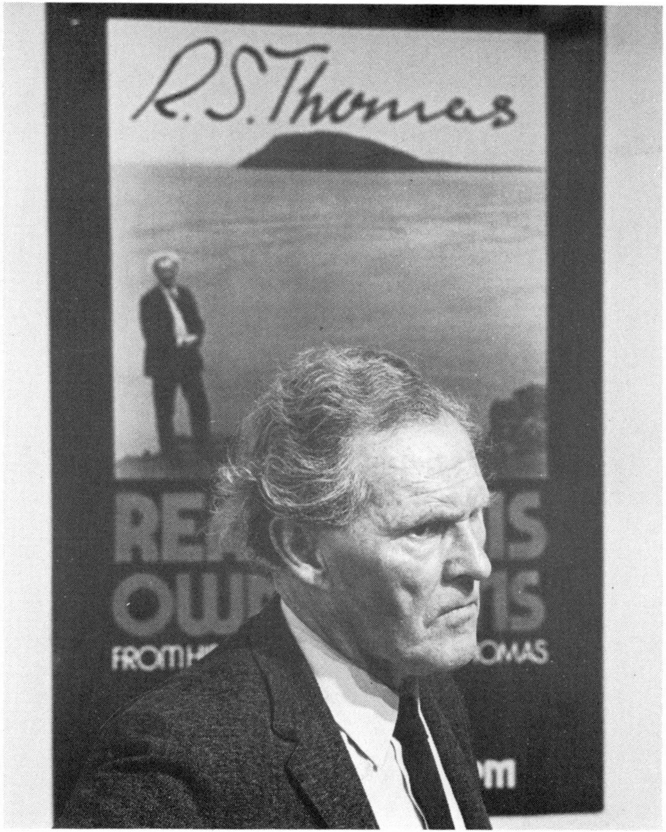

R.S. Thomas

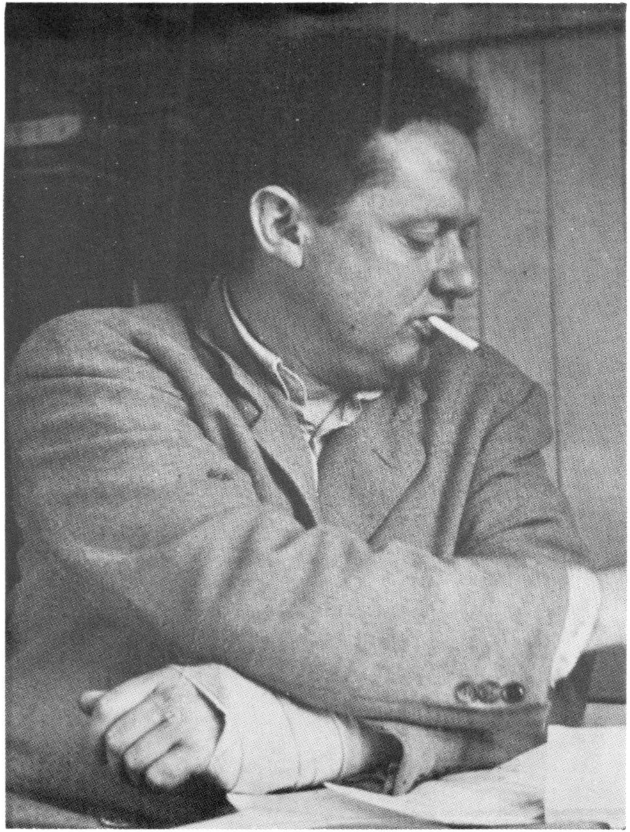

Dylan Thomas 1914-1953

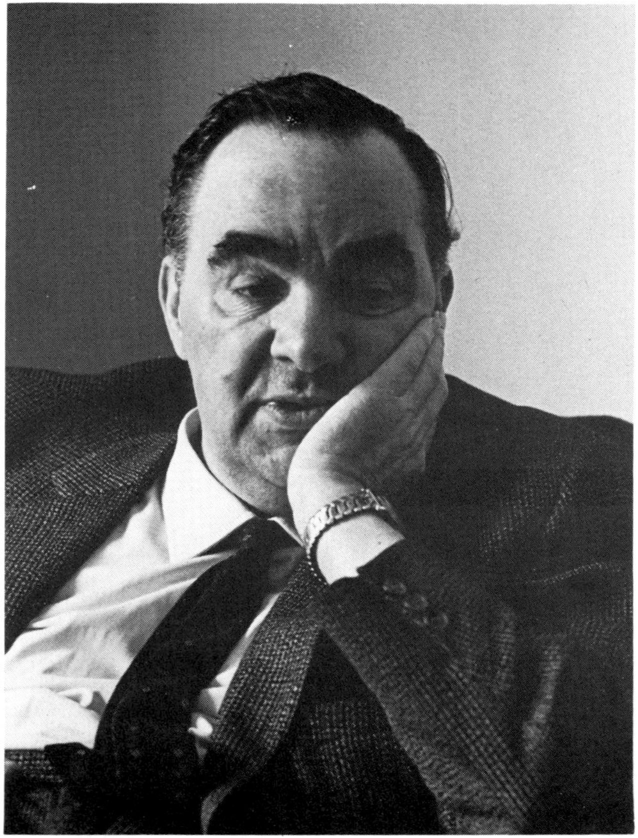

Gwyn Thomas 1913-1981

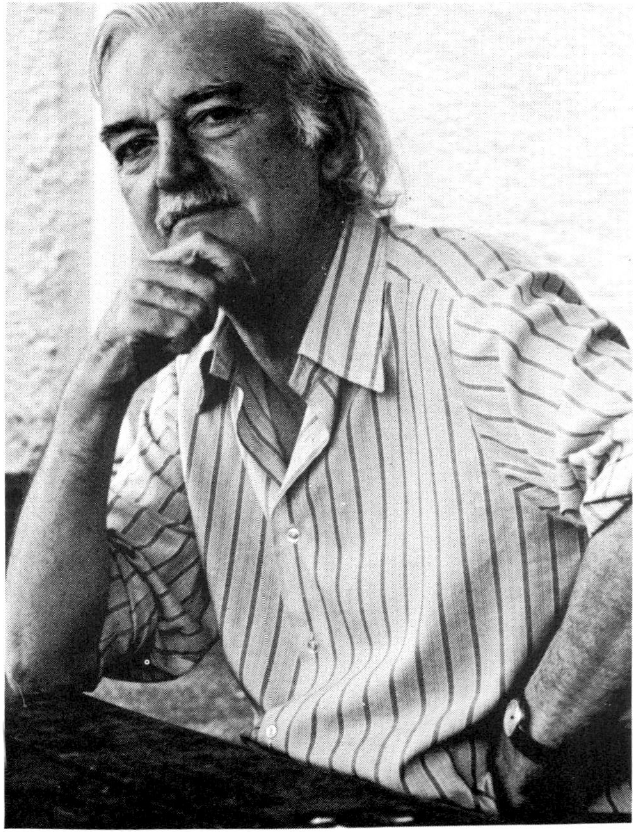

John Tripp

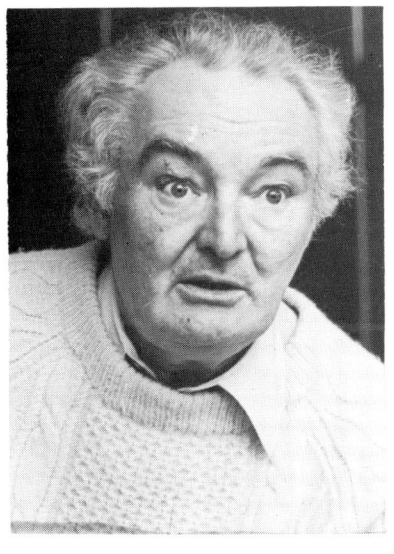

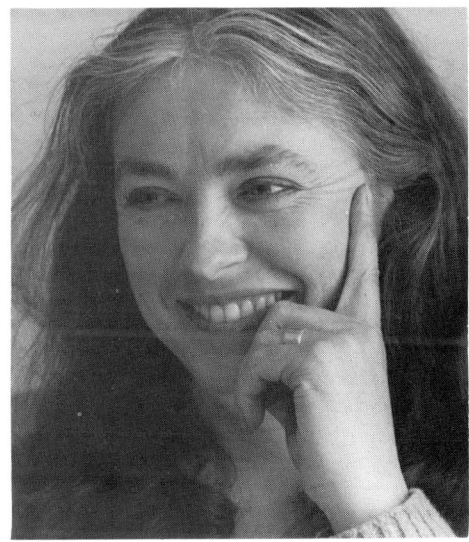

John Ormond

Gillian Clarke

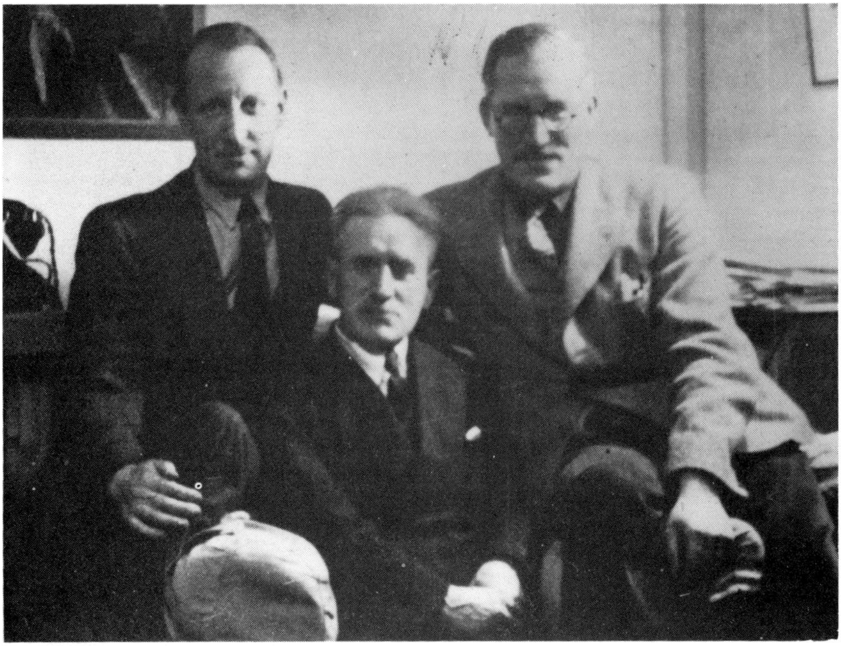

Glyn Jones, Jack Jones, Gwyn Jones

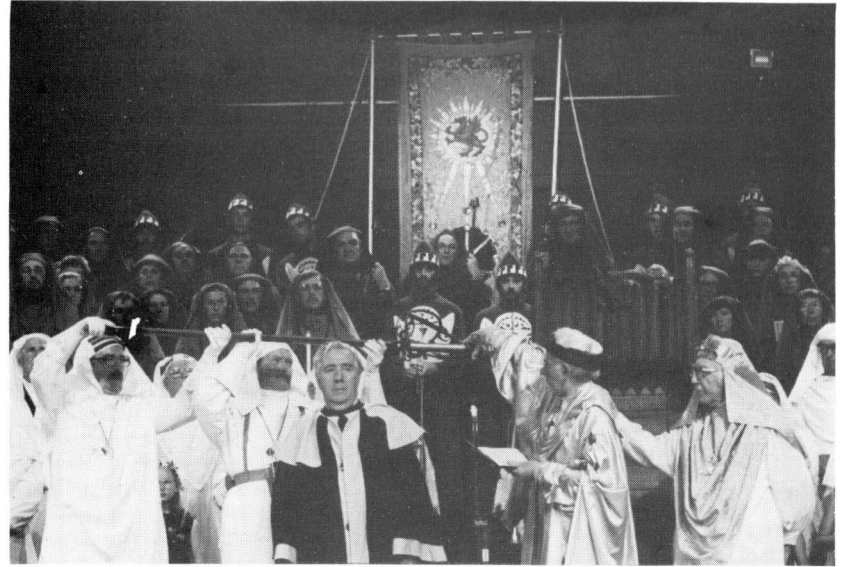

'Is there peace?' – A vestige of Iolo Morganwg's vision of the bard. The chairing ceremony at the National Eisteddfod.

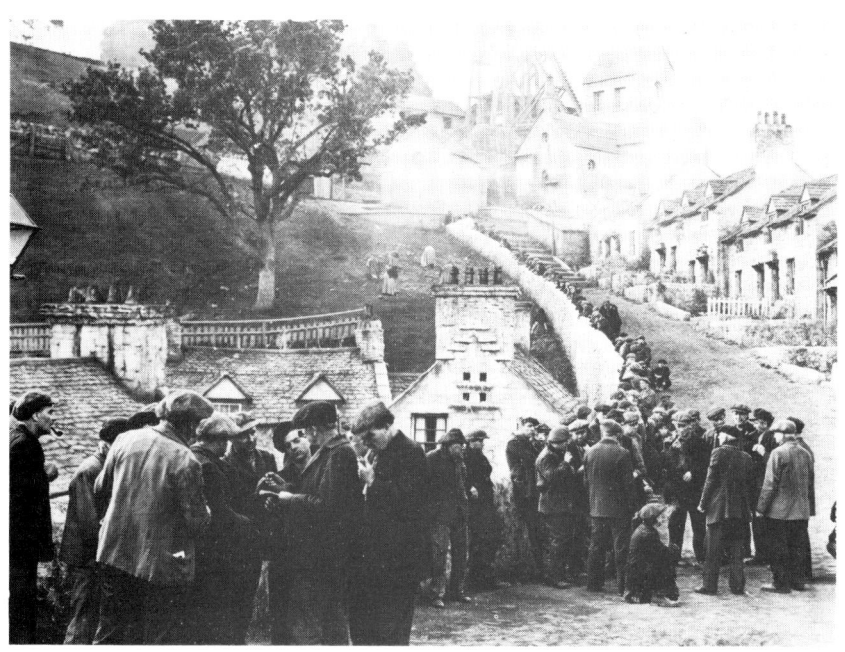

For many *How Green Was My Valley* was unconvincing, but John Ford's film remains one of the fullest depictions of working-class community. Daryl Zanuck demanded that the politics be left out but nevertheless this Californian studio set was destined to become the most famous of all mining villages.

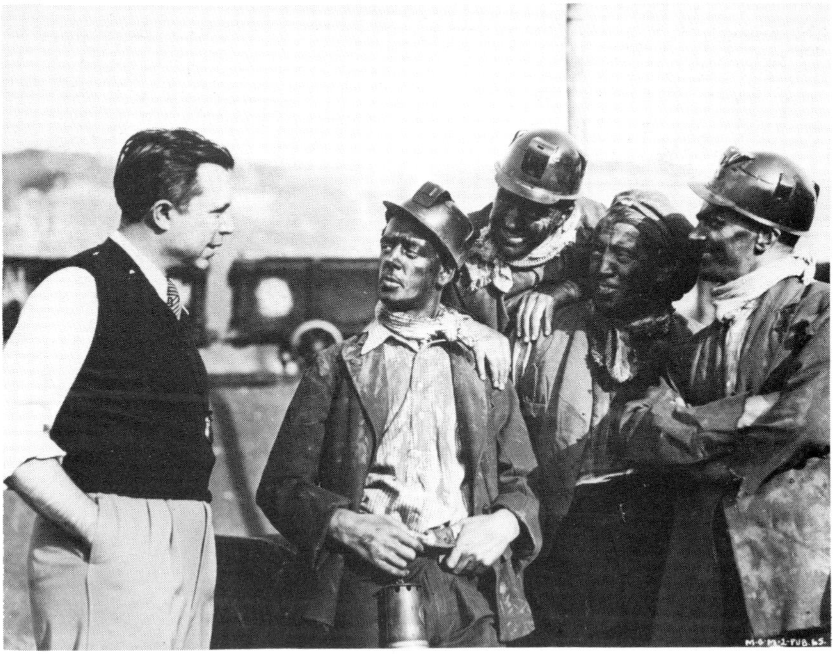

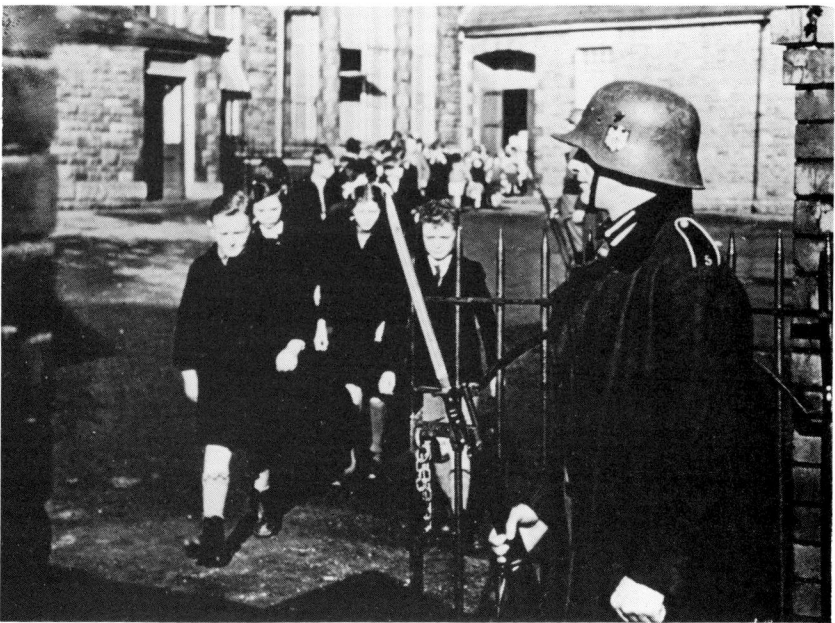

Hollywood shows the way: it was the vastly experienced Texan, King Vidor, who came to Britain to make *The Citadel*, the first feature film about both mining communities and social medicine. Vidor instructs his British actors in how workers should be portrayed.

During the war ordinary people became perfect material for documentary directors: in *The Silent Village* a German soldier stands guard over the schoolchildren on Cwmgiedd.

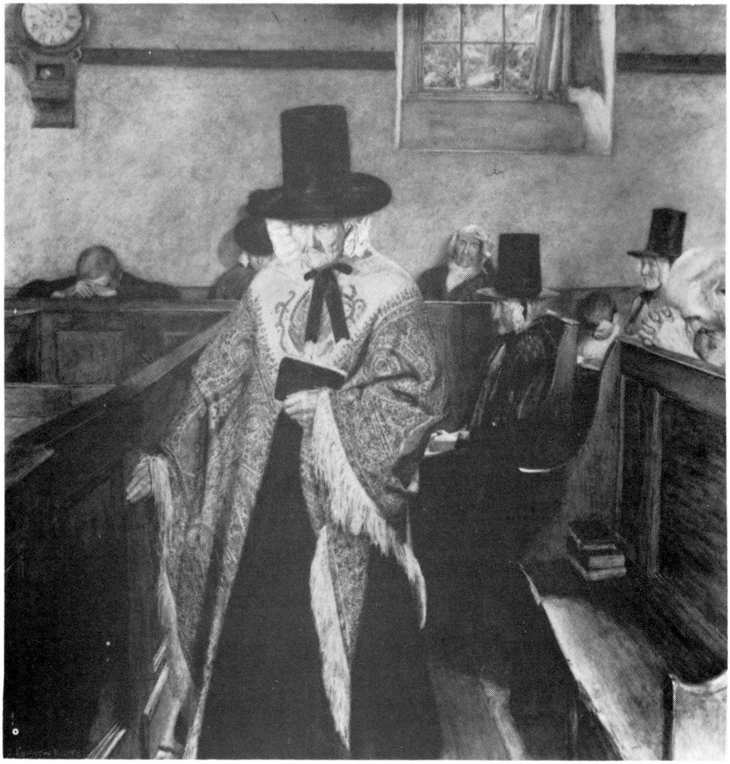

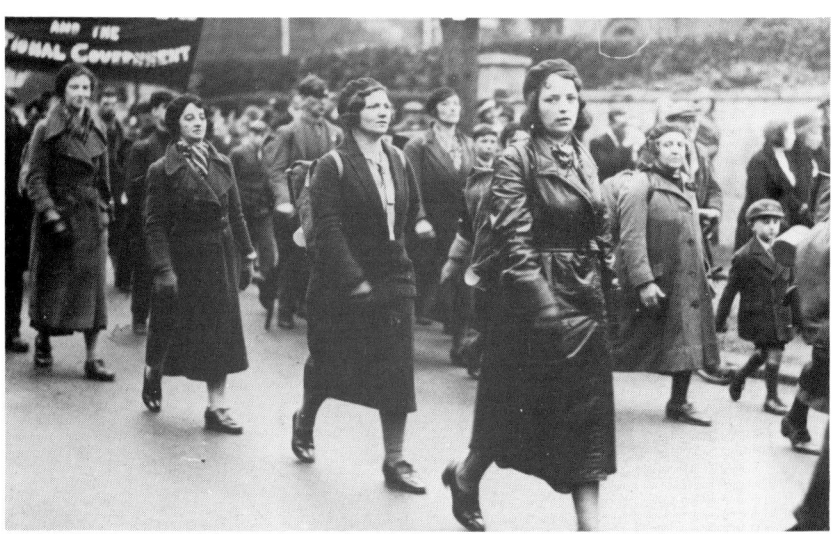

'Salem', S. Curnon Vosper's famous image of the pious Welsh woman.

Another face of the Welsh woman: a contingent in the National Hunger March of 1934.

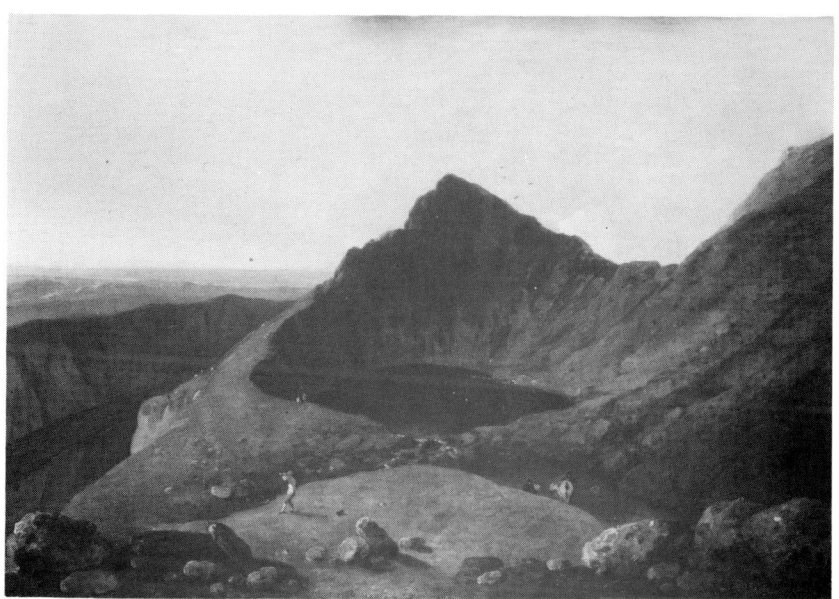

'Cader Idris, Llyn-y-Cau': the most famous landscape by Richard Wilson, generally felt to be Wales' outstanding artist.

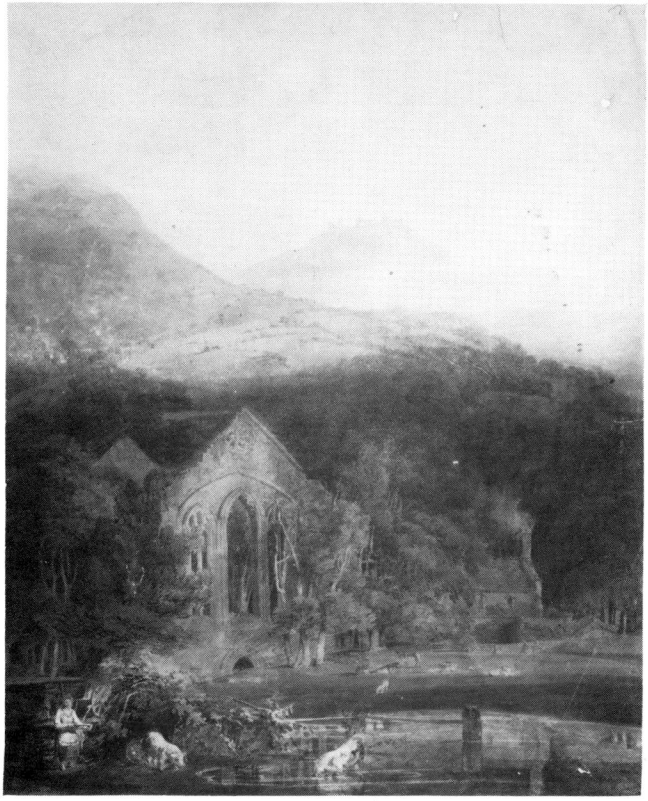

The influence of Wilson: Turner's 'Ruins of Valle Crucis Abbey with Dinas Bran Beyond'.

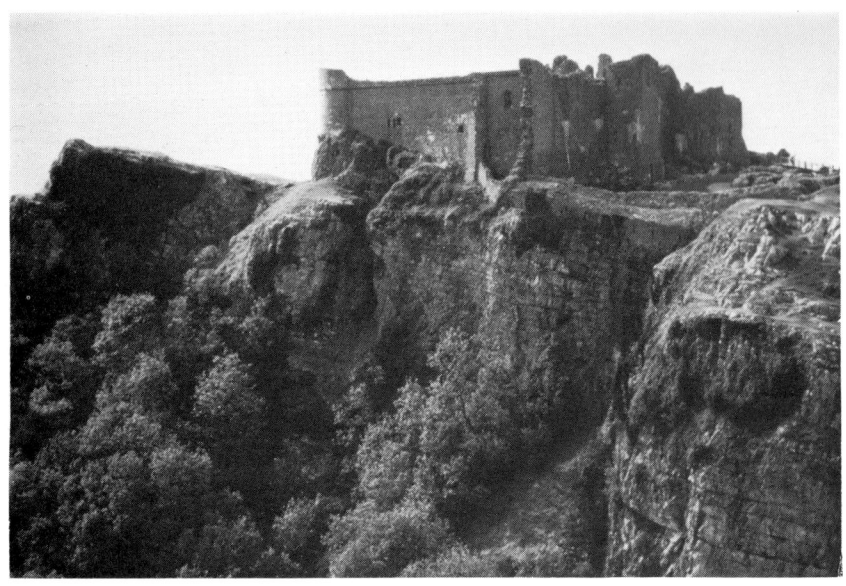

Castell Carreg Cennen, photography in the style of Wilson's art.

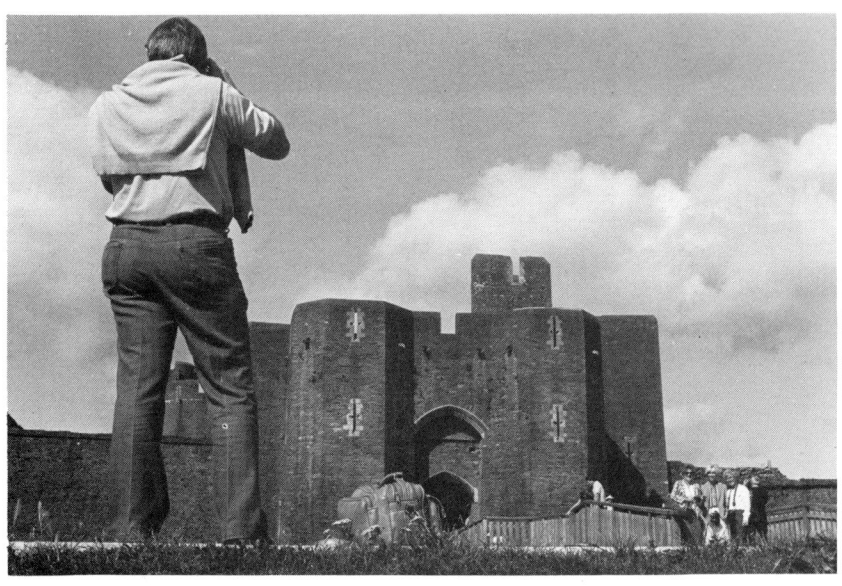

What the castle means today. A more relaxed look at 'The Year of the Castles': Caerphilly Castle by Ian Walker.

societies, art houses and even on television. Within this dispensation an authentic Welsh Cinema emerged. Young film-makers can train in Wales, they can develop their skills at video workshops, they can compare notes with colleagues from a number of other countries; either at Celtic film festivals or in Cardiff itself which has become a centre for film making, and above all television has provided not only jobs, but financial backing for a number of projects. This has been an exciting period which has given film-makers the invaluable advantages of flexibility; video especially has allowed many more people and groups to participate in film making and viewing, and also of subjectivity, for within certain financial constraints directors have been allowed to make their own films, even for television's mass audience. All this vigorous activity in Wales has been duly noted by the outside world and there has been much critical acclaim from London and even recognition from the incredibly metropolitan British Film Institute and National Film Theatre. The work of Cardiff's Chapter Workshop and the Welsh films of Chris Monger and American director Stephen Bayly have all been shown at the National Film Theatre where there was also a short retrospective season of Welsh feature films in March 1985.

These are good times but perhaps for directors the most frustrating aspect of this new film culture has been the question of how their films relate to audiences. For all the commercialism of the Hollywood system there was a way in which the films were made by the people and belonged to them. Independent or "auteur" films are rarely popular in that way and many of them only have any impact within a restricted film sub-culture even if they have been shown on television. After many initial difficulties Karl Francis has certainly succeeded in getting his films shown in art houses and on television but he is acutely aware that he lacks the relationship with a mass audience that the old popular cinema would have given him. In a sense, the films of Francis nicely illustrate both the strengths and weaknesses of the new cinema. As a film-maker he has pioneered a tremendously effective form of what he terms "documentary-narrative", in which people act themselves, but this technique is entirely harnessed to his own choice of narrative and his own rather stark political standpoint. He effortlessly achieves an authentic South Wales idiom but then uses it as his own weapon. In becoming auteurs, modern film-makers inevitably distance themselves from the audiences to whom they want to relate, whereas the old showman knew exactly what qualities defined good entertainment. I sometimes wonder how many Welsh films those Ninian Park supporters have enjoyed since *Zulu*.

BIBLIOGRAPHICAL NOTE

The best discussion of motion pictures within their respective cultures is provided by Roy Armes, *A Critical History of British Cinema* and Robert Sklar, *Movie-Made America*. I have examined the impact of Hollywood on Britain in two articles published in N. Pronay and D. Spring, *Film Propaganda and Politics, 1918-1945* and *The Historical Journal of Film*, Vol. 1, No. 1, 1981.

Haggar's career is discussed by Rachel Low and Roger Marwell in *The History of the British Film 1896-1906* and his films by Roy Armes (*op. cit.*). Documentary films can be viewed at and in some cases hired from the National Film Archive at the British Film Institute and the best introduction to this important chapter of British film history is provided by Paul Rotha, *Documentary Diary*. For film censorship in Britain see articles by Jeffrey Richards in *The Historical Journal of Film*, Vol 1, No. 2, 1981 and Vol. 2, No. 1, 1982. The alternative film culture of the 1930s is the subject of Don Macpherson (ed.) *Traditions of Independence: British Cinema in the Thirties*. Bert Hogenkamp has provided a thorough examination of how the miners have been depicted in the movies in his *Bergarbeiter im Spielfilm*; in an article to appear in *Llafur* 1985,he examines the role of the Miners' Cinemas in South Wales and in a book which will appear in 1986 he analyses the depiction of the whole British working-class in documentary films. The fullest discussion of British films and British film culture in the 1930s is provided by Jeffrey Richards in *The Age of the Dream Palace, Cinema and Society in Britain 1930-1939*. The background to *How Green Was My Valley* is explained in Mel Gussow, *Don't Say Yes Until I Finish Talking. A Biography of Darryl F. Zanuck*.

Charles Barr's *Ealing Studios* remains the best book yet published on any aspect of British Cinema. The best introduction to Jennings is the British Film Institute's *Humphrey Jennings: Film-maker, Painter, Poet* (edited by Mary-Lou Jennings) but see also Alan Lovell and Jim Hillier, *Studies in Documentary* and R.M. Barsam, *Nonfiction Film*. Several major studies of the strangely neglected subject of British society and films in the Second World War are due to appear in 1985 and 1986 but meanwhile there is Ivan Butler *The War Film*. There is a discussion of *Fame is the Spur* in Jeffrey Richards and Anthony Aldgate, *The Best of British: Cinema and Society 1930-1970*. The strange story of that apparent renaissance enjoyed by British Cinema in the 1960s is skilfully analysed in Alexander Walker's *Hollywood England* and a new interpretation is hinted at in an article by John Hill in James Curran and Vincent Porter (eds.) *British Cinema History*. Stanley Baker's fruitful collaboration with Losey in *Blind Date*, *The Criminal*, *Eve* and *Accident* is discussed in James

Keahy, *The Cinema of Joseph Losey* and Michael Ciment, *Conversations with Losey.*
The new Post-Hollywood film dispensation is best explained in James Monaco, *American Film Now*, John Walker, *The Once and Future Film: British Cinema in the Seventies and Eighties*, and Martyn Asty and Nick Roddick, *British Cinema Now.* John Pym discusses Stephen Bayly's work in Wales in *Sight and Sound*, Vol. 54, No. 2, 1958, p.78 and Geoff King had a very revealing discussion with Karl Francis in *The Guardian*, 9 July 1985.

MICHELLE RYAN

Blocking the Channels: T.V. and Film in Wales

Blocking the Channels:
T. V. and Film in Wales

A film and television culture can be an important dimension of any emerging Welsh nation in that it can articulate those progressive notions of national identity, not only to ourselves but to the rest of the world. Wales is still slow to grasp the political and cultural significance of such a culture. During British Film Year 1985, Wales was the only country not represented. Whatever criticisms there may be of the actual films, there is no doubt that Scotland, England and Northern Ireland are taking film far more seriously than Wales, as a way of representing their specific national and regional identity. With films like *Gregory's Girl* and *Local Hero* from Scotland; *Acceptable Levels* and *Anne Devlin* from Northern Ireland and *A Private Function, The Draughtsman's Contract* and *Chariots of Fire* from England, it is possible to talk about an emerging British Film culture that recognises within it strong regional and national differences. What is missing is any sense of a Welsh dimension. Not only do we not have any films to show, but, in 1985, Cardiff, the capital city of Wales could not even find a space for the British Film Year Roadshow, a mobile exhibition and gallery which had been touring all the major centres of Britain. This lack of interest and support for film in Wales was illustrated most sharply at a season of Welsh films at the National Film Theatre in London that same year. There were only three films shown that had been made since the seventies: *Giro City* by Karl Francis, *So That You Can Live* by Cinema Action in London and *Johnny Be Good* by Marc Evans, and only the latter was actually funded from within Wales by the Welsh Arts Council. In fact, of the thirty films shown in the season, less than half were actually made in Wales and most of those were produced for television. It is no wonder that our own perception of ourselves as a nation is so confused and distorted when we are prepared to rely on others to define who we are.

Wales has always been proud of its musical and literary culture but

has seemed to have regarded film as culturally irrelevant. Karl
Francis's film *Ms. Rhymney Valley 1984*, shown on BBC2, made far
more impact in the communities of Wales in terms of the relevance it
had to people's lives and experience than any opera or play, and,
more important, it allowed these people from a mining community to
determine for themselves how they were represented. Karl Francis
is perhaps the most successful and well known of all the film makers
living in Wales, but it has taken him a long time to get any kind of
recognition or support in his own country. The only source of funding
for film in Wales comes from the Welsh Arts Council and the film
budget is pathetically small in comparison to other Arts Council
budgets. Whilst some other regions in Britain have seen an
expansion in their funding for film, Wales staggers on with barely
enough money to produce one good feature film, let alone contribute
to the growth of a lively Welsh film culture. It would appear that our
small middle-class band of Welsh men who control the purse strings,
and who therefore determine existing cultural policies in Wales, are
reluctant to relinquish control of their notions of culture. National
opera and theatre companies hardly relate to most people's lives, nor
do they contribute much to ideas of cultural democracy. In many
countries film is recognised as an important form of cultural
expression capable of reaching a great many people. It is time that
those people who can influence cultural policies in Wales recognised
this fact and began to establish the framework that would allow such
a film culture to develop.

The Scottish experience may be used to argue this point. Scotland
has a film tradition almost as long as film itself. As a result there is
a much greater awareness in that country of the value of film in the
construction and representation of an emerging nation. That
awareness also goes beyond merely attracting money for production
by recognising that an essential part of a film culture is the
infrastructure that sustains and promotes it. Scotland has such an
infrastructure that puts it way in advance of anything we have in
Wales. It established its own Film Council in 1934 which then went
on to open a Film Library in 1939 and now has an impressive film
archive, in existence since 1976. The Scottish Film Council also
established their own National Film Theatre in Edinburgh where they
host an international film festival dating from 1947. It has opened a
number of film theatres throughout Scotland, produced a number of
interesting film publications, encouraged film education and, more
importantly, has been running an equal opportunities training course

for film since 1978.

This kind of infrastructure goes some way to explaining why Scotland can talk about an emerging Scottish film culture and Wales cannot, and why in British Film Year most people could name at least one recent Scottish film and yet be unable to cite a Welsh contribution. Film workers in Scotland would argue that the work is only just beginning, but at least such an infrastructure provides a space to address the problem of how Scotland can best be represented on film.[1] Here in Wales we still have a long way to go before we can seriously talk about a Welsh film culture. The task of such a culture would be to reclaim our past moments of struggle and place them in contemporary debates about Wales and its future, to encourage debate and represent the different policies and strategies of the various political, social and cultural organizations of Wales and to enable us all to have a clearer understanding of the contradictions and complexities of Welsh life. Such a possibility is a long way from realisation in terms of film and it is perhaps television in Wales that offers more hope for such representations.

Television in Wales has been defined as one of the key areas in the struggle for a national identity. As television is an important dimension of most people's lives in that it influences the way we see ourselves and understand the rest of the world, it is here that questions of control of the media and its representations have been articulated. Behind the campaign for a Welsh television channel was the clear understanding that if the Welsh language and its culture were to survive, it would have to have its own communications network linking the separate Welsh-speaking communities and providing the language with a more cohesive identity. Sianel Pedwar Cymru and the rest of the Welsh broadcasting system have shown some success in achieving this. Unfortunately, what has been lost in the process is any sense of the radical and oppositional dimension of the movement that was so successful in fighting for S4C. As S4C is the only channel we have in Wales (and it took a lot of hard campaigning to get it) there has been an obvious reluctance to criticise it, particularly in its formative period. But there are signs that the honeymoon period is coming to an end and many Welsh speakers, to say nothing of the rest of us who have to tune in, are beginning to express dissatisfaction with what is being offered. Some of this dissatisfaction was highlighted by a representative from Cymdeithas Yr Iaith Gymraeg (the Welsh Language Society) who spoke at a recent conference on 'Radical Television' in Cardiff.[2] He pointed to the fact that S4C had not provided any effective consultative structure which would allow the audience to influence or comment on programme output; its location in South Wales prevented people in the Welsh speaking areas from having any access to the station, it was too conservative in its use of Welsh language and it under-represented women, youth and ethnic minorities.

Perhaps this should come as no surprise as from the outset S4C made its intention clear "to be popular and middle of the road" and "to provide a diet of audience-catching shows". Three years later they remain faithful to their original intentions, steadfastly conforming to the dominant modes and conventions of mainstream television. Whilst some of their output, particularly in drama and current affairs, is beginning to display some awareness of the importance of addressing contemporary issues that relate specifically to Wales, and there are a few producers who are trying to be more innovatory, the bulk of their programmes appear dated, conservative and stereotyped. Too much of their drama and features refer back in an uncritical way to a Welsh mythical past or else provides soap opera with a Welsh voice. The rest of the space is filled with sport, quiz shows and light entertainment. I am not arguing that they shouldn't be there, but it does seem to represent a received professional wisdom dominant in the British broadcasting system, that the Welsh audience is an homogenous whole, content with the usual diet of mainstream television, providing it is in the Welsh language. But where are the programmes about women, ethnic minorities, unemployment, rural depopulation and Welsh labour history? There is a real danger that all the radicalism associated with the Welsh language is stripped away and that the language itself becomes a conservative tool used by a "nationalist" elite to justify the exclusion of radicalism. The central concern of those who control S4C seems to be more for how the language is spoken than for what is said. This would seem to echo the BBC's concern for "correct English" which had the function of excluding all but a small group of the Oxbridge-educated middle-class from determining how and what is represented. Surely very few people in Wales would want to see the same thing happening in S4C? It should not see its task as merely preserving the purity of the Welsh language for its own sake. Welsh is a living language that historically has always been associated with radicalism and it belongs as much to the Welsh working class as it does to middle-class nationalists.

The responsibility for this conservatism in S4C must lie within its own organizational structure. It has drawn on a small, white, male, middle-class elite to run it, an elite that runs the rest of Welsh broadcasting and in fact most of our cultural institutions. Their main concern is with preserving all that is traditional in Welsh culture, secure in the knowledge that such a policy will not compromise their allegiance to and security within the British Establishment.[3] It means that many of the professionals engaged in producing programmes are encouraged to merely reproduce their mainstream broadcasting values through the Welsh language, with the result that if the language was taken away very few of the programmes would look any different from the television output of any other part of Britain. This was one of the main criticisms of *Newyddion Saith* made by many Welsh speakers, that it merely re-cycled the network news rather than providing any specific Welsh identity to the programme. To be fair to S4C, this is mentioned in their last Annual Report[4] and an attempt has been made to alter the balance more in favour of Wales. However the same criticism could be levelled at some of their more popular programmes like *Pobol Y Cwm* or *Coleg*, Welsh forms of soap opera that tend to play safe and rarely touch on the more controversial topics that you will find in Channel 4 UK's *Brookside*. Their latest offering in this genre, *Dinas*, is based in Cardiff and looks like a Welsh version of *Dallas* or *Dynasty*. Whilst it may help to boost their ratings it could hardly be described as innovative, nor can it have much relevance to the majority of Welsh speakers living as they do outside South Wales. One of the problems lies in S4C's dependence on getting the majority of its programmes (nineteen out of the twenty-three hours of Welsh programmes a week) from within the existing broadcasting institutions of BBC and HTV Wales. This static professional framework does run the risk of allowing "jobs for the boys" to take precedence over innovative programming and guarantees that very little controversial material filters through the effective censorship of such a structure.

The apparent reluctance of S4C to incorporate into its program-ming an alternative or oppositional voice and its unwillingness to actively participate in the rebuilding of a modern, democratic, Welsh identity can only lead to its own marginalisation within Wales. For S4C to guarantee its own future as a Welsh channel within the British broadcasting system it must have the active support of its own constituency. Wales needs its own channel precisely because it exists on the margins of British political and economic life. Its task must not be to merely reproduce that marginalisation but to represent an emerging nation through its own struggles and contradictions and in a real context rather than through idealised notions of a Welsh identity. But such a task is hampered by the concentration of S4C and its "satellites" in South Wales. This means that many of the programme makers, through geographical location and social background, are out of touch with their audience. This was referred to in a recent report produced by the Welsh Consumer Council[5] which also mentions that the W.F.C.A. (Welsh Fourth Channel Authority) was not representative of S4C's audience and while S4C through public meetings, informal polling and its own *Arolwg* programme did try to keep in touch with its viewers, this did not provide enough consultation and accountability. What is also missing from S4C is any commitment to access to the channel. A scheme like BBC 2's *Open Door* or RTE's *Access Community Television*[6] might help to break down this professional isolation and give Welsh people a genuine sense of S4C being their own channel. It might also bring some fresh new approaches to the channel and even some controversy and debate such as occurred after 'It Ain't Half Racist, Mum' was shown on an *Open Door* programme. Such a scheme might go some way towards increasing Welsh people's loyalty to the channel and might help to increase the ratings, which have never managed to reach the level of the initial months.[7] As long as S4C continues to transmit the views of a small cultural elite in Wales, it compromises the very idea of Welshness that brought it into being and is bound to alienate those very sections of Welsh speakers that fought for it.

S4C is now coming to the end of its three year trial period and is already undergoing its Home Office Review. Owen Edwards (S4C Director) stated that he was pleased that it was going ahead and that S4C "will be seen to have worked to the advantage not only of the Welsh language but of Wales as a whole". [8] It is the latter part of this statement which should be questioned. Yes, it is essential for the Welsh language and Wales that S4C should be allowed to continue. But it is as a Welsh language channel providing a unique service that it must survive. It cannot offer a television service to the whole of Wales because it already has to juggle Channel 4 UK programmes, which has left English speakers dissatisfied. Nor can it allow any more airtime for English language programmes as that would dilute its Welsh language profile. S4C's strength lies in the service and working relationship it can offer to the Welsh-speaking community.

Its advantage to the English speakers in Wales is that it offers an example of what is needed in the English language and puts on the agenda the crisis of representation facing English-speaking Welsh people.

BBC Wales and HTV both appear to have made the mistake of assuming that Wales only exists through the Welsh language and having provided their quota of Welsh language programmes for S4C, fail to deliver anything that addresses the vast majority of us. The huge concrete structure of new studios at Culverhouse Cross is testimony to the kinds of profit that HTV is making, yet hardly any of it is being ploughed back into the Welsh community. It would make a great difference to the growth of a film culture in Wales if only a small part of their profits went towards training and sponsorship. As far as their programming policy is concerned, after producing their nine hours a week for S4C there seems to be very little left for making programmes specifically about Wales. There has been one notable exception to this in their collaboration with Channel 4 UK on the Welsh history series *The Dragon Has Two Tongues* and they are currently producing a series on the history of cinema in Wales. It is a start, but there is a long way to go before they could be described as a Welsh channel. And when HTV do fund drama productions they tend to be of the trans-Atlantic, block-buster variety that might please their shareholders but does little to provide Wales with any pride in its own productions. They could easily channel some of that money into encouraging Welsh writers to write short plays on contemporary issues and provide a showcase for Welsh talent. HTV Wales must stand on its own and not be determined by the decisions taken in Bristol if it is ever going to offer Wales its own television service.

It is the same story with BBC Wales, a state which is even more unacceptable as it is meant to be a public broadcasting service. Outside of the ten hours a week produced for S4C, BBC Wales produces very little for the majority of Welsh people and is even more determined by decisions taken in London. Its new schedule for Autumn 1985 comes up with three new programmes, *Juice*, a rock magazine programme, *Time and Place*, interviews with celebrities and *Don't Break Your Heart*, a look at heart disease in Wales. All of them promise "stars from the world of sport and showbiz".[9] Somehow, I don't think it will be enough to persuade people to turn their aerials back to Wales. It is interesting that BBC Radio Wales produces far more Welsh material than television does and it has managed to find and encourage good Welsh writers. An indication perhaps of how important television can be and why there is such a tight control of the reins from London.

What we are left with is a non-existent broadcasting service for the majority of Welsh people. It is no wonder that most people who have the choice prefer to turn their aerials towards England, nor that the majority of Welsh people have problems in defining themselves as Welsh when so little of the media output offers them any real opportunity to build an expression of their own cultural identity. This lack of representation is not only a problem for English speakers in Wales. There is a real danger that the constant defining of Wales only through the Welsh language will produce a neglect and alienation of the majority of Welsh people which could isolate and jeopardise the Welsh language and its institutions. The Welsh language needs to be defended by all Welsh people as an important expression of Welsh life, but we need to recognize ourselves as part of the Welsh community and to be given a voice in it to ensure that that will happen.

It is certainly the case that any movement for self-determination in Wales will get very little representation from the existing three channels, which means we must look to alternative forms of representation to challenge the cultural hegemony that exists here. The miners' strike of 1984-5 presented the opportunity to see what could be realized within a genuine cultural democracy. Not only did it succeed in bringing the class and national question together through the links between the local Welsh communities and the growth of the Welsh Congress, it also generated a wealth of cultural activities from within local communities. Theatre, poetry, print, film, video and photography were all used in support of the strike and drew many people into a network of cultural activity that expressed their political and national identity. The miners' strike expressed the frustration many of us feel when confronted by the bias and distortions of main stream media, the lack of control we have over their representations and the very real importance of developing alternative forms of cultural activity until such time as the mainstream media begin to take their responsibility to Wales more seriously. The task confronting us is to be engaged in the mobilisation of a Welsh consciousness that addresses people's experiences and provides the means to express that experience so that they can make their own contribution to reclaiming Wales for themselves.

We can see this beginning to happen in the theatre with the demand for more support of Welsh writers and local theatre groups, in the writers' workshops that are emerging in the communities, in the re-launch of the magazine *Planet*, the continuation of *Radical Wales*, in the growth of film, video and photography workshops, in the concern with our history and in the numerous arts and cultural activities that are beginning to mushroom in Wales. Many of these initiatives are dismissed by funding bodies as not being "Art with a capital 'A'", but there must be a recognition of the importance of all aspects of cultural activity whether it takes place in a local community or on a national level, rather than trying to set one against the other.

In the independent film and video sector of Wales there are also positive signs of growth and a concern to become an integral part of the social fabric of Wales. In the last few years Chapter Video Workshop has grown to a point where it is now funded by Channel 4 UK and the Welsh Arts Council. This has enabled it to become the first fully equipped and staffed workshop in Wales capable of responding quickly to community and political interests. It was able to provide the miners with tapes that documented their experience of the dispute and which argued the case of coal in terms of the Welsh economy, an issue which was hardly touched on by the Welsh media. It also developed a very efficient distribution network that allowed people throughout Wales and Britain to see these tapes in the pubs, clubs and community centres and to discuss issues that have a profound effect on their lives and the future of their communities.

Chapter Film Workshop, which for a long time remained isolated and inward looking, is also beginning to build links with its community by training young people, organizing public debates and events and by producing work that engages more seriously with the lives of people in South Wales. There is the Valley and Vale Community Video project based in the Ogwr Valley, the Black Video Project in Butetown and the beginnings of a Women's Film Workshop in Pontypridd. Film and Video Workshops are growing up in Swansea, Aberystwyth, Bangor, Wrexham and all of them are trying to develop an integrated practice of education, production and distribution and working with other social and political groups in their communities.

The problem that all these initiatives are faced with is the lack of interest and support for film and video from funding bodies. The Welsh Arts Council via its film panel does its best to encourage growth in this sector, but is severely limited by its lack of funds and lack of interest from the Arts Council as a whole. Local authorities and County Councils in Wales, who could provide funding, are remarkably slow at recognising the potential in these initiatives for their own communities. In the North East of England which faces in some areas even higher unemployment and deprivation, the County Councils have attracted large sums of money from the E.E.C. Social Fund towards building their own regional film culture. They have done this because they have been persuaded of its importance in terms of the cultural life of their region and because, if properly funded, it can provide jobs, training and a service for the many organizations who want to use the media to get their message across. In other parts of Britain there has been a dramatic increase in the funding of media activities, particularly in the Greater London Council and the Metropolitan Councils, but in the Welsh establishment there still exists an entrenched suspicion of anything but the most traditional aesthetics. These must be challenged if we are to see such initiatives happening here.

Despite this lack of support, the foundations of a national film and TV culture are beginning to be built from within the independent sector. For it to grow and have relevance within a national context it must continue to develop an integrated practice in alignment with other organizations involved in political and cultural activity. In other words, it must go beyond a concern merely to produce "good" films "consumed" in one sitting by an audience undifferentiated by class, race or sex and engage in the activities of exhibition, distribution and education. Welsh local authorities have done little to prevent the decline and closure of local cinemas, so it is essential that alternative forms of distribution and exhibition exist. Different sites must be found which are more integrated with people's lives and where films and videos can be viewed by the people they are made for and in a context which encourages debate and discussion. Such a process can go some way towards deconstructing the myth that the media can only be produced by "professionals" for mass consumption and allows people to question why issues that are relevant to their lives are rarely covered by television.

At the same time production must be involved in the process of constructing new and positive images beyond "talking heads" and documentaries, capable of inspiring people with a real understanding of where they are, rather then merely reflecting what already exists. This work could be facilitated by involving other creative talents such as writers, artists, poets, photographers and musicians who want to contribute to a truly democratic Welsh cultural identity that lives in the communities as well as in the theatres, art galleries and concert halls. This is why the growth of film and video workshops is important because they encourage people from within their communities to have access to an immediate form of communication and enable them to determine for themselves how they want to be represented.

The question of training therefore becomes a central one in the growth of a Welsh national film and television culture because it is connected to one of the few areas of growth in the Welsh economy. BBC, HTV, S4C and the film industry that has grown up around it, need to recruit skilled personnel from within Wales. In the future we are also likely to see cable television and community radio, bringing with them a real opportunity for community groups and organizations to have their own channels and produce their own programmes. Such opportunities will be wasted unless there is an infrastructure capable of providing training and resources. S4C has taken the first steps towards setting up a training scheme in Wales but we must ensure that it is available for Welsh and English speakers and that it is committed to a policy of equal opportunity for women and ethnic minorities in Wales.

The independent sector in Wales is also trying to contribute to the educational areas of film and television culture by creating forums for discussion and debate, connecting with schools and other institutions and promoting the relevance of film and video to popular and radical movements in Wales. The most positive outcome of this work so far is that Chapter is going to house the first Media Education Institute in Britain.

These initiatives are encouraging, but they are mainly concentrated in and around Cardiff and we are a long way from being able to describe it as a national film culture. For that to happen we need a Welsh Film Board financed by the Welsh Office and television companies, representing both languages. It would have to have a wider brief than the existing Bwrdd Ffilmiau Cymraeg which has never moved beyond the issue of language preservation. Its task would be to oversee the development of all film activities throughout Wales from education and training through to workshops, film centres and a Welsh film industry capable of producing films that can be a showcase to the rest of the world.

It is within this framework that questions as to the relationship between television and the Welsh community can be addressed and where intervention for change can begin. Wales needs a single Welsh

Broadcasting Authority that would ensure a truly representative broadcasting service that extended the range of political ideas represented in the programmes and which went beyond the usual stereotype of class, race, gender and nationality. It would need to be democratically elected from the various constituencies in Wales and to encourage positive discrimination in the recruitment and training of women, blacks and other under-represented social groups. As part of this process of democratisation we should call for the setting up of regional monitoring committees both to safeguard the Welsh language channel and to ensure that the service represents all aspects of Welsh opinion.

The English speakers in Wales also have a right to their own channel. The existence of S4C has made that more of a possiblity because the infrastructure is now there to sustain it and because it has brought into focus the absence of a service for the rest of Wales. It is becoming increasingly likely that if HTV does not pull away from the West of England and start to produce a recognisable Welsh service, campaigns will grow to replace it with a company which does, when the franchise comes up for renewal in 1989. Meanwhile all three channels could be making more of a contribution to a Welsh film and television culture by following the example of Channel 4 UK and giving financial support to film and video workshops in Wales and by screening some of their productions. It would also go some way to breaking down the language barriers if more of S4C's programmes were shown on BBC Wales and HTV with subtitles so that the English-speaking Welsh can understand why they should defend it. Only when these points have been taken up can we really start to have a Welsh broadcasting service that effectively engages with progressive notions of a Welsh identity.

The policies of successive governments have allowed Wales to become one of the most marginalised and neglected areas of Britain. Under a strong Conservative government this neglect has accelerated to a point where it seems impossible to imagine even a Labour government doing much to halt the decline. Whole areas of the valleys have already been abandoned, rural depopulation is further exacerbated by the E.E.C. agricultural policy, forcing many small farmers to sell up, and there is only a trickle of new industry to replace the vast ones that dominated the landscape. Wales is being stripped of its assets, leaving in its wake a criminal waste of natural and human resources. But none of us would willingly choose the kind of future for Wales described by Gwyn Alf Williams as a "Costa

Bureaucratica in the south and a Costa Geriatrica in the north; in between sheep, holiday homes burning merrily away and fifty folk museums where there used to be communities".[10]

Such a prospect has to be resisted and there is a much greater chance of success if it comes from within the movement for a strong Welsh national identity. Whilst the establishment of a national film and television culture might not be a major priority for Wales, it is nevertheless an important site for debating and representing what a progressive Welsh identity could mean and it provides an opportunity for people themselves to participate in this process of deconstruction and reconstruction. As the British state becomes more centralised and moves ever further to the right, it is forcing many of us living on the margins to examine again the significance of the national question in relation to the very real need for political and cultural self-determination. However, it is also important not to take for granted what we mean by a national identity. Narrow and conservative notions of Welsh nationalism will not work as they have little relevance to the majority of Welsh people's experience. What we need is a cultural identity that defines Wales not as a one-nation monolith cloaked in bourgeois sentimentality, but forged from within new formations of class, gender, ethnicity and language.

NOTES

1. These issues are addressed in *Scotch Reels: Scotland in Cinema and Television*, published by the British Film Institute. For the Irish experience see: *Television and Irish Society, 21 Years of Irish Television* (RTE/IFI publication); *The Green on the Screen: A Celebration of Film and Ireland* (IFI); *Film and Ireland: A Chronicle*, (A Sense of Ireland Ltd, 1980).
2. The 'Radical Television' conference was held in Chapter on 6-7 April 1985. Speakers from Scotland, Ireland and England attended and there were representatives from S4C and the independent sector in Wales. The aim was to encourage a public debate on the role of television in Wales.
3. David Bevan has documented this process very well in his article 'The mobilisation of cultural minorities: the case of Sianel Pedwar Cymru' in *Media, Culture and Society*, no.6, 1984.
4. Sianel Pedwar Cymru: Annual Report and Accounts 1983-84.
5. Consultation Paper of the Welsh Consumer Council on S4C and viewer

representation, July 1985.

6.   This question of access is dealt with in Kevin Rockett's article 'Form, Content and Irish Television' in *Television and Irish Society, op. cit.*

7.   The audience for the five most popular programmes averaged 115,000 in the first months and fell dramatially in the summer and autumn (to the 50,000's) of 1983. Towards the end of the financial year there was the beginning of a small upturn. See Annual Report, *op. cit.*

8.   *Western Mail,* 24 August 1985.

9.   *South Wales Echo,* 17 September 1985.

10.   Gwyn Alf Williams: *When Was Wales,* Penguin, 1985, p.303.

S4C

Joseph Clancy

There's a brand-new phenomenon in Wales,
    A television channel *yn Gymraeg,*
On which the Welsh-speakers now can view
    Pobol y Cwm and *Gwely a Brecwast*
        And *Dick Van Dyke.*

It's been a long time coming. It wasn't easy
    To get the government to open Channel Four.
It took three decades of protest and petition
    Before they'd broadcast *Rhaglen Hywel Gwynfryn*
And *Mary Tyler Moore.*

It just may be that what will save the language
    Is children watching Sianel Pedwar Cymru
And growing up to be, on *Smyrffs, Wil Cwac Cwac,*
    Sêr and *Arolwg* and *Here's Lucy,*
        Americymry.

TREVOR WRIGHT & JOHN HARTLEY

Representations for the People?
Television News, Plaid Cymru and Wales

Representations for the People?
Television News, Plaid Cymru and Wales

Wales is virtually ignored by the London based news, but when it is covered, the identities that flourish are cultural: wit, sport, poetry and song. The London news is easy with such Welsh identities but has no concepts of Welshness (or Britishness) into which someone like Saunders Lewis can be fitted. Its political concept of Wales stretches no further than mainstream Parliamentary figures and their activities. When Saunders Lewis died it was no surprise that the London news thought it unworthy of a mention as they have avoided all the issues that made up his life for years.

Critics of this situation are answered with the argument that the London news is a national service (whose nation?) and that Wales has its own "internal network" serving its own interests. Wales does have a media network and it is looked at jealously by European minorities such as the Bretons. But what is the point of an "internal network" that is first, dominated by other centralised networks and secondly, has never shaken off the influence of the cultural, political and economic traditions of those networks?

A problem, inside and outside Wales, is the media's relationships with British Nationalism. There are times when watching the London news (like the Falklands or the Coal Dispute) that conflicts of identity arise between what the event is encoded as meaning to the "British Nation" and what it means to be Welsh and part of all this. It is these kind of conflicts that television in and outside Wales fails to engage with consistently. In the face of social upheaval, broadcasters cling to rigid and outmoded notions of news values, production practices and assumptions about the audiences (who we are, what our interests are and how capable we are of making up our own minds). Politics means Parliament, marginalising anyone else into the "un-newsworthy" or the "extra-parliamentary" and "illegitimate".

"Us", the "Nation", means a narrow and select band of right-minded people and excludes questions of race, gender, class and nationalities. Can television in general be opened up to a wider range of progressive ideas, not to give itself over to socialist, feminist or nationalist opinions, but to approach issues with these approaches taken to be as legitimate and important as Parliamentary politics and ask questions relevant to the present? At the beginning of the *Dragon Has Two Tongues* series, Gwyn Alf Williams argued that history depends on what questions are asked – so does the future.

The idea of a study of the media in Wales is nothing new but this project was made possible by a meeting between ourselves and Dafydd Elis Thomas at the Polytechnic of Wales in December 1981. As a result of this meeting we submitted a proposal to Plaid Cymru. It outlined a study of representations of Plaid Cymru and Wales based on the analysis of the weekday news and current affairs television programmes broadcast to Wales. It was to be limited to weekdays only, for the period of one month.

This does not mean that other forms of mass communication (cinema, press, radio), other categories of television (sport, drama etc.) and weekend coverage are of no concern. But a budget of £300 had been suggested and the study had to be tailored to fit it.

The programmes to be monitored were divided into the following categories:

1.   The main daily London news, *News at Ten* and the *Nine O'Clock News*.
2.   The main daily Cardiff news, *Report Wales* and *Wales Today* in English and *Y Dydd* and *Heddiw*.
3.   The daily Cardiff news summaries, *Report Wales* headlines and the *News of Wales*.
4.   The daily London current affairs programme, *Nationwide*
5.   The Cardiff weekly current affairs programmes, *Outlook* and *Week In Week Out* in English and *Yr Wythnos*. There was no BBC Wales current affairs programme in Welsh at the time.
6.   Any regular London current affairs programme that specifically dealt with Wales; *Panorama, World in Action* etc.
7.   Any one-off programme of special relevance such as the hour long *King Coal*, made by Granada and broadcast by HTV Wales on December 17th 1981.

These programmes amounted to over one hundred hours of television.

Owing to revisions of the budget and the inability of Plaid Cymru's executive committee to meet because of the severe weather, the proposal was not approved until February 1982. Since we were anxious to start as soon as possible, the monitoring period began on February 22nd 1982 instead of the proposed January 1st. Therefore the events that are discussed such as Plaid Cymru's water campaign or St. David's Day were not originally or deliberately selected to be part of this analysis.

What follows is an interim report on the state of the analysis so far and it concentrates on the two daily news programmes produced from London. First it discusses the variety of possible approaches and the ones that dominate public debate about the media in order to show why they are invalid for this study. It offers some indication of the problems of the coverage of politics and political parties, the structures of news production and the contradictions of news practices. It also poses questions about the role of television in the relationship between Britain and Wales in terms of dominant and subordinate cultures. It is not intended as another vitriolic attack on broadcasters themselves but as a discussion document which questions underlying assumptions about political television.

THE MEDIA DEBATE

The question of how to analyse the coverage of Plaid Cymru and Wales cannot be separated from the dominant ways of conceptualising the media. Both academic and public debate have centred historically around the questions of the effects of the media upon individuals and on television's assumed bias towards particular political standpoints. Unfortunately analysis that starts from the assumption that effects or bias exist, tends to find them wherever it looks. However, recent research has questioned the assumptions themselves. Television may be influential and it is certainly political, but not in the simple way these approaches suggest.

Effects

The assumptions about the effects of television on the individual are well summarised by Mary Whitehouse writing in the *Guardian* of 6 September 1982:

> Young people today are reared on television. They sub-
> consciously imbibe its values and messages...it is very arguable
> that its effects have sunk deep into the psychology of the people
> and it may take years for the powerful conditioning towards
> violence to be replaced with a more responsible public attitude.

Implicit are the assumptions that television has a direct effect upon
the individual in terms of psychology and behaviour, and that these
individuals passively receive media messages against whose
influence they are helpless. This approach is informed by a
pessimistic view of human nature which, it seems, only needs to be
stimulated by television to produce character defects. These defects
cause violence and a general immorality which therefore needs to be
subjected to control from on high. Mary Whitehouse demands "rapid
and effective counter-measures on behalf of the public at large".

Such counter-measures are posed as a different, neutral and more
moral kind of conditioning of the individual necessary in order to
reach the stage of a "more responsible public attitude". But it is the
approach that suggests the remedy. The proposal stems from the
assumptions, not the analysis.

Bias

When it comes to so-called bias, the evidence can point any way you
like. In evidence to the Annan Committee, *On The Future of
Broadcasting* (1977), the Socialist Party of Great Britain claimed that
news and current affairs were biased against the left, whilst Aims for
Industry thought them to be biased against the right and centre.
There is the work of the Glasgow Media Group who "claim to have
cast iron evidence of bias against the left...complaining that news and
current affairs programmes are anti-union, anti-left and anti-working
class... It is a bias, they say, which is so ingrained it amounts to
distortion" (*Man Alive Debate*, BBC2, Summer 1982). But on the
other hand, during the Falklands War the right exerted itself upon the
BBC. Sally Oppenheimer MP thought a *Panorama* programme to be
an "odious subversive travesty", and the Prime Minister herself
"found the equal weight being given to the information coming out of
London and Buenos Aries offensive" (*Guardian* 12th May 1982).

All arguments about bias assume that there is only one view of the
world (usually one's own) and that this view is being distorted. In the

middle are the broadcasters who, as long as they are being attacked from all sides, can claim this as proof of their impartiality and hence avoid discussion of their practices. In fact, the debate about bias makes it difficult to move from the supposed opinions of individual broadcasters to the more important question of the role of television itself and of professional ideologies in producing not reality, but the only thing television deals in, namely stories.

Statistical Methods

> In politics the assumption of the law of statistics as an essential law operating of necessity is not only a scientific error, but becomes a practical error in action.

Antonio Gramsci, Prison Notebooks, 1971.

One of the dominant methods used in the analysis of television is that of statistics. Relying on the assumptions outlined above and on the law of statistical method, Delwyn Williams MP made his position clear in the *Committee on Welsh Affairs*

> I look at the figures for *Heddiw* (short bulletins), and I see that Labour with over 20 MPs in Wales has only 28% of the coverage and Plaid Cymru has 25%. Now I am taking the gloves off with you. I firmly believe that Plaid Cymru has infiltrated BBC Wales.
>
> *Broadcasting In The Welsh Language And The Implications For Welsh and Non-Welsh Speaking Viewers and Listeners* Volume II, 1981, p.209)

One of the central concerns of the Committee, in fact, is that the new fourth channel in Wales will also be infiltrated by nationalists and biased towards Plaid Cymru. The concern is based ultimately on statistical arguments – the "evidence" submitted by BBC Wales and HTV at the request of the Committee (Vol. II, pp.86 and 178).

Committee chairman Leo Abse made no bones about his reading of the evidence in his questions to Vincent Hanna (representative of BBC TV's NUJ Chapel). He asked if "the extraordinary amount of attention devoted to one particular party does not give you any feeling of unease at all" (Vol. II, p.245). But charges based on figures can be dismissed if you can invalidate the statistics. This the BBC, HTV and the journalists of both NUJ Chapels proceeded to do. Hence, of course, they were able to evade the accusation of bias.

Even so, the *Western Mail* (December 6th 1982) returned to the debate in the wake of S4C's launch. The journalists and broadcasters may have refuted the statistics, but this only goes to show that "allegations that broadcasting in Wales, particularly in Welsh, is riddled with nationalists, have far more truth than the broadcasters themselves will admit – in public".

The argument cannot be settled by statistics. There is an important distinction to be made between being covered and getting fair treatment. Tony Benn, for instance, gets an enormous amount of *coverage*, but is usually *represented* unfavourably. But the Committee, the TV journalists, the *Western Mail* and numerous Parliamentary critics all fail to make this distinction. Our analysis of the way Plaid Cymru is represented in news and current affairs demonstrates that it's not how often you are mentioned that counts. What counts is how television stories make sense of you.

PLAID CYMRU: COVERAGE

Cardiff coverage: All is well?

We began our study by producing figures for the number of times the Parliamentary political parties in Wales were mentioned in our project month. The figures refer to the Cardiff news programmes *Heddiw, Y Dydd, Wales Today* and *Report Wales* in the period from February 22nd 1982 to March 26th 1982. The figures are:

Party	Mentions	% of total	% vote in Wales at '79 election
Labour	63	30.0	46.9
Tory	73	34.8	32.2
Liberal	12	5.7	10.6
SDP	13	6.2	n/a
Alliance	10	4.8	n/a
Plaid	39	18.6	8.1

210

These figures indicate that Plaid Cymru is not limited to an unreasonably small share of *coverage* in the Cardiff news. When a further statistic is added, namely that 60% of their press releases during this period were covered in new stories in some way, it merely reinforces the idea that, for Plaid, all is well.

But getting into this sort of statistical argument places certain questions, and therefore certain political arguments about media coverage, outside the terms of the debate.

For example, what stories about Plaid Cymru are not covered? What are the rules governing newsworthiness? Once Plaid is included, what is the news context that it is placed in? Most important, how is Plaid Cymru signified in news items and what is the overall representation of the party?

If Plaid Cymru has no problem in gaining access to Cardiff coverage, is there a Plaid Cymru not being represented in the news? Using the *Western Mail* as a control, we compiled a list of some of the activities of the party during this month that were not covered in the televison news broadcast from Cardiff. The list was not meant to suggest that particular events *should* have been covered; it indicated that some of these events *could* have been covered following the broadcasting norms of newsworthiness.

What the party thinks

On page 9 of the *Western Mail* of 24th February was a short item on an article by Dafydd Elis Thomas in *Marxism Today*. He argued that Labourism in South Wales has brought socialism into disrepute and that Tony Benn MP "is reported, or perhaps mis-reported, to have told a Labour Party fringe meeting that if he came from South Wales he would be a Welsh Nationalist because of what the Labour Party had done to South Wales". This debate, which concerned both the future of Wales and the future of politics in Wales, was not covered. But it could have been rendered newsworthy as being a nationalism v. socialism argument.

Similarly, there is a debate about the politics of Plaid Cymru following its decision in 1981 to write a Welsh socialist state into the party objectives instead of self-government. Since that decision a group has formed within Plaid (Hydro) whose objectives are to return the party to pre-1981 politics. The *Western Mail* of February 26th 1982 gave half a page to a feature on Plaid and "the left" and there

followed two letters on the subject from prominent party members
(February 27th, March 1st). None of this was covered but it could
have made a story on television as, for instance, being yet another
split in party politics and nationalism in Wales. It seems, then, that
it is not what parties think that is considered important for the
television audience, it is what they do.

What the party does

Plaid Cymru is defined as a party that does some things but not
others. The news covers *some* of its activities – but the ones that are
covered and the ones that are excluded fall into a definite pattern.
The news operates a routine strategy of inclusion and exclusion
which limits and sets a boundary round Plaid Cymru.

There were a number of topical and newsworthy events in the
project month which were covered in the news and in which Plaid
was active. But the news did not cover Plaid's part in these stories.
For example, there was the declaration of a Nuclear Free Wales on
February 23rd. This followed the announcement that all eight of the
Welsh County Councils had declared themselves to be Nuclear Free
Zones. This was covered by all four Cardiff programmes at length.
But there was no coverage at all of "the anti-nuclear stance urged for
Plaid Cymru by Dafydd Wigley" *Western Mail*, 3 March 1982).

"Illegitimate" activities concerning Ireland are always topical. But
there was no coverage of the Plaid Community Councillor's support
for the Wales Sinn Fein organizer imprisoned in Maidstone who had
"been placed in the punishment block... for refusing to make clothes
for the Army" (*Western Mail*, 16 March 1982). There was no
coverage of a speech by Plaid's General Secretary, Dafydd Williams,
who said that the Tories, by refusing to face up to Welsh problems
and showing contempt for Welsh opinion, were encouraging
extremism.

A call by the Barry branch of the party to the Secretary of State
for Wales, Nicholas Edwards, to release unused dockland for
industry and create jobs in the area (*Western Mail*, 26 February
1982) was absent. Also absent was Plaid Cymru's press release
complaining about the shelving of plans for a new mine at Margam
and the lack of investment in the South Wales coalfield.

It could be argued that all of Plaid Cymru's activities can't be
covered, but by its strategy of selective exclusion the news defines

the party as not being involved in international affairs, civil rights, labour and industrial issues. It is not represented as an alternative anti-Tory party and it is not seen as being involved in *British* politics. Many of the events involving Plaid could have been covered since they were already newsworthy, but by exclusion the party identity is denied its full range. When we look at the television stories that did mention Plaid Cymru, the party identity in the news becomes clearer.

PLAID CYMRU: REPRESENTATION

Identity

Plaid Cymru's identity on the news results not only from what is excluded but also from the stories that are included. The majority of stories in the project month that do mention Plaid are on the water campaign where the issue is defined in a traditional nationalist vein. It's about what the *English* pay for *Welsh* water. The support for Wayne Williams in his fight to be reinstated at Llanidloes High School is defined as a *language* issue. And the party's call for an inquiry into the Welsh Arts Council (after its grant to *Arcade* was withdrawn) fits an image of nationalism as a literary issue.

Other items that were included dwelt on Plaid Cymru as a party opposing the various agencies of the British State. Two examples are Wigley's attempts to get the *Home Office* to disclose its guidelines on telephone bugging (March 24th and 26th), and the pressure placed on the *Welsh Office* to get them to relax the rules on second homes enabling local authorities to buy up private housing (February 26th)

Plaid Cymru is identified overall as a party that is still carrying out the nationalist style politics of the past. These Plaid activities are newsworthy because they fit into the historically established images of what nationalism is, and of Plaid as being that sort of nationalist party. A party opposed to the Tories, or to the British state on specifically labour issues, would not make sense within that framework. The news reports what is assumed to be what is already known about Plaid Cymru. Without "bias", but in the routine *practice* of newsworthiness, the news misrepresents Plaid Cymru.

News Values

As we have seen, broadcasters refute statistical balance as the
criterion for deciding on newsworthiness. But the issue cannot rest
there, since the criteria for newsworthiness – the strategies for
inclusion and exclusion – result in the misrepresentation of Plaid
Cymru. So what are these critieria?

> If a journalist is given some information about a political story...if
> in his judgement as a journalist that story is a valid news item
> and is an important story and a matter of public concern, is he
> to say: No, we will not carry that story because the figures at
> the moment are such that we need to balance it up with
> reference to other people?

> G.T. Davies, Head of News and Current Affairs, HTV Wales, in
> evidence to the Committee on Welsh Affairs. Vol.II, page 121).

But how does the journalist know what is important and of public
concern? Vincent Hanna of BBC Television told the Committee:

> The trained journalist knows perfectly well when an event is not
> worthy of reporting...knows perfectly well when to bring the
> values of judgement, of political common sense and good
> reporting to these matters.

> (Vol.II page 244).

The notion of "good reporting" begs the question, good for whom?
Not for Plaid Cymru, certainly.

The trouble with "trained" professional "values" of "judgement"
and "political common sense" is that their uncritical acceptance is
actually *responsible* for the misrepresentation of Plaid Cymru. Using
political common sense, the good journalist will obviously select a
story in which Plaid Cymru is acting as a "nationalist" party. A story
which doesn't fit the established image of the party or of what
nationalism means is liable to be overlooked for precisely these
reasons. The result is that Plaid Cymru and nationalism are reduced
to the strait-jacket of a stereotype.

LONDON

The case from Plaid has been that it is under-represented in the television news and current affairs programmes originating from London. With the SNP, it has been pressurising broadcasting institutions for many years. Much of this pressure has been for, first, the right to have party-political broadcasts which were broadcast in Wales only. Then there was the fight to have these broadcasts transmitted to the rest of Britain.

These demands became more pressing with the resurgence of nationalism and cultural politics of the '60s. Plaid won three parliamentary seats in the 1974 election and the 1974-79 Labour Government was forced to take notice of Plaid and the SNP in order to survive on their Parliamentary support; *Welsh* nationalism became a force in *British* politics.

In March 1982, after a meeting between Dafydd Wigley of Plaid, Brian Wilson of the SNP, Sir Ian Trethowan of the BBC and Sir Brian Young of the IBA, the broadcasters agreed to

> ensure that any guidelines for the next election issued to news editors include a reference to the need to take account of the position of the National Parties in Scotland and Wales in arranging UK outputs.

> (Letter from Brian Young to Dafydd Wigley, 11 March 1982)

But in the same letter Young reiterated IBA policy, stating that Plaid Cymru broadcasts "should only be carried by transmitters sited within Wales itself".

Once again it seems Welsh politics is being refused a British dimension. This is certainly the case when we turn to the "national" news programmes from London. Whatever the "guidelines" for the next election might be, the current situation could not be worse for non-London parties.

During the whole project month thre was not one item on either *News At Ten* or the *Nine O'Clock News* that even hinted at the existence of Plaid Cymru, never mind its involvement in both Parliamentary and extra-Parliamentary activities. The SNP was mentioned but only because of the obligations of broadcasters to be balanced and impartial to all parties during election campaigns. If it wasn't for the Hillhead by-election, the SNP would not have been mentioned at all.

So during the whole project month, Plaid was not mentioned at all. But at the same time the other Parliamentary parties who are active in Wales were all mentioned. The figures are as follows:

Number of items in the London news that mention
the main British Parliamentary Parties

Political Party	Mentions on *News at Ten*	Mentions on *Nine O'Clock News*	Total Mentions
Labour	35	28	63
Tory	31	23	54
Liberal/SDP Alliance	25	18	43
SNP	7	3	10
Plaid	0	0	0

This is not bias against Plaid Cymru. But by not representing Plaid in the London news at all the assumption must be that it does not really matter in *British* politics. First, viewers outside Wales are given no indication that it exists, and second there are many people inside Wales who prefer to tune into the BBC 1 and HTV West transmitters (even after all the Welsh Language programmes have been moved to S4C) and who therefore do not receive news of Plaid from Cardiff. In addition to this there is the fact that the London news is dominant in terms of its authority and audience size. Plaid Cymru is restricted to a small audience in Wales whilst, as the table above shows, the other parties get coverage regularly from London in addition to their coverage in the Cardiff news.

THE WATER CAMPAIGN COVERAGE

When, on March 4th, Plaid Cymru launched its campaign for fairer water charges in Wales it was not covered in the London news. Plaid's General Secretary wrote to both Sir Ian Trethowan, Director General of the BBC, and Sir Brian Young of the IBA to complain at this exclusion. In his letter of March 12th, Dafydd Williams complained that "the water campaign will be one of Plaid Cymru's chief activities during the year and therefore is a first class example of the lack of coverage we receive as a party by the London-orientated news media".

IBA

Colin Shaw, Director of Television IBA, replied in the absence of Sir Brian Young (18th March 1982). "Every day confronts editors in national newsrooms with difficult choices about what to include and what to exclude". As usual, the reason for Plaid's absence is the pressure of other news. But on the day that Plaid's water campaign was launched it was contending with a story about Freddie Laker having his free air travel on other airlines stopped (*News at Ten*, item 11, 32 seconds) and the tale of a karate expert who broke his hand during a record attempt (item 16, 34 seconds). So much for the pressures of the day.

Mr Shaw continues "parties whose interests are almost wholly confined to Wales and Scotland will naturally receive far more coverage in their home regions than across the network as a whole". Does this mean that the Tory Party should abide by the same rule? If so, how much coverage would they get in Wales and Scotland or anywhere outside the south-east of England? What is so "natural" about the way coverage is allotted? Since when have the Tories been the natural party of Wales? Is this the application of the values of "judgement" and "political common sense" that Vincent Hanna said that journalists are ruled by?

Shaw's letter goes on "coverage will also take into account the strength of the Nationalist parties within Wales and Scotland generally". The implication here is that either votes attained or seats held in Parliament are the criteria of "strength" which determine coverage. We have already heard that statistics do not come into it, but as Sir Brian Young told the Committee on Welsh Affairs (Vol. II page 303): "it would not be our view that what is done regionally atones for what is done nationally. We would say that in both you actually do what the subject demands and it therefore tends to happen that the Nationalist parties tend to think that they do not get much coverage".

Plaid's campaign to get fairer water charges in Wales involves a

political party holding two seats in Parliament advocating civil
disobedience in the form of non-payment of water bills led from the
front by its president. The subject surely demands coverage and it
certainly would have got it had the Labour Party thought of it first.

BBC

Sir Ian Trethowan, Director General of the BBC, adds some more
pieces to this jigsaw. In his letter to Dafydd Williams (29 March) he
states that "UK coverage given to the activities of political parties
must have some relevance to the extent to which these parties
engage in UK politics". When Plaid Cymru's strength was "of
considerable significance in the Parliamentary balance of forces...
considerable attention was given to the party's policies and
attitudes". Plaid Cymru is not now considered to be significant in this
Parliamentary balance, so it is excluded again, but on the very
criteria it is in being to challenge. Plaid Cymru exists because of the
failure of Parliamentary politics in Wales.

Trethowan adds "coverage cannot be the same when political
realities are different". Just whose political reality is he referring to?
It is one where Plaid clearly does not matter because its framework
is set by the activities of the three other political parties, by Whitehall
and its elite personalities. It is the politics of government where only
the parties who can participate in it matter. A party having different
ideas about what politics is and being directly opposed to
governmental power over Wales resting in the London Parliament,
Plaid Cymru is excluded from this "political reality".

Yet another assumption serves to exclude Plaid Cymru.
Trethowan continues "It is unrealistic of you to expect coverage on
network programmes whose responsibility is to cover the world at
large". The world at large covered by the *Nine O'Clock News* of 4th
March, when the water campaign was launched, included a 1 minute
44 second item on the auction of war medals (item 15) and a 44
second item on a German dentist's poltergeist hoax. With this kind
of common sense view of the "world at large" no wonder Plaid never
gets covered.

THE WATER CAMPAIGN: REPRESENTATION

Plaid certainly has a case against the London news. What is needed is a decentralised news service, produced in Wales, that is dominated by British governmental politics to the same extent that the existing London news is dominated by French governmental politics.

But since Plaid is not covered at all from London, we must return to the Cardiff programmes to find out how the water campaign was *represented* in television news. This raises the general issues of the way stories are put together and put over. The professional codes of reporting and TV representation determine what a story means – but these codes are so familiar on the screen that it is often difficult for us to recognise them at work.

However, as the water campaign will serve to illustrate, the way they work means that getting coverage itself is not enough. For even when it is included, Plaid Cymru is marginalised and misrepresented by the way it figures in the stories.

Defining Authority

The campaign for fairer water charges in Wales, launched on 4th March 1982, had already been contextualised in the *Western Mail* of February 26th. On page 13 it states: "Welsh water chiefs told MPs yesterday that Plaid Cymru's campaign of non-payment of water rates could mean even bigger increases in the future". This angle on the campaign (not the campaign itself) was picked up by the broadcasters. The first *Wales Today* headline of 4th March announced "The Welsh Water Authority says Plaid Cymru's campaign against water charges *could* [our italics] lead to bigger bills for everyone next year".

The next headline is "After a second arson attack on a North Wales holiday cottage police say they're stepping up their guard on second homes". The third headline begins "An angry village protests". In short, the normal news values of disruption, illegality and anger have all been introduced. Enter the water campaign:

> The Welsh Water Authority has warned rate payers today not
> to put themselves *outside the law* by heeding Plaid Cymru's
> campaign to withold the payment of water charges. The

authority says if the campaign succeeds, it *will* [our italics in
both cases] only mean everyone paying more next year.

In the space of 40 seconds (from the headline to the story) we move
from it *could* mean to it *will* mean higher charges.

The story concerns a Plaid action but the Welsh Water Authority
is allowed to get its oar in first. So the item is about the truth
according to Authority, and Plaid's part in it is represented first as
illegal and second as damaging to the rate payers. The story could
have started with an extract from Plaid's press release – it is a
common journalistic practice to quote verbatim from such releases:

> Water bills for the coming year are dropping through letter
> boxes in Wales this week and should be sent back to the water
> authorities without payment. This was the call made today by
> Mr. Dafydd Wigley MP, President of Plaid Cymru, who was
> lauching the party's water campaign.

> (Opening lines of press release).

Questioning Authority

The presenter gives a brief outline of the campaign before
introducing "our political correspondent" who is said to have asked
Mr. Wigley what he would consider a fair price for Welsh water
(Q.1). Cut to a shot of Mr. Wigley answering the unseen political
correspondent in a film interview. Mr. Wigley is subject to the "but
surely" kind of interrogative interview. The questions asked of him
are as follows:

> Q2. But that's bound to be many millions of pounds?
> Q3. What you think would be a fair price for Wales might not be
> considered fair by people in, say, Birmingham?
> Q4. What's going to happen during this campaign? Are people
> going to end up in jail?
> Q5. But if your campaign is successful, and a lot of people
> withold their water rates, couldn't you end up by pushing up
> water rates in Wales, because you're depriving the Authority?

Plaid is questioned within the framework of the damage that its campaign will cause – disruption and illegality. Mr. Wigley succeeds in fielding the questions and is given time to explain Plaid's position further. There is nothing wrong with interrogative interviewing. But compare the above questions to those asked of the Chief Executive of the Welsh Water Authority:

> Q.1 Mr. Wigley has put himself forward as an example by sending his bill back today. What will happen to him now?
> Q2. Can you ever see a stage though where people in England will be paying the same charges as people in Wales?
> Q3. Do you think Plaid Cymru have a general argument?

These were not the hard questions given to Mr. Wigley. What happened to the interrogation of WWA policy? Giving different styles of questions to different parties in a dispute is typical of television interviews. Once authority – water or otherwise – is allowed to dominate, it sets the framework for what is to follow. A problem is established and the problem here is Plaid. These are the terms that set the meaning of the whole story. Questions of inequality and of the involvement of the British State are never raised because they are outside the terms of the established problem. Authority is privileged and given its own friendly questions, whilst Plaid is marginalised. It was their *event* but the *story* belongs to the Welsh Water Authority.

Marginalisation

We are not suggesting that the news is biased against Plaid but the party and its activities were still misrepresented. Nor does our argument imply that this one moment of television determined the general response to the campaign. There are the other three programmes to be taken into account, together with local press and radio, previous coverage of Plaid Cymru and the way the story was understood by the viewers, if at all.

The story was not typical of the treatment that Plaid received during the project month. But it was by far the most extensive coverage that they were given. What it shows is that the way in which the application of *routine* news practices, which allow both sides access to the story but also allow one to be privileged, disadvantages the party even when it receives generous air-time.

YOU CAN'T HAVE A PLAID WITHOUT A CYMRU?

Stuart Hall has suggested that the media would rightly be seen as partisan if they systematically adopted the view of a particular party and that it is only when:

> certain parties or interests have acquired legitimate ascendency in the state...legitimately secured through the formal exercise of the "will of the majority"...that...their strategies can be represented as coincident with the "national interest" and therefore form the legitimate basis or framework which the media can assume.

(Culture, Society and the Media, 1982, page 87).

The dominant framework of political broadcasting is Parliament and the electoral franchise. Broadcasting is licensed by Parliament and its politics are dominated by it. The assumptions of this narrow definition of politics run deep in news values themselves. In their practical, routine day-to-day operation, the results are specifically ideological.

The news is playing a role in defining what politics is and what Plaid Cymru's part in it is. There is more space for Plaid in the Cardiff news because news values here are informed by different assumptions of the audience from those of the London news. But the narrow definition of politics offered from London is not disputed; it is only localised to include "local" interests. It is still within the same framework.

Well outside this framework is Plaid Cymru: opposed to the British State and the British Parliament and the supposed neutrality of it all. It follows that Plaid operates outside the framework that news values are based on. It is represented then, not as *opposed* to British nationalism, but as "confined" to Wales. But even in Wales a particular definition of Plaid is represented; that of a particular brand of nationalist politics. As a result it is systematically marginalised, pushed out to the very edges of a political terrain that news itself plays a major role in shaping. Plaid's place on this terrain is reduced to little more than minor community politics.

The party is caught in another combination of invisibility and marginalisation – that of Wales itself. As we show in the following sections, Wales doesn't exist in the London news except as a place that is the same as others within the "unity" of Britain. The problem in media representations of Wales is that a *different* Wales, which does exist, is denied. Thus the possibility of a Wales that can be understood as a separate entity is also denied. There cannot be a party (Plaid) Wales (Cymru) if there isn't even a *country* Wales in the news.

SOME WELSH IDENTITIES

The London Welsh

> It would not be our view that what is done regionally atones for what is done nationally.
>
> (Sir Brian Young (IBA) in evidence to the Committee on Welsh Affairs, Vol. II, page 303)

During the project month it became a struggle to locate any items on either *News at Ten* or the *Nine O'Clock News* that could be said to be about Wales. Of course, all the news is of concern to Wales, whether it is mentioned or not. Part of the difficulty lay in deciding whether those stories that did mention Wales were specifically designed to explain aspects of life in Wales to itself and to other regions. However, because we could not find a single unequivocally Welsh story, we decided to report any story that mentioned Wales at all.

Some stories that mentioned Wales were covered by both the BBC and ITN. These were:

1. *Job losses and unemployment figures.* When the unemployment figures for January (BBC February 23rd) are released they are treated as national figures – Wales is mentioned as a British region. In ITN's weekly survey of jobs lost and gained (February 26th, March 5th and 26th) Wales is there as a typical part of Britain, not as a country with its own economic history.

2. *Michael Foot's re-selection for the Ebbw Vale constituency.* This was topical in the light of the current rows over other re-selections (Peter Tatchell, Pat Wall), of the well-known splits in the Labour Party, and of Foot's position in all this as party leader.

3. *A plaque commemorating Dylan Thomas is unveiled in Westminster Abbey* (March 1st). Clearly a "Welsh" story for St. David's day, but nevertheless it was a British occasion in the pantheon of British culture, in London. And the Welshness it celebrates is the supposedly non-political cultural kind.

4. *The "ferry war" between Sealink and B & I Ferries* (March 8th). Mentions Holyhead.

Some stories that mentioned Wales were covered only on one channel. They were:

1. *Sport* The libel case between J.P.R. Williams and the *Daily Telegraph* (BBC February 25th); Boxer Colin Jones pulls out of European title fight (ITN February 26th).

2. *Nationwide student marches* (BBC March 5th); includes film from Cardiff.

3. *Roy Hattersley speaks* (BBC March 5th); in the Rhondda.

4. *The Prince and Princess of Wales are to get a new neighbour* (ITN March 22nd); in the West Country

5. *Home Secretary to extend stop and search laws to England and Wales* (ITN March 25th); this is because "England and Wales" is the legislative unit distinguished from Scotland.

The Two-Minute Silence

> Viewers in one region can have the opportunity to see programmes about life in other regions...but there has to be a process of selection – it would just not be possible to cover every flower show or Gilbert and Sullivan production throughout the land.

> (*IBA Handbook*, 1981)

Both BBC and ITN frequently make use of film produced by the regional services in their national bulletins. Two recent examples from Wales were the Royal Visit in November 1981 and the blizzards in early 1982. In order to show a Wales that was easily available to the national news without much effort and at reasonably low cost, we have compiled a list of the Cardiff news programmes' longer stories. These were stories of over two minutes' duration, and on average they were a third of the total number of stories in the Cardiff programmes.

On St. David's Day there could have been a story on the official opening of S4C, covered by all the Cardiff programmes. Another "language" story was a development in the Wayne Williams case, but the BBC chose to cover the J.P.R. Williams court case instead.

One week before the Hillhead by-election there was no coverage of the SDP's first success in gaining control of a council by elections (Penarth) rather than defections (Islington). This was the topical and amusing kind of story beloved by the news – after five recounts the SDP finally won by drawing lots with Labour. On February 23rd the SDP and Liberals in Wales announced which seats each would fight in the next general election. For the BBC the choice was between this and a man who had to be evicted from prison because he liked it so much (item 11, 20 seconds). On the same day the last of the eight Welsh County Councils declared itself nuclear free.

Report Wales devoted two thirds of its programme on March 5th to a report that the Severn Bridge could be structurally unsafe. On that day both London bulletins gave twenty-four seconds to the robbery of Anne Hathaway's cottage, and both covered Liz Taylor's return to the West End stage. Cottages which didn't get into the London news were those fired at Morfa Nefyn(*Wales Today* February 25th) and the one attacked for the second time in five weeks in North Wales (*Wales Today* March 4th).

Workers staged a sit-in for proper redundancy settlements at the Dunlop Semtex factory in Brynmawr. Peace campaigners succeeded in getting building work stopped at Mid Glamorgan's nuclear bunker. The council agreed that it should be used only for peace time emergencies. These stories were all covered in the Cardiff news, which even included film of contractors pouring concrete over protestors who refused to get out of the way (*Wales Today* March 8th). But all of this was as a flower show or Gilbert and Sullivan production to the London news.

Submerged Wales

Gwyn A. Williams has pointed out at various times how capitalism in Wales has developed in its own distinctive way. Wales doesn't just have a different linguistic and cultural tradition from other parts of Britain – it has its own economic and political history as well. What is conspicuous by its absence from the London news is any recognition of the political and economic distinctiveness of Wales.

In particular, there is an entire submerged Wales of protest: a political history quite unlike the land of song, chapel and rugby stereotypes that serve to identify it within and beyond the news. Recent examples of protests that have national implications are the continuing battle between the state and the language; the peace campaign (the women who marched to Greenham Common started from Cardiff, whilst others marched to Brawdy); and protests against unemployment, attacks on civil liberties etc.

The submerged Wales is invisible in the news from London – not because news is uninterested in protest, but because it simply doesn't have an available notion of a Welsh identity within which such protests make sense as being, among other things, *Welsh*. Wales figures in the news as an aspect of stories that are about something else altogether. Events are covered as and when they are deemed important, not to Wales, but to Britain – they may just happen to occur in Wales.

In fact the identity that submerges Wales in the news and elsewhere is that of *British* nationalism. The news treats Wales from the point of view of a Britain that, despite many internal differences and fragments, is nevertheless held together within the powerful unity of "the" nation – or as it usually says in the news – simply "us". The internal differences that make "us" such a fascinating nation are of course non-political. This means that the news has little difficulty in identifying a Wales of culture, literature and song, and a Wales of sport.

We are not arguing here for any one essential "Welsh Identity" to set up in opposition to the mythical British one. In fact part of the problem lies in the search for just one rallying point, one particular identity that sums up Welshness. It is clear even from the limited evidence of the Cardiff news that there is a wide range of different possibilities and activities within Wales. This needs to be recognised in order to avoid being reduced yet again to stereotypes – like the popular land-of-song stereotype – that no-one in their right minds actually wants to identify themselves with.

However, the London news media are actively promoting the stereotypes and excluding other identities that are just as Welsh. This makes it hard for people in Wales to watch the news and feel themselves to be Welsh at the same time. As Dafydd Elis Thomas has argued "virtually all Welsh people ask themselves what it is to be Welsh and what Wales is" (*Marxism Today* March 1982). For the news, the answer to these questions is simple. To be Welsh is to be

part of Britain. Unfortunately for Wales, this part only offers one role
– invisibility.

Postscript

On the release of this report in January 1983, Plaid Cymru held a
press conference in Cardiff. It was well attended by the media in
Wales and after the usual interrogation and criticism, the journalists
involved showed a genuine interest in the problems outlined by the
report. It received over two minutes coverage in both HTV Wales'
Report Wales and BBC Wales' *Wales Today*. It received no attention
from either *News at Ten* or the *Nine O'Clock News*.

DEIRDRE BEDDOE

Images of Welsh Women

Images of Welsh Women

Welsh women are culturally invisible.

Wales, land of my fathers, is a land of coalminers, rugby players and male voice choirs. Welsh cultural identity is based almost entirely on the existence of these three male groups. Not only are these groups exclusively male but they are *mass* groups. Think of Wales and you think of Welshmen *in large numbers*: at the rugby match, in the mines and in the concert hall. Besides their corporate ranks, the tiny, usually solitary figure of the Welsh woman in national costume pales further into insignificance. She was only ever a bit of trimming on the male image of Wales anyway. Not only is the dominant image of Wales male and mass, it is also macho. Coalminers and rugby players evoke visions of strong male bodies caked with grime and of rippling muscles glistening with sweat: this hard image is brought into somewhat softer focus around the edges by the sweet harmony of tenor, bass and baritone voices (belonging to the same hard men) singing the 'Slaves' Chorus' from *Nabucco*, 'Bread of Heaven' or 'Raindrops Keep Falling'. The picture of Welshness is complete. The amazing point about this picture, is that it is constructed on an extremely narrow base. It has been constructed with reference to only one sex, to only one class and to only one sector of the Welsh economic base: the industrial sector. It is enough for me to tackle only one aspect of this distortion: the exclusion of one sex from the image of Wales, namely women.

In this essay I shall explain briefly why I believe Welsh women are invisible in the context of the national image of Wales. But my main aim is to concentrate upon images of Welsh women themselves. Do specific images of Welsh women exist? What are they? How accurate are they? And finally I should like to suggest what I believe should be the new dominant images of women in Wales in order to reflect more accurately the role of Welsh women in the present day.

First, why are Welsh women absent from the popularly held vision

of Wales? To answer that I need to invoke three mighty factors:
Patriarchy, Capitalism and History. Patriarchy is a system in which
power lies in the hands of men, the father in particular and all men
in general. Within patriarchy men hold economic, political and moral
power, although women are sometimes enlisted as the custodians of
moral power which they enforce in the interests of men. (For
example, the sexual fidelity of a wife must be ensured in order that
the husband may be certain that his offspring, to whom he will pass
his property, are indeed his: "moral" control of erring women was/is
enforced not only by patriarchal laws but by the censure of other
women, who have better absorbed the patriarchal code.) Wales is,
and long has been, a patriarchal society, in which the activities and
views of men are held in far higher esteem that those of women. As
a patriarchal culture Wales therefore projects a male image of itself.
The existence and operation of the capitalist mode of production in
Wales entirely ties in with the patriarchal system. For the most part
male capitalists controlled economic production and hence wielded
political power. To put it crudely, capitalism is about capital, i.e.
money, its generation and its increase through profits. The central
industry generating wealth in Wales in the second half of the
nineteenth century and the first half of the twentieth century was
coal. The male waged worker in coal was the central prop on which
Welsh capitalism rested: the coalminer was the symbol of wealth
generated in Wales and ironically the symbol of rebellion against the
capitalist mode of production. Clearly, in a system based on money,
the male wage earner should be singled out and not the unwaged
female labourer. The contribution of unwaged female labour to
capitalism has always been fully recognized by employers but never
exactly publicized and certainly not celebrated. Women worked for
wages too in Wales, since waged work began and they certainly work
for wages now! The role of Welsh women in the workforce will be
discussed later, but the fact that it has been so neglected until very
recently may be laid squarely at the door of the persistence of an out
of date macho image of Wales. Another contributory factor to that
image is History. There is – as any intelligent person should know
– no such thing as History, that is there is no such thing as an
objective, detached chronicle of facts called History. History is what
historians have selected it to be. Now I have reduced it to that level
I can stop writing it with a capital "H". Historians (mainly middle
class, university educated, men) have made a selection along lines of
class and gender. We have been presented with a package of history

which concerned itself with the deeds and antics of a ruling class: kings, princes, nobles and well-to-do parliamentarians. The lower orders appear only off-stage – as the recipients of paternalistic benevolence – an extended franchise, better drains, shorter working hours, education and moral advice. But our society is not only divided along class lines but along gender lines too. The middle class historian who valued only the record of the upper and middle classes also found only the deeds and lives of men as worthy of inclusion in the study of "History". In short, in Wales, as elsewhere, the writing and study of history has for a very long time omitted women. Welsh history, like English history, has been about chaps.[1] Things are changing now, but the move to investigate the lives of women in Wales is very recent. There is a long way to go. Perhaps, when we get a people's history of Wales we may begin to see the emergence of a people's image of Wales, as opposed to just a single sex image.

Welsh women may be excluded from the formulation of the national image of Wales, but do specific images of Welsh women – as opposed to women in other parts of Britain – exist? I think that they do. Some of these images have echoes or counterparts in other parts of the United Kingdom but I believe that a distinct set of images, or stereotypes, exist with regard to Wales. Those that I shall examine are the Welsh Mam; the Welsh lady in National Costume; the Pious Welshwoman; the sexy Welshwoman and the funny Welshwoman.

I must begin with the Welsh Mam. I have a vivid mental image of her: she is small; she wears plain dresses and an apron; her hair is in a bun. She looks like the Welsh actress Rachel Thomas. She is hardworking. She is as clean as she is pious: she scrubs her floors and her husband's coal-black back. She is, of course, a mother, mainly the mother of sons who like her husband are also coalminers. She has responsibility for and in the home: she is given her husband's wage packet every week. This is how she is depicted in Richard Llewellyn's *How Green Was My Valley* (1939):

> As soon as the whistle went they [the women] put chairs outside
> their front doors and sat here waiting till the men came up the
> Hill and home. Then as the men came up to their front doors
> they threw their wages, sovereign by sovereign, into the shining
> laps, fathers first and sons or lodgers in a line behind. My
> mother often had forty of them, with my father and five brothers
> working.[2]

In good times she keeps a fine kitchen. This is *How Green Was My Valley* again:

> We always had hams in the kitchen to start with, all the year round, and not just one ham, but a dozen at a time. Two whole pigs hanging up in one kitchen, ready to be sliced for anybody who walked through the door, known or stranger.[3]

In bad times it was she who scrimped and went without. The Welsh mam was the moral custodian of the home, keeping drink and trouble out.

Of course the Welsh mam *existed*, to be more accurate I should say bits of the picture of her I have painted existed. She is an historical fact. She can be located historically. In fact, she *must* be located historically, lest people think she has always been around. She is a nineteenth century invention. As Gwyn A. Williams stated:

> Two archetypal and quasi mythical figures loom through the mist of our memory of Wales; the Welsh miner and the Welsh Mam. Both were invented by the nineteenth century.[4]

We do not come across the Welsh Mam in the seventeenth or eighteenth centuries. Working class women in pre-industrial Wales contributed to the economy of their household. They worked on the land. Lipscomb (1792) tells us that in Wales women shared "the most arduous exertions and business of husbandry, and they are commonly seen either driving the horses affixed to the plough, or leading those which drew the harrow".[5] In 1851 agriculture was the second largest employer of female labour in Wales: 29.3% of employed women in Wales were in agriculture as opposed to 7.5% in England.[6] The housewife of pre-industrial Wales, like her counterpart in pre-industrial England, often managed a large household and ran a specialist area of the farm, particularly the dairy. In some households, indeed, the spinning done by women may have brought the only actual cash into the house. In contrast to this, the Welsh Mam was economically *dependent* upon her husband's and sons' wages. The fact that the industrial revolution in South Wales was dominated by heavy industry meant that there was no work – or next to no work – for women in these heavy industries. In Wales there was nothing really comparable to the industrial out-work done at home by the women chain and nail makers of the West Midlands.

By 1911 only one in five of the female population over ten years old in the old county of Glamorgan was in paid employment and the majority of those were in Domestic Service or Dress, to use the census categories. In rural Cardiganshire, at the same date, one in three women were economically active.[7]

The economic dependency of the Welsh Mam upon her husband and the strict division of labour along gender lines (men went out to work for money and women worked at home for no money) was actually in strict harmony with the ideology of the times. The first half of the nineteenth century saw the rise of the domestic ideology: the Revolution in France, coupled with social problems in Britain caused by industrialization, greatly alarmed the British middle classes. To avert similar revolution occurring in Britain, they sought to stabilize society. One of the chief ways that the middle-class sought to bring about such stability was through strengthening the idea and the role of the family. They advocated a bourgeois view of the family: male breadwinner, dependent home-based wife and dependent children. It was this version of the family that the middle class wished to impose upon the working class and which indeed the working class came to aspire to: the dependent wife was to become a symbol of working class male success. The message that "women's place is in the home" was consequently trumpeted from the pulpit and reinforced by religious tracts, poems, magazines, paintings, prints and manuals of behaviour for women.[8] The first Welsh periodical intended principally for women, *Y Gymraes* (1850-1), consequently aimed to create:

> faithful girls, virtuous women, thrifty wives and intelligent mothers who would instil Christian morality and virtue into the men and boys of Wales.[9]

The domestic ideology, like the Welsh Mam herself, is an historically locatable phenomenon and not a tradition.

There is one point central to the myth of the Welsh Mam which I must address. The Miner and the Mam are the stereotypes: the myth is that they had equal power or even that the Mam was the dominant power. The business of the miner handing over his pay packet to his wife is often cited as evidence of this. Actually in doing this the wage earner was passing over the burden of managing the household on his wages. Can you imagine coal owners or iron masters giving their wives their profits intact? The point must be made that women's authority was entirely limited to the domestic sphere of the home. Her power was confined to the private sphere. Not for her the big world of the public sphere outside! Her province was as limited as that of the Jewish mamma or the Indian woman in purdah. Did she have a vote? (Women over twenty-one in Britain were not granted the parliamentary vote until 1928.) Did she have economic power? Did she have control over even her own body and its reproductive functions? The pathetic letters from Welsh women to the Women's Cooperative Guild, published in 1915, which tell of hardship and broken health caused by successive pregnancies testify to her lack of control over even her own body.[10] When in the early 1920's the birth control campaigner, Stella Browne, toured Monmouthshire, she recorded:

> How often in this tour have elderly women not said, "you've come too late to help me, Comrade, but give me some papers for my girls. *I don't want them to have the life I've had.*"[11]

Miners were oppressed by coal-owners and poverty. For their wives it was a double oppression. As one woman said, "We were slaves because they were slaves to the mine-owners".[12]

Another image of Welsh women which requires consideration is the picture of the Welsh lady in national costume. There are Welsh lady dolls, Welsh lady pots of jam, Welsh lady ornaments and pretty young women in national costume smile out at us from postcards and plates. Of course nobody actually wears this costume anymore except little girls on St. David's day or singers at Eisteddfodau. The costume is now just a device of tourism. Welsh costume – the tall black hat and the big red cloak worn over a pretty petticoat – was the invention of Augusta Hall, Lady Llanover, 1802-96.[13] She was one of the leaders of a romantic revival of Welshness which flourished in the early and mid nineteenth century. She studied and made drawings of a variety of Welsh peasant costumes and came up with her version of what Welsh national costume ought to look like. She urged women to wear it especially on "national occasions" such as eisteddfodau: she was also keenly aware that in urging its adoption she was helping the Welsh woollen industry. One of the by-products of Lady Llanover's fashion designing was the emergence of "Dame Wales", a cartoon figure who represented Wales in much the same way as John Bull stands for England or Uncle Sam for the U.S.A. The fact that Wales is represented as a female figure is, I believe, of no significance beyond being convenient for cartoonists. France too is represented by a woman, as are the abstract concepts of justice or socialism, but when has there been a woman president of France, a Lady Chief Justice or a woman head of the Labour Party?

The reality of the issue of Welsh costume, is that at the time when Lady Llanover was advocating her newly designed outfit, the old peasant costume was dying out. Women had actually worn the tall beaver hat, basically a man's hat of the style worn generally in the seventeenth century. The tall hat was popular especially in the towns of South Wales and there are many prints and paintings showing women wearing them. By the late nineteenth century however it was rarely worn. Wirt Sykes, American consul in Cardiff, writing in the 1880's, bemoaned the fact that the tall beaver hat was rarely seen although it gladdened his heart to find one market-woman in Merthyr wearing a beaver:

> There are, however, some specimens still to be seen of the Welsh peasant costume as it has been for generations past: notably a comely young woman behind a vegetable stall, who wears the full costume in all its glory. She is a pink of neatness, and her beaver is superb. [14]

She glows from his pages. What is so delightful about her is that she is a genuine working woman who may well have grown the vegetables she is selling. She is *working* in her costume. What Lady Llanover did was to produce a "twee" version of what was really the gear of working women. Today the image of the *lady* in Welsh costume – she is far too genteel, far too demure to be a woman – is sweet, decorative and innocuous. The visual images of these ladies in costume compound this by always showing them sitting or standing and smiling, or at most singing or playing the harp. The donning of national costume seems to render their limbs useless and reduce them to the status of ornament. The lady in Welsh costume as a symbol of Wales is interchangeable with the daffodil. There is, incidentally, no male equivalent "national" costume. There are several other characteristics attributed to the standard image of Welsh women, as I perceive that image. Welsh women are pious and passionately religious. They are also regarded as sexy and even sexually wanton. Maybe there is a connection between these two feature of the image.

Perhaps I regard the religious devoutness of Welsh women as important because the few women normally given mention in standard histories of Wales were models of piety. There is Mary Jones who saved her pennies and walked bare-foot across the mountains to buy a Welsh Bible from Thomas Charles of Bala. There was Madam Bevan of Laugharne who helped Gruffydd Jones with his circulating schools. There was Lady Charlotte Guest, who was engaged in philanthropic works amongst the poor and labouring classes of Merthyr Tydfil. Then, of course, there is that powerful visual image of Welsh female piety, *Salem*: Curnon Vosper's famous painting of 1908 depicts an aged Welsh woman, wearing a tall hat and magnificent shawl, in chapel. She is the central figure of the painting and she clutches a Bible under her arm. The painting should be viewed as a piece of bourgeois art; it is a genre painting, a piece of "biedermeier", presenting a homely and comforting view of Wales in the same way that Norman Rockwell's paintings present us with a folksy and reassuring image of America. Some people in Wales read Vosper's painting somewhat differently and pointed to the old woman's lateness and the proud finery of her dress: they saw the devil's face in the folds of her shawl. This is a tortured and nonsensical interpretation but its very existence is an interesting confirmation of Welsh religiosity. We have plenty of statements too on the deep religious fervour of the Welsh. These came thick and fast in the mid-nineteenth century, following upon a vicious attack on the state of morality in Wales in a government report on the state of education in Wales of 1847. The Welsh response was to assert that the people of Wales were highly moral, virtually free of crime and they were intensely devout. Wales emerged as a non-conformist nation and the image of Welsh women projected at this time is devout and god-fearing. The rise of the domestic ideology, coupled with this development, was to mean that the chapel was practically the only public assembly which respectable women could attend.

If part of the image of the Welsh woman is that she is pious, another part of it is that she is passionate. She may have adored the Lord on Sunday but the rest of the week it was the turn of the local boys. Where has this image come from? The old Welsh custom of bundling, (of pre-marital "courting in bed", or quite simply the Custom of Wales) is I think the chief contributor to this image. Pre-marital sex between couples who intended to marry seems to have been normal practice in old Wales, especially before the rise of nonconformity. The commissioners sent by the government to investigate the state of education in Wales in the 1840's singled out this practice as particularly appalling and to be righteously condemned.

> But there is one vice which is flagrant throughout North Wales,
> and remains unchecked by any instrument of civilization. It has
> obtained for so long a time as the peculiar vice of the principality,
> that its existence has almost ceased to be considered as an evil;
> and the custom of Wales is said to justify the barbarous practices
> which precede the rite of marriage.[15]

As one vicar testified:

> The want of chastity is the besetting evil of this country, but
> especially of this district of Lleyn. In the relieving officer's books
> out of twenty-nine births I counted twelve which were
> illegitimate. This was in one quarter of a year... What is worse,
> the parents do not see the evil of it. They say that their
> daughters have been *unfortunate* and maintain their illegitmate
> grandchildren as if they were legitimate.[16]

The commissioners laid the blame for this "gross and bestial
indelicacy" upon overcrowded living conditions and mixed sex
evening prayer meetings.[17] The response from Wales was a spate of
denials and contradictory statistics on illegitimacy. As one Welsh
writer, righteously and indignantly wrote, "There is no bastardy in
our country without a good deal of courting goes on before".[18]

It is clear what the English view of Welsh women was in the
nineteenth century, but what about today? Are Welsh women
regarded as sexy? If we look at Welsh stage and T.V. performers
there are Cardiff's exuberant and sexy singers, Tessy O'Shea and
Shirley Bassey. But if we look at fictional representations of Welsh
women on British television (and we have to look hard) there is
Nerys Hughes' *District Nurse* and Ruth Madoc's Gladys Pugh, the
chief Yellowcoat of Maplin's holiday camp in *Hi De Hi!* The district
nurse is a dynamic social campaigner but she is also attractive and
she has the skeleton of an illegitimate child in her medicine chest.
Gladys Pugh has dark Welsh good looks and she aspires to being
sexy – but not to being too sexy: she is a respectable girl. She has
romantic designs on a succession of the holdiay camp's managers but
she always fails to get her man. I think that she is very funny indeed
– perhaps in the tradition of Welsh funny women like Gladys Morgan
and Maudie Edwards – but she is also rather a figure of fun. Some

English people still regard Welsh people, along with Irish people, as inherently funny. It is funny to have a Welsh accent especially if you are a woman. British Rail ticket collectors at Temple Meads or Paddington call you Blodwen.

I am not happy with the fact that women are excluded from the national image of Wales. I am equally unhappy with the constricted and nowadays inaccurate images which I have outlined above. But we are not necessarily stuck with them. It would be nice if the image projected of Welsh women were nearer reality. I would like to make two suggestions as to how this can be done.

First we should discard the housebound Welsh Mam – she has had her day: Welsh women today are Welsh workers and if current trends continue they may end up being the only Welsh workers. Before the heavy industrialisation of Wales they had worked in agriculture in large numbers: women from West Wales used to *walk* regularly from, say, Tregaron to London, knitting as they went, to work for the season in the market gardens of Chelsea and Fulham. Then came the era of heavy industry and this together with the rise of the domestic ideology placed Welsh women firmly within the home. They stayed there too – although many thousands of them stayed in *other people's* homes, in Weston-Super-Mare or Surrey or London – as poorly paid domestic servants. As late as 1961 the economic activity rate of women in Wales was only twenty-eight per cent, the lowest in Britain by a long way. From that date, however, things began to change rapidly. The deconstruction of Welsh heavy industry together with a rise in service industries and the arrival of multinational or American or Japanese companies has meant jobs for men have disappeared and jobs for women created. By 1977 fifty-seven per cent of Treorchy's workforce was female. Whilst husbands are thrown out of work, wives and daughters are getting jobs – albeit often part-time and underpaid. By 1981 even in Gwynedd fifty-two percent of women were economically active and the figure for South Glamorgan was up to sixty per cent.[19]

Similarly I think the coy little Welsh lady, the doll-like little creature, gives a false impression of Welsh womanhood. Welsh women have never been demure little objects. In 1795, "the year of the housewives' revolt", as it is known, throughout Wales women took direct action against the high price of food: they led protests at Haverfordwest and Hay-on-Wye.[20] They were there too in the Merthyr Rising of 1831 and in the Chartist movement of the 1830's and 1840's: in Llanidloes in 1839 women rescued the Chartist leaders who had been arrested and were being held by policemen who had been specially brought in from London. In the late nineteenth and early twentieth century Welsh women were active in the women's suffrage movement: militant Welsh members of the Women's Social and Political Union cut telegraph wires between major towns, blew up pillar boxes and carried out hoaxes: territorial army members in the Pontypool district turned up for duty as the result of a suffragette hoax-summons. As we move into the inter-war period poverty and unemployment became the key issues. Welsh women marched in hunger marches to London: Dora Cox, Ceridwen Brown and other women left Tonypandy on the 1934 Hunger March to London. In 1935 the women around Merthyr organized a march on the offices of the Unemployed Assistance Board (UAB) in response to a new UAB Act: they smashed the offices. The next day the government backed down on the Act. In the summer of 1981 a women's march left Cardiff. It went to Greenham Common airbase in Berkshire. When the women got there they simply refused to go away. In the miners' strike of 1984-5, miners' wives have stood along side their husbands in that struggle. It is this reality which I find impossible to square with the demure and passive Welsh doll of the posters and postcards. It is this reality which demands that we jettison false images.

NOTES

1. See my 'Towards a Welsh Women's History', *Llafur: The Journal of the Society of Welsh Labour Historians*, vol.3, no.2, 1981, pp.32-38.
2. Richard Llewellyn, *How Green Was My Valley*, London, New English Press, 1984, p.7.
3. *ibid.* pp.7-8.
4. Gwyn A. Williams, 'Women Workers in Wales, 1968-1982', *Welsh History Review*, vol.II, no.4, 1983, p.530.
5. G. Lipscomb, *Journey into South Wales*, London, 1792, pp.111-12.
6. L.J. Williams and Dot Jones, 'Women at Work in Nineteenth Century Wales', *Llafur: The Journal of the Society of Welsh Labour Historians*, vol.3, no.3, 1982, p.24.
7. *ibid.*
8. For a fuller account of the domestic ideology see C. Hall, 'The early formation

of the Victorian domestic ideology', S. Burman (ed.), *Fit Work for Women*, London, Croom Helm, 1979, pp.15-32; C. Hall, 'Gender divisions and class formation in the Birmingham middle class, 1780-1850', R. Samuel (ed.), *People's History and Socialist Theory*, London, Routledge and Kegan Paul, 1981, pp.164-175. The detailed impact of the rise of the domestic ideology in Wales has not yet been studied. I have begun an analysis of Welsh town directories with a view to making comparisons between the businesses run by women in the early and late nineteenth centuries. Welsh women were however subjected to the same propaganda barrage as their English sisters.

9. See Sian Rhiannon Williams, 'Y Frythones: Portread Cyfnodolion Merched y Bedwaredd Ganrif ar Bymtheg O Gymraes yr Oes', *Llafur: The Journal of the Society of Welsh Labour Historians*, vol.4, no.1, 1984, pp.43-54.

10. M. Llewelyn Davies, *Maternity: Letters from Working Women*, London, Virago, 1978.

11. S. Rowbotham, *A New World for Women Stella Browne – Socialist Feminist*, London, Pluto, 1977, p.31.

12. See the film *Women of the Rhondda*, distributed by Circles, London.

13. For a fuller account of the creation of Welsh tradition in the nineteenth century see Prys Morgan, 'From a death to a view: The hunt for the Welsh past in the Romantic period', in Hobsbawm and Ranger (eds.), *The Invention of Tradition*, Cambridge, Cambridge University Press, 1983, pp.43-100.

14. Wirt Sykes, *Rambles and Studies in Old South Wales*, Barry, Stewart Williams, 1973, p.51.

15. *Report of the Commissioners of Inquiry into the state of Education in Wales*, PP 1847 XXVII, vol.III, p.67.

16. *ibid.* vol.III, p.68.

17. *ibid.* vol.I, p.21.

18. Evan Jones, *Fact, Figures and Statements in Illustration of the Dissent and Morality of Wales: An Appeal to the English People*, 1849, p.38.

19. For a fuller discussion of the role of Welsh women in the workforce see Gwyn A. Williams, 'Women Workers in Wales, 1968-82', *Welsh History Review*, vol.II, no.4, 1984, pp.530-548 and Gwyn A. Williams, *When Was Wales?*, Harmondsworth, Penguin, 1985, pp.255-60.

20. For this and other actions by Welsh women see *I'll Be Here For All Time* (Boadicea Films, 1985), distributed by Circles, London.

CARL TIGHE

Theatre (or Not) in Wales

Theatre (or Not) in Wales

Indeed, all I know about the history of the theatre and everything that my modest experiences as a dramatic author have taught me, confirm that the best theatre is and always has been naturally political.

Vaclav Havel, *Politics and the Theatre.*

In the nineteenth century the national struggles (of the Poles, the Hungarians, the Czechs, the Slovaks, the Croats, the Slovenes, the Romanians, the Jews) brought into opposition nations that, insulated, egotistical, closed off – had nevertheless lived through the same great existential experience of a nation that chooses between its existence and its non-existence; or put another way, between retaining its authentic national life and being assimilated.

Milan Kundera, *A Kidnapped West or Culture Bows Out.*

In the Warsaw Ghetto a child wrote in its diary: "I am hungry, I am cold; when I grow up I want to be a German, then I shall no longer be hungry, and no longer cold."

George Steiner, *Postscript.*

When we go to the theatre we indulge in a ritual that has its roots in the most distant recess of human history. From the magic of hunting dances, through the mediaeval religious plays, to Shakespeare or Harold Pinter, right down to the Sherman Theatre in Cardiff, the business of making theatre has always been a response to differing social pressures.

Theatre is a part of a binding social process. It creates and reinforces a common identity in a public act. In effect theatre says: "This is who we are, these are the things that worry us, these are our neighbours, these are our gods, our dreams, this is how we live and this is our language". Theatre reflects social reality in ways that poetry and the novel cannot, and there is a subterranean tunnel that connects theatre and the national consciousness. Whether that theatre is in China or India, Poland, Nigeria or even Wales, that connection is present. In the words of Raymond Williams, "Theatre not only creates but reflects and reinforces consciousness". Theatre, the most socially and politically sensitive of the arts, is a "major and practical index of change and the creator of consciousness" (*The Long Revolution*).

Having said this we are right to ask what kind of consciousness the theatres of Wales have created and fostered over the last fifteen years. First though, it is necessary to emphasise that, apart from the last fifteen years, Wales has almost no theatre history to speak of. Wales has produced several dramatists of distinction – Dylan Thomas, Emlyn Williams, Gwyn Thomas, Saunders Lewis – but these have all been the exception rather than the rule, and have written without any tradition behind them, without any specific Welsh theatre context. The departure of the gentry to London after the "Tudor" victory at Bosworth, the small, scattered population, the language division, poor transport network and the advent of Methodism have all played their part in preventing the development of a Welsh theatre. Apart from the above mentioned writers and a few Welsh language interludes there are very few Welsh plays. In 1947 Elsbeth Evans wrote: "If a historian were to undertake to read every Welsh play extant the task would neither tax their health nor wealth – only perhaps their patience" (*Y Ddrama Yng Nghymru*). Clearly the fact that Wales has no theatre history of its own is of enormous importance.

It is worth looking very briefly at what Welsh theatre history there is, if only to see the size of the problem and its historical roots, which are indeed, long and confused. It is not just the matter of making new plays that is difficult in Wales, but the whole business of theatre itself. After the battle of Bosworth in 1485 the Welsh gentry removed themselves, their money and their potential patronage to the wealthy court of the Tudor king Henry VII. English companies did visit Wales from time to time, and this was mainly as a result of the increasing Anglicisation of the remaining gentry. In 1503 Welsh players performed at Shrewsbury, and in 1574 Welsh players were seen as far away as Leicester, but in general, even as late as 1660, the trend was not for Wales to create or export its own drama, but to import it from Shrewsbury, Chester, Ludlow, Hereford, Gloucester and Bristol. Even though Charles II explicitly instructed that the Master of Revels should devolve his powers to control theatre in Wales onto the local authorities, there was in fact very little theatrical activity to regulate. Wales was, compared to the comparable English towns, backward in its civic development and had very few of the wealthy nobles who could stimulate an interest in the theatre through patronage. Unless English companies chose to explore out from the English border towns, or unless a company was on its way to Dublin, Wales was regarded as not worth the trouble or expense of visiting. As Professor C.J.L. Price points out, Wales was not "good business", and if we take the possession of a coach and horses as a measure of wealth sufficient to qualify the owner as a potential patron of theatre then "there were more coaches in the county of Sussex than in the whole of Wales". (C.J.L. Price, *The Professional Theatre in Wales*).

Wales lacked wealth, ease of transport, gentry and civic and social organization sufficient to support a theatre industry of any size, but that did not mean that theatre was unpopular. Twm o'r Nant criticized the mad scramble to see the English companies that did stray into Wales, and he in his turn was criticized for the Interludes that he penned, which according to English observers were full of doggerel, popular horseplay and obscene mimes. It is interesting to note that the only sizeable body of dramatic literature from Wales dating from before the twentieth century consists almost entirely of Interludes – a form which had died out in England with the Dissolution of the Monasteries, but which persisted in Wales until Twm o'r Nant's death in 1810. The surprising popularity and durability of this form, and the very sharp social and satirical skills of Twm o'r Nant mark one of the very few attempts to create a specifically Welsh dramatic art form, however limited the scope of the form might be.

From about 1630 onwards the growth of Puritanism in Britain as a whole brought pressure to bear upon potential theatre audiences. Later this pressure was taken up and reinforced by the Methodist ministers and a whole range of Evangelical chapels, all with their own belief that theatre was both unGodly and unWelsh: to read some of the anti-theatre sermons of those days is to realise that to many preachers the two were synonymous. By the 1770's magistrates began to fear that a taste for theatre among the labouring classes would engender a taste for lounging around. In 1787 John Byng, after criticising the theatre at Llwynygroes as being little short of a barn possessed of wigs and truncheons, went on to express the opinion that the Welsh were better off without good roads and theatres, since good roads only allowed people to wander from place to place, that so far the Welsh had been kept innocent by being homebound and by speaking Welsh, and that once they had learned English, moved out of their home territory and acquired a taste for theatre they would simultaneously acquire a taste for luxury that their language and their country could not satisfy, with a resulting decline in their morals, language and culture.

By the 1840's sufficient Welsh people had been convinced by the arguments of the Methodists that theatre, such as it was, went into decline. The only kind of activity to persist was the private and the amateur theatre. Indigenous professional theatre just did not exist, and this meant a number of theatre buildings closing down. Monmouth had no touring players for ten years: Abergavenny and Carmarthen had none for seven years; Aberystwyth had no touring company for eleven years; Brecon, being nearer to England suffered this drought for only four years. Only Swansea, Merthyr and Cardiff maintained any kind of show beyond the fairground booth, but even here the show was always given by an imported group from England, and the show was specially "fitted-up" for Welsh audiences by alteration of the title to include a local reference, by including rather more clowning and fighting than usual, and by enlisting the services of a local singer to lead the finale. And this was the general situation throughout the Victorian era.

The years immediately before the Great War saw "music hall" alternate with Shakespeare, Ibsen, Shaw and Yeats, but there was still nothing worth speaking of from Welsh writers. In 1908 Harley Granville Barker, in an irate letter to the *South Wales Daily News* (10 October 1908) outlined the productions of the previous seven months at the Cardiff New Theatre: five Shakespeare, six Musical Comedy, four French translations, five adapted novels, ten original English plays less than five years old, seven English plays of more than five years old, a Sarah Bernhardt matinee and one light opera. He complained that there had been no comedy, no foreign masterpieces and no grand opera. He concluded by saying that his main criticism of the theatre was that it lacked works of either national or local significance. Nearly eighty years later the same could be said of Cardiff New Theatre, Swansea Grand, Theatre Clwyd, and, until recently, about The Sherman Theatre.

The developments of the last fifteen years, particularly in relation to new writing, have been hailed by some as a Renaissance. But you cannot have a Re-naissance where you have had no naissance in the first place, and it would be more accurate to describe this period as a long drawn out first birth, with all the attendant fears, miseries and mistakes. While it is true that there has been an enormous growth in the theatre industry of Wales, it must also be said that it has been growth of particular kinds of theatre. Experimental theatre, Theatre in Education and Community Theatre Companies – all of whom generally devise their work without writers – all thrive in Wales, despite the difficulties of finding adequate funding. And if we believe the publicity of Theatre Wales there is a massive audience for "mainstream" work too. For various complex reasons the only area which has done relatively poorly is the area of developing new writing for the theatre.

Of late Radio Wales has taken better advantage of the wealth of Welsh writing talent than either TV or the theatre. Until recently BBC Radio Wales was something of a joke for the playwright, but over the last two years the output has risen steadily, and now tops twenty plays per year. Radio production is relatively cheap though, and that is of vital importance in a country which is almost by tradition poor, where transport is a problem, and where the act of going to the theatre is seen to be alien, bourgeois, and unnecessary. Radio is available to all at the twist of a knob, it is free and in its search for an audience and its subject matter it is wide ranging. Almost by default the sheer output and flexibility of Radio drama makes the medium a serious contender for the coveted title of Welsh National Theatre.

The advent of S4C (and the sudden flow of money) has meant that Welsh language writers, who were in short supply anyway, have more work than they can handle. They can afford to work in live theatre once in a while. For the English language writers this is not the case. Large numbers of English language writers are chasing the very few opportunities to write professionally in Wales. They are still out in the cold, and even though some of them will be able to work for S4C through a translator, the general effect has been to highlight the inadequacies of the Welsh live theatre scene. The levels of subsidy involved are such that live theatre, even with handouts from the Welsh Arts Council, cannot compete with the finance available from TV work. Not only that, but the sheer numbers who watch any TV show dwarf to the point of insignificance those who attend any show at a Welsh theatre, with a resulting discrepancy in the level of the royalty payments that writers may expect: it takes a writer about as long to write a stage play as it does to write a TV play, but the latter is infinitely more rewarding in terms of finance, audience, acclaim and quality of production. It is possible to paraphrase G.B. Shaw's famous comment: "Those who can, do it on TV; those who can't, do it in England; those who can't do either write stage-plays in Wales".

There are a number of well established writers working in Wales – Ewart Alexander, Elaine Morgan, Sîon Eirian, Alun Richards – but their main effort goes into TV rather than the stage. It is not simply that TV is far more lucrative, or that there are too few openings in Welsh theatre to sustain professional stage writers (though both of these are true). It is a question of whether or not the theatres *want* these people to write for them, and in general the conservative and unadventurous Welsh theatres do not want anybody to write for them. Alun Richards, even though he has published a volume of stage plays, and has worked on both *Ennal's Point* and *The Onedin Line*, has never had a stage play premiered in Wales.

No matter how active a theatrical environment, it needs the full range of operations if it is to be healthy. Welsh theatre, particularly in the English language, is rarely penetrated or even touched by the talent of the individual writer. Why is that? It must mean something. But what? Given that theatre holds a central position in the psyche of any nation's culture, the absence of home-grown new writing for Welsh theatre and a general reluctance to face up to the implications of the problem, are a clear indication that all is not well.

Of course, it is possible to say: "What? Look at the money the Welsh Arts Council spends on new writing every year,and what about Made in Wales?" There is some truth in this: after much struggle we do have a company where the directors are interested in developing new writing. However, they are severely handicapped. Generally they produce only about three shows per year, and one of those is often an adaptation, rather than an original play. Even so, those three plays represent, in the average year, about half of the opportunities for commissioned work in the English language in Wales. That is in an average year there will probably only be about six new plays from Anglo-Welsh playwrights. Made in Wales' policy of staging adapations cuts this even further.

It must also be said that Made in Wales is not a writers company. It is a company which has a special interest in writers, but it is an interest that is determined by the tastes and predilictions of directors. Perhaps that is inevitable. However it does mean that those plays which do get staged are not the direct response of writers to the world they see around them, but the response of a writer whose work appeals to a particular director as accurate, acceptable, exciting, etc. The director's taste is interposed in the selection of the work that will be accepted or rejected. The company is now approaching its fourth season and already the limitations of this approach can be seen in the uniformity of work done in the initial three seasons. In general, the work has been very closely linked to scaled down versions of TV naturalism, with strictly linear plots, and a very keen avoidance of theatrical and political controversy. In this the company represents an extension of the general characteristics of Theatre in Wales into the area of new writing, rather than a radical new departure. Ironically parallels are often drawn between this company and The Royal Court, and yet for precisely the reasons that The Royal Court can do adventurous and politically sensitive work, Made in Wales finds it cannot, and as a result is more likely to become a stepping stone for playwrights on their way to the Royal Court, than a rival organization. What does that mean? Well, it is not possible to give a simple answer, since this involves exploring the precise relationship of theatre in Wales to Welsh society, and an assessment of the real interest that both the society and the theatre show in the business of new writing.

In the current financial year WAC has allocated only £25,000 for a combined new writing and training budget, and feels that, given the current level of interest among Welsh companies, this will be adequate to cover both areas. This is a reduction of the finance available for new writing. The awful thing is that this is probably a fairly accurate assessment of the interest in new writing and it must be said that until the recent cut-backs a large slice of the money allocated to new writing by the WAC was unspent at the end of the year – it had remained unspent simply because there had been no demand from the companies to employ writers.

In the two financial years 1982-84 the Torch Theatre and Theatre Clwyd *between them* only managed to spend less than six per cent of the WAC's new writing budget. In the five years of its existence Theatre Wales commissioned only three new plays, and performed only two. The refusal to stage new works by Welsh writers is a deeply ingrained habit, and when questioned the theatres wriggle around with all sorts of excuses. However, the plays that a theatre *does not* stage and the subjects it *does not* talk about can be as revealing as the things it *does* stage.

There is a huge list of subjects missing from the theatre of the last fifteen years – subjects which in the right hands could make excellent theatre; the presence of tank-proving grounds in Pembroke, Nuclear Free Wales, the Cardiff Women at Greenham, Civil Liberties after operation Tân, and the Miners' Strike, Welsh Soldiers in the Falklands and in Northern Ireland, the dilemma of the Labour Party under a Welsh leader, the demise of the Welsh Socialist Republican Movement, local government corruption, holiday homes, the death of the rail, steel and coal industries, the death of Ports and Docks, the growth of sunrise industries, the advent of Swansea *Bay* City...the list goes on. Sîon Eirian, Jon Preece, Greg Cullen and some of the devising companies have touched on these subjects, but these are exceptions to the general silence. In any case, most of the writers I have shown this list to have been unimpressed; the subjects do not interest them very much. And yet all these issues are, or have been, vital to the political life of Wales. The quesion I ask is: Why are these subjects of little interest? What does it mean that these subjects are absent from the stage? What does the absence of individual talent writing on, for, in and about Wales mean for the inner life of this social and political and cultural complex? I divide the answers into three overlapping effects: The Margin Effect; The Audience Effect; and The Experience Effect.

The Margin Effect is sometimes called Home Counties-itis and applies generally to the large scale repertory and main stage companies, but has serious implications for the work of virtually all the companies operating in Wales, including those working in the Welsh language. Theatre, historically, is marginal to Welsh culture in both languges. Wales is marginal to the British state. Directors appointed to Welsh theatres are generally the products of a strong, rich, powerful and attractive centralist cultural environment. No matter how sympathetic, it is an enormous effort for them to see beyond the mad panic of getting bums on seats to the underlying problems of Wales.

Faced with a complicated situation the response is stock: the "real" work of these theatres is defined, very conveniently, as being the supply of *mainstream* theatre. New work, where it is undertaken at all, is at best an annual sop, involving writers who have already been successful elsewhere. Novelists, travel writers, comic authors or, at a push, playwrights who have had West End successes are the preferred item. Local playwrights may be offered a workshop, or a reading, but they can hardly ever get a look in at a mainstage full production of their work, since local experience is by definition not Mainstream.

In the absence of a strong and vital Welsh theatre writing tradition the term "Mainstream" is suspect. The term can only be shorthand for work developed elsewhere, and taking its cultural and political bearings from outside Wales. Home Counties-itis is part of the general situation of the Anglo-Welsh. They are caught between a Welsh language culture that has been fairly hostile to them, and an English language culture that regards them as absurd deviations from the Home Counties norm. They are marginal to both; essential to neither. They are easily trivialised and ridiculed. As Dr. Dai Smith recently observed, there are large numbers of extremely talented writers in Wales, and yet because they write in English they are overlooked. If they had written in Welsh they would have been very quickly snapped up and absorbed into S4C. But as they write in English they are ignored.

But what kinds of plays are presented on the stage in Wales, and why is artistic success so elusive? One of the major problems is the lack of any historical development in indigenous theatrical forms. Writers are faced with the task of developing their own forms under very harsh economic restraints in conjunction with an indifferent theatre industry and with audiences who don't know what they are missing because they have been trained by TV and by established notions of British (London) theatre norms. The writer in Wales has no tradition, nothing out of which to develop, nothing to fight against and nothing to disagree with. The temptation is to opt for the already established patterns of British theatre, but they are not quite adequate to the different demands of the Welsh cultural situation, and in the absence of any serious thought about theatrical forms in a specifically Welsh environment the author all too frequently lapses into "The Welsh Play". Where this is not a rewrite of Dylan Thomas or Emlyn Williams, it follows the essentially amateur idea of a "local" play, or uses Wales as a stepping off point, a convenience, before moving on to themes which are more important/less parochial/less dangerous/great/international/etc. Using Wales in such a way is not too bad an idea if the the play then reflects on the life of Wales, and those reflections are made to work in and through ideas about Wales, but often Wales is the convenient location, the point of departure, the token gesture to interest theatre companies whose conscience pains them enough to feel a Welsh (but not too Welsh) play is called for once in a while. The varieties of tokenism are endless.

Since Wales is marginal to England, and theatre is marginal to Wales, and the playwright is marginal to Welsh theatre, it is clear that the business of being a playwright in Wales can be a very unrewarding experience. In order to get work in Wales it is often necessary to be a success outside Wales first. Material which would not titillate a Home Counties audience is simply not wanted. Even plays about Wales have to conform to a Home Counties image of Wales. As most (but not by any means all) writers in Wales do not find this an exciting prospect, they often find that they are seriously out of joint with their potential employers. When it comes to theatre traffic over the Severn Bridge, then it is all too often "One Way Only".

The general effect of Home Counties-itis is to be felt throughout the Welsh theatre industry. There is a horror that Wales should be seen as in any way dissident. The theatres are anxious not to offend or disturb. The suppresion of Howard Brenton's *The Romans in Britain* by Swansea Councillors and the Dylan Thomas Memorial Theatre was only one of the more visible aspects of this mentality. Ironically, Brenton had challenged and beaten the narrow-mindedness of his Home Counties London audience, only to be defeated by the entrenched narrow-mindedness of his Swansea audience. Open Cast Theatre had problems in the late 70s, Action PIE has had problems recently, and there have even been cries of censorship from the Welsh language Eisteddfod. The general effect is to create a theatre of the barely engaged, where the bland lead the bland. If theatre is to accurately reflect life in Wales, and if it is to reflect on the nature of life in Wales, then it is inevitable that it will come into conflict with WAC and with other bodies in authority, and will challenge many of the assumptions and principles, both moral and political, by which Wales is run. If theatre is doing its job, then some conflict is inevitable. So far conflict, and hence accuracy of observation and portrayal by the theatres themselves, has been minimal. The WAC is an organ of state, and we must remember that. It funds theatre, and nourishes ideas, that are helpful to the state. It does not willingly finance dissidence, so its influence is rather like that of financial genetic engineering. The possibility of a Welsh company losing its grant because of its politicality is still quite a way off.

The second effect, The Audience Effect, is sometimes called "No Welsh Theatre Please, We're British". Of course the Theatres themselves are not entirely to blame for their attitudes to new writing. Theatre is a social art, and it depends on its audience. Theatres respond to audience demand, as much as audiences respond to theatre output.

The enormous social and political and industrial changes that have swept over Wales in the last ten or fifteen years have changed the face of South Wales - the area where the bulk of potential theatre audiences reside. The growth of the public sector and the attendant growth of the Cardiff-based Civil Service, the growth of Sunrise industries, the death of the coal and steel industries and the sudden growth of S4C have all substantially shifted the political and social thinking of South Wales. And this has been reflected in the votes cast at the last two General Elections, and at the Referendum of March 1st 1979. In Professor Gwyn Williams' view Wales has voted decisively to ditch a specifically Welsh identity and assume a British one.

Certainly attitudes are polarising at quite a rate. The election of a Welshman to the leadership of the Labour Party has served to emphasize how limited that party's understanding and commitment to Wales is now, and probably always has been. The Communist Party, always small in Wales, but highly influential in the thinking of certain sectors of the NUM, is being forced to reconsider its base in Wales. Plaid Cymru has substantially altered its stance with regard to both socialism and the Anglo-Welsh. The growth of theatre audiences on a large scale has coincided with the growth of the SDP-Liberal Alliance, the swing to the Conservatives and the long drawn out stage death of Labour in Wales.

Surely these things are not unrelated. The growth of theatre audiences over the last decade is part of the upwardly mobile, white collar, increasingly Anglicised surge that first started as Henry Tudor's knights filtered off Bosworth Field and onto the roads to London. As in most colonial situations the act of prodding around in the collective memory (or collective amnesia) is a dangerous business. When it is done on stage audiences can, and do, vote with their feet. And yet the fact remains that Variations on these basic themes can be seen in the output of new plays over the past four to five years. Ken Jago's play *A Touch of the Sun* produced by The

Torch Theatre, was advertised as a "harmless farce". It was in fact a damaging misrepresentation of Wales and Welsh politics. It dealt with a decaying aristocratic household in West Wales and the sequence of events unleashed when a red dragon hatches from an egg in the basement and procceds to set fire to second homes with more efficiency than the local nationalists can manage. The play doubtless appealed to the very English audiences around Milford Haven, but in terms of its relation to harmony and understanding within a bilingual community it was not a success. Nor was it a success in dramatic terms. One could have wished for rather more sensitivity on the part of The Torch Theatre, who toured the piece through South Wales. The production was part of the Festival of Welsh Castles, which gives a fair indication of the sensibilities of those involved.

Alan Vaughan Williams' *Matchplay* produced by Theatre Wales, was exactly the kind of play that had been rejected from the Welsh Academy's Play for Wales play writing competition in 1981 as being "all about artists returning to Wales – awful". The theme was the well worn and predictable contrast between the cold wealth of English entrepreneurs and the soulful Celtic poverty and passion of the Welsh. The possibility that it was not so much what the English had done to Wales out of malice, but rather what the Welsh had done to themselves out of indifference did not arise. Nor did the possibility that much of the damage to Welsh cultural life arises not out of the power of English money, but out of a thoroughly understandable desire to lay hands on that money (see Byng 1787) come in for much exploration. It was an attempt at a Welsh-play-for-all-time. It was a play which simplified matters to a national and dramatic convenience.

Theatre Wales' other new play, *The Blood That Sings* by Roger Stennett was so poorly constructed and possessed of dialogue so wooden that it must have been apparent to all concerned at a very early stage that the piece was not ready for production. The play deals with a group of Welshmen returning from the fighting in the closing days of the Spanish Civil War. In so far as the conflicts of that war are still relevant to Wales, and that the conflicts that sent the Welshmen from Wales to fight in the first place are still largely unresolved, the play had enormous scope and potential. Yet it collapsed almost immediately because the writer had no clear idea of what Wales meant to his characters, or why such a thing should be of interest to his audience. Instead of spiralling and complicated personal and political difference revealed through the collapse of the

Republican cause, we were presented with six monologues, and once again we were back with the damaging and limited sentimental vision of the exile.

For the Welsh writer Wales is often a selling point, a bargaining chip. The notion of Wales and the idea of a Welsh writer are more important than the actual execution of a particular project, and all too often those seeking some real connection have willed themselves to believe that a play is better than it really is. In all the cases mentioned above this seems to have happened. There are other examples. Dick Edwards' *Canned Goods* purported to explore the conjunction of Poland and Wales in the period just after the Solidarity era. The play itself was reasonably funny and had a number of interesting plot twists, but the interest in Wales or Poland was a mere dramatic convenience for the story since the play had nothing much to say about either. Made in Wales seems to have peculiar difficulties in this area since they made a very similar mistake with Sîon Eirian's *City*. In both these plays Wales is a token presence, there is no real engagement with Wales as a place. In *City* the subject was local corruption seen through the boardroom machinations of a local football club. It could have been set anywhere, and I suspect that the location was left vague for ease of adaptation to TV, where audiences would expect an English setting.

The search for suitable form and for suitable subject matter in theatre goes hand and hand with the search for political and cultural forms. Politics and theatre are two aspects of the same personal and general involvement. The success of the theatrical form depends on the honesty, the integrity and the depth of the playwrights' understanding of and engagement with their own culture. How can it be otherwise? There is one subject which is crucial to the development of theatre in Wales and to the individual talents of the writers who should form the backbone of that theatre. The subject is so deep in the psyche that there is as yet only a vague perception of it in the theatre industry. The subject is the relation of Wales to England and to the British state. Only from the full and merciless confrontation with this, and the attendant examination of Welsh history, can theatre in Wales generate matter suitable for a Welsh theatre and devise the forms to convey it. This subject underlies all others; it is the one constant factor in the whole range of Welsh life and new work that does not deal with it in one way or another is consigning itself automatically to the margins of both English and Welsh theatre. In the end, the only way to avoid the subject is by remaining silent – and that is something that theatre in Wales has done very nicely by instinct.

Failure to come to terms with this central issue lies at the heart of the disappointing development of Made in Wales over the last four years. The company is still young, it is also severely restricted financially, and it is still learning about itself as an entity. Yet it must be said that so far the work it has produced has had a predictability that goes beyond establishing a House Style. The plays presented so far have been "safe" both politically and theatrically. Almost a third of its work has been on adapatations of classics or novels; it has chosen to work with established playwrights, writers of note, or writers that it knows and trusts, so there has been little sense of challenge beyond the *idea* of new work. Also the company has slowly begun to appreciate that it is not producing the work it feels it should, nor is it generating the work it needs through the workshops, readings, script services and classes. The ancillary services of the company operate as a machine for telling writers that they are not good enough to be commissioned, while the company gets on with commissioning work from writers who by-pass this part of the company's activity by virtue of their experience. Those plays which the company has chosen to commission display remarkable similarity in their a-politicality, the "literary merit" of the texts, their linear plotting, their TV-Naturalist style of presentation, and in their uneasy relation to this thing called Wales which has somehow to be satisfied. So far, only Sîon Eirian's *Crash Course* and Nigel Jenkins' *Strike A Light* have been uncompromising in their relation to Welsh political life. This "sameness" indicates an uncertainty that can only be resolved by a much firmer grasp of the company's function within the Welsh theatre industry, and by a much more rugged appreciation of the relation of theatre to the political and cultural life of Wales on the part of the company's directors.

The third of these effects, The Experience Effect, is sometimes called "Daisy Pulls It Off (Again!)". In the past couple of years, Theatre Clwyd, The Torch, Masquerade, Action PIE and Theatre Powys have all employed writers from outside Wales, in preference to the writers available here. I have no wish to impugn the talent or the integrity of the writers involved, but it must be said that every time a writer from outside Wales is employed, the talent, the energy and the experience of local playwrights suffers a severe blow. At best we are talking of perhaps one or two Writers in Residence per year, and maybe six or eight possible commissions as the sum total of professional opportunities for live theatre writing in Wales. And there is no shortage of playwrights in Wales either. *The Playwrights' Register* lists over one hundred and twenty, and it is still far from complete. Eight commissioned plays between one hundred and twenty writers is not a good average. Given the limited opportunity the importation of talent has a devasting effect on local development in that it denies legitimacy, denies valuable experience, and generally degrades the cultural life of Wales. This situation is reflected in other areas too. Much has been said and written about the position of the Anglo-Welsh in relation to poetry and the novel and short story. In TV a similar situation prevails, where Welsh audiences find it easier to watch an English "soap" than they do to identify with the characters in, say, *Taff's Acre*.

There is a general refusal to engage with the idea of Wales, and this extends to the employment of writers. It is surely no accident that Theatre Wales – the company which in its own opinion was the most likely contender for the accolade of National Theatre – existed on a diet of English and foreign plays, with only two very poor productions of new plays. One of the Board of Directors was once heard to remark that for this company to stage new plays was rather like putting a Mini in a Rolls Royce showroom. The company saw its work in creating a National Theatre as lying solely in attracting a large audience for a cast of stars. Their idea of theatre was of an actor's theatre, and at an early press conference a leading company member treated assembled journalists to a discourse on the parallels between Theatre Wales and The Abbey Theatre, where he said, the Fay Brothers Acting Company had come down to Dublin from the north and had got Yeats to write them a play. It was an interesting, wilful, wishful re-write of The Abbey Theatre's history. Yeats and Edward Martyn had in fact begged money from Lady Gregory, had hired The Ancient Concert Rooms, and because there was no company of actors of a high enough calibre available in Ireland had imported a company from England. Theatre Wales would have done well to study the Abbey closely as a corrective to their own narrow focus and their even narrower understanding of the function and formation of a national theatre.

The Anglo-Welsh writers, but particularly the playwrights, are at the mercy of prevailing middle-class taste, fashion, ambition, language and politics. The mental map of the dominant culture is probably the toughest nut the playwright in Wales has to crack. Let me give two examples of the thinking that this mental map engenders and its effect on the playwright. The first is a comment from a North Wales theatre director, explaining why he was not very interested in new writing: "Welsh writers?... No... It is not possible. They are too parochial. Too dangerous". Parochial *and* dangerous? Only in Wales could that combination be fatal. The second comment was made by a writer who after several years of trying to get a production was seriously thinking of giving up the theatre altogether: "They won't do my plays. You see, they think I'm too mad or too Welsh". Again, only in Wales could there be such a conjunction.

These three effects combine upon the Anglo-Welsh playwright with uncommon complication. But for the full magnificence of the result it is to Dylan Thomas' masterpiece *Under Milk Wood* that we must turn. For all its comic brilliance and poetic charm the play presents a Wales peopled by barmy eccentrics, loonies and no-good boyos. For many people the play has become the real Wales, and that is a tribute to the power of Thomas' imagination, his perception and his writing skill. Just as the real Africa lay in the novels of Sir Rider Haggard, after which Africa itself was a disappointment, so the real Wales is different from the Wales of Thomas' creation. The play is acceptable to the centralist British culture because it is seen to be safe, remote, poetic, alien but utterly charming. Wales is seen as quaint but harmless. I'm certain that it was not always so. When the play was first produced the BBC in Wales refused to broadcast it, saying that it was too lewd and lascivious for Welsh ears. And that also is testimony to its power.

Under Milk Wood is *the* most popular Welsh play. And yet it is not a stage play at all. It is a radio play. Things have changed since Dylan Thomas wrote the play, and yet it remains with us on stage, its static and untheatrical qualities notwithstanding. As there is no theatrical context to set the play against, no environment which might serve as a corrective, or offer other ways of looking at Wales, other avenues of theatrical exploration, this play stands now as a powerful piece of damaging and limiting propaganda for a centralist attitude to Wales, and it invites and enjoys the complicity of audiences, actors, directors and writers throughout Wales.

How fair would it be if we were to judge Irish theatre and culture, if the only play to have emerged from that country was *The Playboy Of The Western World*? Synge's play is one among many fine plays. Thomas' play stands almost alone, and in the absence of a rapidly developing writing tradition it has become *the* Welsh play to which all others must be compared. It has been hijacked with ease and the elements of parody intended by Dylan have become a ludicrous travesty. Worst of all, in the autumn of 1984 the New Vic Company, with a London based all-Welsh cast under the direction of the exiled Welsh director Michael Bogdanov, attempted to import a production of the play that included a barefoot cast, clowning and looning unrelated to the text, an interpolated song and male voice choirs on tape. It was a production that put sentimental twaddle on the stage and which reinforced the damaging limitation of possibilities for playwrights at a time when they were desperately seeking to extend the horizons of the theatre companies and go beyond this kind of thinking. One might add that Emlyn Williams' *The Corn is Green* has been subject to the same pressure, and that this kind of attitude has surfaced in Bill Ingram's adaptation of Gogol's *The Government Inspector* produced by Made in Wales. In the original version the satire on corruption was so pointed that Gogol spent the next twelve years in voluntary exile rather than face the wrath of the Czar. In this version, in spite of the fact that South Wales has seen some very interesting and far reaching examples of corruption in local government, the savagery and accuracy of Gogol's satire was replaced by a gallery of lovable rogues, not so very different from those of *Under Milk Wood*. Not only that but the power of the "here and now" was abandoned when the adaptation was set in the vague era of "by-gone days". Gogol would never have approved.

The tendency to sentimentalise the odd characters is a common one in Wales. It hovers in the work of Frank Vickery, and it is a powerful force in the works of Alan Osborne. In both *Bull, Rock and Nut* and in *In Sunshine and in Shadow* we are presented with a gallery of nutters, freaks and alcoholics whose sense of their individuality is seriously out of joint with that of those around them. There is very little of what is usually thought of as plot in these plays, and clearly it is the warped "individuality" of these damaged minds that we are being invited to admire and sympathise with. It is not just the oddity of their character that is glorified. We are invited to mourn the passing of Merthyr, the town that created these peculiar characters. Public reaction to these plays has been very favourable indeed. This may mean that Alan Osborne has found a suitable vehicle for his explorations, which just shows that the borderline between accuracy of observation and easy sentiment is a particularly difficult one to pin down with any degree of certainty.

The mentality that fosters a limiting and sentimental attitude to Wales and to the potential of Welsh theatre is not so very different from the mentality that produced the stage Irishman – all tugging forelock and "Top o' the morning to ye", or the negro mammie of American films, all rolling eyes and slices of "Wahdy Melon". It is about as adequate as that, but unfortunately it is an image of Wales that sentimental exiles, retiring civil servants and the dispossessed Anglo-Welsh all seem to agree on, and it takes its place with the other debris of national identity. This is a phenomenon which is well known in political history and in sociology. It was the basis of Joyce's story *The Dead*, and of Franz Fanon's *Black Skins, White Masks*; it is a constant theme of Eastern European literature and it was a theme that Antonio Gramsci returned to again and again: "What is the meaning of the fact that the Italian people prefer to read foreign writers? It means that they undergo the moral and intellectual hegemony of foreign intellectuals, that they feel more closely related to foreign intellectuals than to 'domestic' ones, that there is no national intellectual and moral bloc, either hierarchical or, still less, egalitarian" (*The Concept of 'National Popular'*). In Fanon's terms this results in schizophrenia, both cultural and personal. Certainly, if the Anglo-Welsh who pander to this vision of Wales were black we would have little hesitation in labelling this "Uncle Tomism". But since they are not black perhaps it is best if we simply call it Dylan Thomasism, with apologies to the poet.

Much of what has passed across the stage in Wales in the last few years has been frankly irrelevant to the lives of the people who live here – though of course a great deal more relevant to their ambitions. At worst it has been a parade of West End copies, examination texts and amnesiac froth. One thing is certain: theatre in the next fifteen years will be quite different from the theatre of the last fifteen years. Political and economic change are set to test the integrity of the theatre, its writers and its directors.

In some ways the process has already begun. In 1984 the WAC's proposals united companies of all kinds, both English and Welsh language, in a storm of protest and demonstration – even five years ago it would have been hard to imagine such commonality and direction. WAPA, TWU and Equity are stronger, better organized and better informed about their business in Wales than they have ever been, and that brings with it a level of political understanding that WAC and the managements have not yet had to contend with. There are already rumblings of disappointment at the apolitical and rather unadventurous approach of Made in Wales. Kim Howells, the Research Officer of the South Wales NUM, has soundly berated the writers of Wales for their failure to engage with the issues of the Miners' Strike. In Welsh Cwmni Theatr Cymru is bankrupt for the second time in five years, and the small scale companies are expressing concern at the effects that the plush ghetto of S4C is having on their audiences. At a conference hosted by Brith Goff in September 1985 the question was openly asked: "Why is it that Poland can produce such spirited, engaged and inventive work, while Wales cannot?" And in its "keynote" opening production of *The Winter's Tale* the new Sherman Theatre Company has grasped the milk-cow firmly by the udders and gone for decadence of style and content.

It is clear that Welsh theatre is in a transitional phase, and it is highly likely that the changes will make it a very politically aware business in future. All concerned will be acutely aware of who they are playing to and why, and the obligations of theatre, especially a national theatre, will become increasingly obvious. And this is devoutly to be wished for, because this very basic level of thinking, understanding and debate has been missing from Wales and from theatre in Wales for so long. Now that the row about the allocation of the WAC's funding has died down a little, it should be possible to get down to the business of forging a Welsh theatre, rather than just performing theatre in Wales.

But what does the future hold in store? The present certainly holds clues. The Welsh theatre industry reflects the difficulties of making theatre in Wales not only in the subject matter that it does or does not prefer, but in the very structure of the industry itself. Wales has no writers company. It is significant that the "Capital City of Cardiff" should have to wait until 1985 to get its own resident main stage company at the Sherman. There is no overtly political theatre company, such as 7:84. There is very little in the way of serious theatre criticism. And it is also significant that twice within five years the WAC should find itself subject to the scrutiny of a House of Commons Committee. Perhaps the most interesting and most ignored fact about theatre in Wales is that it is not the main stage companies, the TIE, touring or community companies who have won international acclaim for their work, but rather the adventurous experimental companies. It is they who, in a country where audiences are divided on linguistic and geographical and social lines to an extraordinary degree, have found ways of exploring themes and narratives through the language of image, sign and gesture, frequently dispensing with "words" altogether. It is these companies who have responded most adequately to the totality of their environment, and perhaps they are the real "political" theatre of Wales.

There is more than one "perhaps" though. Perhaps we have been looking to theatre companies and writers to do the impossible in Wales. Perhaps theatre writing is not a viable concern under these conditions. Or perhaps we are the victims of that centralist education I mentioned earlier. Perhaps our traditional concept of a writer's place within a theatre is too wooden, too out of place here. Perhaps we need to forge an entirely new relationship. Perhaps our appreciation of writers in a national theatre is too close to the English model after all. It may be that as the Cardiff glitterati come to dominate the taste of companies like The Sherman and Made in Wales, and after them (but not very far behind) The Torch and Theatre Clwyd and Swansea Grand, the audiences will not be able to bear any great level of politicality. It may be that the touring theatres will remain too small or too marginal to take on major themes in new work with any hope of winning an audience. Either way, there is no reason why the experimental companies should not be persuaded into a closer relation with writers. Polish experimental theatre, which on some levels has had an important influence on theatre in Wales, has a profound, flexible and productive relationship with writers of all sorts. One has only to think of the subject matter of Grotowski's various experimental work, and of his relation to the Wroclaw Laboratorium's literary adviser, Ludwik Flaszen, to see the possibilities.

There are those who persist in seeing the possibility of a Welsh National Theatre company. Usually they see it as either a theatre without writers, or as a theatre modelled upon the Abbey. I cannot imagine a theatre without writers. Nor can I imagine an Abbey in Wales. Such a theatre as the Abbey cannot exist in Wales simply because the national feeling that created the Abbey does not exist here. Theatre is one of the ways in which a nation is responsible for itself, its history and its future. It may be that Wales already has the theatre it deserves.

I said at the start that there is a tunnel that connects the theatre in any nation with the national consciousness. In Wales the connection exists. Compromised and deeply schizophrenic, it exists...

ROD JONES

Out of the Past:

Pictures in Theory and History

Out of the Past:
Pictures in Theory and History

One of the most important changes now taking place in the social sciences, based on the realisation that social insitutions cannot be examined in isolation from economic and political ones, is the growing recognition of the importance of communication, art and language in any consideration of social structures and processes. Up until quite recently the sociology of culture was a relatively neglected area within the general field of sociology. Within the prevailing economism cultural phenomena were regarded as marginal, or at least secondary and derived, social processes, always themselves epiphenomena of the underlying economic order. But now we can say without underplaying the theoretical problems, divisions and disputes which continue to inform the discipline, that cultural phenomena are seen to be firmly connected with the structural characteristics of society and that they play a much more active and determining role in social reproduction than they did hitherto within earlier approaches. Culture produced by the social structure, in turn, helps to maintain it. In the related area of the history of art, which has run a very different course from that of other histories, the picture is much less encouraging. There is some evidence to suggest a broadening of approaches even to the point of considering art in its socio-historical context and in relation to its political and economic mainspringing where previously it was isolated in some remote area of the superstructure within orthodox art history. But this change is less than widespread, being uneven and frequently resisted. What little work has been carried out on the visual arts in Wales is limited by the fact that it has largely failed to take account of these much-needed changes in method and approach.[1]

If the visual arts in Wales are to be considered in other than the most superficially formalist terms then, within these new approaches, whatever can be said about any particular image or view of Wales, in terms of its capacity to project some ideal or representative view or even simply to reflect some individual aspect of its physical appearance or make-up, must ultimately concern the social totality and thus the relations of power which invest the image or view itself, motivate it, set it to work and give it currency. If power is coextensive with this social totality and everything comes within its reach then appearances too have to be considered from the point of view that they are always related to and informed by the broader functioning of power in society and heavily enmeshed within its networks, as relations of power are maintained and consolidated by the mobilisation of appearances. Some practices may be relatively autonomous when compared with others within the social super-structure but they are never out of reach of relations of power and consequently, in their functioning, always reproduce its effects.

In the profusion of its representations the overwhelming impression of modern Wales is one which is organized around that publicly instituted image of national consensus within a wider British orbit, that would-be democracy of the image projecting in numerous and familiar ensembles of faces, places, events, rituals and customs, a country at once industrial and rural, radically nationalistic and loyally British, ancient and high-tec. Like its English or British counterpart it extends from the glossier effusions emanating from institutions like the Wales Tourist Board and the Welsh Development Agency to colonise and recuperate, in a variety of discourses, acutely contradictory aspects within controversial areas of contemporary reality and experience as it similarly draws on a transformed, idealised and confirming past to constitute what Colin Mercer calls, "a self-confessed heterogeneity enveloped in a silent and persuasive voice which effectively says 'this is how it hangs together'".[2] Society and history are regulated and unified around visions of social diversity, evolution, living continuity, organic development and the progress of consciousness. But in relation to the functioning of power the reproduction of this "natural" order in the realm of the image is simultaneously the reproduction of the effects of dominance. "Wales" as a mode of address, a set of images, a discursive unity, is rule governed: a determinate ordering of social relations in the logic of dominance; a projection of unequal and mobile relations in the guise of a fundamental and unchanging unity. Like the classic realist text, it depends for its effectiveness upon a fundamental identification. The moment of ideological recognition – that this is indeed the way things are – occurs when the viewer accepts the position offered by the text. Dominance is secured in what, following Gramsci, may be called the active generation of consent. By concealing its basis in the economic and political power of the dominant group this consensus view legitimates itself as part of the dominant ideas of the dominant group and by so doing it not only reflects but reinforces this dominance. It is a component part of an arbitrary cultural scheme which is actually, though not in appearance, based upon power; it is generated by an arbitrary power whose interests it serves. It should be emphasized that the state apparatuses are not the unique instrument of power of one class over another. Legitimation is secured by means of direct domination in motions laid on from above by the state and also by means of consent by the governed through the institutions of the civil society. Hegemony is never entirely triumphant but always in a state of becoming. It is never guaranteed but has to be reproduced in political and cultural struggles at each new historical juncture. Consequently, the significance of these cultural struggles has always to be calculated in relation to their political efficacy.

At this point the questions crowd in. How is this particular version of Wales produced, regulated, distributed, circulated and operated and what are its effects? What are the positions and viewpoints of those whose interests it serves? What are the mechanisms, tactics and strategies of power which produce it and what are the effects of power which it intensifies and excites? What is the basis of its institutional support and what is the movement of its historical formation? How are alternative versions invalidated or subordinated in this process? What kind of challenge do these alternatives pose and in what circumstances could they be mobilised and raised to the point of overthrowing the dominant version? What form would resistance take in the realm of power? Clearly the field opened up here extends considerably beyond the possible scope of this present enquiry and consequently what follows is set to fairly limited objectives. The opening section takes up some of the issues already touched on in the introduction in a more general consideration, reflecting current thinking, of the theoretical issues raised by the agenda of questions above, especially in relation to dominant cultural forms and modes. The middle section considers some contemporary popular cultural forms and surveys a few historically significant points in relation to this initial discussion, and the third and concluding section considers some of the problems encountered in attempts to support and mobilise popular history and culture and working-class experience by independent cultural initiatives.

Central to the analysis of capitalist culture is the problem of values and ideology in the legitimation of capitalist domination. Culture plays a crucial role as a source of values (as opposed to knowledge) in the process of social reproduction. Since culture establishes itself as legitimate by masking the power relations which are its force, then the manner in which social relations are experienced in terms of available appearances, is misleading. These appearances can only be understood in the light of some theory – such as historical materialism, for example – which can lay hold of the underlying and actual relations and structures which give rise to them, which can explain the relationship between these appearances and the relations and structures they are appearances of. The question then raised concerns the relation of theory to history – between the inner coherence and consistency of the former and the latter as a profusion of fragmented occurrences. How are contingent historical events accomodated to the logic of theory? The precise form which culture takes is not theoretically predictable in the sense that it derives from static and theoretically consistent notions of social structures and domains such as those characterised in Frankfurt School and Marxist Structuralist thinking. Rather, its particular configuration is determined by the wider historical circumstances in which it is forged from its material basis in the mode of production, by the development of communication within this mode of production, by the particular nature of the institutions and associations which produced it and by the social institutions and associations which reproduce and mediate it. Most obviously, appearances are open to empirical observation as the effects of reality and as such they become objects of historical research. But at the same time they are also liable to explanation in theories which reveal the causal mechanisms between them and the underlying reality of which they are the effect. Theory, then, is indispensable to cultural history in the sense that it enables historical research in the domain of power.

From this point of view, in relation to the requirement of a theoretically informed approach, most of the existing studies of the visual arts in Wales emanating from national cultural institutions and agencies like the National Museum, National Library and Welsh Arts Council and indeed most of those produced outside Wales would have to be described as less than adequate. Empirically based, they lack the conceptual reach to move beyond available appearances. Instead, the visual arts are severed from their basis in production and transformed into some autonomous realm. Issues of class, domination and power rarely, if ever, figure. By analysing culture apart from its specific determinations in the social formation and in history, these studies project an idealist view of culture which eliminates the genetic approach to analysis – they beg, if not all, then certainly the most important questions. Given that these institutions were originally set up to establish a tradition of Welsh historical and cultural studies which would give support to the state and existing power relations, then it could be confidently predicted that institutions like the National Museum would continue to be underwritten by standards of "excellence" and notions of "quality" applied in the depoliticised, and thus neutral realm of a fully worked-out national culture. Skill and the aesthetic impulse combine to elevate art above the level of contingent needs – the privilege of art becomes a function of its lack of power. Within the class-related conventions and protocols of the academic fine art tradition "good" and "bad", the historically interesting and significant and the meretricious are easily identified and the cultural division of labour is secured. In this way a bourgeois version of culture is naturalised and generalised into a Welsh national culture as part of hegemonic practice.

A couple of recent studies on Welsh culture and nationalism have centred on narrow considerations of the changing nature of the nationalist movement in the nineteenth century and the nationalist party Plaid Cymru as the primary focus of nationalist activity after 1925, on the one hand in relation to its complex interactions with British state activities, which variously bring into play a range of issues from religion, national history and the Welsh language to the economy and the bureaucracy[3] and on the other in comparison with similar nationalist movements on the European periphery and elsewhere.[4] What opens up a quite distinct terrain and instigates a separate line of enquiry is the fact that nationalist issues are not likely to be exhausted by nationalist movements, however diverse they may be. Functioning even more generally and below the level at which the nationalist movement operates in terms of ideas, as it serves to transmit and circulate new values and concepts in an informal and diffuse manner through the wider society, is a broader, more sublimated, more mystifying and largely independent national-ism which always opposes structure as an implicated tactic in the reproduction of the relations of dominance. One of the most powerful articulations of this broader nationalism which is generalisable across a range of media and indicates a dazzling array of discourses and images, is constructed around what Foucault calls "the national history-geography".

In the following remarks I draw substantially on Michael Bommes' and Patrick Wright's description and analysis of the constitution and effects of what they take to be the dominant representations of the past in "National Heritage" and the "national past"[5] as they bear on the national history-geography. I draw this discussion out in the specific terms of the local Welsh experience and with particular regard to the representation of the Welsh landscape. "National Heritage" is a public articulation or staging of the past of immense extent, variety and ubiquity which appears to involve nothing less than the abolition of all contradiction in the name of a national culture. It functions both at the point of its individual sites and forms and in terms of how they configure togther. The former has to do with the production of consent and the eradication or transformation of other forms of organisation and the latter has to do with the way these forms are appropriated in everyday life as part of the collective will, democracy and participation, to create a shared social horizon which acts as a front of legitimation. In this sense "National Heritage" is a constituent part of the broader hegemony involving the individually negotiated components of culture and social experience and the impression of their unity: how "it all hangs together". As such it has to be analysed as a publicly instituted structuring of consciousness. Thus contemporary events are articulated within the public sphere and thematised in order to understand them in terms of national identity, culture, history and tradition. It is at the level of this public thematisation of events that the "nation" assumes considerable and increasing importance. The most fundamental element of the "nation" is the historically produced sense of the past. This "national past" is an accomplished presence: not just residue, precedence or custom but grounded in the active and concrete terms of "National Heritage", history and a tradition which is increasingly divorced from people's experience as it is generalised and diffused as a national identity. The diverse articulations of past and nationhood offer the serene and apparently natural unity of a "national" subjectivity to those who identify with them, they postulate a collective subject overriding contradictions.

Heritage has long been understood as a legacy of knowledge and culture essential for the continuity of civilization. But over the last two hundred years it has become increasingly identified with property rather than with knowledge and culture; with paintings and cultural artefacts and through these, as Raymond Williams has shown, with actual landscapes and views themselves. The vast enterprise which has grown up around this yoking of landscape and history began as far back as 1773 with the publication of Thomas Pennant's *Tours in Wales* which brought together all the interests of the period in Welsh history, topography, geology and literature. According to Andrew Wilton:

> The essential quality of the Welsh landscape, in its uncultivated grandeur, was its immediate evocation of history: it brought into startling juxtaposition *the present and the unaltered past* [my italics]...the vision of raw nature as a kind of basic antiquarian topography was an innovation of the 1790s.[6]

Since then, educational instruction in public institutions like schools where history and geography have had the task of implanting and inculcating the civic and patriotic spirit, to promote a belief in continuity and identity with the national past, and reverence for national heroes and the commemoration of great national events, together with popular and other forms of history writing, poetry, literature, folk-lore and legend, art photography, film and television have all evidenced the wealth of opportunities offered by the Welsh landscape for overdetermination and restaging as the national history-geography. In its most familiar modern form of presentation – fixed and framed in high-resolution, full-plate colour photography and installed in topographic, pastoral, picturesque or romantic guise – the landscape now reads like an historical pageant. Beyond their individual importance ancient sites such as cromlechs, tumuli and some of the more dilapidated of the ubiquitous castles of Wales sign-post the fact of the landscape's historical significance and content. As they are naturalised into the landscape and become coextensive with it so they have the effect of opening up a perspective in which the landscape itself becomes an extended record of the history with which it is saturated, an infinity of traces without an inventory, visible confirmation of a "national past" which is as unreadable in any rational sense as it is physically undeniable. In the accumulating terms of the photographic record the process cuts both ways – if the castle is made to look like some rocky outcrop or prominence then the prominence takes on the appearance of some ancient fortress.[7] At the heart of this monumental national geography are the mountains of Wales, symbolising a legitimate national impulse as the bastion of Welsh history, culture and identity – the unchanging and enduring hinterland of Welsh-speaking Wales, continuous with the remote past, a sign of difference as a point of vantage over the lowly and alien Midland plain and a wild and rugged, if stunningly beautiful, place where the fitful, unpredictable, dramatic and spectacular weather conditions form the basis of the national temperament and character. Welsh history becomes a matter of given environmental and meteorogical factors.

This tendency to concretise history and treat the past as a simple existent has its basis of support in nineteenth century historiography and in particular in the influential Rankean school of history and earlier in the work of Hegel.[8] As a positivist Ranke argued for a rigorous scientific approach to history. History, for Ranke, was like science to the extent that the events of history were liable to sustained and objective scrutiny in the concrete form of the document. In this view history reduces to the document – always anterior to the present in the sense of being given as an accomplished past but always existing in the present in the sedimented strata of recorded events. Even within the narrow terms of this pseudo-scientific definition, and on the basis of eliminating history as a problem except as one of recovery, it was perfectly possible to develop records and order antiquities so as to provide the basis for the systematic study of national institutions as one of the principal tasks of nineteenth century history. However, history differed from science in that the events of history, unlike those of science, were unique and unrepeatable. History could not explain its objects as science could explain the natural world on the basis of discovering laws which governed the relations between repeatable events. The event in history was considered as the site of the irrational, the unthinkable, that which cannot be analysed because it is in the realm of absolute contingency. Consequently, for Ranke, the historical event could only be understood intuitively by the individual historian in a way which was not accessible to public discussion. Later historians took on board the scientific aspect of Ranke's approach but argued to contextualise, and thus uncover, the regularities, connections and causes between events to enable explanation in knowable, and therefore publicly debatable, terms.

Within the public sphere, the articulation of the national history-geography has much in common with the Rankean approach to history. The national history-geography is defined and concretised as a succession of unique artefacts and understood only in the most limited and irrational sense of their "historical" aura and talismanic significance. In these circumstances history evaporates in social myth and since social myths, as Alan Singewood says, "are politically right-wing and reactionary and their social function is to conserve the structures of domination vested in the ruling class or bureaucratic stratum",[9] then reality is defined and authorised as a pre-given structure of social relations, objective laws and tendencies. For a number of reasons to do with anti-industrialism, Romanticism, the Gothic Revival and nineteenth century historicism in relation to the development of the British nation state, our origins in the distant recesses of pre-history are given a peculiar and disproportionate emphasis in the formation of our understanding of the past and the nation. As John Ingamells so aptly puts it, "We still ask of art the satisfaction of our surviving mystical feelings, and we may find this satisfaction best catered for by those functional works of art from the distant past."[10] Ideologically motivated accounts of the remote past, however indiscriminate they may be with regard to truth and falsity, legitimate the structures of dominance at the level of theoretical content – they enable us to make sense of the world in which we live and of our place within it and within history in such a way as to overlay practical concerns and contradictions at the level of everyday reality. If, as Gramsci says, ideology is an epistemological and structural matter, if it is material and ideal then we would have to say that the emphasis in the dominant understanding of our origins is placed on the latter as the basis of its effectiveness. In this burgeoning concern with origins an inconvenient intervening history is elided with the present as evidence of that mysterious past to which we all belong. Underneath social difference, in that vague if nonetheless powerful sense of our beginnings, is the distant figure of some tribal unity or ancient tryst, a special kind of pleading for an implicitly racist community of experience which always, ultimately, returns us to the assurances of blood and soil.

If landscape and history are combined in the terms of "National Heritage" and the "national past" as a national history-geography, then this combination is frequently fashioned and projected as an appeal to beauty, style and the aesthetic in the conventions of High Culture. Where even fifty years ago princes, kings, the odd saint and sundry other national military heroes were pressed into service on the side of this national history-geography, now, in a more cultural vein, artists, writers and poets (it goes without saying that all of them would be men as far as Wales is concerned) are similarly

commandeered and valorised in the same cause. One of Wynford
Vaughan Thomas' numerous books on Wales illustrates the point.[11]
In terms of organisation and content it is clearly designed with the
purpose of promoting tourism in Wales; the opening and closing
chapters entitled 'Welcome to Wales' and 'We'll Keep a Welcome',
respectively, signify the tourist visit that the rest of the book
simulates. Apart from the usual interlocking of historical and
landscape themes expressed in the terms of a familiar rhetoric as a
mystic evocation of the Celtic Twilight – 'Land of the Setting Sun',
'The Island Spell', 'Castles, Princes and Kings' and 'Cromlechs and
Chapels' – we are also given 'Dylan's Wales' and 'Kilvert's Country'.
Now "the heron-priested shore" captions a suitably rhapsodic view
of the Laugharne Estuary. In the intensifying terms of the cultural
hype everyday reality becomes a source of creative inspiration and,
by *fiat*, the creation itself; the landscape of the creative imagination
concretised, remorselessly re-invoked in a welter of cultural
resonances and safely ghettoised in the separated regions of a
national culture for the literary pilgrim.

Popular literature on Wales is often constructed around this
combination of art and the tourist visit. A number of regional cultural
guides, for example, are arranged in terms of an inventory of places
associated with the artists who either lived or worked there, rather
than chronologically or according to individual artists, as is more
usual.[12] Facilitated by a map indicating the main routes between the
individual sites, they probably quite intentionally take on the
appearance of the gentleman/artists tour which became popular in
Wales in the last quarter of the eighteenth century. And they have
the same effect, displacing the region to the aesthetic and reducing
history to an act of discovery. Even more striking in this respect is
the Powys Sculpture Trail which is being initiated in Llandrindod
Wells, "by far the most important spa town in Wales". Under the
auspices of the Welsh Sculpture Trust, the Welsh Arts Council and
Powys County Council, and with material provided by local
companies, the trail will, "combine outdoor pursuits with discovering
modern sculpture" in "the landscape of writers" in a stupefying
demonstration of cultural overdetermination which brings together
tourism, business interests, culture and history.

In order to indicate the "timelessness" of the Welsh landscape and
acquire some cultural gloss along the way, comparisons are often
invited between the modern photographic view and earlier
representations.[13] Notable among the artists who are most

frequently invoked for these purposes is Richard Wilson – the first, and probably the only, "great" Welsh painter according to established cultural values, and the only Welsh painter to achieve international recognition as the father of British landscape painting (the fact that Geoffrey Grigson refers to Wilson as "an Anglo-Welshman" is perhaps an indication of his secure position in the pantheon of great British artists). In his attempt to assess the accuracy of Wilson's *Cader Idris Llyn-y-Cau* c.1765, Grigson effects a familiar conflation of art and landscape.[14] Both painting and landscape are approached in the equally familiar terms of the tourist visit but now appropriately expressed in the quasi-religious and reverential terms of a responsiblity to be carried out. Thus,

> There are duties I should like to perform – if only there were life enough and time... Whenever I have driven in sight of the blue summit of Cader Idris, I have thought of Wilson – guiltily because I was always on the way to other mountains and loftier ones around Snowdon. One day, I have always thought, up Cader Idris I must go, if only for Wilson's sake...[15]

In view of the fact that, as Grigson argues, "particular country does have its particular effect upon artists", presumably as a source of inspiration, then, inevitably, the landscape is caught and reflected in the eye of the artist. Thus,

> Welsh valleys, Welsh rivers, Welsh tints sparkled certainly to Richard Wilson's eye. Blue mountains – Welsh and not Italian mountains – serenely straddle more than one of Wilson's major landscapes.[16]

The landscape, then, is taken over, grasped in the creative act, possessively expressed in terms of ownership and consequently nationalised as part of a common heritage which is indiscriminately "ours". Thus,

> If one mountain in his native country really belongs to Wilson, if one Welsh mountain really owes a great deal of its celebrity to Richard Wilson, it is Cader Idris, on account of that picture, which is his masterpiece, in my opinion.[17]

Any attempt to develop an alternative historical account of Wilson's picture would have to confront the relations of power which always already traverse the terrain of historical discourse in its articulations with the national history-geography as part of the general politics of truth. It is not a matter of establishing some "true" account existing in a privileged domain and independent of those relations of power which invest the dominant versions of the past to which Grigson's and most other accounts are habitually recuperated. Nor is it a matter of installing some additional alternative version to put alongside all existing versions in a benign pluralism based on some conventionalist theory of knowledge. Historical truth is linked in a circular relation with the systems of power which produces and sustains it and to the effects of power which it induces and which extend it. The problem with academic work is always to do with the possibility of an historical truth which could have political effect; with the possibility of a discourse which is both true and strategically effective. Just as Grigson's account serves to support bourgeois relations of dominance through the national history-geography, so any true historical account of Wilson's picture would need to have political meaning, utility and effectiveness as part of a broader academic project being worked out in relation to the contemporary political agenda and in relation to contemporary issues, struggles and experience. In extending and modifying the work of David Solkin this next section sketches out in what can only be very summary fashion some of the political and other factors surrounding the production and early functioning of Wilson's picture, opening up a number of possible lines of enquiry which would need to be followed up in more sustained and detailed historical study.

Wilson's current reputation as an artist, and even the integrity of his work, rests on the considerable influence that he exercised on artists like Girtin, Turner and Constable in pointing the way and providing the basis for the development of realist painting in the nineteenth century. As early as 1781 Thomas Pennant described Wilson's *Snowdon from Llyn Nantlle* as "a view as magnificent as it is faithful"[18] which the modern commentator reiterates in a demonstration of the remarkable continuity of appeal as, "an honest account of the appearance of the actual place".[19] Constable appreciated the observation in Wilson's painting and he described Wilson as "one of those appointed to show the hidden stories and beauties of nature".[20] Wilson's appeal lay in his combination of scientific investigation and deep poetic sensibility. While Ruskin, in a more moral vein, believed that, "with the name of Richard Wilson, the history of sincere landscape art founded on meditative love of nature begins in England".[21] Wilson's "historical" significance, then, is constructed around this complex web of essential continuities, interconnections, reinforcing influences and transformations which is at the centre of the history of art as the history of styles. Working in the opposite direction and synchronically, John Barrell suggests that the increasing demand for realism in English painting after 1750, to which Wilson himself was responding, was a consequence of the growth of the mobile power of money, the coming together of landed and monied interests and of the breaking down of the hierarchical coherence of the paternalistic society by a new economic individualism.[22] Broadly, classicism came to represent the conservative values of the older patrician class in its projection of unchanging universal laws, order, continuity, stability and harmony, as against the idea of change and development and even discord associated with those who favoured realism in the visual arts. In the 1760s Wilson began to tone down the Italianate flavour of his British landscapes in accordance with the requirement to produce more credible representations while at the same time retaining something of the classical idealisation and order demanded by his politically conservative patrons. In his painting of Cader Idris Wilson's ability to effect a compromise between the desire to impose a "measurable and secure order" on the landscape, to "subject irregular nature to strict classical control" on the one hand and yet produce a plausible topographical account on the other, is stretched to the limit. Solkin suggests that the evident difficulties Wilson had with the figures suggests hostility between natural form and pictorial structure. Yet, Solkin argues, by using the conventional devices of landscape art, Wilson succeeds in producing a universal ideal of order and stability. We look out over the prospect from a position outside and above the scene and consequently we are not threatened or dominated – "nature submits to our command".[23] He goes on to suggest that such views of Wales by Wilson and by others "as a paradise of primitive simplicity" and particularly as "an embodiment of modern liberty" acquired a particular resonance in the turbulent years of the 1760s because they projected an acceptable form of "liberty without licentiousness" in marked contrast to the potentially disruptive liberty being demanded by John Wilkes and his urban middle-class supporters in their striving for political power.[24] But more than this, they provided reassuring evidence of tranquillity and the absence of rural discontent where elsewhere there was widespread unrest as a result of the disturbances caused by the aftermath of the Seven Years War and the succession of bad harvests in the middle years of the decade when, briefly, the country replaced the town as the greatest threat to social order.[25]

Rather than pursue the intriguing line of argument opened up by Solkin I want to suggest that a number of other issues need to be taken into account which relate to rather broader tendencies in eighteenth century society. When Wilson painted the first of several versions of *Cader Idris Llyn-y-Cau* sometime between 1765 and 1768, Great Britain had been in the process of unifying around both merchant, and later industrial capitalism, imperialism, naval power, a modernised agriculture and liberal oligarchy for the best part of fifty years.[26] The conflicts of the seventeenth century had given rise to a powerful civil society and an oligarchical Parliament, which, after disarming the provinces and limiting the franchise, were able, according to Gwyn Williams, "to ride commercial and agrarian growth into an extraordinarily relaxed and informal system of government"[27] based on property laws, a web of libertarian traditions and notions of the Freeborn Englishman. Wales was not unaffected by this process and frequently instrumental in bringing about change. Williams tells us that the Glamorgan gentry, for example, were totally dedicated to modernisation: developing copper, coal, iron and textile industries which, typically, brought them into contact with monied groups among the middle orders. And in connection with these enterprises they supported a massive rebuilding programme, introduced new concepts of property, law and order and even devised a new model prison. On the basis of this commitment the "community achieved a comfortable political consensus from mid-century onwards" as an indication of the wider moment of consent in British society in the eighteenth century.[28] This process of modernisation was most marked in, but by no means confined to, Glamorgan and the South East. In Flintshire and Denbighshire agricultural modernisation had generated considerable disruption through widespread enclosure and given rise to massive estates like that of Sir Watkin Williams-Wynn who was one of Wilson's patrons. Add to this the gradual transformation of the rural communities in Mid and North Wales which had been taking place since Tudor times with the introduction of wool manufacturing, "creating pockets of modernisation and reservoirs of technical skills",[29] and the development of copper mining in Anglesey, and we move some distance away from the usual picture of a backward and isolated region based on subsistence farming.

Under the impact of economic change and modernisation, and as the industrial enterprise began to open up the regions of Britain, there developed a need for a new technology of power which was capable of an individualising, exhaustive analysis of the social body so as to ensure the development of productive forces characteristic of capitalism. By being exercised over consolidated social groups or imposed by means of infrequent, spectacular, exemplary and very costly military and penal interventions, the system of power before the eighteenth century had little hold on detail and was progressively replaced by a system based on surveillance with no need of arms, physical violence or material constraints, which could ensure the circulation of the effects of power through progressively finer channels of the civil society, gaining access to individuals themselves, to their bodies, their gestures and their daily actions. Power is instituted in "the gaze" and exercised by virtue of things being known and thus controlled. There are good reasons to suppose that the development of topographical landscape painting in the second half of the eighteenth century is intimately bound up with this trans-formation in the economy of power. During the seventeenth century topographical draughtsmen and estate cartographers were employed to produce accurate records of places of interest like houses, towns, agricultural and industrial enterprises and local customs. In the following century interest shifted to representations of uncultivated scenery largely in relation to the management of collective space by doctors and the military, but still in the interests of economic initiatives. Several water-colourists were employed by the military and since the military were chiefly concerned to think the spaces of campaigns and thus of passages and that of fortresses, it is hardly surprising that we see evidence of these concerns – roads, bridges and castles – in the work of military draughtsmen like Paul Sandby and others.[30] Moreover, there is growing evidence to suggest that the general upsurge of interest in landscape and fortifications in the visual arts after 1750 is often connected with and instigated by this same desire to control territories and organise domains.

From this point of view Wilson's attempt to reduce the scale of the topography of Cader Idris by exaggerating the size of the figures in accordance with the general fear of space and magnitude, the fact that "he does not give the sense of drop between himself and the lake",[31] the fact that Cader Idris is "coarser, less aerial and more intensely formidable",[32] the fact of his attempting to impose "a measurable and secure order" on this inaccessible and fearsome terrain, and most importantly, the obvious concern for accuracy in representation, are consistent with this same impulse to control. The landscape is mapped out, demarcated and distributed in the privileged and controlling gaze of the artist. The continuous exercise of power is instituted in a relentless process of surveillance which is doubly inscribed in the picture as an artist paints the scene and a man scans the cliffs of Craig Goch and distant Cardigan Bay through a telescope. The new status of the private individual which is usually posited in the growth of topographical realism as evidence of a more personal response to landscape, can now itself be seen as the product of a relation of power exercised over bodies and over populations. As the circuits of tourism opened up in North Wales in the 1760s and 1770s and followed the circuits of commodity exchange and profit, so the circuits of commodity exchange and profit combined with the circuits of power in an ingenious and self-amplifying system which has never since lost its hegemonic grip.

The development of mechanisms of power for the regulation of the growth and mobility of population as the objects of relations of dominance and as a principal resource of the capitalist industrial enterprise in the nineteenth century, opens up a perspective in which Romanticism, as a kind of cultural dialectic, could usefully be assessed. Whatever else Turner's sombre, brooding pictures of Wales were intended to evoke in the consciousness of British connoisseurs and exhibition visitors, they have to be understood as a kind of obverse of the visible and transparent society represented by Wilson. Like the imaginary spaces of the Gothic Novel which so influenced Turner, the dark spaces of his Welsh pictures symbolise the blockages and obstacles placed in the way of the exercise of power. The fear of dark spaces in the nineteenth century is simultaneously the fear of ignorance, superstition and privilege which they symbolise in the minds of those who subscribe to the reign of public opinion as the mode of operation through which power is exercised. Turner's work on Wales articulates a whole complex of meanings constructed around the project of Romanticism. A number of these meanings provided the basis of contestation and opposition to the dominant cultural and discursive forms of the nineteenth century originally applied to the consequences of the specifically capitalist forms of industrialisation on human beings. And it is to the actual and possible development of cultural initiatives as alternative to or in opposition to the hegemonic in present-day Wales in relation to some of the relevant broader issues of cultural politics that I briefly turn in this last section.

Given the specific determinations of visual culture in the social formation and its material basis in the mode of production as described above, and having come to some general understanding of the role of visual culture in the reproduction and legitimation of the relations of dominance, then any survey of contemporary art in Wales would have to be mounted from what would constitute an unorthodox angle of vision in order to take account of these relations and interactions. The concept of hegemony and the processes of domination and subordination, struggle, resistance and recuperation that it implies, provides a perspective in which contemporary art can be adequately assessed as it also furnishes criteria for possible future developments in the direction of a wider socialist project. Any such assessment would have to extend beyond considerations of individual artists and their work to engage with the constituencies of support, the whole institutional aspect of the visual arts – production, reproduction, distribution, display, training, administration and financing – in as much as they bear on and determine both what is produced and how it functions. All artists are confronted by the enormous recuperative power of this system which is deployed predominantly in the interests of the bourgeois hegemony. It may well be the case that there are many artists in Wales who wish to give genuine and committed expression to the values and aspirations associated with human freedom and dignity in their work which could be set against the alienated structure of people's needs and substitute satisfactions. But ultimately, in terms of its political efficacy within this system as part of the cultural struggle which reproduces the bourgeois hegemony, most of this work is worn down, commodified and transformed in the circuits of cultural exchange and display and it eventually serves to underwrite the world both ideologically and economically as it is given in the phenomenal forms of the political economy. Even avowedly political work, and especially committed documentary photography, of which a good deal is now produced in Wales, if it simply points to areas of concern among the underprivileged and dispossessed in some naively empirical and essentially regressive notion of documentary realism, if it engages with reality at the most superficial level of available appearances, if it never adequately addresses the structural inequalities and divisions both within the region and between the region and the wider British and European context, then it is always caught in the terms of an ideological proposition which isolates it and recuperates it to a reformist position to leave the global situation intact. Commitment is not in itself sufficient to prevent such work from serving to support the idea of cultural diversity, pluralism, democracy and participation on the front of bourgeois legitimation.

Even given the power of the system, both politically motivated and other artists and photographers must take some responsibility for this state of affairs. If left artists and photographers tend to work off social realities which have already been or are in the process of being transformed and eradicated, if their work gives only partial and contradictory expression to contemporary social reality, it is probably less to do with nostalgia for the now vanished solidarities of the past or loyalty to social and socialist realist cultural traditions than to do with their failure to come sufficiently to terms with the essential dynamism of the capitalist process itself, to interrogate the continual transformation of the production context necessitated by the dictates of capital accumulation and the social consequences of this. Put very simply, what was available and politically effective for photographers like James Jarche working in Wales in the 1930s or artists like Josef Herman in the 1940s is no longer an option for those artists and photographers working in the radically altered circumstances of today. As far as artists and photographers who are not themselves socialists are concerned, they may share with socialists an awareness of the poverty of desire and a concern for the quality of life in modern capitalist societies and even the need for human emancipation, freedom and spiritual happiness. But, unlike the socialists, they imagine that human freedom can be attained on an individual basis and in isolation from the social system that is, in fact, both the source of its conspicuous absence and its basis in the superseding of the existing state of things. From a Left standpoint, only in some radical socialist transformation of society, in some fundamental rupture of the historical process itself, is this emancipation possible when individuals become the full subjects of their own history and can undertake self-determined actions which alone can give human happiness. Here non-socialist and socialist aspirations intersect at the point where the commitment to radical discontinuity and change deriving from some general humanism is mapped out in the specific and unique terms of a particular cultural intervention at a particular historical juncture.

What then are the particular terms in which culture can be reorientated and mobilised in pursuit of these human needs and in the interests of the majority? What kinds of initiatives and interventions can be envisaged, and how would they be mounted? And what evidence for the development of such initiatives is there in the Welsh context? To take the last question first. Institutions and agencies of culture, even some of those funded directly by the state, are often sufficiently open and heterodox, sufficiently committed to a liberalist policy based on notions of cultural diversity, to allow for the limited provision of support for radical oppositional initiatives. Most interesting in this respect as far as Wales is concerned is the U-Print Workshop at the Chapter Arts Centre in Cardiff. Organised on a collective basis, the workshop is centrally concerned with issues of self-representation, as the name indicates. To this end it provides access to graphic media and skills which are developed in discussions, lectures and debates and directed in projects which often centre on local community issues. As a focus of support for photography in Wales, the recently formed ffotogallery in Cardiff has also initiated a number of projects on Welsh themes. The gallery's most ambitious undertaking to date is a three-year project to document the crisis-ridden valleys of South Wales. Using archive and community arts as well as professional material, and drawing on the support of historians, writers and poets, they hope to establish a material resource on the basis of this collaborative mode which will foster and instigate further study and debate. Like the projects being developed at U-Print and the ffotogallery the independent work of a number of artists and photographers, among them Ian Walker and John Podpadec, also give cause for some optimism. Walker's "alternative" photographic view of the Welsh castle, as a gentle and ironic debunking of the official representations produced in 'The Year of the Welsh Castle', demonstrates the importance of humour to politically effective work as it draws attention to the selective and synthesising processes which underlie and give rise to the official image. More than this, the series raises important questions about notions of the ordinary, about the ways in which ordinary people in their everyday lives are excluded or marginalised or otherwise misrecognised and misrepresented in the actual histories which are symbolised in this monumental imagery.

Walker's work returns us to the question which was raised earlier to do with the relation between power and resistance. At the outset we would have to say, almost as a matter of definition, that resistance is not in a position of exteriority with respect to power. It is not as if resistance comes from elsewhere in being exercised against power, but rather that it exists all the more by being in the same place as power. Given this relation between power and resistance then the struggles around popular history and popular culture, to repoliticise history, tradition and culture and reinvest knowledge with new relations of power in the interests of the majority, need to be addressed in local, regional, national and international terms and especially in relation to the forms and tactics of the national history-geography. To the extent that the world is already exhausted by relations of power, the development of a politically effective oppositional culture is not simply a matter of devolving, proliferating or diversifying the existing culture nor even of marking out and colonising some new areas of practice based on new principles; as Walker's work demonstrates it must be crucially concerned with the structures and mechanisms of domination and subordination. Some of the possibilities of a photography mounted on the terrain of a fully worked out socialist practice are posited in the work of John Podpadec. In a spectacular combination of high quality colour photography, intentionally reminiscent of modern advertising imagery, Podpadec's more recent work interrogates particular themes in Welsh history and politics in relation to their specific power relations and the struggles which surround them. In one series of photo-texts, for example, he relates the themes of land and labour exploitation during the industrial revolution in such a way as to provide the theoretical basis for the politicisation of popular memory in the context of local history workshops.   ·

With such forms of cooperation and interchange, individual points of resistance and local struggles, as a multiform of objectives, means and processes, can be built up and integrated into the figure of a global strategy. As culture itself is socialised, as it undergoes a fundamental transformation in its production and institutional deployment (a transformation, as Walter Benjamin recognised over fifty years ago, of what is recognisably artistic practice) so it integrates with, articulates and intensifies this broader strategy. Initially this would involve the democratisation and collectivisation of the relations of artistic production in ways which are suggested in germinal form by the current community arts programmes such as are being fostered by the South East Wales Arts Association and in the collectivised projects associated with the U-Print Workshop and ffotogallery. Following Paulo Freire's notion of cultural synthesis artists adopt a collaborative mode and work in collective authorship, thinking through projects collectively and collectively taking initiatives. Work produced in this way is argued to have greater impact and political effectiveness than that produced by individuals in relative isolation as it also provides a wealth of opportunities for reciprocal learning and teaching across class barriers and between workers and intellectuals. This process of restructuring along democratised and collectivised lines would need to be carried through, as Hans Magnus Enzensberger has argued, into the institutional spaces of culture within which cultural forms are published, distributed, used and seen. Implicitly hierarchical and divisive critical values would need to give way to concepts of quality conceived in terms of social utility and social action and a much wider agenda of issues than those usually associated with community schemes – bad housing, unemployment and lack of social services provision – would need to be engaged. By reaching out beyond the traditional boundaries of culture, the policies put forward by Freire and Enzensberger could be taken up into broader forms of consensualist action suggested by Habermas' theory of "communicative action", for example, – the development of practical discourse which is unconstrained and works towards mutual understanding, or Rudolf Bahro's reworking and generalising of the "historic compromise" of the Italian Communist Party which aims to transform the state machine and thus make it an instrument of rational administration that no longer operates as a mode of domination. Both the basis of support and the will to develop culture along these lines in relation to the existing state of affairs certainly exists in Wales. Those of us who are concerned with culture – with its history, theory and politics; those of us who believe that the cultural alternative very swiftly leads to political articulation in contemporary society, must, as Bahro says, organize our self-conception and our theoretical work more effectively and more cooperatively to this end.

NOTES

1.   The notable exception is David H. Solkin, *Richard Wilson. The Landscape of Reaction*, Tate Gallery, 1982.
2.   Colin Mercer, 'Generating Consent', *Ten 8*, No.14, p.4.
3.   Charlotte Aull Davies, 'Welsh Nationalism and the British State' in Glyn

Williams (ed.) *Crisis of Economy and Ideology: Essays on Welsh Society, 1840-1980*, B.S.A. Sociology of Wales Study Group, 1983, pp.201-214.

4. Phillip M. Rawkins, 'Uneven Development and the Politics of Culture' in Glyn Willaims, *ibid.*, pp.214-231.

5. Michael Bommes and Patrick Wright, '"Charms of residence": the public and the past' in Richard Johnson et. al. (eds.), *Making Histories, Studies in History Writing and Politics*, Centre for Contemporary Cultural Studies, Hutchinson, 1982, pp.253-303, and Patrick Wright, 'A Blue Plaque for the Labour Movement? Some Political Meanings of the "National Past"' in *Formations of Nation and People*, Routledge and Kegan Paul, 1984, pp.42-68.

6. Andrew Wilton, *Turner in Wales*, Mostyn Art Gallery, 1984, p.17. Wilton's uncritical acceptance of this idea is worth noting. Thus he describes Wales as, "a country whose landscape and history are inextricably fused in the eye and mind of the visitor". Wilton, *ibid.*, p.11.

7. See, for example, the photographs of Carreg Cennen castle and Worms Head, Gower in Wynford Vaughan Thomas, *Wales*, front cover and p.29.

8. See Georg G. Iggers, *New Directions in European Historiography*, Wesleyan University Press, 1975, *passim*. See also Michel Foucault, *The Archaeology of Knowledge*, Tavistock, 1972, p.7 ff.

9. Alan Swingewood, *The Myth of Mass Culture*, Macmillan, 1977, p.123.

10. John Ingamells, 'The Evolution of Art' in Eric Rowan (ed.), *Art in Wales. 2000 B.C. - A.D. 1850. An Illustrated History*, Welsh Arts Council, 1978, p.14.

11. Vaughan Thomas, *op. cit.*

12. Michael Jacobs and Malcom Warner, *Art in Wales*, Phaidon, 1980.

13. See, for example, Vaughan Thomas, *op.cit.*, pp.116-117.

14. Geoffrey Grigson, 'Cader Idris in Art and Actuality', *Country Life*, May 12, 1960, pp.1038-1040.

15. *ibid.* p.1038.

16. *ibid.*

17. *ibid.*

18. Jacobs and Warner, *op.cit.*, p.23.

19. *ibid.*

20. Quoted in William Vaughan, *Romantic Art*, Thames and Hudson, 1978, p.185.

21. Quoted in William Gaunt, *A Concise History of English Painting*, Thames and Hudson, 1970, p.88.

22. See John Barrell, *The Dark Side of the Landscape. The Rural Poor in English Painting 1730-1840*, Cambridge University Press, 1980, pp.1-35.

23. Solkin, *op.cit.*, p.97.

24. *ibid.*, p.100.

25. *ibid.*, p.102.

26. See Gwyn A. Williams, *When Was Wales?*, Penguin, 1985, p.142.

27. *ibid.*

28. *ibid.* p.148.

29. *ibid.* p.145.

30. Sandby was employed as a military draughtsman on an ordnance survey of the

Scottish Highlands, helping to build General Wades' roads for the Duke of Cumberland in the year following the Jacobite Rebellion in 1745. After this Sandby retained his associations with the military, becoming drawing master at the Ordnance Depot of the Tower of London and later drawing instructor at the Royal Military Academy in Woolwich. Wilson might well have been influenced by his friend Sandby's clear and precise style of drawing and his frequent use of vista and silhouette which were obviously suited to and reinforced by the needs of the military.

31.   Grigson, *op.cit.*, p.1040.
32.   *ibid.*

A Welsh Wordscape

Peter Finch

1

To live in Wales,

Is to be mumbled at
by re-incarnations of Dylan Thomas
in numerous diverse disguises.

Is to be mown down
by the same words
at least six times a week.

Is to be bored
by Welsh visionaries
with wild hair and grey suits.

Is to be told
of the incredible agony
of an exile
that can be at most
a day's travel away.

And the sheep, the sheep,
the bloody flea-bitten Welsh sheep,
chased over the same hills
by a thousand poetic phrases
all saying the same things.

To live in Wales
is to love sheep
and to be afraid
of dragons.

A history is being re-lived,
a lost heritage
is being wept after
with sad eyes and dry tears.

A heritage
that spoke beauty to the world
through dirty fingernails
and endless alcoholic mists.

A heritage
that screamed that once,
that exploded that one holy time
and connected Wales
with the whirlpool
of the universe.

A heritage
that ceased communication
upon a death, and nonetheless
tried to go on living.

A heritage
that is taking
a long time to learn
that yesterday cannot be today
and that the world
is fast becoming bored
with language forever
in the same tone of voice.

Look at the Welsh landscape,
look closely,
new voices must rise,
for Wales cannot endlessly remain
chasing sheep into the twilight.

Select Bibliography

Nationalism and Welsh History

Gellner, Ernest: *Nations and Nationalism*, Oxford, Basil Blackwell Ltd., 1983.
Hobsbawm & Ranger (eds.): *The Invention of Tradition*, Cambridge, CUP, 1981.
Humphreys, Emyr: *The Taliesin Tradition*, London, Black Raven Press, 1983.
Morgan, Kenneth O.: *Rebirth of a Nation: Wales 1880-1980*, Oxford, OUP, 1981.
Osmond, John (ed.): *The National Question Again*, Llandysul, Gomer, 1985.
Smith, Dai: *A People and a Proletariat: Essays in the History of Wales 1780-1980*, London, Pluto Press, 1980.
Smith, Dai: *Wales! Wales?*, London, Allen & Unwin, 1984.
Thomas, Ned: *The Welsh Extremist*, Talybont, Y Lolfa, 1973.
Williams, Glyn (ed.): *Social and Cultural Change in Contemporary Wales*, London, Routledge, 1978.
Williams, Gwyn A.: *When Was Wales?*, London, Black Raven Press, 1985.

The Arts

Adams & Hughes (eds.): *Triskel One* and *Triskel Two: Essays on Welsh and Anglo-Welsh Literature*, Llandybie, Christopher Davies Ltd., 1971, 1973.
Butler, Susan (ed.): *Common Ground: Poets in a Welsh Landscape*, Bridgend, Poetry Wales Press, 1985.
Conran, Anthony: *The Cost of Strangeness*, Llandysul, Gomer, 1982.
Garlick & Mathias: *Anglo-Welsh Poetry 1480-1980*, Bridgend, Poetry Wales Press, 1984.
Jones, Glyn: *The Dragon Has Two Tongues*, London, Dent, 1968.
Mathias, Roland: *A Ride Through the Wood: Essays on Anglo-Welsh Literature*, Bridgend, Poetry Wales Press, 1985.
Rowan, Eric: *Art in Wales*, Cardiff, UWP, 1985.
Stephens, Meic (ed.): *Artists in Wales*, Llandysul, Gomer, 1971, 1973, 1977 (in three volumes).
Stephens, Meic: *Linguistic Minorities in Western Europe*, Llandysul, Gomer, 1976.
Stephens, Meic (ed.): *The Arts in Wales 1950-1975*, Cardiff, Welsh Arts Council, 1979.

Stephens, Meic (ed.): *The Oxford Companion to the Literatures of Wales*, Oxford, OUP, 1986.

Solkin, David H.: *Richard Wilson: The Landscape of Reaction*, London, Tate Gallery, 1982.

Tighe, Carl: *The Playwright's Register*, Cardiff, The Welsh Academy, 1985.

The Media

The Annan Report on the Future of Broadcasting, London, HMSO, 1977.

Antonio Gramsci: *Selections from Prison Notebooks*, eds. Hoare & Smith, London, Lawrence & Wishart, 1978.

Second Report From the Committee on Welsh Affairs: Broadcasting in the Welsh Language and the Implications for Welsh and Non-Welsh Speaking Viewers and Listeners, vols. I and II, London, HMSO, 1981.

Stuart Hall: 'The Rediscovery of Ideology' in *Culture, Society and the Media*, ed. M. Gurevitch, London, Methuen, 1981.

Television and Radio 1981, London, IBA, 1980.

The Media in Wales – A Campaigning Handbook, Cardiff, Wales Campaign for Press and Broadcasting Freedom, 1985.

Index

Nationwide, 202;
Nine O'Clock News, 202, 211,
214, 219, 223; *Open Door*, 188;
Panorama, 202, 204.
B.B.C. Wales, 50, 113, 187, 189, 193,
194, 205, 206. Broadcasts *Don't
Break Your Heart*, 189;
Heddiw, 202, 205, 206; *Juice*,
189; *News of Wales*, 202; *Poems
and Pints*, 89, 105; *Taff's Acre*,
255; *Time and Place*, 189;
Wales Today, 202, 206, 215-17,
221, 223; *Week In Week Out*,
202.
Brown, Ceridwen, 237.
Browne, Stella, 232.
Burton, Richard, 99, 176.
Bwrdd Ffilmiau Cymraeg, 193.
Byng, John, 244, 252.

C

Cadwaladr the Blessed, 24, 26, 33.
Cavalcanti, Alberto, 167.
Channel Four U.K., 188, 191, 194.
Broadcasts *Brookside*, 187;
Wales: Landscape and Legend,
99.
Chaplin, Charlie, 162.
Chapter Arts Centre, 193, 281.
Chapter Film Workshop, 177, 191.
Chapter Video Workshop, 191.
Chariots of Fire, 183.
Charles II, 243.
Charles, Thomas, 35, 234.
Citadel, The (film), 169.
Clancy, Joseph P., 'S4C', 197.
*Twentieth Century Welsh
Poems*, 76.
Clarke, Gillian, 83, 106, 110-18. 'Blaen
Cwrt',91, 113-14; 'Chalk
Pebble', 112; 'Clywedog', 112;
'Fires on Llŷn', 114, 116-17;
'Harvest at Mynachlog', 115-16;

Letter from a Far Country, 115;
'Letter from a Far Country',
113; 'Miracle on St. David's
Day', 117-18; 'Ram', 112;
'Scything', 112; *Selected Poems*,
111; *Sundial, The*, 111;'Water
Diviner, The', 112; 'Welsh
Blacks', 112.
Cohn, Norman, *Pursuit of the
Millenium, The*, 23.
Communist Party, The, 123, 167, 251.
Conrad, Joseph, 134. *Victory*, 131.
Conran, Anthony, *Cost of Strangeness,
The*, 59, 73, 75, 89, 99.
Conservative Party, The, 206, 208,
209, 212, 213, 251.
Constable, John, 274.
Cook, A.J., 142.
Coombes, Bert, *These Poor Hands*,
135.
Cordell, Alexander, *Rape of the Fair
Country*, 137
Cox, Dora, 237.
Craigie, Jill, directs *Blue Scar*, 175.
Cronin, A.J., 169. *Citadel, The*, 169;
Stars Look Down, The, 170.
Culhwch and Olwen, 88.
Cullen, Greg, 248.
Curtis, Tony,101.
Cwmni Theatr Cymru, 259.
Cymdeithas Cymru Newydd, 76.
Cymdeithas Dafydd ap Gwilym, 79.
Cymdeithas Yr Iaith Gymraeg, 187.
Cymru Fydd, 37.

D

Dai Jones – A True Story, 172.
Daily Worker, The, 168.
Dale-Jones, Don, ed. *Twelve Modern
Anglo-Welsh Poets* (with
Jenkins, Randal, q.v.), 85, 89.
Daniel, J.E., 82. *Welsh Nationalism –
What it Stands For*, 78.

Acknowledgements

Poetry

We would like to thank John Davies for permission to reprint 'How to Write Anglo-Welsh Poetry', taken from *At the Edge of Town*, published by Gomer; Harri Webb for 'Synopsis of the Great Welsh Novel', from *The Green Desert*, published by Gomer; Joseph P. Clancy for 'S4C', first published in *Poetry Wales* vol. 21 no. 1; and Peter Finch for 'A Welsh Wordscape', from *The End of Vision*, published by John Jones, Cardiff.

Illustrations

The following acknowledgements must be made.
To the Welsh Arts Council for photographs of R.S. Thomas, Gwyn Thomas, John Tripp and Gillian Clarke.
To the BBC for the photograph of John Ormond.
To Glyn Jones for the photograph of himself, Jack Jones and Gwyn Jones.
To the National Eisteddfod for the photograph of the chairing ceremony.
To the British Film Institute for stills from *How Green Was My Valley*, *The Citadel* and *The Silent Village*.
To the Lady Lever Art Gallery for 'Salem'.
To the Tate Gallery for Wilson's 'Cader Idris, Llyn-y-Cau'.
To the British Museum for Turner's 'The Ruins of Valle Crucis Abbey'.
To Derry Brabbs and Michael Joseph Ltd. for the photograph of Castell Carreg Cennen, which first appeared in *Wales*, by Wynford Vaughan Thomas, published by Michael Joseph Ltd.
To Ian Walker for his photograph of Caerphilly Castle.

Notes on Contributors

DEIRDRE BEDDOE was born in Barry, South Glamorgan. She was educated there and at the University College of Wales, Aberystwyth, where she obtained a Ph.D in History. She is currently Principal Lecturer in History and Art History at the Polytechnic of Wales, Pontypridd. Her main interest is in women's history: she has lectured and written widely on many aspects of this subject. Her publications include *Welsh Convict Women: A Study of Women Transported from Wales to Australia, 1787-1852*, (Barry, Stewart Williams, 1979) and *Discovering Women's History: A Practical Manual*, (London, Pandora, 1983). She is currently preparing a study on women in Britain between the Wars. Deirdre Beddoe is a director of Boadicea films and has just released *I'll Be Here for all Time* (Wales, 1985, 25 mins.).

TONY BIANCHI was born in North Shields in 1952. He was educated at St. Cuthbert's Grammar School, Newcastle-upon-Tyne, and St. David's University College, Lampeter, where he learned Welsh, graduated in English and Philosophy and received a doctorate for research into the works of Samuel Beckett. He subsequently became a lecturer and later a Fellow of the University of Wales, and is now Literature Officer for the Welsh Arts Council. His publications include a monograph on Richard Vaughan and essays on Idris Davies, Waldo Williams and other Welsh writers; he is currently editing an anthology of Welsh poetry in support of the Anti-Apartheid Movement.

TONY CURTIS was born in Carmarthen in 1946. He is Senior Lecturer in English at the Polytechnic of Wales. His critical work includes a book on Dannie Abse, and he edited *The Art of Seamus Heaney* for Poetry Wales Press. His *Selected Poems 1970-1985* appeared from the same publisher in 1986 and a collection *Poems: Selected and New* from the Story Line Press in America. He won the National Poetry Competition in 1984 and was shortlisted for the 1985 Arvon Prize. He is Chairman of The Welsh Academy and directed the first Cardiff Literature Festival in 1986.

JAMES A. DAVIES is a member of the Department of English, University College, Swansea. Though born in Llandeilo, Dyfed, he was brought up in Glamorgan at Tonyrefail, Tonypandy and Pontypool. A University of Wales Ph.D, he is a founder member of the Association for the Study of Welsh Writing in English. In 1981 he was a Visiting Professor at Baylor University, Texas. he has published two books: *John Forster: A Literary Life* (1983) and *Dylan Thomas' Places* (1986), and numerous articles on various aspects of nineteenth century literature. Other articles include critical work on Dylan Thomas and R.S. Thomas, and he is presently writing *The Textual Life of Dickens' Characters* for Macmillan.

JOHN HARTLEY was formerly Senior Lecturer in Communications at the Polytechnic of Wales, and is now Lecturer in Human Communication at Murdoch University, Australia. His publications include *Reading Television* (with John Fiske), *Understanding News*, and (with others) *Key Concepts in Communications*.

ROD JONES was born in Ebbw Vale in 1940. Initially trained as a scientist, he worked for a brief period in the steel industry before turning to visual arts in his mid-twenties when he studied to be a painter. He has since spent most of his time as a lecturer of visual culture and communication, and is at present lecturer in Art History at Newport College of Art and the Polytechnic of Wales. His articles and reviews have appeared in *Ten8*, *Creative Camera* and *Art Monthly*. He is currently working on popular imagery associated with the medicalization of the female body.

PRYS MORGAN was born in Cardiff, educated there and at Oxford. He has lectured in history at Swansea for many years. He has published a volume of poetry and a novel in Welsh, and was for some years the deputy editor of *Barn*, and chairman of the Literature Committee of the Welsh Arts Council. He is at present editor of the *Transactions* of the Honourable Society of Cymmrodorion, and is the author of several works on Welsh History, the two most recent being *Wales – The Shaping of a Nation* (with David Thomas, 1984) and *Welsh Surnames* (with T.J. Morgan, 1985). He is currently at work on two longer surveys of Welsh history.

MICHELLE RYAN was born in Cardiff in 1949 and is a Lecturer in Media Studies at the Polytechnic of Wales. She has worked as an

Equal Opportunities Producer-Presenter at CBC Cardiff, and published a book on the work entitled *Shut Up and Listen: Women and Local Radio – A View From the Inside* (Comedia, 1983, with Helen Baerh). Previously a film editor at Teliesyn and HTV she is currently working on a film about Welsh men and their mothers. Co-ordinator of the First National Feminist Film and Video Conference (at Chapter, 1982), she was a founder member of the South Wales Women's Film Group, and is a member of the editorial board of Radical Wales.

DAI SMITH is Senior Lecturer in the History of Wales Department at University College, Cardiff. He has written widely on the culture and society of South Wales and has lived most of his life in one or other part of the area. His most recent books are *Lewis Jones* (1982) and *Wales! Wales?* (1984). He has recently prepared for publication Gwyn Thomas' novel *Sorrow For Thy Sons* (1986) and is now working on the politics and culture of Aneurin Bevan. He now lives on the world's edge at Barry Island.

PETER STEAD was born in Barry and educated at Barry and Gowerton Grammar Schools and University College, Swansea. Since 1966 he has been a member of the History Department at Swansea. He is the author of *Coleg Harlech: The First Fifty Years* and numerous articles on Welsh Labour History and more recently on Film History. He frequently visits North America, where has has been a Fulbright Fellow and Visiting Lecturer at Wellesley College, Massachusetts.

CARL TIGHE was born in Handsworth, Birmingham and graduated in English Literature from University College, Swansea. After working in a mental hospital and as a Butlins Redcoat he took an M.A. in Nigerian theatre. After some years teaching in Poland and at the West Glamorgan Institute of Higher Education he took an EFL qualification and returned to Poland as Assistant Director of English at the Jagiellonian University, Krakow. A free-lance writer since 1981 he has written for several theatre companies and for Radio Wales. He has been Secretary to the Wales branch of the Theatre Writers Union, writes a regular column on theatre in Wales for *Drama*, and is editor of *The Playwright's Register*.

TREVOR WRIGHT was born in Nottingham in 1957 and is a graduate of the B.A. Communications course at the Polytechnic of

Wales. He lives in Cardiff where he has worked variously for the F.P.A. and the Wales Campaign for Press and Broadcasting Freedom. He is co-author with H. Goulden and J. Hartley of 'Consciousness Razing' in *What's the Channel Fo(u)r*, eds. S. Blanchard & D. Morley, (Comedia, 1982).